By now the round, red winter sun was descending and the sky exploding with glorious flashes of crimson and silver, like a firework display to honour their departure. Every rope and spar was thrown into sharp relief against this final glow, and the *Countess* shivered and shifted as ropes were cast adrift, so slowly at first that the movement was hardly perceptible. The emigrants surged towards the bulwarks; those left behind ran alongside, shouting and waving, while the oarsmen in the tugs pulled with all their strength and turned the *Countess* into the river . . .

'Raise tacks and sheets.'

'Helms a-lee, all clear for'ard?'

The answer was a shout of 'Ay, ay, sir' and a great clattering as canvas, ropes and blocks heaved above them like a second sky. The sun had set by now and a slight breeze filled the sails. The ship was alive!

SWANSDOWNE

Daniel Farson

ARROW BOOKS

Arrow Books Limited
62–65 Chandos Place, London WC2N 4NW

A division of Century Hutchinson Ltd

London Melbourne Sydney Auckland
Johannesburg and agencies throughout
the world

First published 1986

© Daniel Farson 1986

Photoset in Linotron Baskerville by
Rowland Phototypesetting Limited
Bury St Edmunds, Suffolk
Printed and bound in Great Britain by
Anchor Brendon Limited, Tiptree, Essex

ISBN 0 09 944810 6

For all the laughter we have shared together,
I dedicate this book to my dear friend
Sandy Fawkes
May she triumph for ever.

Acknowledgements

I am indebted to numerous books for my research, though it was often the dullest tome which provided the most valuable information. In the mid-1960s I bought a battered paperback outright for £100 – a considerable sum for those days – *Martin Cash, The Bushranger of Van Diemen's Land in 1843*, assured that this was the only copy in Britain apart from one in the British Museum. As it described Port Arthur as well as Cash's escape over Eagle Hawk Neck and his subsequent raids on the settlers, I expected to use this extensively, but in the event only a couple of chapters proved relevant. My other earlier reference was a copy of *Stories of Australia* by Marcus Clarke (Hutchinson 1897) which I particularly admired, but I was careful not to read his classic novel of Australia *For the Term of His Natural Life* which I feared could prove too overwhelming an influence. However, by chance someone posted me a copy of the recent paperback (Penguin 1980) at the very moment I had reached my chapter on Port Arthur and the temptation was irresistible.

At first I was dismayed to find certain similarities in our stories until I realised that Marcus Clarke would have used the same source as myself: his own *Stories*. I believe I would have dared attempt this book even if I had read *Term* beforehand; as it is I am happy to acknowledge my debt to Marcus Clarke.

Other books which helped me:

Report from Select Committee on Transportation 1838 (photo-copies supplied by London Library)

English Prison Hulks, Branch-Johnson

Convict Ships, C. Bateson

Diary of Royal Movements & Personal Events (from *Official Records 1883*)

Hurrah For the Life of a Sailor, John Winton (Michael Joseph)

East End Underworld, A. Harding

The Worm in the Bud, Ronald Pearsall (Penguin)

Sailing Ships and Emigrants in Victorian Times, Alison Grant (Longman)

Punishment and Profit, J. D. Ritchie

Governor Arthur's Convict System, W. D. Forsyth

The Adventures of Ralph Rashleigh (fiction), (Jonathan Cape)

Convicts & the Colonies, A. G. L. Shaw (Faber & Faber)

Unwilling Emigrants, Alexandra Hasluck (Oxford University Press)

The Tasmanians – The Story of a Doomed Race, Robert Travers (Cassell, Australia)

Dry Guillotine, Rene Belbenoit (Dutton, New York)

Early Australia With Shame Remembered, Bill Beatty (Cassell)

Thirty-Three Years in Tasmania and Victoria, G. T. Lloyd, 1883

Australian Genesis, J. S. Levi (Robert Hale)

Historical Records of New South Wales IV, Hunter & King, 1896

Tasmania, Lawrence Collings & Lawrence Durrant (Jack Pollard)

Menace at Oyster Bay (fiction), Vivienne Rae Ellis (Antelope)

Heritage of Stone, Charles Barrett (Lothian Publishing)

Hobart Sketchbook, Max Angus & Patsy Adam Smith

and James Backhouse's *Visit to the Australian Colonies*, the invaluable account of life in Van Diemen's Land in the last century.

For my chapters on board the *Countess of Bath*, I am particularly grateful to the splendid recent account of migration contained in *The Long Farewell* by Don Charlwood (Allen Lane) which gives an extraordinarily detailed account of voyages to Australia around this time.

Always on the lookout for personal detail, I purchased two limited volumes of *Some Private Correspondence of Sir John and Lady Franklin, Tasmania 1837–1845*, compiled by George Mackaness, which provided the background for my chapters on Government House. I am indebted to Judith Hewitt who was brought up in Tasmania and has been consistently generous in loaning documents, photographs, and books such as *Pioneers of the East Coast* by Karl von Stieglitz, which helped me understand the life of the early settlers.

Following a broadcast made by Judith Hewitt and relayed in Hobart, similar assistance was offered by Don Norman, a fourth-generation Tasmanian, who was kind enough to send me his privately printed booklet: *So Soon Forgotten – A Story of Two Tasmanian Families*.

I should also like to express my appreciation for the booklets supplied by G. J. Dean, the Director of the Department of Tourism, Tasmania; and the encouragement offered by Geoff Pearsall, the Minister for Tourism, Hobart.

As always, I thank the London Library for their exemplary service in supplying me with many of the above books; and special gratitude to Mrs Jane Lindsay whose skill in coping with the final typescript has made my work much easier.

After twenty-five years, it is time to record my affection and admiration for my agent, Irene Josephy, who has sustained me all this time and has never lost faith though I have frequently given her cause to do so. My debt to her is beyond words.

In the case of this particular book, I have been helped throughout by Peter Lavery and Nancy Webber, my editors, whose guidance has proved indispensable. I am deeply grateful to them for their constructive advice and encouragement.

Foreword

When I visited Tasmania in 1961, I had the good fortune to meet Miss Carrie James. She lived in a sloping house in Bathurst Street made from the timbers of a convict ship and though she looked scrawny and bird-like her use of gesture was dramatic and her eyes were neither pale nor watery but almost fierce in their intensity. At the age of ninety-four she had difficulty in coping with the present but enjoyed a total recall of her childhood, which meant that she remembered Hobart as a convict town – an eyewitness of one of the most shameful episodes in British history.

Until I met her, I had little idea that Tasmania, which looked so peaceful, had been one of the bloodiest places on earth. The genocide of the aborigines speaks for itself, and the punishment of the convicts was cruel even by the standards of the time. Nor would I have learnt the truth from the Tasmanians in 1961, most of whom preferred to forget that transportation had ever taken place, though they are prouder of their convict ancestors today, and rightly so. Their reticence was understandable, for the penal settlement of Port Arthur can be compared to Devil's Island, though the calculated brutality of the model prison was closer to Belsen. Altogether 130,000 convicts were sent to Van Diemen's Land – today the population is little more than 400,000.

Miss James, however, had no compunction in describing the 'sad old days'. When she was a girl, the freed convicts still regarded Hobart as their town, the women leaning over their fences with pipes in their mouths swearing at the few settlers who passed by. 'They hated the migrants,' she declared. 'They hated everyone – a hate in their hearts.'

She remembered the flagellator from Port Arthur, Sam Burroughs, on his visits to Hobart Town: 'We all got on our doorsteps and watched the man go by with our little eyes. We hated him – quiet, the street was quiet, then we'd all spring out and have our games again when the flagellator had gone. He had a red handkerchief' – Carrie James swayed, holding an imaginary handkerchief between her fingers – 'he liked the colour of blood. They get used to it, their heart gets hardened.' Her vivid recollections made me appreciate the enormity of the convict's punishment: to be transported to the other end of the world, with little chance of seeing friends or family again. 'I never saw a happy one,' she told me. 'Homesick and broken spirit. They realised there was no hope.' She remembered two convicts with special affection: 'There was Charles, tall man, he got subservient you know, mother wouldn't have that. If he came to our home he was treated like a gentleman, but my uncle was a rich man and thought Charles should stand up when spoken to. Poor fellow. He was going along a street in London, only a boy of nineteen, when an old man with a barrow full of stuff said "Give us a lift, lad" and of course he did, one of the softy sort! And the man ran away when he saw a policeman who found the boy with the barrow which was stolen. He was never flogged, he came of a good family, but they wanted men out here so they assigned him to a grazier up country. But his spirit was broken. He left a comfortable home and a loving mother, you see. He said "I wish I'd never been born".'

The other convict was a British sailor called Richard Stanton who had been transported to Van Diemen's Land, as Tasmania was known in the first half of the last century, and assigned as a convict servant. She gave me a page of notes which Stanton had scribbled for her: 'The first day after my arrival I was given two large baskets of ladies' underclothing to wash and iron. I looked in astonishment. I remarked I would not disgrace the flag I sailed under, and danced "Jack's the lad with a horn-pipe" on top of them.'

This impertinence earned him twenty-five lashes and a sentence to Port Arthur. When he returned to Hobart Town, Carrie James saw the scars on his back: 'Dick would only show it to our boys, he didn't like the girls looking.' Suddenly she mimicked the boys in a high, squeaky voice: '"Show us your back, Dick!" I crept up behind them one day, I thought I'll see that back and I did. Oh . . . *shocking*.' Her hand sketched the cuts across the air: 'Like a piece of leather, scored, scored, great weals, cross to cross.'

Her jauntiness vanished as she remembered the cruelty: 'Oh, can't they ruin a life.' She described her own, unhappy childhood succinctly: 'Never a cuddle, never a kiss, always a cane on top of the Bible. Father read the Bible and mother held the cane. Mother was cruel: "If you can't break their spirits," she said, "break their backs." But you break the spirit of a child and you ruin it for life.'

The following day I drove down to the Tasman Penin-sula to see the ruins of Port Arthur, with a splendid swim beforehand off the beach of a sweeping bay with dense, dark virgin forest rising behind me. Then across the infamous Eagle Hawk Neck which features in this story, and finally to the remains of the settlement set in another bay of almost delicate beauty. Yet I shivered from the sense of melancholy. Probably this was due to my new knowledge of the suffering which had taken place, but it felt as if the anguish of Port Arthur had left an imprint on the land. I opened my film on Carrie James and the convicts (the first in a television series *Farson in Australia*) with the admission: 'If I believed in ghosts, I'd expect to find them here.'

That was my introduction to this little-known period in history. On and off, I have researched the convict days in Van Diemen's Land for the last twenty years, ever since my meeting with Miss James. It seemed only fitting that I should use the name of Richard Stanton for the convict in this book, and when someone suggested that his original offence was too trivial to be convincing I was able to reply that this was the literal truth. Stanton's notes began: 'Richard Stanton of Her Majesty's Navy, at your service. After service of twenty months an event happened that altogether altered the course of my life's career. Her Majesty, Queen Victoria, who had been Queen of Great Britain for some seven years, paid an official visit to the Fleet.' It was during this visit that Stanton fell from grace and was sentenced to two years' transportation – which meant a sentence to Van Diemen's Land for life. In the name of colonisation, men, women and even children were transported for such pathetic crimes as insubordination; stealing a cheese or pilfering meat; obtaining eight shillings and sixpence by false pretences. One convict known to Carrie James was sent out for stealing a piece of ribbon. Little wonder that her tombstone was inscribed: 'Farewell old world, I've had enough of thee.'

After Stanton's 'fall', the rest of my story comes from imagination but is based throughout on fact. It's a hazardous business attempting to write the truth in an historical novel, running the risk of getting a detail correct while defaulting on the whole. I consider it more important to get the *feel* of the period right rather than give a correct date; consequently I have altered a few points to the advantage of my story. Queen Victoria's inspection of her Fleet took place in Portsmouth and not Plymouth as I have it here; and I have prolonged the Governorship of Sir John Franklin by several years. Occasionally the truth is unconvincing: the Franklins sailed for England on the *Flying Fish*, which sounds a bit like 'a trip round the bay on the *Saucy Sue*', so I have used the name *Rajah* instead, which was the vessel they were going on in the first place until a change of plan.

Occasionally the truth sounds unconvincing because it

is too horrifying, but the convicts *were* forced to wear masks in the model prison and this is not my fiction.

Historical figures are not intended to be photographically accurate: the name of O'Hara Booth conjured up a particular image in my mind, different from the dark, unsmiling man in the engraving I eventually obtained.

Apart from such minor alterations, *the mass of historical detail is correct.*

Miss Carrie James is dead but we kept in touch after I left Tasmania. She posted me an excruciating pair of vivid pink bedsocks which she had knitted herself, and wrote that she still kept the flowers I had brought her. They must have been brittle by then but my memory of this remarkable woman is still bright. She was the inspiration for this book.

PART 1

— 1 —
The convict

'He looks a rough diamond.'

Usually the face gives everything away. Not so with Dick Stanton. The belying scar which crossed one cheek promised belligerence, as did the angry colour of his hair which was red when he was a boy, though it grew darker with age. The hair came from his mother's side. 'Ah,' said the neighbours knowingly, 'there's no doubt that he's his mother's son,' with the suggestion that the same could not be said with such certainty about his father. This was the inevitable consequence of the unexpected marriage between 'old man Stanton' and the young Irish girl, Maureen Daley. Old man Stanton was barely forty, a punctilious man who kept himself apart, working as a clerk in Raxleigh House on the hill above Bideford, as if he was one of 'them' rather than working class. Sideboards which were prematurely grey, and the need for rimless spectacles after years devoted to the scrutiny of documents and ledgers, gave the impression of pedantry – 'a bookish sort of cove'. This was not a compliment, neither was it wholly true, for Stanton's reticence masked a natural modesty, 'a born bachelor if there ever was one'. Consequently, his neighbours were surprised to learn of the marriage ceremony after it had taken place privately in the tiny church of Landcross Parish. Tongues wagged as they are wont to do in the West Country: 'How on earth did the likes of they meet in the first place?' – 'What is a man like 'ee doing with a chit of a girl like she?' –

1

and the whispered reproof 'They do say she's no better than she oughta be!' This last remark made little sense, for people are seldom better than they ought to be, but was typical of the gossip in a small community which can be cruel.

However, it must be admitted that the excess of curiosity was understandable. Where *had* she come from? How had they met? It was rumoured that the toothy but attractive girl had run away from her family in southern Ireland and 'bought' her passage on a boat from Cork to Swansea, though her means of payment could only be guessed at. Finding the Welsh too sullen for her high spirits, Maureen Daley had taken another vessel across the Bristol Channel to the new resort of Ilfracombe – but after that the scent was lost. It was two years before she surfaced in the whitewashed town of Bideford whose ancient bridge spanned the River Torridge. She told several people that she had 'fallen in love with the place', but they found it harder to believe the same affection for Stanton, who may not have been as senile as his reputation but was twice her age at least. They seemed happy enough, which provided further fuel for the caustic comments of the women who envied young Mrs Stanton her radiant spirit and the men who envied Stanton his enjoyment.

Sadly, the nudges and whispers were proved correct. Before a month had passed, it was evident that the young Mrs Stanton was pregnant. Five months later she gave birth to a son – Richard Stanton – and the local tongues would have wagged again except that even 'they' were muted in sympathy, for as the boy entered this world on the first day of September 1828, the radiant spirit left it. In the first part of the last century such misfortunes were common.

It is claimed that in such cases the father can hardly bear to look at the child who has caused his grief, but this was not so with Stanton. After the wet-nurse had departed he employed a local girl to act as nurse, and when he returned from work, which he did more eagerly now, he fondled the baby, played and gurgled, as foolishly and lovingly as any mother. As the boy grew up, however, his scrupulous – some might say exaggerated – sense of duty caused him anxiety lest he spoil the child, and Stanton made the mistake of withdrawing, not merely giving the boy his independence but thrusting it upon him. In a large family this would have been wise, but Dick was an only child with an 'old' man for his father and no fussy aunts or grandparents to dote on him.

One of the rare occasions when Stanton revealed his feelings was when Dick was carried home at the age of seven after falling from the loft in a barn where he had been playing hide-and-seek with some of the local boys. Landing on the hay below he struck a scythe which had been left there carelessly, invisible beneath the straw. The accident was bad enough but the quantity of blood made it seem worse at the time. Luckily the boy's cheek had been sliced by only the tip of the blade; unluckily the new doctor who had set up his surgery around the corner made such a botched job of the stitches that when they were removed they left a criss-cross track which marred Dick's appearance. Stanton's own doctor, older and wiser and less intoxicated than the newcomer, examined the scar when he returned from his holiday in Exeter and shook his head regretfully. 'A shame,' he concluded, 'a damned shame. You should have called in the butcher – he'd have sewn him up better. As it is, the boy has lost his looks and that's the end of it.'

This was said in front of the child, who felt guilty at having been the cause of his disfigurement in the first place. No one realised that the scar hardened his appearance to advantage, for it had trespassed on prettiness before.

The solitary boy was popular with the local fishermen, who took him on board in the summer when they sailed from Bideford on an ebbing tide. Past the wooded coves and the footpath to the village of Appledore, where the Torridge joined the Taw. They dropped the boy and his dog at Crow Point on the opposite shore and continued on their way to Bideford Bar and the point where the two rivers clashed with the advancing sea, wavered, and poured at last into the vast Atlantic.

With the dog barking wildly, and the shouted promise to be waiting there when they returned, Dick gave a parting wave and climbed over the first ridge of dunes into that strange Arabian landscape known as the Burrows. Boy and dog walked for miles through the windswept valleys of sand, arid-looking from a distance yet in reality rich with fields of wild flowers – miniature orchids after rainfall in spring, viper's bugloss blue and bristling in the summer.

They seldom saw another human being and Dick revelled in the privacy as if the dunes belonged to him alone. Even at the age of eleven, he knew they contained the grace of life, so varied that they never failed to surprise him. There were times when he lost his way and had to find his bearings by climbing to the top of the highest hillock nearby. His destination remained the same – a natural pool where the dog swam for a stick after drinking fresh water, and Dick lay down beside the bullrushes and opened his favourite book. *Robinson Crusoe* had already given him an uncontrollable desire to follow a seafaring life.

When he was tired of reading, he put the book aside to contemplate the scene – the horizontal dragonflies hovering beside the rushes, the blue butterflies above the water-lilies which never flowered, the pair of wild duck disturbed by his arrival, circling again.

The freckled and fiery appearance of the boy belied a nature that was more contradictory than it seemed. He valued solitude, but felt such an itch for adventure that he had set his heart on joining one of the most crowded professions on earth – the Royal Navy – where men at sea are cooped up together like hens in a hatch and solitude is unattainable except inside oneself.

His father dreaded Dick's departure, but he made no protest. It became imminent with the sudden death of the dog when Dick was fifteen years old. The boy's tear-stained grief was hurtful, for Stanton doubted whether his own death would have caused such distress, and the suspicion was confirmed by Dick's thoughtless announcement: 'There's nothing to keep me here now. Please let me enlist in Her Majesty's Navy.' Stanton had succeeded too well in allowing his son his independence, even at the risk of estranging him. There seemed no point in denying the parental permission necessary for any boy enlisting under the age of sixteen. When they parted, they shook hands with stiff formality.

The driver came up to say that the coach would be delayed for several minutes, held for an important gentleman who had not yet arrived, so they continued, awkwardly, to wait. 'Old man Stanton' felt old in truth as he saw the elation on the boy's face. Everything lay ahead for him. Dick knew with the certainty of youth that everything would be all right for him. He shared none of the deep anxiety of his father, who knew that advice is pointless on such occasions yet felt, suddenly, that he had to say something, alarmed by the boy's wistful innocence.

'Dear Dick,' he murmured, yielding to the emotion he usually kept in check, 'you can always depend on me, whatever happens. When I am no longer here to help you, turn to yourself. You will be your own best counsellor – you will know if you are doing right or wrong. It's fashionable these days to scorn the old traditions, but try to be a man of honour. It doesn't matter how wretched your circumstances as long as you retain that.'

'Yes, father,' the boy replied respectfully, hardly listening.

William Stanton smiled, realising that his words were too heavy for a boy overwhelmed by the present, with scant thought for the future.

'I sound exactly like Polonius.' He laughed. 'That's what fathers are for. And Shakespeare's advice was good enough. "This above all: to thine own self be true"; he said it all. There is another thing, now that I'm in full flood. Emulate the python.' The boy looked up, surprised.

'That reptile has the most extraordinary strength,' his

father explained, 'but I'm told it can only be used to the full extent if its tail fastens round a branch or treetrunk which gives it the purchase to strike at any passing animal, crush it to death as the muscles constrict – and devour it whole. This is how it survives.'

The boy did not see what his father was getting at, but was interested nevertheless by this unexpected piece of information as intended.

'You see, Dick,' Stanton continued, 'it is the same with us. We need some support to hang on to in life, to give us strength. It may not be visible, it can be as vague as a point of honour, or the security of a happy marriage,' – he sighed here – 'the spur of ambition, the comfort of religion, or the passion of a cause. Then, like the python's tail – or, rather, the branch it coils its tail around – it will support you as well.'

The two of them laughed simultaneously, for no special reason except that this belated intimacy was welcome, and the little allegory of the python's tail was rather absurd.

'Does the snake really do that?'

'Frankly, Dick, I haven't the faintest idea!' Stanton admitted, with a rare flash of humour. 'But I'm sure it makes sense to have a purpose in life – something to rely on. There, the coach is ready. Just as well, or my little sermon might have gone on for ever. Do look after your-self, my dear boy' – he leant down and kissed him on the forehead – 'and may God be with you.'

They waved and waved until the coach turned out of sight. Stanton remained outside the hotel, wondering what on earth would happen to the boy, loving him as much as if he had truly been his son.

Where was he? Who was that beside him? Dick woke with the sudden shock which comes from too much drinking on the night before, the eve of his seventeenth birthday – not that he could remember much of it apart from flashes of celebration, fights and laughter. He lay motionless for a moment, realising he was not in his hammock on board the *Juniper* but in a sort of bed, covered with sacking. A furtive glance towards his companion revealed a face largely composed of nostrils, belonging to a girl he had never seen before. A closer scrutiny showed that she was not a girl but a woman, neither clean nor beautiful. Dick remembered setting out with his mates to celebrate his birthday on the run ashore in the taverns along the Barbican, armed with two florins sent him for his birthday. Had his mates abandoned him and gone back aboard? Was there a brawl? An image leapt up of a raised fist, but his face felt much the same. He wriggled out of the sackcloth and stared down at his nakedness, but to his relief that looked much the same as well. The last birthday present he needed was pox from a Barbican girl. Yet something nagged at his mind. Sounds of activity from the street below made him turn to the attic window. As he looked out at the bunting strung above the cobbles, he remembered the great occasion. How could he have forgotten! He had thought of little else the last few days.

Struggling into his naval dress, fearful that he might be late, he wondered for a moment whether he should leave any payment for the old drab, but the problem was solved when he discovered he had no coins to leave her. Presumably he had spent his florins and she had stolen the rest. He crept out of the tiny room, his bare feet crossing the wooden boards without a sound, and hurried down the circular stairs into the bottle-strewn bar. He smiled with relief as he recognised the tap-room of the Anchor Inn, for its emptiness was proof that the day had scarcely begun. Undoing the latch, he stepped into the street and blinked in the shocking sunlight before starting to run towards the naval dockyard. Strangers turned to smile at the exuberant young sailor clutching his straw sennet hat with 'H.M.S. *Juniper*' embossed in gold letters round the ribbon.

1 September 1845 – the day of Queen Victoria's first visit to Plymouth to inspect her Fleet. With twenty months' service behind him Dick had grown accustomed

to discipline, but life had become almost intolerable since the announcement of Her Majesty's visit: it is doubtful whether any event could have imposed more strenuous duties on the ship's company, short of war. Standing-gear had to be overhauled; decks already as white as stone could make them were given extra scouring; and the brass, of which there was a warship's profusion, came in for such burnishing that Dick thought it was in danger of being polished away altogether. Yet, in spite of the work and the officers' commands, he would not have wished it otherwise. He had been looking forward to the royal visit with growing excitement, and now he was on the point of missing it. He increased his pace, but the crowds were gathering already and he was forced to zig-zag his way through them. Country visitors who had travelled overnight from distant parts of Devon and Cornwall stared around them, eager and awkward in their finest clothes, overawed by such sophistication.

All were making their way towards the Hoe where sightseers had been assembling since dawn, seeking the finest vantage point with a view over Sutton Harbour. A flotilla of small boats and private yachts bobbed up and down in anticipation, while the warships beyond were laid out in lines with a frowning precision worthy of ruler and compass. Hundreds of them, flags fluttering up the shrouds to the top of the main mast, riding stiffly at anchor as if standing to attention.

It was a spectacle of such grandeur that even the most cynical republican had to conceal his choke of emotion, while patriots gazed with pride at the visible proof of Britain's naval supremacy following her triumph in the Napoleonic wars.

The gentry and the local members of Parliament sat on the benches provided for them. The Mayor was desperately rehearsing his speech, though the words were meaningless from repetition. Soldiers of the 84th marched up and down and the strains of their military band were absorbed into the general clamour. Vendors jostled with the crowds: 'Pies all hot, hot baked potatoes', 'Gingerbreads, threepence a packet and one over', 'Sheeps' trotters, penny each, all hot'; while others persuaded the visitors to buy souvenirs in the form of a broadsheet with woodcuts to help them identify every ship taking part, or a 'panoramic lithograph' which gave the clever illusion that the assembled Fleet had been drawn from the air above.

Older citizens declared with authority that this was the largest multitude Plymouth had ever seen: at least 100,000 people.

Eyes raked the harbour for the arrival of the new steam-driven royal yacht, named *Victoria and Albert* after the Queen and her consort, and there were sudden shouts of 'There she is!' followed by ripples of excitement fading away in disappointment as the 'swells' shouldered their telescopes as if they were rifles, aimed them out to sea, and reported with superior shakes of the head that there was nothing yet in sight, while their lady companions, bedecked and befrizzed for the occasion, laughed affectedly.

More adventurous spirits gathered on the shore below, waiting to clamber on board the pleasure boats which would take them for a closer view of the steam-yacht, clutching their hats with one hand, steadying themselves with the other, to cries of warning and encouragement from passengers already aboard.

Children ran wildly through adult legs, and even the dogs knew that something special was happening, adding their contribution by barking furiously. A small, bandy-legged terrier snapped ferociously at Dick's ankles but fell back as his quarry ran through the formidable columned gateway of Devonport dockyard.

Inside the dockyards the activity was less carefree than the holiday atmosphere on the Hoe, and Dick was ignored. He had the luck to catch one of the gigs taking stragglers back to their ships, but as he pulled on the oars he dreaded the punishment ahead. By now he was several hours adrift, for his day should have opened at four with a piped awakening followed by the inspection of hammocks which had to be rolled so tightly they could pass through a ring. At the best, Dick could hope for a black-listing, set to work while the rest were enjoying their meals, shaken before anyone else was up, restricted to six-water grog – six parts of water added to the tot of rum instead of the usual one to one. He hoped he might be able to sneak to his place unnoticed in the confusion, for he knew that punishment would be severe on such a day, with the slightest misdemeanour reflecting on the ship's reputation. Flogging was still far from obsolete and Dick had enough sensitivity to be scared, not so much of the pain of having his 'back scratched', but of the degradation of being tied down, gag in mouth. Some of the younger sailors thought of a flogging as something to be proud of, proof of manhood so long as it was taken 'four bag' without a cry, but Dick was not so hard, though his appearance misled people into thinking otherwise. Dick had been sought after by older seamen who offered to look after him as his 'sea-daddy', though they left him alone when they sensed his reluctance. Without the blemish they might have persisted, but the scar made them uncertain.

Dick knew he had to assert himself or be placed apart, and did so by making the ship's company laugh, 'acting the giddy-goat' as his father called it at home. There were 300 men on board, in a world where you stood on your merits alone, with neither family, class, nor money to assist you. Dick was different because he failed to use his fists or swear like most of his companions, and because he was one of the few who could write. Dick hardly saw this as an advantage until he discovered that it gained him gratitude when his help was needed in writing letters home. Gradually he became aware of the respect below decks for any man who managed to better himself, a yearning for the higher things in life. This was particularly noticeable among the so-called 'hard cases', for they could afford the sentimentality of the strong. When posting time was due, Dick was asked to write letters for as many as twenty of his mess-mates, and when they received letters in return he read them aloud, which placed him in a position of trust. One sailor had brought the latest Marryat novel, *Masterman Ready*, on board, and Dick read to the men at night while they sat listening in the candlelight. All this won him a place in the intricate hierarchy on board, based on favour, and when he protested one evening that he needed time to mend a tear in his canvas trousers several volunteers offered to do this for him if he would read as usual. Consequently, his life on board was proving better than he had dared to hope.

His arrival alongside the *Juniper* was ill-timed. The ship was ready for the captain's inspection. A final scouring with holystone and sand had left the decks as white as bones bleached by the sun. The men were mustered in their white frocks and trousers, the marines stiff from pipeclay and soap, the drummers waiting with crossed sticks, while the officers paraded the quarter-deck in dress uniforms, cocked hats and swords. Dick had been hoping the gig would take him to the far side, but the coxswain seemed determined to thwart such subterfuge and steered the craft to the port entry. Dick's scramble up the steps on the starboard side was spotted by Midshipman Haynes, generally known as Pompous Percy, a plump boy even younger than Dick himself.

This miniature Napoleon informed Dick that he would be placed on charge the moment the Queen's inspection was over. Meanwhile, he was ordered to join ranks without further delay. This was a fair rebuke in the circumstances; unfortunately, the pompous midshipman was so tightly buttoned in his full dress coat that his voice was reduced to a squeak and Dick was unable to suppress a smile. It was noticed instantly.

'I'll deal with you later,' came a shriller squeak, and Dick grinned openly as he ran towards the mainmast. Sailors were starting to climb the shrouds to man the yard-arms in salute. Soon they rose in tiers from the lower yard to the topsail in diminishing lines, their hands touching as they held on to the ropes.

Dick was exhilarated as he waited for the royal yacht to approach, listening to the cannon and the cheering increasing in volume as the yacht drew nearer. An officer waited on the maintop, hat in hand, to wave the signal as the royal yacht came in line. In the years to come, Dick often pondered on what happened next. Was it too much excitement that made him dizzy, or a sudden heave of the drink consumed the night before, encouraged by a swell which rocked the *Juniper* herself? Standing on the mainyard, the widest spar of all, he saw – or thought he saw – some loose halyards swinging towards him and as he sprang forward to catch them he lost his balance and fell.

Two things broke his fall: the shrouds, which he managed to clutch as he flew past; and Midshipman Percy Haynes, who was sent bowling down the poop deck towards the main like a nine-pin in a game of skittles.

The guns roared their salute! The drums beat their tattoo as Midshipman Haynes scrambled to his feet, all dignity gone, and confronted the fallen sailor in a rage of humiliation. Accusing Dick of deliberate assault, he became hysterical when Dick vowed it was an accident.

'How dare you answer back,' he screamed. 'You assault me and now you call me a liar.'

'I did not intend to do that, sir,' said Dick evenly, while the *Victoria and Albert* continued its way from bow to stern. As the roar of the guns faded, the midshipman's treble could be heard on the bridge. The marine band struck up the anthem and the entire crew of the *Juniper* stood rigidly to attention, Haynes staring angrily at his tormentor. The drums started rolling and the ship's company rent the air with three tremendous cheers for Her Majesty, and waved their hats, and then the yacht had gone and Dick was put in guard by two men and taken below.

The crowds had cheered along the Hoe from the moment they saw the first faint puffs of smoke from the Admiral's flagship, followed a few moments later by the echoing welcome from 120 guns glinting in the September sunshine. Carrying sail as well as steam, the paddle steamer proceeded smoothly as well as swiftly, outstripping the flotilla of inquisitive small boats which tried to follow her. The Queen's main pleasure in the day, however, stemmed from her family. Without realising her lack of tact, she declared that the appearance of her son gave her more satisfaction than the sight of the entire British Fleet laid out for her approval. Prince Edward wore a tiny sailor suit made for him by a member of the crew: summer rig, with a white frock and blue cuffs, a broad blue collar edged with the three blue lines commonly, but mistakenly, attributed to Nelson's naval victories, and white bell-bottomed trousers.

'What curious names they do have!' she exclaimed, as the garments were explained to her. A striped shirt and a black handkerchief and lanyard completed the naval uniform, together with the broad sennet hat. The small boy saluted gravely as the royal yacht sailed past, the towering warships so high that the Queen's party was scarcely discernible from their decks. From the royal viewpoint little could be seen except the figureheads, the gilded quarter galleries, and the guns peeping from the lower gun deck which made 'far too much noise for the royal pleasure' as they fired their salute. No one caught sight of the sailor falling from the mainyard of the *Juniper*.

When the inspection was over, the *Victoria and Albert* anchored below Mount Edgecumbe, and the Queen and her consort transferred to the *Fairy*. They steamed up St Germans River, passing Trematon Castle, which belonged to Prince Albert as part of his command as the Duke of Cornwall.

'It reminds me of the Rhine,' said Victoria, trying to please him.

'The Danube,' he corrected her.

'Of course, Bertie, that's what I meant.'

No hint of disagreement could spoil such a perfect day, and that night she recorded her happiness in the pages of her diary:

13

We drove back by our carriage, another way under beautiful trees and above the fine valleys, so reminiscent of the Rhine whatever Bertie may say to the contrary. How happy I was to see him so proud on such an occasion as this. Then we re-embarked on the *Fairy* and proceeded down the river in the perfect light of evening, the sun bright and the sky and sea so blue. We returned to the yacht surrounded by the myriads of boats, crowded with waving figures, grateful for the chance to see us, which gave us much pleasure. How dear everyone has been today, though tomorrow will be tiresome with the duty of attending to our Admirals who arrive with their despatches to be received by oneself. How grateful I am to have Bertie to assist me on such occasions, for he can talk to them with greater ease while we intimidate.

As the Queen retired to her cabin, she could hear the distant cheers that still rang out along the Hoe, renewed as five great bonfires were lit in honour of the most powerful woman on earth.

— 2 —

A family disgraced

That same September day, on the northern side of Devon, another young man was about to celebrate his birthday, with the difference that he was a gentleman and this was his coming-of-age. His family, all of whose lives would be altered before the night was over, lived in Raxleigh House, an imposing Georgian mansion on top of the hill above Bideford. The head of the family was Augustus Stowe, generally known as Gussie, who had married Sarah Raxleigh. Their son – the young gentleman – was Roland, known as Roly, and his sister Sally was four years younger.

The odd man out was Lionel Raxleigh, Sarah's brother, who sometimes felt an interloper in his own house, though he was happy to leave the running of the estate to his brother-in-law and the faithful family clerk, William Stanton. Usually smiling, his eyes crinkling as if he was uncertain but anxious to please, Lionel flinched from responsibility. Living as part of the family, he had remained a bachelor, though he was now thirty-seven. His sister Sarah, five years older, had always felt protective towards him, a feeling intensified by the suspicion, which she did not fully understand, that he was somehow flawed.

To an outsider, the family had nothing in common. They might have been residents brought together in a lonely hotel, or travellers stranded by a storm.

The Italianate garden was the pride of Raxleigh, a tribute to the unselfishness of Sarah's father who knew he would never see its ultimate splendour except in his

15

mind's eye. Sir Thomas Raxleigh had been a ship-owner, like his father before him, able to instruct his captains to bring back exotic shrubs and trees from distant corners of the world. Many of the plants died on the journey home, but more survived, often the most seemingly delicate. Like Sarah herself, they possessed an inner strength belied by their gentleness.

On the morning of her son's twenty-first birthday, she rose early and walked through the gardens, stopping from time to time to touch the trees, many of which she had planted herself. She knew every turning of the paths so instinctively that she sometimes day-dreamed of an old age with her eyesight almost gone, yet able to find her way with ease.

The garden was her solace. She turned her head for her favourite view over Bideford, less busy now than a hundred years ago when twenty customs officers were required to cope with the highest import of tobacco in Britain. Now the cargo was less romantic, largely salt cod from the New Found Land, but the sight of the sailing ships moored to the quay never failed to give her satisfaction. She recognised the masts of a large vessel due to leave for the New World and thought how courageous people must be to abandon their native country for somewhere unknown.

While his wife walked through the gardens, Gussie dressed himself carefully, viewing the day ahead with apprehension. He deplored the cost of any celebration, even Christmas, but he was devoted to his difficult son and determined to rise to the special occasion of Roly's 'coming-of-age'. Gussie's life had become a struggle to maintain the façade of prosperity, for he was a man with a faltering grip on life. When he married Sarah Raxleigh he was prosperous in the timber business, but though the price of wood rocketed after the Baltic blockade a recession followed and the business failed. This was the pattern of his life, with his highest expectations ending in disappointment, until he wondered if he was born unlucky. He was not bitter or envious by nature, but there were times when he thought it unfair that someone as scrupulous as himself should see his ambitions thwarted while charlatans invariably met with success. Recently he had suffered the severest loss of all, investing in the new canal from Bideford to Torrington. This had looked splendid in the drawings shown to him by Lord Rolle, and his lordship assured Gussie that he had invested heavily himself. The scheme included an elegant aqueduct over the Torridge, a mill, and various lime kilns. Most imaginative were the ramps and rollers over which the barges were hoisted by chains to avoid a series of locks. The basic flaw was ignored, that this was an absurdly ambitious large-scale project for small-scale traffic bringing coal from Wales which scarcely covered costs and showed no profit whatsoever.

When Gussie tried to cut his losses by withdrawing his investment, he was hampered by some preventive clause in the agreement which he had failed to understand. Lord Rolle was not so guileless after all.

'You might as well have thrown our money down the drain,' Roly told him. 'After all, you've thrown it into a canal.'

The loss had placed Gussie in a delicate position, forced to borrow money from the bank and to make as many economies as possible in order to maintain the repayments. Some of the economies had been embarrassing, like the dismissal of the clerk who had served the family all his life. Stanton had enjoyed the absolute trust of Sir Thomas Raxleigh; his son, Richard, even shared the same birthday as Roly though he was four years younger. When Gussie broke the news of his dismissal, Stanton wept openly. But the tears were not shed for himself. 'I pray you have better fortune, Augustus, for you deserve it,' said the clerk, using his employer's Christian name for the first and last time, now that their business association was over. The dismissal had not been allowed to pass so simply, however. Gussie had been upset, bewildered, and finally aggrieved by the ferocity of Sarah's reaction when she heard of it.

'What have you done?' she demanded, though she knew perfectly well. Gussie stammered out his reasons for 'parting' with Stanton, but his explanation was ill-received.

'When you say you're parting with him, you mean you've dismissed the old man after all these years? How could you?'

'As you say, my dear,' Gussie said unwisely, 'he is an old man, getting on in years.'

'Nonsense!' she exclaimed, reversing her attack. 'He's less than sixty, and as bright as ever. I don't know how you'll manage without him.'

'You don't understand, my love,' Gussie continued patiently. 'I'm trying to make economies to keep us on an even keel.'

'But not at the cost of Stanton, of all people. He's part of the family.'

'No, he is not,' Gussie reproved her. 'He's our clerk.' She gave him such a look of scorn that he flinched. He was genuinely puzzled. 'I don't understand why you're so upset.'

'No, you don't,' she agreed enigmatically. 'If you did you wouldn't dream of letting him go,' and she swept from the room leaving him more confused than ever.

Relaxing in the garden afterwards, Sarah regretted her outburst. How foolish to go so far when she was unable to go further. To tell him the truth would be a betrayal of her father too shocking for comfort. There are some aspects of life which are best kept concealed, but she hated hiding the truth from Gussie when it was of such relevance to their lives.

As she knelt by the flower bed on the piece of matting she always carried with her, Sarah remembered the events that led to the birth of Richard Stanton.

'Try not to make too much noise, Sarah, there's a good girl.' These softly spoken words echoed through her childhood,

followed by an upward look towards the bedroom where her mother was imprisoned after the riding accident. As Lady Raxleigh disliked hunting, 'foolishly fond of the fox!' according to her husband, she had only taken part to please him. Consequently, he bore the blame for her wretched bedroom existence because she held him responsible, until the grievance festered between them.

Sarah had sensed her father's relief when they left Raxleigh House and rode down to Bideford. Had she seen the Irish girl? She could hardly be sure of that, though she seemed to recollect a picture-book image of white teeth, laughing eyes and an abundance of fine red hair one day on the quayside, and her father's response: alert, playful, mischievous.

By then, Sarah must have been the same age as the Irish girl. Indeed, she might have been older, for she was still unmarried at the age of twenty-one, tormented by questions from aunts who wallowed in archness as they insisted she had a secret romance. When she protested that she had no intention of marrying a man she did not love, they shook their heads knowingly. When she pointed out that Lionel had no wish to get married, it was greeted with merry laughter and the reminder that 'men are different'. Consequently, it was a relief to all concerned – even to Sarah, though she would have denied it vehemently – when she fell in love with Augustus Stowe and accepted his proposal. 'Too quiet a chap for my taste,' said her father, 'but dependable, and that's what counts.' When the banns were read the words 'spinster of this parish' seemed to reverberate around the church as if to remind Sarah of her narrow escape.

For the next five years, life had been too full for Sarah to notice that her father spent most of his time away from Raxleigh House, as if he hated the place. First there was the honeymoon: her visit to London followed by the cross-channel sailing to Paris, and to Lake Geneva where they explored the lower slopes of the towering Alps, or took the ferry along the shore-line of the lake. Everything was new and Sarah was blissful. With no comparison

19

to go by, she assumed that their love-life was normal: unexciting, rather unpleasant, to be endured for Gussie's sake alone; but if this side of marriage was disappointing she loved him all the more for his fussiness and obvious devotion. In such exquisite surroundings it was easy to feel romantic. Roly was born on 1 September 1824 at Gussie's family home in Torrington. Sally was born four years later – in the same year as William Stanton's son, Richard – and during this time Sarah was so absorbed in her family that she lost touch with her former home.

She never thought of her father as an old man, but he was nearly sixty when he died from a heart attack. Conscience-stricken over her neglect, Sarah tried to atone by becoming close to her mother for the first time in her life. Until then she had felt excluded by her mother's obvious devotion to her brother, and transparent indifference to herself.

The effort came too late. By now Lady Raxleigh, frustrated by years of restriction and pain, was in a state of desperation close to madness, but one day Sarah was startled to find her mother in a chilling state of lucidity. 'Do not think I have any intention of *joining* your father wherever he might be. I pray to God I shall die soon, but if he's in heaven I'll go straight to the other place. Heaven would be hell if he is there.'

'Don't say such things,' Sarah said, shocked. 'You know you don't mean them.'

'Don't I?' Lady Raxleigh summoned her strength and turned from the pyramid of pillows to stare at her daughter as if she had never set eyes on her before. 'How little you understand about your father. What a fuss he made of you! It never occurred to him how much I envied him that, unable to do so myself. He stole your childhood away from me as he stole everything else. The two of you were inseparable. I hardly saw you except when you were brought to my bedroom to say goodnight – our roles reversed! Your father deceived everyone with that awful charm of his. So bluff on the outside, so . . . so rotten within. Your wonderful, wonderful father . . .'

'Please,' Sarah protested. 'He was a *good* man. You know that.'

'A good man!' her mother echoed mockingly. 'A saint! – as far as I was concerned. He told me everything. "No secrets between *us*," he used to say, like the sinner at confessional. Everything nice and tidy because he didn't have the courage to bear it on his own. You know he fathered another child after Lionel?'

Horrified, Sarah shook her head.

'More, for all I know, but in his saintly way he confessed to this one. I knew about the Irish girl because he told me from the beginning. She proved more serious than most, because he was older by then, I suppose. Told me how he doted on her, how she made him feel young again. Usual stuff. Feckless, feckless, feckless. There was *nothing* he didn't tell me, punishing me for his own guilt, but when she discovered she was carrying his child, my goodness he sang a different tune. Panic! What should he do? He came to me in a state of sheer funk.' Her mother chortled, a mirthless sound. 'It's a funny thing, but men who behave badly often have an exaggerated sense of honour. "As a man of honour" – if I heard him say that once I heard him say it a hundred times. "As a man of honour, I could not do this", "As a man of honour, it's my duty to do the right thing". He dreaded that people would find out about the child and laugh at him. He couldn't stand the thought of scandal, and came to me whimpering like a child. Could I save him?

'I thought it all rather funny. Don't look shocked, Sarah. What else was I to feel? No point in my panicking as well. I never saw the Irish girl, of course, so I had nothing against her – a pathetic serving girl picked up and flattered by a rich old goat who got her into trouble. So Tom came to me for advice and did not even see the harm in *that*! He mentioned some nasty things, but I wouldn't listen. Told him to go away for a week or two; I'd cope. He tried to thank me, I remember, but I told him to get away – *shoo*!' She made a dismissive gesture with her gnarled hands, almost translucent apart from

21

the large brown liver spots. 'He looked so ashamed. I was glad of that.'

'What could you do?' Sarah asked. In spite of her distress, she had to hear everything.

'That was simple. I summoned the family clerk, whose loyalty would have shamed the disciples, and asked *his* advice. Of course I knew what he'd suggest, and he did. He married the girl a week later. I doubt if they slept together but I believe she was good to him, and he was fond of her at the end. It wasn't her fault, poor soul, that she died in childbirth.' The mockery had left her mother's face, replaced by desolation. 'Yes, Tom was the father of the boy known as Richard Stanton.' She said the words so quietly that they seemed to hang in the air between them. 'An old man's last fling to prove he still had life inside him. Dick is your own half-brother.'

'Does he know?' asked Sarah at last.

'Does who know?' said her mother impatiently. 'Of course the boy doesn't know, and don't you ever tell him. Of course his father knows, but he wouldn't tell anyone. In fact Stanton acted oddly over the entire business. Not that you could call it business, for he refused to accept a farthing piece, blushed when I mentioned a sum towards the boy's upkeep. A point of honour, and all that. Must have rubbed off on him from Tom, always worshipped Tom. Still, that was what Stanton wanted . . . I rather admired him. Who else is there to know?' She looked at her daughter sharply.

'Gussie?'

'Gussie!' Her mother gave a contemptuous sigh. 'Why on earth should *he* know?' Her tone confirmed her indifference towards her son-in-law.

'I suppose Lionel knows?' Sarah said without thinking.

'What do you think I am?' Lady Raxleigh stared at her daughter accusingly. 'I'm not like your father, spreading his guilt around. No one knows. I shouldn't have told you except that I didn't want you to be totally taken in. Lionel must never be told. You understand?'

Sarah nodded, wishing that she had been spared as well.

'Promise me you'll never tell anyone.'

'I promise.'

'Good.' Her mother's drawn features relaxed and she released a long, sad sigh. Sarah felt a pang of compassion and kissed her mother gently on the forehead before she crept out of the darkened room.

The preparations had been completed for the party to be held that night, and now it was time for Roly to open his presents. His mother smiled as she thought of the waistcoat embroidered so lovingly by Sally, hoping that Roly would be in one of his better moods and not find fault with it, nor with his portrait which the artist was about to unveil in the dining-room after breakfast.

No one could have denied that Roly's looks were striking, with hair as dark as his sister's. Unfortunately, the artist had revealed the hint of petulance as well, the mouth turned down in impatience, a suspicion of ill-temper in those opaque eyes. The likeness was excellent and Roly stared at his image with unconcealed dislike. The artist waited with an anxious smile, unaware that he had revealed the truth, a fatal talent for a portrait painter.

Roly gave his verdict. 'Not the least bit like me.'

'I like it,' said his wife defiantly, recognising the latent irritation which the artist had caught so successfully. A cheerful local girl, Matilda Stowe still felt awkward when the family came together on occasions like this.

'I like it too,' Sarah agreed gratefully. She saw the truth as well – dear, lovable, *difficult* Roly!

'And so do I,' Gussie declared. Even he could see the truth beneath the varnish. 'Yes, I *do* like it,' he repeated.

'Yes,' said Lionel. 'I think it's remarkable. He's caught you admirably.' He said this with a crinkled smile which was not lost on the subject, who stared at his portrait and then turned away.

'I don't like it at all.'

The wretched artist gave a sickly, sycophantic laugh. His opinion of the sitter was even less complimentary than his brush-strokes, but his bill had not been paid so he bowed politely as he ventured to wish the young gentleman 'many happy returns of this auspicious day' before he was shown out.

Sarah suppressed one of her sighs in the silence which followed, but Roly surprised her by a sudden recovery of his good humour. He insisted that the first gift he opened should be Sally's, and wore the waistcoat with approval. Fortunately it fitted. Matilda's small silver snuff box was accepted graciously and she blushed with pleasure when Roly kissed her, casting a look of gratitude towards Lionel who had helped her choose it.

The pile of packages delivered by dutiful aunts and cousins over the last few days proved much as everyone expected, useful gifts of quality. Then came the moment everyone had been waiting for. The breakfast plates were removed and Gussie pushed back his chair. Rising to his feet, he surveyed his family with obvious affection.

'What a happy occasion this is, and how lucky we are to be together on such a day.' He turned towards his son. 'Our love and admiration is probably the finest present we can give you, so this is a more transient gift to mark your coming-of-age,' and he presented Roly with a leather purse containing twenty-one golden sovereigns.

'I'm sorry my gift cannot be more generous, but you know that times are hard . . .'

Roly interrupted cheerfully. 'Don't go on, father, or you'll make me feel I ought to give them back!' Everyone laughed with relief as he went round the table to embrace his mother and shake his father's hand. Matilda smiled, thinking it was so like him to behave unpredictably. She knew how he detested ceremony and family get-togethers.

Now it was Lionel's turn. He rose shyly from the end of the long refectory table, polished so smoothly that he could see his reflection on the surface. With the familiar crinkling of the nose, he blinked, coughed and made his announcement:

'My dear Roland,' – this was not the moment for the usual abbreviation – 'I hope your father will understand when I say that I, too, regard you as a son.'

'Hear, hear,' cried Gussie, trying to conceal the flush that was rising to his face. He knew that his brother-in-law enjoyed a special trust from Roly which was denied to himself. As Roly's father, he represented authority and discipline, qualities his son had little time for.

Lionel gave an awkward nod, and continued: 'I love you all very much.' He said this impulsively, immediately lowering his eyes at the shame of such emotion. Sarah leant across and squeezed his hand. 'My brother-in-law has always been generous in making me feel you are *my* family too . . .'

'No!' Gussie broke in emphatically. 'It is you who are the soul of generosity. After all, this is your home. You're the owner of Raxleigh House.'

Lionel gave him an odd, lop-sided smile. 'No longer.'

'What do you mean?'

'I mean that I am presenting the deeds of Raxleigh House to my nephew now that he has come of age. I hope our present happy arrangement will continue, but that is something Roland and I will have to discuss.' Reaching down, he produced a small bundle of beribboned documents and slid them across the table to Roly on the opposite side.

If he intended to take the family by surprise, he succeeded. They were appalled. Roly was dismayed by the responsibility, and thought of the complications. Sarah wished that her brother had asked her advice before acting so impulsively. Sally ran round the table and hugged her uncle, feeling this was expected. Gussie sat rigid, as if turned to stone. Then he left the room hurriedly. Lionel was going to call after him, puzzled by his reaction, but Sarah gave a warning shake of the head and went out as well, following her husband upstairs. She found him in their bedroom, his back towards her as he gazed out of the window.

'How could Lionel do such a thing?' he whispered. His voice sounded so desperate that she rested her hands on his shoulders to give him comfort, waiting for him to explain. After a minute of alarming stillness, he continued: 'Now that I've let old Stanton go I run the estate with no help from anyone. Certainly not from Lionel, who leaves *everything* to me.'

Distressed by this note of bitterness, she murmured, 'That's because he values your judgement,' but her husband turned round angrily.

'If he did, he would have had the decency to consult me before he transferred the deeds.'

'You mustn't look at it like that. Lionel meant well.'

'It's the people who mean well who cause the most harm!' he exclaimed, unaware that this often included himself. 'What could have induced your brother to do such a dreadful thing?'

'I don't understand,' she said with genuine bewilderment. 'After all, he's given the deeds to Roly.'

Gussie nodded. 'That's what's so unfortunate. He might as well have given them to Rufus.' Rufus was his beloved dog. 'Dear Roly. We seldom talk about him and we're wrong in that, but we know in our hearts that we've spoilt the boy – unless he was born lazy.'

'He wants to be occupied with something worthwhile.' Sarah defended their son instinctively.

'He doesn't want anything of the sort. He's naturally idle, and now that Lionel has given him the deeds to Raxleigh . . . well, it will go to his head. I dread to think of it. If the deeds should go to anyone, they should have come to me. I need them. I'm having the devil of a time. I try to keep the worst of it from you.'

'I wish you wouldn't. It's so silly, this old-fashioned idea that women don't have a head for business.' She hesitated. 'How bad is it?'

Gussie shook his head and groaned. 'Usually I'm optimistic enough, but suddenly every single thing's against me. I've been forced to borrow from the bank, and they've turned hostile. The deeds were the only security I could think of.'

Sarah felt a chill of premonition: obviously their affairs were in a worse way than he admitted, but she thought she saw the means to comfort him. 'Then Lionel's gift is just what you need. If we explain the situation, Roly will be glad to transfer the deeds to your name. I know he will.'

'How could I!' Gussie laughed sarcastically, though he wanted Sarah to convince him. 'How can I ask my own son to give the deeds to me? It would look as if I'm robbing him on his birthday.'

She smiled at his show of outrage. 'Don't exaggerate! But you're right: it *is* his birthday, and they'll be wondering where we are. Come on down and put on your best brave face.' She kissed him fondly. 'We'll have our serious talk with Roly tomorrow.'

The atmosphere was frozen like a tableau when they returned to the dining-room. Lionel looked up apprehensively; Sally had been crying; Matilda stared fixedly in front of her. As for Roly, his eyes hardened as they came in, though his father tried to break the tension with a laugh that sounded far too cheerful. 'Congratulations! To the new squire!'

'No,' said Roly bleakly, his eyes empty of expression. 'You don't get away with it so easily, *father*.' Whenever he intended disrespect Roly called Gussie father. 'You don't think I'm up to running the estate. That's why you walked out.' The others listened guiltily, recognising the truth in his accusation.

'That's not fair, Roly,' Gussie protested feebly. 'My one concern in life is to make you all happy.'

But Roly was unable to leave his grievance alone, picking it at like a scab until he exposed the rawness underneath: 'You think I'll make a mess of things. Let me tell you, father, everything you touch goes wrong, yet you grudge me my chance of independence. Uncle Lionel has given me the deeds because he has more faith in me than he has in you.' Lionel started to protest, but Roly brushed him aside. 'Instead of being pleased for my sake, you had to hide in your bedroom until mother fetched you down. A fine start to my birthday, I must say. I'm going into town. I may ride to Plymouth to see the review

– yes, and miss my party – and no,' he turned on Matilda, 'no, no, no, I do not want you with me. Can't I ever enjoy myself on my own?'

'I haven't said a word,' she pointed out, but by this time Roly was out of the door. The rest of the family remained around the table, mocked by the abandoned gifts.

'I've made a mistake, haven't I?' asked Lionel. It was an anguished admission.

'If only you'd spoken to Gussie first,' sighed his sister. 'There's so much he could have explained.' Noticing her daughter's confusion, she told her: 'Run along, Sally. We're going to be serious for a moment, which you'll hate!' She gave her a reassuring smile and the girl left the room reluctantly. Sarah waited for the door to close before she continued: 'It's not your fault, Lionel, you couldn't have known. Gussie's in trouble with the bank . . .'

Gussie interrupted, feeling obliged to answer for himself: 'They've been asking for security against my borrowings and I more or less guaranteed the deeds of Raxleigh. It's ironic, but I was going to discuss it with you once today was over. Just short-term, of course.'

Flushing with embarrassment, Matilda sprang to the defence of her husband. 'Excuse me, Mr Stowe, but aren't you being hard on Roly? You haven't given him a chance to help you out. I'm sure he'll hand those papers over to you, once he's calmed down. It's only fair to hear what he says.'

'Well done!' cried Sarah. 'We're assuming the worst. Leave it for a day or two and then we'll sort it out. We mustn't allow it to spoil today.'

'You're right, my dear,' Gussie agreed with relief, and turned to Matilda. 'Well done, my dear, speaking up for your husband like that. Most proper.'

Lionel Raxleigh was less content, and, after a shrug which suggested an apology, he made his excuses and walked down to the King's Arms in Bideford, which served excellent French cognac. It might have been the unpleasantness at Raxleigh House which caused the drink to overwhelm him so quickly, though his transition to a beatific haze was hardly discernible. Sarah could never appreciate that sense of well-being which eased every strain, the glorious thought that something marvellous might happen. No one understood the ecstasy he gained from alcohol.

Around midday, he glimpsed Roly in the opposite bar and gave him a cheerful wave, followed by an exaggerated shrug of mock despair. Both of them laughed. A moment later, Lionel frowned as it occurred to him that Roly was celebrating his ownership of Raxleigh while he, the benefactor, was being punished for his generosity. 'To hell with them,' he muttered, 'they're such *little* people . . .'

A few moments later it struck him that the place was unusually empty. 'Where is everyone?' he demanded.

'Have you forgotten?' the barman asked. 'Most of our regulars left at dawn for Plymouth, and the rest have gone to Barnstaple Fair.'

As if in confirmation, Stanley Yeo, a farmer, came through from the back. 'Are you'm coming to the Fair along of us? The trap's outside and we're leaving now, so quick about it.'

Lionel was moved by the air of gaiety when they arrived at Rolle Quay: little boys laughing, young men with smiling girls dressed in their finest clothes and local youths grinning as they fired guns at a jack-in-the-box. He pressed forward through the clowns and harlequins, paused at a stall to buy some sweetmeats, and shook his head smilingly when a jovial barker implored him to enter a tent where they were performing *A Ghostly Tragedy*. He stopped instead to join the crowd surrounding a fire-eater whose tricks were so dangerous that one girl swooned, or pretended to, while less sensitive children roared their enthusiasm for more. Lionel acted on a sudden impulse and gave a tow-headed girl one of his sugar-plums, patting her hair. A furious glance from the child's father made him move on.

Music conflicted – fiddlers from Ireland, a band from

Germany – but the greatest attraction of the travelling Fair was the chance for the Barumites to gaze at strange animals they had never seen before, as well as the two Russians from Cardiff with their dancing bear. This mournful animal was held by a heavy chain, subjected to the taunts of boys who darted forward to prove their bravery, jumping back 'just in time', while the bear yawned with Siberian indifference. At least the bear was free to move, unlike the wilder animals in the cages of the menagerist, where the African lion paced, and the frantic Indian mongoose hopped a few feet, this way and that. In one of the cages, lit from above by a large chandelier, an evil-looking hyena laughed at the crowd. It sounded like a cry of loneliness to Lionel. When the animal looked towards him, he turned away guiltily. He was tempted to remonstrate with the keeper who prodded the animals with a long wooden pole when they tried to lie down, but the crowd looked so cheerful that he decided against it, and moved on to join a family group staring at the young Indian elephant with sores on its legs. Most beautiful and majestic of all was the Royal Bengalese Tiger, scowling at the humans with disdain yet unable to escape their ceaseless scrutiny, trapped in that tiny space, surrounded by a noise so alien to its nature. Lionel felt sickened by the ill-treatment of animals, even a rat caught in the iron jaws of a gin-trap, and the sight of the tiger denied its freedom was so disturbing that he left the fairground and made his way to the Market Inn on the other side of the bridge.

An hour or so later Lionel rose with an effort and went outside for air, which he drank as deeply as the brandy in the smoke-filled tavern before making his way back to the Fair to join his travelling companions. It was time to go home to Raxleigh. But after this moment of clarity the evening dissolved into a nightmare in which torn faces laughed at him silently. No sign of familiar friends, but glimpses of the raree show: a grotesquely tall woman billed as the Giantess of the Modern World, and a group of unfortunate dwarfs mouthing into his face with such mockery

30

that Lionel shouted at them, to the amusement of the crowd, which gathered round him as if *he* was the exhibit. Escaping, he stumbled into a booth where travelling wrestlers challenged the local bloods. As to the cause of what happened next, Lionel was never sure; though he never forgot the shame of it. His fine clothes were torn off him by a dozen hands which pulled and twisted his body into a pair of stinking leather trousers, and when this was accomplished they pushed him upwards into the makeshift ring, where he pranced like a comic, encouraged by the shouts of the spectators. *That* was the hideous thing, that he enjoyed making a fool of himself, at one moment embracing the dark, gipsy-looking traveller as he held on to him, kissing him on the mouth. A roar of delight from the crowd, and then a moment of silence as the traveller struck Lionel a terrible blow and the good humour was replaced by sniggering derision. His body was carried from the ring and dumped in a corner of the tent. Two men from Bideford came to his rescue, lifting him to their cart nearby and taking him to the back door of Raxleigh House, for guests were leaving at the front. He was helped to bed by the servants, still wearing someone else's trousers, the blood congealed on his face.

'Poor Mr Lionel,' said the footman, shaking his head.

The next morning the story of his wrestling bout was told in the taverns of Bideford. A few people laughed good-naturedly but others shook their heads and shook them again before the day was over. There is a satisfaction derived from the misfortune of others, especially the privileged.

When Lionel set out for Barnstaple Fair, his nephew had continued to drink, settling down at last to a game of cards in the elegant room above the Colonial Buildings at East-the-Water, next to the prison. The afternoon proved disastrous. He was rarely lucky when he gambled but guilt had made him reckless. He knew he was expected at Raxleigh, but he convinced himself he had a

31

genuine grievance against his father. The deeds to Rax-leigh were still in his greatcoat pocket.

'Let them wait,' he decided. 'Serve them right.'

It is astonishing how quickly you can lose when luck is against you. There was a point when Roly should have pulled back, but he was unable to do so. When his last coin had vanished – fortunately, the birthday sovereigns had been left at home – Roly scribbled his markers for larger and larger sums until his friend Charlie Cleveland cried out, loud enough for everyone to hear, 'Dash it, Roland, this isn't good enough! Your signature's not worth a sixpence.'

Humiliated by the taunt, as he was meant to be, Roly left the table without a word and headed for the cloakroom. Everyone laughed, assuming he had thrown in his hand, but when he returned a few minutes later Roly threw down the bundle of deeds on the green baize cloth. 'These good enough for you, Charlie?'

Young Cleveland studied the documents intently: 'With security like this,' he smiled, 'I should say! We'll raise the stakes, shall we?'

His party proceeded without him. The rooms where people gathered near the fires were properly heated for once, with the additional brightness of red and golden flowers. The footman opened the front door in his canary yellow livery; the best wax candles cast their reflected light on the highly polished tables; and Sally was radiant as she exchanged her rough pelisse and thick shoes for silk stockings and a frock of India muslin which bore a 'London' label, bought at Wyatt's in the High Street.

In the cascade of greetings the absence of the guest of honour was hardly noticed at first, then Sarah had to run a gauntlet of enquiries: 'I don't see Roly anywhere? I do hope he liked our present?'; 'Where's Lionel hiding himself?'

Sarah shook her head knowingly as if she shared a secret which she was not prepared to divulge. She dared not say that Roly would be late, for she had the dreadful suspicion that he might not arrive at all. So she smiled and waited, with an occasional look at Gussie who was doing his best to appear jovial and unconcerned, laughing heartily at the silliest excuse.

Soon, Roly's absence became inescapable, and the guests grew silent. Sally ran up to her father and whispered rebelliously: 'I *knew* he wouldn't be here when you made it "family". He *hates* family!' Yet, how could he be so cruel? And Uncle Lionel too. Where was *he*?

When the footman whispered the news that Roly was gambling with Lord Cleveland's son in the Colonial Buildings and losing heavily, Gussie pressed the claret bell and clapped his hands.

'Good friends and family,' he announced, 'we shall not wait any longer for Roland, who has been delayed and sends you his regrets with the hope that you will enjoy this evening without him. Let us go in to dinner.' This was the signal for the musicians to start, accompanying a rustle of silk and a murmur of surprise as the guests entered the dining-room arm in arm.

Before dawn the next morning, long after the last guest had left the party intended to celebrate his twenty-first birthday, Roly broke into the silence of Raxleigh House, and ran up the stairs crying out something unintelligible. The sound was daunting enough to keep his mother awake for the rest of the night.

Entering his room he clutched Matilda as she tried to undress him, and then fell into a deep though tormented sleep, calling out several times from some distant, inner anguish.

Matilda lay beside him, saddened by the disappointment of the evening. Neither Roly nor his uncle had been present at the party everyone had been looking forward to. She knew, by now, that the upper classes were different. Even so, she wondered how people could do such things.

— 3 —
Days of reckoning

Vice-Admiral Sir Henry Harvey was a fair but impatient man who had little time for society or etiquette. Arriving on board the royal yacht at nine in the morning on the day after the Queen's inspection of her Fleet, he kicked his heels until midday when he received word that Her Majesty was unable to thank him in person for the Address presented on behalf of Plymouth Naval Command, which she accepted graciously. In other words, he had wasted the morning for nothing. To make it worse, Prince Albert came forward to apologise on his wife's behalf, explaining with an appeasing smile that the Queen was busy playing with her two-year-old son, the Prince of Wales – a fact confirmed by squeals of childish laughter. Regarding this as a deplorable confusion of priorities, the Admiral returned to his flagship in a poor temper, disappointed at losing this opportunity of meeting his sovereign face to face.

The first lieutenant was standing at the top of the ladder, providing further irritation in the reminder that six Captains of the Fleet had been waiting for the signal to join him on board.

'Dammit!' the Admiral exclaimed. 'The court martial.'

'I'm sure,' the lieutenant said with a knowing smile, 'that they welcomed the wait if Her Majesty ...' He received such a glare that he stopped in mid-sentence. The Admiral gave orders for the gun to be fired and withdrew. In a short time the longboats of the six naval captains pulled alongside the flagship and the escort of marines presented arms. A few minutes later the officers filed into the courtroom and the court martial began. Admiral Harvey waited at the head of the long table as president of the court; standing on his right was Captain Holloway as prosecutor; the six captains assembled in order of their seniority. At the other end of the table stood the judge advocate, and the defence counsel was isolated behind a small table close to the prisoners. After the court was sworn in, everyone sat down with a scraping of chairs, and the provost-martial brought in the prisoners. The men were brought to attention to the left of the judge advocate, while witnesses stood at his right.

The distinguished nature of the court was explained by the appearance of the first prisoner: a second lieutenant accused of absenting himself without leave. As the officer pleaded guilty there was little delay in finding the charge 'proven' and the verdict declared him 'incapable of serving in the naval service of Her Majesty, her heirs and successors for ever', though he was recommended for consideration by the Lords Commissioner of the Admiralty.

The officer was followed by a corporal and private in the marines, from H.M.S. *Cambridge*, who were convicted on a similar charge, receiving the lesser punishment of fifty lashes each, and they were followed in their turn by two seamen from H.M.S. *Indus* accused of 'unnatural crime'. When this was found 'proven' too, in spite of their plea of not guilty, the president spoke of their 'atrocious depravity' before passing sentence. The two prisoners were to be hanged aboard their ship the following morning to 'expose the enormity of such an offence'.

Dick Stanton was the next prisoner, and came to attention beside the judge advocate staring rigidly ahead.

'Seaman Richard Stanton, you are charged with insolent and contemptuous behaviour towards a midshipman.' The charge was confirmed by Pompous Percy who, with his staring eyes and brick-red complexion, looked as if he was about to burst from his tight-collared jacket. The defence claimed that Stanton had slipped in his attempt to catch some loose halyards, but this was denied by the young midshipman, who described Stanton's late arrival on board the *Juniper* on the morning of the Queen's inspection. He concluded that his insubordination was deliberate.

'But the man could have slipped?' asked Captain Rudolphus Bryce, representing the *Shannon*.

Midshipman Haynes hesitated, but recovered as he remembered the sailor's smile after the incident. 'I believe not, sir,' he stated firmly. 'He has claimed there was a swell which made him lose his balance, but it happened to no one else. I believe he fell against me deliberately because I had rebuked him.'

Captain Bryce turned his gaze to the criss-crossed scar that stretched over Dick Stanton's cheek and concluded, as others had before him, that the man was a trouble-maker.

'Dumb insolence,' murmured Captain Webley of the *Triumph*, reaching the same conclusion. With several more prisoners to deal with, the president conferred quickly with the captains beside him, suggesting a punishment of a hundred and fifty lashes and forfeiture of pay, to be followed by two years' solitary confinement in the Marshalsea Prison.

Captain Algernon Ward, who commanded the *Juniper* and knew that Stanton was not a trouble-maker in spite of the conspicuous scar, whispered in the man's defence: 'He's not a bad lad. Intelligent. I believe some leniency is in order.'

They looked towards the president, who remembered a recent instruction from the Admiralty and beamed with a sudden benevolence. 'Then I have the solution. He looks strong enough and they need such men in Van Diemen's Land. Give him a chance to start again, eh? Two years' transportation, agreed?'

'Agreed.'

When Dick Stanton was taken back to the *Juniper*, the provost-martial treated him sympathetically as he placed him in detention. Resenting the arrogance of Midshipman Haynes, he warmed to the sailor who had dared to send him flying across the deck. When Dick asked him if Van Diemen's Land was an island off Holland, he was genuinely concerned.

'No, lad, she's a far cry from Holland. You're off to the other side of the world – to Australasia. They call the place that because some Dutchman discovered it. You'll make out all right if you behave yourself, like the convicts who get a ticket of leave to settle there. About a thousand of them go there a year.'

Stanton's face clouded over at the mention of 'convict'. Was this to be his label from now on?

'Anyways, no cause to fret – you're not being hung!'

That was the fate of the two seamen from the flagship charged with 'unnatural crime' as Dick was taken to Plymouth dock at ten the next morning. When they passed the *Cambridge*, the longboat drifted with oars at rest as the crew watched the prisoners being led along the gangway to the forecastle. Ropes were strung around their necks, and they knelt before the naval chaplain until their prayers were shattered by a gunshot and their bodies leapt up the foreyard-arm. They were left hanging there as a warning to the men before being lowered an hour later and taken for interment to the Royal Naval Hospital on shore.

A shocking sight, but Dick forgot it as he concentrated on his own future. Two things worried him: the friends he left behind on the *Juniper*, and the pain his father would suffer when he learnt of his son's disgrace and transportation. But the resilience of youth is limitless. Two years. Only two years! he thought, and a chance to see the other side of the world. By nightfall he was dressed in grey, one of twenty men sentenced to transportation, with a number on his jacket and rings round his legs. His carefree days as a sailor were finished.

Dick's natural curiosity helped him during the march through the English countryside after the convicts disembarked at Portsmouth. By day there was the glow of autumn, the leaves turning colour before they fell, a warm display of browns, reds and yellows, and by night they slept on the floor of a local prison with straw as a mattress and a roof to shelter them from the cold. Being chained to another man was vile as well as slow, but Steven Boucher was a cheerful lad of his own age, of farming stock from Hatherleigh. His black sense of humour, which became his dark appearance, stemmed from his days as a grave-digger, though this had been his undoing: "'Tis awful waste, burying good things with dead 'uns,' he told Dick unrepentantly. He had been caught by the vicar in the act of taking a ring from a corpse's finger, and been put in charge, resulting in his transportation to Van Diemen's Land. The joint destination, like the chain which bound them together, forged an immediate friendship.

Reaching London nineteen days later, the convicts were marched through the city along the banks of the Thames, past Westminster and Wapping, through the turbulence of Ratcliffe Highway, past the kiln at Limehouse Dock, on to the loneliness of the Isle of Dogs where a solitary windmill rose from the marshland, until they reached the slipway opposite Greenwich and were rowed to the *Indomitable* moored in the centre of the river.

This grandly named vessel had known glory as a Spanish 32-gun warship until she was captured by the British, but now she was ignominiously referred to as a hulk: the right word for this floating dungeon, described by one misguided official as 'an academy for reformation'. In spite of this euphemism, it remained a *hulk*, all base and no top except for two spindly masts with washing strung between and six rickety smoking chimneys. The inferno lay in the density below.

This was to be Dick's home until his transportation along with 500 other men, most of them double-ironed. Once on board, his arrival was recorded in a minimum of words: date, name and age. Condition: male. Position and institution: convict. STANTON CONVICT 982. Then he was stripped and dipped in two vast vats of water, the first soapy and the next supposedly clean though it re-sembled a sewer by the time Dick arrived. His clothes were taken away to be sold and he was issued instead with the obligatory coarse, grubby ship-dress. Though he was re-ironed with light fetters round each ankle and a chain between, he was spared the chain stretching from the waist to the throat inflicted on the more dangerous criminals. Then he was taken below, guarded by soldiers with drawn cutlasses ready to stop anyone with the desperate idea of diving overboard. The stench was sick-ening and grew worse, for new arrivals were taken to the bottom of the hulk to work their way upwards by virtue of their good conduct in this murky world. The stench did not come from the prisoners alone; it crept out of every crevice in the timbers which retained a putrid mixture of ballast, damp, rot, and seeping human excre-ment which had festered over the years until it was in a state of ferment. Dick gasped, choked, and gagged as he struggled to breathe in such airlessness. The upper deck had been warm from the sun and positively airy compared to these lower depths where the black liquid seeped through the wood. The chance of escape to the pleasanter decks above was seen by the officials as a spur to good behaviour, so they allowed these wretched conditions to continue in the name of 'encouragement'.

At this depth, the river outside added its own rich, dank aroma, and it was said locally that even the famous Greenwich whitebait were blackbait until they were rinsed in fresh water.

A passage ran down the middle of each deck with rows of cells on either side containing twenty to thirty prisoners. The cells resembled cages, rows of impen-etrable iron bars enclosing the convicts. Though lanterns protected by metal grilles lay in the bulkheads dividing each cell, they shed little light, and candles were one of the luxuries exchanged for tobacco and other goods smuggled on board. It was extraordinary that so much bartering went on between men who apparently possessed nothing.

After supper in convict ward, Dick and Steven were locked in their cells at seven thirty. Lights-out was at nine. With hardly the room to stand upright, the familiarity of the hammocks was a relief, though they were barely inches apart.

Prisoners appointed as watchmen relieved each other every two hours, but made no effort to enforce the rules. Even after nine there was no silence, but an uproar of cursing, swearing and depravity. Dick was accustomed to the noisy companionship of the lower decks, but the noise was hostile here. Whenever he felt himself slipping into sleep, he was woken by shouts as fights broke out over games of dominoes or pitch and toss. Hour after hour the obscenities continued. The man in the hammock next to Steven masturbated openly in a fantasy world of his own, and Steven turned his face away, muttering to Dick: 'It's like a hell on earth.'

Dick nodded, for once too disheartened to speak. The man the other side of him, ancient in Dick's eyes as he must have been all of forty, gave a sarcastic laugh. 'This is a paradise compared to some,' he informed them. 'In the *Ganymede* they have three tiers of hammocks, one above the other. That *is* hell, if you like. Mind you, if you have anything of value, don't let on, for they'll strip you clean if they think there's anything to rob. Don't even tell *me*, for I'll be tempted. Keep yourselves to yourselves. If anyone makes up to you, raise your fists and tell them to bugger off so they know where you stand from the start.' When Dick told him of his transportation, the 'old' man laughed. 'Lor, you're a lucky one,' he said surprisingly. 'To be sent abroad. I'm sentenced here and doubt if I'll live to see the end of it. And if I do I won't come out the sort of man I'd want to meet myself. You worsen here. You young'uns look honest enough but you'll lose all that if you stay here long. Things I've seen! I wouldn't tell you!' He offered them tobacco though smoking was forbidden and proffered some fatherly advice: 'Take care if the watchman's lantern is blown out. That's a signal for trouble.'

'What sort of trouble?' asked Steven.

'Trouble trouble. Every kind of trouble,' said the man mysteriously.

A blessed stillness replaced the pandemonium for a few hours around midnight. Soon after three, the treadmill turned again as the convict cooks began the prisoners' breakfast, though why such a meagre meal required such a lengthy preparation remained a mystery. When Dick was confronted with the mess of boiled barley he was unable to finish it, spoiled by the fresh farm produce enjoyed on the march to London. His fastidiousness lasted for two days; then hunger conquered taste.

Breakfast was eaten, if not enjoyed, after a rapid visit to the troughs and buckets of the wash-house. Even if there had been all the time in the world, Dick's visit would have been brief. The closets were never properly drained, owing to the scarcity of water, and the stink was appalling. After breakfast there came the call for 'all hands' to muster, and the prisoners swabbed down an entire deck, a different level each day. An hour later, at seven o'clock, Dick presented his hammock for inspection, stowed it away, and came up for air to face his first full day in London.

He looked around him eagerly, having learnt of Greenwich Palace, birthplace of Henry VIII and Queen Elizabeth, but the hulk was anchored discreetly around the bend of the river, sparing the gentry of Greenwich the proof of its wretched existence. The swells who ate their whitebait dinners in the new Trafalgar Tavern did so with no qualms of conscience to spoil the taste.

As the prisoners lined the upper deck, they were roughly searched by the guards before being divided into groups of ten and ferried ashore. Even in this stretch, the river was alive with every type of craft: white sails and rowing boats, swaying masts and paddle-boats; all the traffic of the Thames.

The Isle of Dogs was not an island but a horseshoe-shaped peninsula. Great walls were being erected along the shore to hold back the floods from the seven mills, and most of the convicts were marched in this direction. Dick and Steven were taken past Cold Harbour to the other side of Black Wall stairs, and then to the marshland beyond the River Lee where the foreshore had proved so treacherous that the land was being reclaimed for the public benefit. It was energetic work overlooked by hard-faced soldiers, and though the days were cold their efforts kept them warm. The luxury of bread and cheese at noon was provided by the cheerful wife of the man who owned the orchard north of the river. A kindly, home-loving woman, sympathetic to any 'transport', she allowed them to pick up windfalls under the apple trees afterwards.

Back on the *Indomitable* by nightfall, Dick was searched again before a supper of 'smiggins': a dirty-looking broth thickened with barley and a few scraps of meat from the fatless carcases of elderly cattle. There was broken biscuit to supplement the bread, which was made with sea-water and either unbreakable or so gluey that it stuck to the wall when the convicts threw it away in disgust. Each man was given a pint of beer on four evenings a week. After 'smiggins' and another dash to the wash-rooms, Dick and Steven were locked up again.

This was their routine, and there was no indication when their transportation would end it. Autumn made way for winter and conditions grew worse. Now they were incarcerated for sixteen hours a day, with so little supervision that the uproar below acquired a new ferocity. The 'London Particulars' descended, remorseless fogs especially dense along the river, penetrating the lower depths, suffocating the precious candles which struggled faintly against the fumes already seeping through the timbers, blackening men's throats and leaving them gasping. When the fog was particularly bad the food grew better in compensation, with generous portions of broth, and boiled ox-cheek made into soup.

On Saturdays the men were ordered to shave in readiness for Sunday when they were mustered on the main deck for kit inspection. The Divine Service which followed was performed by a chaplain who came on board with a lavender scented handkerchief which he pressed constantly to his nose.

The fog also brought disease. Many of the prisoners died from one ailment or another – including the 'old' man in the hammock next to Dick, released at last by typhus – but Dick suffered no worse than dysentery caused by drinking the water filtered from the Thames. Steven suffered from a graver complaint. Raised in the west country, he had spent his days in the open air. Now, like a caged animal, he pined away for no apparent reason, though the surgeon understood. 'What a cruel irony!' he muttered to his assistant. 'He's one of the few with nothing wrong with him, yet it's plain the boy is dying.'

A week later Steven was shifted to the hospital ward – the forecastle separated by a few nailed partitions – and when Dick received permission to visit him he found his friend lying listlessly on a straw mattress inches away from a man with scurvy. His leg irons had been removed and he smiled faintly when he recognised Dick. After that Dick was allowed to see him every day. He was given rice gruel and a little wine to raise his spirits, but a few days later he died.

Dick was told of his friend's death by one of the guards. He was silent, for he had been expecting the news, but he shuddered when he saw the naked corpse of his friend being washed on deck; buffeted by a broom on the bare planks before it was dumped in a coffin and taken ashore.

Even more distressing was a visit from his father. William Stanton had been notified of Dick's imprisonment in the hulk and made the four-day journey from Bideford to say farewell before he was transported. To the dismay of both, the father broke down when he saw his son in such surroundings. The boy looked well enough, in spite of the initial shock of that shaven head, but the cuts on his hands, the filthy clothing – above all, the hideous all-pervading stench – were so overwhelming that Stanton turned away for a few moments. Trying to compose

43

himself, he feigned a coughing fit: not difficult in such conditions.

They spoke formally of inconsequential subjects at first. Hoping to amuse Dick, Stanton described the 'goings-on' at Raxleigh, though he shunned gossip as a rule.

'You'll scarcely credit it, but they say that Mr Lionel . . .' He referred to the sly editorial in the *Bideford Gazette* which alluded to 'rumours regarding a well-known local family', though it was careful to name no names. Dick started to laugh when told of the antics at Barnstaple Fair and Roly's disastrous loss at cards – 'probably the most substantial gambling debt the town has ever known' – and the old man regretted his indiscretion.

'I know it has a humorous side, but I feel for that poor family. Their disgrace reflects on us all. I dread the outcome.'

Dick had never understood his father's loyalty to the Raxleighs, wondering at times if it might have been misplaced – after all, they dispensed with his services when it suited them – but he listened and nodded respectfully, delaying the inevitable lecture.

'Do tread carefully,' William Stanton implored him, when it came at last. 'I know how impetuous you can be, but try to work for your own advancement – especially at first, when everything will be counted, for you or against. Don't make the silly mistake of swimming against the tide. Go with it. I'm told they need decent, educated young men to colonise Van Diemen's Land, so a pardon is not hard to come by. You could make a fine life for yourself out there.'

'Never,' Dick interrupted emphatically, trying to make their separation seem less final. 'As soon as I'm free, I'll come back. My home is here with you. And don't worry, I'll behave myself. To tell you the truth, I'm looking forward to getting there. Anything will be better than this!'

'I can understand that,' nodded Stanton, looking around him.

'A mate of mine called it hell,' Dick replied, remembering Steven, 'and he wasn't far wrong.'

44

Neither was aware that this was the last, painful gasp of a system which had failed. Originally the hulks were intended as a resting place for 'transports' before the journey overseas, but the hulks had deteriorated into floating conveniences for others too: prisoners held on suspicion, not yet convicted; old lags who were irredeemable, though hardly criminal; young boys whom nobody knew what to do with. All were victims of the morality of the time which swept such unfortunates out of sight, and forgot them. Like most reformatories, no one left there reformed.

Dick had been shocked to see children condemned to such a place. Judges in their mercy sentenced boys to the hulks 'for their own good', with little idea that they were sending them to a place more miserable than prison itself. It was worse for the very young and the very old because there seemed no hope for them. The boys were treated with special harshness, kept in silence for hours on end, birched for the slightest disobedience, or, in the case of one boy of nine, locked in darkness in a solitary cell after being labelled 'incorrigible'. The judge offered to release another boy, John Cowley, if his mother would take him home. She refused, saying he was too old to come home at fourteen, and he was sentenced to transportation 'in the hope of offering him a new chance in life'. Learning that he was destined for Van Diemen's Land Dick befriended him, snatching a few words whenever this was possible.

Why were the hulks retained when their original purpose was lost? The answer, as it is so often, was mercenary: it was cheaper to maintain them than to build new prisons on shore, especially as Britain was still paying the price for winning the Napoleonic Wars. The cost of living was rising all the time. Even so, the unworkable system was nearing its end: earlier that year it had been denounced in the House of Commons by Thomas Slingsby Dunscombe, the member of parliament for Finsbury, who claimed that 'the cruelty was so excessive, the medical treatment was so brutal, and the manner in

45

which the prisoners were treated when alive, as well as when dead, was such that it was utterly disgraceful to a civilised Christian country'. Suffering from a bout of conscience, Parliament set up a committee of investigation to look into the conditions on board the hulks, and their first official visit took place on board the *Indomitable* the day after William Stanton's emotional farewell to his son. This was a lucky chance for Dick. Encouraged by the four golden sovereigns pressed into his hand by the old man from Devon, Superintendent Snaipe included Dick's name among a dozen convicts recommended for early release. William Stanton had behaved most courteously when he implored him to help his son, should the opportunity arise. If Snaipe was going to be bribed he liked it to be done properly, with politeness.

'The lad's a transport,' he explained to the MPs, 'but the Navy has washed its hands of him and the Colonial Office doesn't seem in any hurry, either. It could take years before they shift him, and by then he'll be no use to anyone.' The distinguished gentlemen nodded gravely, still shocked by the number of diseased and dying men they had seen while inspecting conditions below decks.

'And he's got a home to go to,' added the superintendent, 'which is more than you can say for most of 'em. I suggest his sentence be quashed.'

The shaken committee departed, promising to implement his recommendations, and Superintendent Snaipe expected to tell Dick the good news before Christmas.

Dick had no hint of this. He believed he was doomed to stay in the hulk for months, and ideas of escape began to fester. He was also preoccupied with the bullying of John Cowley by a boy called Nobbs, notorious for his simple method of intimidating those around him. He punched them. Though he was no more than fifteen Nobbs was gigantic for his age. His arms swung to his knees, and his fists and fingers were red and swollen from so much sport. His pale face was covered with red spots and most of his teeth were broken and discoloured.

Rations were small for the tiniest boy and totally

inadequate for Nobbs, who seized whatever meat he could lay his hands on. He needed it, but this meant that his victims were left even hungrier. 'Blessings' at mealtimes became a mockery as the scraps were snatched from their mouths. Some boys were so desperate that they inflicted wounds on themselves in order to reach the safety of the hospital ward; one persuaded a friend to break his left arm by dropping a wooden beam on to it, pretending afterwards that he had fallen down a ladder. When his arm mended, the boy was sent to work in the garden on the Isle of Dogs. The surgeon encouraged the provision of fresh vegetables for the convicts suffering from scurvy, though most of the produce found its way to the officers. 'That garden's worth a twisted arm,' John Cowley whispered.

One cold, grey day, working on a new machine which drove piles deep into the mud to fortify the embankment against the tides, Dick noticed a festering gash on Cowley's arm. The boy had resorted to the desperate trick of burning the skin with a red-hot copper button, rubbing soap into the wound, and covering it up with a dirty bandage until it was septic. Dismayed by the gash, which looked worse than it was, Dick was ashamed of the boy until he was told about Nobbs. Touching the pus-filled skin around the wound, he said, 'You should have stuck it out.'

'Anything to get away from Nobbs,' the boy replied. 'You don't know what he's like. Anything to get to the garden.'

Dick had the chance to see the persecutor for himself two days later, when Nobbs was assigned to the pile-driver because of his unusual strength. Then he understood John Cowley's reluctance to fight. Dick had no wish to do so either, but when he heard other convicts refer to Nobbs that night he agreed when someone suggested it was time to teach the young monster a lesson.

—''Tis not fair,' said one, 'the way Nobbs helps hisself to the meat, leaving the little'uns the gruel and shavings. No wonder they're no more than skeletons.'

'And they daresn't say a word against him,' said another.

'If they tell the officers they'll be known as noseys, so Nobbs gets away with it,' declared the first man. 'Time to stop him.'

Dick thought vaguely of a ducking in the polluted Thames, which was nasty enough, but Nobbs's punishment proved more permanent. One day in November, Nobbs was pushed forward as they turned the machine which punched the piles into the mud off Chinns Mill, though who shoved him nobody ever told. With a cry he went under the murky water and the pile plunged down after him, rising again with blood and flesh and sinew sticking to the base. The water reddened. A hand rose to the surface and disappeared.

Dick dived after it while the others stopped the machine and crowded round. For a moment he thought Nobbs had been swept away by the currents, but a few seconds later he grabbed something which proved to be hair and brought him to the surface. At first it looked as if he was dead, but though his arm had been crushed to a pulp the rest of him survived.

However much they hated Nobbs, they admired the way he told no tales, although he was cross-examined by Superintendent Snaipe after the surgeon performed the final amputation. Snaipe guessed the truth of the 'fall' and wondered who was responsible. He was on the point of elevating Dick to a higher deck to reward him for the rescue, but he hesitated. 'For all I know it was Stanton who pushed him in the first place. Anyhow, he'll be gone before long.'

So Dick stayed on the bottom of the hulk while Nobbs was removed to the hospital ward. Eventually both he and John Cowley were transferred to the prison garden on shore, where Nobbs appointed himself in full, if single-handed, control.

Christmas approached. Even in that godforsaken dungeon it was something to look forward to, a break in routine, and the bartering went on more earnestly than ever. Tobacco was smuggled on board by the guards. Snaipe turned a blind eye to the practice, which kept his officers and the convicts happy, and acted as a fumigant as well.

Unfortunately, a newly appointed overseer who was unaware of this 'arrangement' was rash enough to impose a search on the morning of Christmas Eve. As the men filed ashore for work, they were searched and a number of articles removed. But the grumbling was nothing to the convicts' fury when they returned at dusk to find that their lockers in the wards had been broken into – tobacco, coffee, salt, sugar, alcohol; all had been seized. Locked in their cells, they spent the next few hours in mutinous revolt, swearing obscenities at the guards, throwing whatever objects they could lay their hands on through the iron bars. At last Superintendent Snaipe came down to restore order with the promise that all their possessions would be returned on Christmas Day, along with a special issue of ale.

After he left the fury erupted again. Men claimed that Snaipe had lied in order to deceive them. 'They'll keep us locked up tomorrow.' 'We've been tricked. Just you see.' The lanterns went out.

Dick fell asleep around midnight, dreaming of home. Suddenly, he woke up and listened. Something was wrong. The murk seemed murkier in the darkness, the dankness danker, the wetness wetter. With a shout he fell out of his hammock into two feet of water. The hulk was sinking. The yells of other waking convicts followed, rising to the decks above, as everywhere men sensed danger from the different lie of the ship. The hulk shifted slowly on to her beam end, where a section of timber had been chiselled loose an hour earlier by a group of prisoners in a desperate, suicidal act of revenge.

Superintendent Snaipe ran from his cabin; a gun was fired in distress; ashore the bells rang in warning, though people stirring in their beds at Greenwich assumed they were welcoming Christmas morning. In the depths of the hulk, men struggled for their lives, frantic in the rising water.

Many died, trapped in their cells on the lowest deck. As the water streamed down the timbers they clutched their hammocks, lifting their heads above the swirling blackness. A timber cracked, leaving a gap, and Dick seized his chance, though the weight of the rushing water forced him back at first. Somehow, a few moments later, naked and bleeding, he rose to the surface of the River Thames.

A faint, flickering light came from the looming hulk as the currents swept him away towards Greenwich. He glimpsed the lanterns of lightermen hurrying to the shore, and knew that soldiers would be running too from the army garrison. He tried to strike out to the opposite side of the river but the weight of his irons pulled him down. Surfacing again, spluttering and coughing, he saw a ship in the middle of the river ahead of him displaying a strong blue light, the helmsmen peering into the darkness.

Dick had no choice of direction. The tide carried him forward with a speed that saved him from sinking, but his strength was ebbing in the freezing water. He would have drowned but for the floating timber which curled up beside him, broad enough to rest on as he grabbed it.

Dick had no concept of time. It could have been a moment or eternity before the tide swept him round the bend of the river at Limehouse. He saw a twinkling of lights on the shore. The timber veered in their direction as if it was guiding him to safety; there was a sudden clang as it struck an iron ladder. He clutched at the lower rungs as the shock threw him into the water.

Shouts from a balcony above, faces peering down as a lantern was held above him, a girl's scream as she saw his nakedness, then silence as they noticed the glint of iron round his feet. Hands reached out, dragged him up the last few rungs and pulled him on to the verandah where he collapsed.

'Bloody hell,' said one, 'it's a convict.'

'Poor soul,' said the girl.

— 4 —

The fall of the House of Raxleigh

The autumn sunlight was weak but well meaning as Squire Stowe cantered along the banks of the Torridge on his way to Kane House, the home of the Clevelands. He knew Lord Cleveland in the course of business, and thought of him as a friend. In this Gussie was as foolish as the victim of the confidence trickster who is vain enough to believe he will be the exception, though he knows his friends have been cheated. Lord Cleveland was effusive with a smile and an outstretched hand, but the smile was that of a predator. Augustus Stowe was an innocent, relying on such vague terms as 'decency' which have no currency in commerce. That was why his fortunes had waned, while those of Cleveland had risen.

As he rode through the gates, Augustus Stowe saw no cause for anxiety; after all, he was dealing with a peer of the realm, who would never take unfair advantage of a boy's indiscretion on his coming-of-age. However, he was startled to find he was expected. A stable-boy tethered the horse, while the butler took his coat and gave him a sympathetic smile. Gussie always made a point of asking servants how they were and enquiring after their families, and though this was a courtesy rather than genuine interest it was appreciated.

'I believe his lordship's ready to receive you,' said the manservant gravely, leading the way into a spacious, low-ceilinged drawing-room where Lord Cleveland was seated at a desk, writing busily. He made his visitor welcome with a firm handshake and the offer of a glass of madeira. Gussie relaxed.

'How nice to see you, Gussie,' his lordship exclaimed. 'But what brings you here? Nothing wrong, I hope?'

Gussie stiffened.

'Young Roly . . .' he began.

'Yes?' said Lord Cleveland innocently. Surely he *knew*?

'I gather he played cards with your son last night.'

'Did he!' exclaimed his lordship.

'I think the boy was very drunk. Roly, I mean. It was his birthday, and he had some papers which he gave your son as security. Stupid of him, of course, but he didn't know what he was doing. I thought if you could have a word with . . .' His voice tailed away as he saw that Lord Cleveland was staring at him angrily.

'You're not accusing my son of cheating him, are you?' he demanded.

'No, no, not at all . . .' Gussie protested, and Lord Cleveland smiled again.

'That's all right then! All's fair in love and cards, eh? But if you're worried, we'd better have a word with young Charlie. I think he's around.' He pulled a cord, and when the butler appeared he sent him off in pursuit of his son and heir. While they waited, Lord Cleveland spoke of such trivialities that Gussie found it hard to concentrate. Surely Charlie Cleveland had told his father what had happened?

Apparently not, for when the young man appeared he spoke to his father as if it was the first time they had met that morning.

'You know Squire Stowe . . .?'

'Yes, of course, sir.' The future Lord Cleveland held out a hand and bowed respectfully. 'I'm a friend of your son, Roland,' he added. 'I saw him last night.'

'That,' said Lord Cleveland, 'is why Squire Stowe has called. He says you have some papers belonging to Roland.'

'No, sir,' Charlie beamed, 'they belong to me. I won them last night, if you mean the deeds of Raxleigh House.'

'The deeds to Raxleigh House,' echoed Lord Cleveland with astonishment. 'A substantial win for you, sir, though I fear a considerable loss to my old friend.' He turned to this 'old friend' with concern. 'I assume, Augustus, that you have come to buy them back?'

Gussie realised the extent of his naivety. He had walked into a trap, totally unprepared, while the Clevelands played charades. Idiotically, he had been hoping that the deeds would be returned with some humorous remark warning young Roly to be more careful in future. He replied as calmly as he could: 'Of course I shall be happy to buy them back. How much did Roly lose last night?'

The Clevelands looked at each other, apparently confused.

'The deeds,' said Charlie, frowning. 'I just told you.'

Lord Cleveland turned to his heir. 'How much would you be prepared to sell them for? Remember, the Stowes are our friends.'

'Having won them fairly and squarely, sir,' said Charlie dutifully, 'I had not thought of parting with them so soon. But if it is your wish, I should do so for the exact sum which Roly lost – seven thousand pounds.' Young Cleveland started to choke, raising his hand to his mouth.

'It seems a lot of money,' said Lord Cleveland, shaking his head. 'How about it, Gussie?' The enormity of the sum was surpassed by their deceit. There was no way he could pay it.

Gussie gathered the shreds of his dignity around him. 'Of course I shall have to think about it before I let you know.'

'Of course,' said Lord Cleveland agreeably. 'No hurry, is there?' he asked his son.

'Take your time, sir,' Charlie assured him. The two Clevelands grinned as they bade their visitor farewell.

While Augustus Stowe was enduring this mortification, his brother-in-law tried to remember the night before.

The images of Barnstaple Fair crept into his consciousness, but so fleetingly that it was hard to tell if they were true or not. When he staggered to the glass above his dressing-table he gazed at his reflection. One eye was almost closed by a purplish swelling, and dried blood lingered on his cheekbone.

'God help me.' Like most men he turned to God in moments of personal despair. 'Let it be all right.' Though Lionel Raxleigh was excessive in drink, he was puritanical at heart and suffered deep remorse. Ironically, he only drank occasionally, but as this invariably happened in public he was seen to be drunk continually. The pattern had a fearful inevitability: he drank because he was shy and drink made him less so, but one drink was not enough. He continued until he reached that carefree state of oblivion and finally obliteration. Usually the only cure was another drink, but today he would stay in bed. He could not face the prospect of company, feeling the utmost guilt at missing the party.

Roly groaned when he woke up. Then he had a fit of coughing. Then he moaned. Then he made love to his wife, violently, as if he was trying to relieve his guilt. When he was finished, he rolled away, exhausted, leaving Matilda with the feeling that she had just been raped. She had enjoyed the violence once, but now she dreaded that meaningless excess of passion. Yet she loved him. Insecure, snatched from a different class with no money and no social graces to recommend her, possessing looks which were pleasing rather than elegant, she did not 'belong' in the Stowe family. Her husband told her so frequently, causing the inevitable scream of anguish: 'Then why did you marry me?' and his inevitable reply: 'God knows! I must have been mad', followed by her heartbroken sobs as she wondered why she had married anyone so cruel.

She knew, of course. She thought he was the most attractive man she had ever seen. Not for a moment did she resent his vanity, which seemed natural in someone so handsome. Of course he was pleased with himself, with his cluster of dark curls falling over his forehead; no wonder he walked with a superior swagger and a sardonic smile. He stood out from the rest of the crowd like a peacock among pigeons. With the scarlet waistcoat which she had embroidered herself, he had the arrogance of heroes. The knowledge that he was so remote from her own background made him all the more tantalising. Among all the girls of Bideford society, why should he have noticed her? She was conscious that she lacked conventional beauty, unaware that she possessed the rarer quality of radiance, with her tumbling auburn hair and lovely eyes of darkest blue. She had exuded a sense of fun before her marriage, and it was this gaiety that made him notice her among the girls who hoped for his attention.

One perfect day in early summer, when the tides were high, he had set out down the Torridge with a party of friends for Weare Giffard, to buy some of the strawberries for which the village was renowned. As his boat passed under Bideford Bridge he had looked up and seen her smiling face as she leaned over the parapet, and acting on a sudden impulse had called out to her to join them. No further persuasion was needed. Laughing with excitement, she ran across the bridge to the steps where he had steered the boat, and clambered into it.

Like people who live near the sea yet never swim, few made the journey by boat when they could do so on horseback, and she savoured every moment of this unexpected outing on the water. The heat-haze lifted slowly, revealing a perfect sky above an unspoilt landscape. Large, lazy herons rose slowly from the mud banks and flapped their way across the meadows, vexed by the disturbance of voices from the five approaching boats. Otters surfaced, stared, shook their whiskers in consternation and disappeared. Brightest of all, a flash of vivid blue and green raced ahead of them, a kingfisher darting for cover. As Roly, stripped to the waist, took the oars, he smiled at the girl facing him. She smiled back, understanding his intentions completely.

Having fetched their punnets of strawberries, they sat outside the solitary inn devouring hot pasties washed down with ale, until there was a shout of warning that the tide was starting to ebb again. Then they ran, laughing, hand in hand across the fields, knee-deep in grass and wild flowers, and pushed the boats into the receding water which would take them back to Bideford. The other boats went ahead with distant, fading cries of encouragement.

Left on their own, for Roly had held back, they moored the boat at one of the bends of the river and he led her into the woods and made love to her. Because he was kinder then, he took her gently, and she gave herself wholly for the first time in her life. It was dusk when they reached Bideford, gazing at each other in silent wonder at the marvellous thing that had happened.

As they passed under the bridge, several of their friends leant over and cheered, guessing what had taken place, and because of this unfortunate display the whole of Bideford gossiped the following day. Yet it was not a sense of duty that made Roly ask her to marry him. It was a gesture of contempt for the life mapped out for him, which included a conventional wife from his own class, and preferably one who would bring him a dowry. The more his father pleaded, the more his audacity grew. 'I'm damned if I'll be told whom to marry, even by you. It's my decision, no one else's.'

'Yes,' said Gussie wearily. 'But don't rush into it, please. That's all I'm asking.'

Gussie had been shaken by the announcement. He suspected that Roly was being perverse, which was foolish, or had made the girl pregnant, which was disgraceful. Outwardly, he maintained his phlegmatic façade, but when they were alone together he asked his wife incredulously: 'He can't love her, surely?'

'One never knows where love is concerned,' she replied. 'The oddest people love the oddest people.'

'But she isn't a *lady*!' Gussie protested.

'She's a nice girl.'

'I think it's all a game on Roly's part,' Gussie exclaimed with a glimmering of hope. 'All done to annoy us, for he swears that she isn't with child. I wish I could believe that, I really do.'

He suggested to Roly that it might be a good idea to delay the wedding, knowing this would end the rumours that the marriage had been rushed through for reasons of necessity. It would also give Roly time to think again. Detecting the ruse instantly, Roly insisted on an immediate, private ceremony, to the disappointment of the relatives who had been looking forward to a splendid wedding. The knowledge that the arrogant Roly was marrying out of his class provided a glorious chance for gossip. On this score, at least, Gussie was relieved that the wedding was private.

Few people bothered about the girl's feelings, but Matilda did not hesitate, though she knew his faults by now. She wanted him and now she had him, and it was this feeling of being possessed that turned Roly against her. Only in moments of dread, as on this disastrous morning, did he turn to her for the loyalty he knew she would never deny him.

Sarah Stowe appreciated this loyalty now. To begin with, she had been downcast with disappointment over a marriage so alien to the one she had planned. Poor Matilda had none of the desirable attributes of family or dowry. Her father had drowned near Lundy Island when she was nine, leaving a wife and three headstrong girls, of which Matilda was the eldest. She brought no fortune, no brother to defend her honour, no family connections. It was the lack of these practical advantages which had dismayed Sarah at the beginning, rather than snobbery. Once she accepted Matilda as her daughter-in-law, she did her best to absorb her into the unfamiliar world of Raxleigh House, teaching her the basic rules of etiquette, stopping her from becoming too friendly with the servants or doing tasks which were beneath her now. Matilda who was active by nature, used to washing and cleaning and shopping, found that her new life as a lady of leisure became boring, so Sarah encouraged her to help in the garden, and the bond between the two women strengthened as they picked and pruned and grew to know each other.

Sarah admired her daughter-in-law's loyalty, which never wavered, though she suspected there was ample cause for complaint. There were times when Roly's selfishness shocked even her, but she never heard Matilda say a word against him.

When Gussie failed to return from the Clevelands' Sarah waited with growing anxiety, replaced by a dread that something terrible had happened to him as the light faded and darkness began to fall. She stayed in her armchair, dozing from time to time, refusing to go to bed though Matilda and Sally implored her to.

It was dawn when her husband entered the room, closing the door behind him quietly for fear of waking the household. He hurried towards her, begging her forgiveness as they embraced.

'I am so sorry, my love,' he whispered. 'After I saw the Clevelands I went straight to the solicitor. When I heard what Mr James had to tell me I acted on the spur of the moment and took the subscription coach from the Bush Inn at midday. It was six o'clock when I reached Exeter, with that dratted change of horse at Barnstaple, but I saw the man I was looking for. I caught the midnight coach back and have only just arrived.'

He paused, placed his hands gently around her and told her sadly: 'Sarah, I am afraid it is bad news.'

When the first of the servants made a starched appearance an hour later, Gussie gave orders that a family conference was to be summoned for midday in the dining-room. Then he went upstairs to snatch some rest.

The news of the conference was relayed by the anxious housekeeper, who could tell that the matter was serious. She knocked on Roly's bedroom door, in case he intended leaving the house early, but she need not have bothered.

58

He was spending his second successive day in bed.

'Christ,' he moaned. 'I hope it's not a lecture. I couldn't stand that, the way I'm feeling.' Matilda looked at him coldly.

'Thank you for letting me know,' said Lionel Raxleigh weakly after the knock on his door. 'I hope to God,' he muttered to himself, 'that they're not going to blame me.'

Sally was beside herself with curiosity. No one would tell her what was going on, although she knew her brother was in disgrace. She suppressed a gasp when her uncle entered the dining-room and she saw his swollen eye, but she held her tongue for once, though she whispered a moment later to her brother: 'What has happened? Why won't anyone tell me?'

'Stow it, Sally,' said Roly. The phrase was a family joke, though humourless now. He, too, avoided Lionel's eye, now the colour of an over-ripe fig.

His father entered the room a moment later, making an effort to appear more confident than he felt. 'Do sit down, everyone,' he said, 'and help yourselves to a drink if you feel like one. The claret's on the sideboard.'

Lionel and Roly shook their heads indignantly.

'Good,' said Gussie, sitting at the head of the dining-table. 'Then I had better begin. I spent most of the night wondering how I should break the news, but I think it best in the long run to be absolutely honest and tell you the whole truth, which is why I have called you here together.

'You know that Roly used the deeds to Raxleigh as security in a game of cards with young Cleveland?' There was a gasp from Sally, who had been spared this information.

'Let me say at once,' Gussie continued firmly, 'that I am not attaching blame to anyone for what has happened. I am merely telling you the facts. It was Roly's birthday and he didn't know what he was doing. Certainly he did not know the calibre of the gentleman with whom he was playing. Nor did I, till I spoke to Lord Cleveland. He has offered to sell the deeds back to us for seven thousand pounds.' Sally gasped again.

'Surely he has no legal right?' asked Lionel. 'If nothing is signed?'

'They hold the deeds.'

'Only as security, surely?' exclaimed Roly.

'That's what I assumed,' sighed his father. 'I went straight to my solicitor, who turns out to be Cleveland's solicitor too. Apparently his lordship had already sent his clerk with the deeds while I was on my way to see him. He lost no time in having them re-registered in his name.'

'He can't do that!' Lionel protested.

'I know he can't,' said Gussie patiently, 'but he *has*, and that's the end of it, for there's no hope of raising the money to buy them back. None of you has the faintest idea of the struggle I've been through these last few months. I wanted to spare you. No one likes to be the harbinger of bad news, and I suppose I thought the run of bad luck would come to an end. I reproach myself.' He looked towards Lionel who had given Roly the deeds on his birthday, and then at his son who had lost them so recklessly. Though he was prepared to shoulder the blame he knew in his heart that most of it lay with them.

Matilda looked confused, Sarah despairing, but Sally stared around her as if her real family had been spirited away and replaced by strangers.

'I don't understand,' she cried out. 'How is it possible? You can't lose your home, just like that, in a game of cards . . .'

'Several games,' Roly muttered, a comment which was so exasperating that no one deigned to notice it.

'This doesn't mean we'll have to leave Raxleigh, does it?' she asked beseechingly. The silence confirmed that it meant exactly that. She thought of the future mapped out so carefully, of the ball for her eighteenth birthday, and started to sob. Gussie sighed. The family conference was proving even more distressing than he had expected.

'If only . . .' he began, but stopped abruptly. 'No, it's too late for that. When you so generously gave the deeds to your nephew' – there was no taint of sarcasm in Gussie's voice – 'you had no way of knowing that I am in debt to the bank to the tune of nearly twelve thousand pounds.'

Roly looked up furiously. 'How could you run up debts like that without consulting us? How could you?' Somehow, he had become the aggrieved party.

Lionel came to Gussie's defence at last. 'I understand all too well. The estate's been running at a loss for a long time. It's the way of things today. What I don't understand is this figure of seven thousand to buy the deeds back. Surely Raxleigh's worth more than that?'

Gussie nodded. 'That's perfectly true. The deeds are for the house alone.'

Roly cut in triumphantly: 'Then you can raise money on the estate?'

Gussie sighed. 'You don't imagine I haven't thought of that? I've thought of nothing else these last two days – how to find a way out.'

'You say you've been to the bank?' asked Lionel. Like the rest he found it hard to absorb the full extent of the catastrophe.

'Oh, yes. I went there at once to ask for more time, but Cleveland's clerk had been there too. I was told the bank will foreclose unless it receives its repayment by the end of the month. The manager must know I have no hope of raising such a sum by then. He was sympathetic,' Gussie managed a pained smile, 'he always is, but I could sense the atmosphere had shifted. I asked him if he was still prepared to accept the deeds as security against the loan if I could buy them back from the Clevelands, but he says this will have to be discussed once they are in our possession again. He is not prepared to accept the land as security in the meanwhile, for he says that is inseparable from the house. I suppose he's right.'

'Surely we can fight?' Lionel protested.

'*Fight?*' echoed his brother-in-law. Gussie's voice contained such anguish that they fell silent. 'There were witnesses who saw Roly lose to young Cleveland. There is no evidence that Charlie cheated him. It's just an unbelievable sequence of bad luck that Roly happened to have the deeds with him.'

But Lionel had to ask once more: 'Then you mean there is no point in fighting?'

'Will you tell me what with? Do you have nineteen thousand pounds? If you have that sort of money you can save us.'

'God forgive me,' came the reply. 'All I have is a couple of thousand.'

The silence was such that they could hear the tick-tock of the grandfather clock. Turning to her husband, Sarah asked Gussie if he had finished, knowing there was more to come.

'There was one last chance, a man I know in Exeter, a broker of impeccable reputation and a true friend. I went to ask him if he would advance us a loan of twenty thousand pounds to reclaim the deeds, which I would give him as security. I was sure he would allow us to continue living here until we were able to repay him.'

'That makes sense!' Lionel agreed.

'Wait. He was the only person I could think of who might help us. His office was locked when I got there, but I knew where he lived and knocked on his door. I saw him all right, but he barely saw me. It must have been longer than I realised since we last did business. He suffered a stroke a year ago. He didn't recognise me.'

'Oh, God,' sighed Lionel. 'What an ordeal it must have been for you,' he said compassionately.

'I was so shaken I went to the White Hart for a drink. And then the most extraordinary thing happened – as if it was fated. Who should I see but cousin Tony! You've heard me speak of Sir Anthony Payne?'

Indeed we have, thought Lionel, you've bored us for years with talk of your famous cousin. Every family boasts one influential friend or relation, and Sir Anthony was Gussie's proudest connection.

'Cousin Tony was dining there on his way to Plymouth. He was kind enough to ask me to join him. Seeing my distress, he asked what was wrong and I confided the whole story after supper.'

'And *he*'s lending the money?' exclaimed Roly, who knew there had to be a way out.

'Not a bit of it,' said his father impatiently. 'Only banks and brokers have that sort of money to spare, so be realistic. But he offered us help in another way. He's been appointed Assistant Secretary for the Colonies, a position of considerable influence, and he's made a suggestion . . . he'll do everything he can to assist us if we agree to his proposition.'

'Agree to what?' Roly asked suspiciously.

His father hesitated, hardly daring to go further. He cleared his throat and wiped his brow with a napkin. 'How would you feel,' he asked, looking round the table, 'about starting a new life, somewhere else?'

'Where?' demanded Roly.

'Van Diemen's Land.'

Lionel laughed. 'You're not being serious, Gussie?'

'The Governor in Hobart Town will give us land to settle on. He'll help us in every way.'

They sat there, stunned, until Roly astonished everyone by laughing. 'Why not!' he exclaimed. 'Why jolly well not! I'm sick of it here. It could be fun.'

'Fun?' cried Sally. 'To leave our home and all our friends?'

Gussie ignored her outburst and turned to his son gratefully. 'You really wouldn't mind?'

'Why not? There's nothing left here, is there?' Gussie flinched from the bitterness. 'Van Diemen's Land? Sounds just the place for losers like us.' He scraped his chair back savagely. 'Well, I'm off. Might as well go into town and say goodbye to the old place, run up some credit before we leave.' He turned at the door. 'Van Diemen's Land? Other side of the world, isn't it? Should be far enough.' He slammed it behind him.

Seeing her father-in-law's face, Matilda ran to his side

63

and kissed him impulsively. 'I think it's a wonderful idea,' she declared passionately. Inwardly she blessed the chance to make a new life with Roly, in a new country where no one would know or care about her background, and where she would be judged on her merits alone.

Gussie put his arms around her. 'Bless you, Tilly. What a good, unselfish girl you are!'

Sarah, who recognised Matilda's reaction with greater accuracy, left them without a word, as if she was going to fetch something. Instead, not trusting herself to speak without breaking down, she sought the solace of her garden and sat on the bench under the oak tree overlooking the river, trying to analyse what had happened.

It is madness, she concluded. To see her future destroyed in a matter of hours; to lose her home and all she valued; to sail across the world as if they were transports, into an exile of their own volition. All her senses told her to run back to the house, to hold them back at any cost from this absurd, precipitous venture while there was time. Yet she resisted the impulse. Her duty lay in support of her husband's decision, however misguided. Poor Gussie. Poor Lionel. Poor Roly. She sighed deeply. At that moment she detested the weakness of men.

— 5 —

Love in Limehouse

After Dick Stanton collapsed on the wooden verandah of the Two Brewers, his body was carried upstairs to the attic overlooking the Thames and wrapped in blankets for decency's sake and to keep him warm. The temperature had fallen and the freezing fog tried to creep through every door and window, but inside the bar there was a crackling fire, tobacco smoke, and the genial sound of a fiddle.

The gathering consisted of the landlord and his wife, the buxom barmaid Rosie whose voice was the last sound Dick had heard, and a dozen or so regular customers who had been singing and dancing their way into a carefree state of intoxication. With a fire to give them warmth, and nourishing ale at a penny a pint, the pub was more homely than their own miserable dwellings. No wonder that those who could afford it preferred to spend their evenings in one of the small taverns scattered along this stretch of the waterfront, especially on Christmas Eve.

On this particular festive night the tavern was filled to bursting point. Mrs Fossett, the landlady, moved among her customers, from the bar to the tap-room at the back which overlooked the verandah, dispensing a jug of ale mulled by a red-hot poker. On Christmas Eve there was more genuine goodwill in the East End than behind all the respectable façades of the City. Of all the places in London to be washed ashore, Dick could not have found one where more generous hands waited to help him.

His arrival did not cause the sensation it would have done along the grander reaches of Cheyne Walk. Plenty of bodies were cast up on this particular stretch of the waterfront, though it made a welcome change to find one that was still alive. Mr Gubbins wondered if they should send the pot-boy for the doctor, but there is an instinct in this district which advises caution in seeking help from doctors or clergy, who consider it their duty to inform the police of anything suspicious. The mousetrap man pressed a finger to his long red nose, as if to imply 'the less said the better'.

'I'll go and see how he is, ma'am,' Rosie volunteered. Taking a pewter mug of the rum-punch with her, she went upstairs and did not come back to the bar again that night. But it was Christmas Eve, when such behaviour is overlooked.

Rosie was the right name for her. She was twenty, soft and blooming, with a mass of fair hair. The attic bedroom where Dick lay was her own, so she found her way easily up the narrow, circling stairs in the darkness. Once inside she lit the stump of yesterday's candle and leant over the young man who had swept into the Brewers like some celestial Christmas present. She drew back the blanket and winced as she saw the iron rings which chained his feet together. She slipped downstairs to the scullery to fetch some goose-fat, which she rubbed gently on the sores when she returned. His eyes opened but he shivered so convulsively that she slipped between the rough blankets to keep him warm, trying to calm the shuddering with soft words. The caressing medicine worked and the shuddering ceased, but it was replaced by fever and his brow glistened.

'You're safe,' she whispered, 'whatever you've done you're safe.' Gradually the fever eased and he crossed into a calm sleep. She kept watch beside him, wide-eyed at such adventure.

When he woke in her arms he looked around him

wildly, for he could hear the river, and smell it too. He remembered the scuttling of the hulk but little after that, and hoped it was not a dream as he clutched the girl beside him. She bit her lip as the iron cut into her flesh, determined not to break the moment by crying out. When they fell apart they pressed together again, savouring the closeness, and after a few minutes Dick fell asleep with a smile on his face. Soon she was sleeping too, his arms stretched instinctively around her.

It was snowing heavily when they woke on Christmas morning and he hobbled across the floor to stare with astonishment at the water below. It was barely visible, as grey as the sky above. He welcomed the falling snow like the hunted animal who wishes to cover his tracks, and she watched him from the bed, drowsy from their intimacy, admiring the width of his shoulders and the deep cleft of his spine above the towel which was fastened round his waist.

Curiosity always got the better of her. 'Who are you?'

His face clouded as he wondered how much to say, but with the manacles as evidence against him it was pointless to pretend and he told her the truth. When he finished his story she vowed to help him, and they lay in mutual warmth until she heard the distant chimes of Limehouse church reaching an accusing count of ten. She leapt out of bed, pulling on her clothes frantically, alarmed at being so late.

'Thank the Lord it's Christmas!' she exclaimed.

'Christmas?' he echoed. 'Crikey! It's Christmas Day!'

— 6 —

A Raxleigh departure

When Lionel Raxleigh left the dining-room after that fatal family conference, he went to his room. He lay on the bed, trying to absorb what had happened. My life is over, he decided in a surge of self-pity. There was every advantage in leaving Bideford, but not for some godforsaken island on the other side of the world. London would be another matter. As he thought of the stimulating conversation and the opportunity to fulfil his ambition as a writer, he realised he had been given the chance to start life again, on his own terms.

There was a soft knock on the door and his sister came in without bothering to wait for his reply. 'Sarah,' he said, holding out his hand, distressed to see she had been crying.

'Oh, my dear,' she murmured, drawing up a chair beside him, 'I am so sorry.' They sensed each other's thoughts so well that there was little need to express them, and they remained silent for a while, holding hands.

'I assume there's no hope,' he said finally.

'Gussie's going to look into everything in case there's a way out. He's sent for Stanton to go through the books.'

Lionel frowned with irritation. 'Stanton's a sensible man, but that won't help.'

'It's Sally I'm sorry for,' said Sarah, breaking the uneasy silence which followed. 'She's taken it so badly, but I should have been prepared for that. So *silly* of me not to warn her! We've had our chances, but her life hasn't begun. I was looking forward so much to seeing her come of age, with dresses and parties and admirers. She could have made a splendid match.'

Sarah looked at him wistfully as she sensed his guilt. Wondering how she could ease it, she decided to make the greatest sacrifice of her life.

'Lionel,' she said softly, 'I'm relying on your help so much. Please come with us, for my sake. I'll find it so much easier to bear if you're with me.'

Oh, God, he thought, looking at her anxious expression. How can I refuse?

Oh, God, she thought, let him refuse. He won't be able to manage out there.

London, he thought, pulsating with life. How can I endure the wilderness they're going to?

Lionel looked at his sister with great sadness. 'You silly old thing,' he told her lovingly. 'Of course I'm sailing with you, if that's what *you* want. I'd never let you down, you know that.'

'Yes, I do,' she said.

For once brother and sister misunderstood each other, victims of their good intentions.

Matilda, however, was transformed. In the gloom that settled on Raxleigh House she was the shining exception, although Roly did his best to extinguish her good humour. To her amazement, the unattainable had fallen within her reach at last: she *belonged*. The knowledge that she was needed gave her a new incentive in life.

'For God's sake stop humming.' Roly scowled at her. 'There's nothing to sing about. Are you too stupid to understand what's happened to me? I've lost my inheritance.' He magnified his grievance with every farewell to his fair-weather friends in the district until Matilda found it hard to tell if his twisted version of events concealed a deep sense of guilt.

Outwardly indifferent to their future, he was scathing when he referred to it when they were alone. 'Can't think why you're so damned cheerful. We'll be little better off than convicts sent to a penal settlement.'

'We'll manage,' she replied gleefully.

'You amaze me.' He stared at her, genuinely surprised. 'I'd have thought a Devon dumpling like you would be scared out of your wits. I can't take you anywhere here, yet you think nothing of crossing the world.' That's why, she thought. He'll *have* to notice me out there. We'll be equals then. 'I hope the cannibals like their women fat,' he added.

'Why do you always have to be so cruel?' She broke down at last, not at the thought of cannibals but at the reference to her size. There was no need for her to be self-conscious about her buxom appearance, but she was, and Roly knew it. On the rare occasions when he tried to be nice, he reassured her: 'I like you the way you are. I *like* fat little girls!'

But she was more resilient now that she had a future of her own to look forward to. She, alone, dreaded a last-minute reprieve.

Augustus Stowe was not a religious man, though he took his family to church, said grace before dinner, and saw that his servants attended their prayers. But he prayed now as he had never prayed before. 'Please, God, let us stay here. Let us stay.' But God turned a deaf ear.

Gussie spent an exhausting week visiting his influential friends and was shocked to find how they had changed. Friendly, yes; helpful, no! Word of his misfortune had preceded him, and a friend in such desperate need was someone to be avoided. Some were open in their contempt for his brother-in-law, having heard of the fracas at Barnstaple Fair, dismissing Lionel, in that self-righteous condemnation, as 'his own worst enemy'. No one dared refer to the feckless son.

At the end of the month, for the bank was 'lenient' in granting him further time to buy back the deeds and redeem his debt, Gussie signed the necessary papers.

Lord Cleveland was generous in victory, allowing him six months to settle his affairs and vacate the property. He possessed it now; that was all that mattered.

When Gussie climbed the hill afterwards, as desolate as any soldier in retreat, a new worry overwhelmed him. What would happen if cousin Anthony's tempting offer of assistance proved no more than idle talk, an example of that fatal tendency people have of cheering someone up with false promises without the slightest intent of taking them further? Why had he clutched at this drastic solution to their problems when they might be able to stay in the district on a lesser scale in some rented establishment? Perhaps he should abandon the madcap scheme altogether and look nearer home.

Yet the challenge of starting again in a strange land attracted him. He wrote a second letter to cousin Tony in the optimistic belief that cousins did not let each other down, confirming his readiness to emigrate.

He received his reply ten days later. To Gussie's infinite relief, Sir Anthony Payne proved as good as his word. No wonder he's done well, he thought, admiring his cousin's exemplary efficiency. To his astonishment, everything was settled. After receiving Gussie's first letter, Sir Anthony had discussed the matter with Lord Bathurst, the Secretary for the Colonies, who promised to write a personal letter of recommendation to Governor Franklin requesting that land should be settled on Augustus Stowe and his family on their arrival in Hobart Town. This letter, and other relevant documents, would be waiting for him at the Colonial Office in London. However, Lord Bathurst wondered if Augustus Stowe was right in choosing Van Diemen's Land. Was not New South Wales 'more civilised'?

Sir Anthony disagreed. 'Confidentially, I have received good reports of Van Diemen's Land from other settlers, in spite of the alleged dangers from bushrangers and hostile natives. If you and your family are agreeable, I shall book passages on a ship which is due to sail from Gravesend on 20 January. Would you, my dear cousin, kindly supply me with full details concerning the number and sex of passengers and approximate weight of cargo. Because of the need for ballast, there is ample room for freight, although animals are strictly limited. However, I do stress the importance of transporting the maximum livestock allowed. I enclose the name of the shipping company. You should contact them at once for all the relevant details. May I impress upon you the necessity of selecting your possessions with the greatest care, as little can be purchased on arrival. Rest assured that I am entirely at your disposal and wish your family well on their "brave venture".' It was a *fait accompli*.

·Now that the die was cast, Gussie's optimism infected the rest of the family. Raxleigh House burst into activity: cupboards were emptied, chests filled, lists made, lists altered with constant additions. Hopeless at big business, Gussie was excellent at detail, and supervised the preparations with practical common sense but also an imagination which surprised them all.

'Music,' he declared at one of the family conferences which he summoned each morning. 'We must have music. The organ must be dismantled and packed in a crate, together with the flute, the violin and the best of our sheet music.'

Another time he startled them by announcing: 'We must be prepared for death; I shall order two oak coffins to be made from our own wood . . . wait' – he raised a hand to stop Roly from protesting – 'these will serve as chests to be filled with pewter, cooking utensils, iron-mongery, and lead. No point in taking much glass. Bound to be broken on the voyage, though we'll pack our best pieces carefully.

'Work!' he exclaimed, and Roly flinched. 'Apart from our sheep, we must go prepared with tools of every sort; saws and axes; corn mill; cider press; blacksmith's anvil and bellows; thick cedar doors.'

'Cider press,' Roly echoed approvingly. 'And we'll take our wine?'

'Yes, Roly, we'll take our wine. And vines as well.'

'Thank God for that!'

'Attack!' cried his father, but changed this quickly to 'defence' as he saw his wife's expression of alarm. 'To be on the safe side, my dear, in case of the natives. A chest to be filled with five swords, five guns, five pairs of pistols and flints, and a barrel each of gunpowder and shot.'

'Just as well,' said Roly gravely, turning to Matilda. 'Those cannibals would like a tasty Devon dumpling in their stew.'

'Good,' she replied, refusing to be provoked. 'Then we can shoot them, can't we? And put them in the pot instead.'

Matilda was in her element as she helped the servants pack the household goods and count the sheets and blankets, the soap and vital medicines. 'I don't know how I'd manage without you,' Sarah told her gratefully, realising how shamefully she had underrated the girl. Gussie felt the same remorse, shocked to remember that he had been ashamed of her when his son brought Matilda to Raxleigh for the first time. Since the end of that terrible family conference, when she had put her arms around him and given her support, Gussie regarded her as an ally. Her enthusiasm and astonishing capacity for hard work made him aware that he had ignored her true qualities in searching for those she did not possess, like social poise. It no longer mattered that she was not 'their sort'.

'That girl's going to be an asset,' he told his wife.

'She *is* an asset,' said Sarah.

By contrast Sally punished everyone with an air of martyred melancholy, to show them that she felt betrayed. She disappeared whenever she was needed, but Sarah made no protest. It was preferable to her daughter's accusing presence. Sally's selfishness was part of her nature, but she was suffering from genuine shock. For the first time in her young life, she realised that parents can be as weak and fallible as their children, and the disillusion was bitter. Sarah tried to kindle her interest in their new life by describing it as 'an adventure', but

Sally refused to be cajoled, declining to look at the maps and documents laid before her.

'Don't be upset, my dear,' Gussie comforted his wife, concealing his own sense of guilt. 'Of course she's upset. Only natural at her age. She'll recover, wait and see — she has youth on her side.'

Sarah nodded, wishing that she possessed the armour-platedness of youth herself. The map of Van Diemen's Land had been brought by William Stanton, who, most surprisingly, seemed to have some personal interest in the territory too.

'I like the *look* of it!' exclaimed Matilda, admiring the outline.

'How can you tell from a map?' Roly rebuked her scornfully.

'I don't know . . . it looks nice . . . like a strawberry!'

'God help us,' Roly addressed the others, 'she likes it because it's got a nice shape. You silly pudding!' But for once his tone was affectionate, and everyone laughed. Matilda joined in, grateful to be a cause of merriment.

'I know what she means,' said Gussie loyally. 'I wouldn't fancy going to Australia; far too big. Easier to feel at home where we're going. I'm told it resembles England . . .' At this a silence fell as they wondered what sort of life lay ahead. 'Sounds a fascinating place,' he said finally with his eternal optimism. 'Tremendous opportunities.'

As the day of their departure approached, a change took place. Few places are so forlorn as a house whose owners are on the point of leaving it for ever.

Treasured possessions were assembled for the auction in heaps across the floor as if they had been dumped by interrupted burglars, to be prodded and criticised by strangers or seized with glee by those who thought they had found a bargain. Furniture was fingered and even sat upon while the departing family watched fleetingly from doorways or the tops of stairs like reproachful ghosts.

This was the hardest punishment, the alien faces marching through the corridors of Raxleigh House, frequently guided by Lord Cleveland. Sally could not bear to watch and went to her room – 'It's like seeing an animal die.'

Even Matilda's enthusiasm faltered when the time came to say goodbye to her mother. She looked at the exhausted woman as if for the first time instead of the last. Because she had brought up her daughters without complaint, Matilda had taken it for granted that she had nothing to complain about. Now she noticed the lines of worry, the work-worn fingers, the mended shawl, and knew how selfish she had been.

'Oh, ma,' she sobbed, 'I don't want to leave you. I won't, I'll stay here . . . somehow.'

Her mother smiled, stroking her hair tenderly, knowing that Matilda did not mean it.

'Nonsense,' she said firmly. ''Tis your duty to go with your husband. And I'll have the maids to look after me.'

'I suppose so,' sniffed Matilda, doubting if her younger sisters were capable. 'I'll miss you so much, I don't know how I'll bear it. You've been so good to me and I've done nothing for you since I married.'

''Tis only natural.' But her mother smiled wistfully, thinking it was a pity that children appreciated their mothers most when they were leaving them. In this case it was worse than leaving home, for Matilda could well be saying goodbye for ever. This thought was so painful that her mother tried to fend it off with false optimism. 'You'll come back,' she whispered, 'when your husband's made his fortune, and what a lot you'll have to tell us then.' As they imagined Matilda's possible adventures the pain of her departure lessened for the girl, but after she had gone her mother sat there as motionless as stone.

Sally gained no comfort from the knowledge that she would be travelling with her mother and father, for she continued in a state of rebellion against them. Her former friends proved stiff and stilted when she called to say farewell. The young are sensitive to failure and did not wish to be contaminated; after all, Sally was leaving them for ever, so they could afford to be detached; especially if the nasty rumours concerning her uncle and her brother were true, if not fully comprehended.

Hurt and angry, Sally moped in her room. When the time came to pack personal possessions, Sarah tried to excite her curiosity by insisting that her best dresses should be wrapped carefully in tissue paper.

'What is the point, mama? There'll be no call to wear them.'

'Of course there will,' her mother replied enthusiastically. 'Why! Government House in Hobart Town is famous for its dances.' She gave Roly a swift, warning look as he happened to pass by, and for once he took the hint and did not deny the fantasy.

'Yes,' he said. 'I've heard that too; Lady Franklin's keen on parties. As for you, young sister, you'll be the belle of the ball out there with all those dashing young officers and so few decent girls for them to dance with. Ma's right. Take all your fancy dresses and dazzle them.'

Sarah smiled at him gratefully, delighted that he could still surprise her.

'Really?' asked Sally, in spite of herself. 'You mean there'll be parties?'

Sarah suppressed a sigh of relief as she saw the kittenish, almost sly expression return to her daughter's face.

Though they had been counting the days to their departure, it crept up on them suddenly, taking them unawares. The last full day was spent in a panic of remembering vital objects to be squeezed into the few remaining chests. Most of the freight and all the livestock had begun their slower journey already, due to arrive in London before them and be stowed on board.

Lionel Raxleigh faced his responsibilities at last. He emerged from Raxleigh House to pay his respects to his few friends in Bideford and collect three pairs of stout shoes ordered in advance. The rest of his shopping, such as the notebooks and stationery and latest novels so necessary for a voyage, could be obtained during their week's stay in London. This was a treat Gussie insisted on; if they were going to leave England, at least they would do so in style, with a taste of high-life to remember in the years to come. The possibility that such a taste might whet their appetites for more did not occur to him. Gussie spent that final day wandering about, checking luggage with endless lists, supervising the final details, getting in everyone's way. He could hardly look his servants in the face, loyal friends about to be discarded through no fault on their part. Though Sarah made no complaint, the thought of his wife travelling without her faithful maid made him deeply ashamed.

Sarah escaped from his guilt and the accusation of the curtainless rooms into the garden. With her trowel, a small wheelbarrow, and numerous flower-pots she knelt on her mat beside the gravel paths transferring roots and saplings, regretting that this was not the best season for cuttings. Already, she was thinking of a garden in their new home in Van Diemen's Land. The gesture was more symbolic than she knew: she was leaving her roots, but determined to take the seeds with her to be replanted. This relieved her tension for an hour or two, but the pain returned.

Sarah went slightly mad that final night at Raxleigh. It was New Year's Eve. While the rest of the district celebrated the start of another year, she mourned the end of everything she held dear. When her family assumed she had gone to her bed she returned to the garden. It was raining heavily, and she saw it revealed by vivid flashes of lightning. For once she allowed bitterness to overwhelm her. She ran up the paths crying, falling to the ground, scratching at the earth wildly with her fingers, holding on as if she was being torn away. Struggling to her feet, she flung her arms around a tree, imploring it to save her.

For the first time in her life she despised her husband, until she remembered Gussie's return from Exeter, his utter exhaustion and despair, so that when he mentioned Van Diemen's Land as a lifeline she did not have the heart to voice her opposition. She sighed deeply as she thought of their chances in the future. Would Van Diemen's Land give them the opportunities her husband believed in? Of course not; Gussie would bring his weakness along with his coffins – and so would Lionel. If only she had summoned up the strength to tell her brother to take his chance in London. What a liability he would be.

She fell to the ground again, weeping uncontrollably, unaware of the shadow in the shadows as Gussie turned away, his steps noiseless in the pouring rain. He knew there was no way he could alleviate such grief.

Gussie's own moment of grief had passed unnoticed by the family earlier in the day. Already his beloved stallion had gone with the livestock to London; now he led his aged labrador towards the wood at the top of the hill. The dog had shown him greater loyalty than his friends or his son. She could sense his moods instantly, lying beside him on the bed at night now that Gussie and Sarah slept apart. He watched the animal moving slowly, loose-jointed and slack-bodied. The eyes were lack-lustre with age but more loving than ever, and they climbed the hill at a gentle pace, in perfect harmony, until they stopped at their favourite seat overlooking the river. The dog subsided on the earth beside him with a satisfied sigh as he stroked her under the chin in the way she liked. Then she turned towards him, struggled to her feet, rested her grey muzzle on his knee and licked his hand as if to reassure him.

Oh, my God, he thought, she *knows*. She slumped to the ground, sighed again, and closed her eyes for ever as he returned the pistol to his overcoat.

Afterwards, finding a spade, he buried the dog carefully in the wood where she would never be disturbed. No cross or tombstone should mark the final resting-place of his faithful friend.

The entire family was united in the morning, presenting a confident face to the watching world. In the final reckoning, the Raxleigh estate had been worth far more than anyone expected. A piece of land registered in Sarah's name had been overlooked, and the total yield was almost twenty thousand pounds. Gussie had settled every debt and paid off the servants with handsome compensation, and now had hired a private carriage at considerable expense to take them all the way to London, explaining that with their fares and luggage it would work out much the same in the end as public transport. 'Also, make the journey a damned sight more comfortable,' he told his wife. 'No need to rush after breakfast in the morning to catch the coach; tomorrow we can have a walk around Exeter and see the Cathedral with no one to hurry us.' He was trying to turn their journey of necessity into a holiday.

Relatives said goodbye; so did the last remaining servants. Tears were shed and lace handkerchiefs produced, the final luggage was stacked by the liveried coachmen, and Sarah, Matilda and Sally in their best travelling clothes seated themselves inside, with Lionel and Roly opposite. Gussie insisted on joining the coachman outside for the first part of their journey at least, clutching a wicker basket of fresh food for a picnic. The one remaining paid servant sat forlornly on the rumble. He was to make his journey back to Bideford alone once the Stowes arrived in London.

When they were on the point of leaving, the crowd was forced to step aside as Lord Cleveland galloped up the drive on his black mare. He thrust his face inside the carriage and demanded to speak to Roly, who had thrashed his son in a Bideford tavern the night before. Gussie forgot his usual good manners.

'Out of our way,' he shouted at Cleveland, before he turned to the people watching. 'I warn you,' he cried, 'do not trust this gentleman or his son. They will cheat you as surely as they have stolen Raxleigh House from me.'

Lord Cleveland tugged at his reins, and his horse reared. When the coachman saw the gentleman grasp his riding-crop he realised it was time for their departure – and not a moment too soon.

As the carriage lurched forward, so did Cleveland, intent on dragging Gussie to the ground. His intention was forestalled as he drew abreast and received a whack across the shoulders.

'Out of my way, sir!' cried Gussie with relish. 'You have no part of us now!' He waved to the well-wishers, who cheered at Lord Cleveland's humiliation, though many would regret their loyalty in the days to come. 'Goodbye . . . goodbye.'

None of them had the heart to turn round a moment later for a final look at Raxleigh House.

PART 2

— 7 —

The melting-pot

When Rosie returned to the attic room she found Dick Stanton sleeping, and watched him for a while in the timid light which crept through the window. Then she touched his shoulder, lightly at first, before shaking him more roughly as she thought of the men waiting downstairs.

A council of war had been held throughout the morning in the parlour below, convened by the landlord and his wife and the regulars drinking their medicinal Purl, accompanied this festive morning by slices of cheese. Purl flip was a speciality of the Two Brewers, which sported a sign in Fore Street proclaiming it as the Early Purl House. Purl had the advantage of easing any queasiness inherited from the night before, ensuring such an instant recovery that the customer was encouraged to return to the very spirits which had made him ill in the first place, a vicious circle which was excellent for business. On this morning, however, business was forgotten as Mrs Fossett (no customer dared to call her Mabel) ladled out Purl in the generous tradition of Christmas, while her regulars offered their advice regarding the convict in the attic. They were grateful for this diversion, for it meant that their glasses were filled with absent-minded frequency.

'We're not going to split on the lad,' declared Mrs Fossett. 'Not on Christmas Day.'

'What's the day got to do with it?' asked her husband.

'Indeed,' echoed the mousetrap man, who came from

Cork, 'the day's irrelevant!' This earned him a glare from Mr Fossett, displeased that someone else should dare to contradict his wife, a privilege reserved for himself.

'Get along with you!' she exclaimed with spirit. 'Christmas is a day of goodwill to all men, so I've been led to believe.'

'Indeed it is,' said the mousetrap man, switching sides easily. 'To think of betraying the poor young man on Christmas Day. That's just what they did with our Lord.' Because Mrs Fossett was in the middle of refilling their mugs with free Purl the regulars murmured their agreement with this novel idea, anxious not to interrupt the movement of her elbow, and the mousetrap man went further, exclaiming piously: 'It could be God's will, bringing the lad amongst us on a Christmas morning.'

'I don't know what's got into you,' sighed Mr Fossett. 'You sound like a lot of Salvationists. It was the tide what brought him here and I wish it would take him off again. It's no light matter, harbouring a criminal.'

'You don't know he's a criminal!' cried Rosie, flushing with anger. She had been listening carefully while she tended the fire.

"That's right, Rosie, you tell him orf,' cried the jovial ferryman who rowed passengers across from Limehouse Dock to Cuckhold's point.

'Oh, no,' said Fossett sarcastically. 'I don't *know* he's a convict. He wears those manacles for the fun of it. Anyhow, what do you care? Keen on him yourself?' He said this with a certain bitterness, and Rosie suspected that he knew what had taken place in the attic at dawn. To her surprise, Mrs Fossett came to her rescue.

'And why not, might I ask? A good-looking chap like that. I wouldn't be shy if I was ten years younger!' Everyone laughed, thinking silently that she should have said *twenty* years younger.

Mrs Fossett knew that her husband fancied Rosie. His eye had grown increasingly lustful in recent weeks, but if the girl was occupied with a lad her own age it might bring him to his senses. Anyhow, it *was* romantic; Rosie's lover washed up on their doorstep, naked and manacled. Those manacles! The thought of them made her shiver. She was excited by the idea of his naked body in chains, but she was aware of the danger involved in hiding him. Handsome rewards were offered for information which led to the capture of escaped cons, though she trusted those present.

'Them manacles,' she announced. 'They'll have to go.'

'Of course, my dear,' said Mr Fossett sarcastically. 'Do you have the key?'

'Always so clever,' she retaliated, to the delight of the regulars. 'Have you *no* decent feeling on a day like this? He can't sit down to dinner like a trussed Christmas turkey hisself.'

Mr Fossett spluttered ineffectually. 'Gawd, what a lot of sanctimonious hypocrites you are! Christmas – I'm starting to loathe the bleedin' day. Thank the Lord we only suffer it once a year. But if that's what you want, my dear, we'll have the lad down and someone will have to do something about them irons.'

'That's true,' echoed the ferryman. 'But who can we trust?'

The Purl was replenished to help them decide. It was agreed that Joe, the pot-boy, should be sent to the nearby smithy to ask the smith to join them as soon as possible, with a note of apology for disturbing him on the day of rest.

'Send the fugitive down, Rosie,' Mr Fossett commanded. As soon as the girl had left the room he confided to the others: 'No good will come of this, mark my words. Did you get a butcher's at his face? A trouble-maker and no mistake. That's why they put him in chains.'

'Won't he need to be carried down?' asked Mrs Fossett, ignoring her husband's warning, which she dismissed as jealousy.

'Get along with you,' a customer explained with infinite knowledge. 'Them convicts wot got fetters on can leap abaht like monkeys. More to the point, what's he going to wear? He can't go gallumpkin' in a blanket.'

Mrs Fossett lifted her husband's greatcoat from its peg. 'For the time being he can wear this.'

The customer's estimate of a convict's agility was proved correct, for Dick knew how to hop and shuffle with surprising speed, preserving his decency by clutching the blanket around him. He slipped into the coat gratefully and greeted the watchful group with a broad smile.

'Now, my lad,' demanded Mr Fossett, who was unimpressed, 'who are you?' The hostility was lost on Dick, used as he was to harsher voices.

With an honesty which impressed everyone, Dick told them the truth. He told them of his childhood in Bideford, how he fell against the midshipman when the Queen came to visit the Fleet, and how he was interned in the hulk in consequence. He finished his story by describing the scuttling of the hulk the night before, and thanked them all for saving his life.

'Lord bless you,' Mrs Fossett whispered tearfully, 'we only did what was right.'

'Thought as much,' said the ferryman, for once more solemn than jovial. 'Heard there was trouble down river. Most of your mates was drowned. You're lucky to be here to tell the tale.'

'I know I am.'

'Well,' Mrs Fossett declared. 'If we give him up, we're as bad as criminals ourselves.' Rosie dared not speak for fear of saying something wrong, but she gave Dick a smile of encouragement.

'We can keep quiet,' Mr Fossett told the small assembly, 'but can we be sure the smith will do the same?'

'Yuss,' said the rat-catcher. 'He's done time hisself. He'll understand.' But when the pot-boy returned with him, the reluctant smith was far from pleased.

'Leave orf!' he exclaimed with disgust when he caught sight of the chains beneath the coat. 'It's as much as my life's worth to be caught messin' around wiv them things.'

'It's Christmas,' said Mrs Fossett.

'There's another thing,' exclaimed the smith. 'I've let my fire go out, 'aven't I, because it's Christmas, when by rights I *should* be home in bed.'

After a moment of dispirited silence Rosie came forward, producing a purse from under her dress. 'I'll make it worth your while,' she said, knowing the language the smith understood. Opening the purse, which had been used so seldom it looked as good as new, she produced a gold sovereign.

'Ah, well . . .' The blacksmith's eye grew smaller with greed. For a man who spent most of his days tending horses, he bore a disconcerting resemblance to a pig. His mind chewed slowly as he reckoned the amount which he owed the pub.

Reading his thoughts, Mrs Fossett exclaimed: 'And we'll wipe his slate clean, won't we?' She turned to her husband, who sighed in surrender. 'That's in order, Mr Jones, so how about it?'

The smith was taken aback by this unexpected good fortune, for there was no need to relight the fire at all – the breaking of the fetters was the work of moments – and who would be keeping a look-out for convicts in the snow on Christmas Day? But his innate cunning warned him not to appear too eager, so he drummed his fingers on the counter while Mrs Fossett poured a further measure of Purl and everyone waited.

'I'll do it,' he conceded, as if he had come to a grave decision, and Rosie squeezed his hand, transferring the sovereign to his palm as she did so. 'If I'm going to get me collar felt, might as well be in a good cause.' He flashed the broad smile of insincerity.

'Get a move on, then,' said Mr Fossett, unimpressed.

'You're right there,' agreed the matchbox man; 'while it's snowing and all's indoors.'

There was a burst of activity. Rosie and Mrs Fossett collected a strange assortment of clothes, discarded over the years, and Dick struggled into them as best he could. There was laughter all round when it came to the trousers, for these had to be slashed up the leg in order to pull them over the fetters, and looked grotesquely comical in consequence.

With surprising strength for a small man, the smith threw Dick over his back and dropped him on to the cart outside, where the mule stood patiently with a layer of snow forming on his back. Dick quickly tunnelled his way among the bales of rags as they left the Brewers and the cart thudded softly down the snow-covered street. The smith's smile was genuine now: apart from the sovereign lavished by the love-sick girl, the Fossetts were useful people to keep in with, frequently sending him gentlemen who stopped at the tavern because their horses were lame. Now they had wiped out his debt – happiness all round! He looked behind him and quickly threw a sack over an incriminating foot, not that the few ghostly passers-by would have noticed, with their heads swathed in scarves, and their eyes cast down to see where they were stepping.

Having driven up Ropemaker's Field to his hut in Salmon Lane, the smith filed through the iron links, and within an hour Dick Stanton was back in the Brewers with the dignity of new-found freedom. His beaming smile added to the general enjoyment as all sat down to generous helpings of turkey followed by plum pudding with brandy, washed down with claret and port. The favoured regulars who had no homes of their own included the matchbox man, the ferryman and the rat-catcher, who entertained Dick with his stories of the rats who poured in their thousands out through the cracks in the sewers on the highest tides in the year. The others told Dick that the rat-catcher provided grisly entertainment by biting off the rats' heads.

'Aren't you afraid of being poisoned?' Dick asked, astonished.

'Lor, no! The rat wot bit me would get poisoned hisself!' the rat-catcher replied with glee.

They talked far into the afternoon. When the guests started to fall asleep in their chairs the Fossetts staggered to their room, and Dick and Rosie climbed to the attic to lie quietly together. After months in the rotting hulk this was luxury: the closeness of their bodies now that the manacles had been removed; the lazy feeling of completeness; the elation of knowing he had been spared transportation to Van Diemen's Land.

When he woke Dick realised something had happened. There was a different sound, a stillness. The snow had stopped falling. Moving quietly to the window, he gazed out on an altered scene, discernible by a slight glow in the pewter-coloured sky, though it was growing blacker by the second. A few figures appeared on the shore below, venturing delicately on to the ice and withdrawing swiftly as it cracked beneath their weight. Later, when Dick and Rosie left the Two Brewers and walked towards Limehouse church and Commercial Road beyond, they joined hundreds of East Enders revelling in this transformation of their usual landmarks, slipping, laughing, throwing snowballs. Lights started to come up on every side – the warm red glow from the holes beneath the stoves of the street vendors; gaslights flickering in the breeze outside the butcher's; hundreds of stalls brightened by the glare of self-generating lamps. The street echoed with music from the hurdy-gurdy men and the cries of costermongers:

'Three a penny – Yarmouth bloaters.'

'Beeyootiful whelks – a penny the lot.'

'Sixteen a penny – fine walnuts to take home to the wife. Chestnuts 'ot to warm the cockles of yer hearts!' Dick stopped to buy a bag of chestnuts out of the coins slipped him by Mrs Fossett when they left the Brewers, and they warmed themselves by the fire, slipping the scalding nuts from hand to hand as they peeled off the skins.

Dick was astonished to find the streets so crowded and noisy on a Christmas night, but Rosie explained that East Enders never stayed at home when there was fun to be had outside. Because of the holiday and the snow the crowds and costers were in generous mood, and beggars grinned as coins fell in their boxes. Blind street singers marched three abreast with white sticks, led by a colleague and another who hurried among the crowds with an outstretched cap while a hurdy-gurdy woman tried to elbow him out of the way. Half-noticed in the shadows were the destitute nomads, the raddled prostitutes who had known younger days, and the darting pickpockets. A few white-faced children were jostled as they offered their pathetic wares of two or three onions or a turnip, but they were hardly noticed in the swarm.

Unused to such a tumult, Dick found the markets of Commercial Road as strange as an oriental bazaar described in some romance. Rosie had seen it all before, and led him into a tea-shop with a hundred globes of light outside, to sip the thick, sweet drink.

'Let's have a spree!' she pleaded. 'I've got a bit of splosh, with my Christmas money. I'll show you the town!'

She guided him through the crowds which filled even the darker alleys, tramping the snow into slush, faceless people who clutched their scarves to their noses to block out the smell from the dustheaps underneath the rickety houses. Mingled with that of the refuse running in the gutters, it poisoned the freshness of the winter air. Even on Christmas night, now that the snow had stopped, men ran with buckets of human excrement to empty in the sewers: the despised midden-men, in the lowest profession of all. Dick was amazed to see so many people, though he knew of the rumours that the population of the city had surpassed the staggering total of a million souls and was growing all the time. Now he was able to believe that thousands of Londoners roamed the streets at night, sleeping wherever they could, huddled together for warmth, turning to opium and laudanum for escape. He was startled by the contrast in the passing faces: Lascars from West India Docks; Swedes from Spitalfields; and the latest arrivals, the Russian and Polish Jews who were starting to settle in Whitechapel in large numbers, chattering to each other in their native tongues, unable to speak the language of their new country.

Every few yards, they made way for foreign sailors in

search of drink and women, rich from their months at sea. Many would be rolled and robbed before the night was over.

Passing a penny gaff, Dick stopped to gaze at the garish pictures which supposedly illustrated the turns, though they bore little resemblance to the truth inside. The barker noticed Dick's hesitation and shouted aggressively: 'Come inside! Fabulous entertainment – theatre for a penny, reserved seats twopence!' The more people he could tempt inside, the sooner the performance would begin – and those who had paid already were growing impatient.

'Wonderful entertainment!' he continued. 'Comedy and tragedy, singing and dancing! Special tonight, seeing it's Christmas, the country clown and his good lady – or maybe not so good as you'll find out . . . you're in luck tonight, you are, young man . . .' He came straight up to Dick and placed a heavy paw upon his shoulder as if to push him inside if necessary.

'How about it?' Rosie asked.

'''Tis not fit for a maid like you,' Dick replied, feeling himself the chivalrous protector. The girl had been hardened by life, but the boy retained innocence in spite of all he had endured. It did not occur to him that Rosie was not as demure as that angelic face suggested; that a nature as promiscuous as Casanova's lurked behind the milky brow. There was no harm in Rosie, but in her perpetual search for the right man she was becoming increasingly dissatisfied.

She had always been careful not to take any of her gentlemen friends back to the Brewers, leaving a false address when she promised to meet them again. So far fate had not caught up with her, but there were men who had waited hours for her and would not take it kindly if they happened to meet her again. Dick suspected none of this, though her skilful tuition the night before should have given him some warning.

'Where are we going?' he asked, as she led him down a dimly lit alley filled with people.

'Paddy's Goose.'

'Paddy's Goose?' he echoed. 'What's that?'

'A tavern. What do you think it is?'

He laughed, but wondered if a public house was a wise destination for a convict on the run.

They entered even narrower streets. Rickety houses loomed over them as if the chimneys were trying to embrace each other. There was no colour anywhere, even when the thin moon slipped between the clouds. The snow had turned to slush, trampled by thousands of feet. The few white patches that lingered were swept fiercely over the cobbles into the cleft of the street where the snow joined the running refuse. Every doorway was filled with huddled waifs and strays, draped heavily in black rags, the children shoving their freezing feet into the depths of the sacking which formed their beds.

Down the overhanging streets the couple went, clinging together for warmth and fear of being separated in such a hurly-burly of activity. Most of the men had hats pulled down over their ears to keep themselves warm. Dick did the same, in case he was recognised, though there was little chance of that in such a faceless multitude, away from the bright lights of Commercial Road. He was saddened by the atmosphere of misery, the scores of hollow-cheeked men who moved with vacant eyes, their whole appearance signifying a hopelessness belied by some pathetic attempt at neatness, such as a bruised top hat, ragged gloves or a battered umbrella. Dick felt for these people, who refused to accept humiliation, for he had known the depths himself. He pulled Rosie aside sharply as a coster forced his barrow towards them, shouting obscenities as a warning to jump out of the way.

When they reached Ratcliffe Highway, Dick peered into the gloom and wondered for an astounded second if a forest lay ahead of them. The illusion was created by thousands of masts rising from the ships anchored along the docks which fingered their way inland along the shore; an illusion enhanced by the effect of Christmas trees tied to the tops of the masts. Centuries ago this stretch of the

90

river had been noted for the reddish cliffs which gave Ratcliffe its name, but now the waterfront was notorious for its dens and violence.

'Buy, buy, buy,' cried a vendor at a smoking baked potato stove, and they stopped to warm themselves inside and out. Dick looked at the two ill-clad, shivering girls beside it and noticed their bare feet. He pointed to them and whispered to Rosie: 'They must be freezing.'

'They're used to it,' said Rosie. 'Their feet are as hard as they are.' But when he looked at their pinched faces he bought them a potato to share between them and the children ran off giggling.

'You're daft, you are,' said Rosie. Vexed by his extravagance, her face took on a sullen look as she asked him what he intended to do during the next few days. 'How are you going to live, Dick?' She found it necessary to add: 'You'll have to do something. I can't look after you.'

'The rat-catcher told me of the sewer-men,' muttered Dick. 'Seems they make a good living fishing up coins and things from those sewers. I thought I'd have a go at that. At least it would keep me underground, out of the way.'

'Ugh!' exclaimed Rosie, screwing up her face. 'I don't think I'd like that. Not much better than a middy-man, that ain't.'

'But as you say, I'll have to do something.'

'Yes,' she sighed. 'You owe me a sovereign.'

'I'll work. I'll pay you back,' he said angrily.

She looked at him closely. 'All right.'

The moon, suddenly bolder, revealed a tangle of taverns. Dick sensed an atmosphere of violence, almost a trembling in the ground, as if the place was about to erupt. A moment later they saw a group of people sprawling outside a lighted doorway, watched listlessly by several figures slumped on the ground and a few black shapes which slouched away into the shadows. They had arrived at Paddy's Goose.

The White Swan was owned by an Irishman called Patrick Gogarty, a massive, greasy, bald man who laughed incessantly though his eyes remained mirthless. As they had to rove all the time, keeping a look-out for trouble, the lack of humour was understandable.

The people sitting on benches near the entrance looked as if they were waiting for a fight to explode. Fiddles scraped wheezily like the racking coughs of old men, for the centre of Paddy's Goose was a dance-floor where dozens of women clasped sailors of different nationalities. Dick peered through the dense smoke, astonished that Rosie should feel at home here, as she plainly did. A group of old women put down their clay pipes to swear or swallow their half-pints of gin, and to Dick's surprise they hailed Rosie as an old friend.

'Wotcher, Rosie!' one of them called. 'Got yourself a nice bit of stuff tonight and no mistake, even though you've gone and scratched his phiz!' This reference to Dick's scar struck the others as the height of wit and Rosie flushed with annoyance.

'Come on,' she shouted to Dick. 'Let's have a dance.'

'I don't know how.'

'You don't have to in here. Jog abaht.'

Rosie was right: there was no art to dancing in this scrum; no dainty minuet or decorous quadrille, but a stumbling free for all as couples collided and collapsed on the floor.

'Vicky!' said a voice, close to. Dick turned to see a dark-haired man staring at Rosie with undisguised resentment.

'Lor,' she said nervously. 'I thought you was at sea.'

'Damned right you did. I've been looking for you.'

Dick smiled uneasily, not sure of their relationship, until he saw the fright in Rosie's eyes. It prompted him to step in front of her in case she needed help.

'Anything the matter?' he asked the American.

'Plenty,' snarled the man, drawing back his fist, but at that moment the room fell quiet, as several 'toffs' sauntered in, escorted by a detective officer and a sergeant of police who would be rewarded for their protection when the night was over. The toffs stared around them with the startled curiosity of travellers visiting a strange country. Their finery, the vivid yellow-topped hats, the silver-topped canes, the costly pearl buttons and gold watch-chains: their utter elegance constituted an affront in such surroundings, where toffs were resented as much as the Bible-hawkers who ventured self-righteously into taverns to preach on the evils of alcohol. The crowd fell back, and jeers and obscenities greeted the 'slummers', together with a swelling chant of 'gin, gin, gin'. The police sergeant recognised the threatening tone and whispered something to the toff with the monocle.

'By jove,' said the toff. 'Why not push the boat out? It's Christmas after all! Eh?'

A cheer replaced the jeers as the police sergeant announced that the visitors had ordered gin for everyone – 'To wish you all a merry Christmas.'

'Any unripe fruit?' one of them whispered to the detective.

'You won't find much of that in here, sir,' said the sergeant respectfully. 'The fruit is old and rotten. Look about you.'

At this the toff made the fatal mistake of laughing, except that the sound which rang out in one of those sudden, inexplicable silences which can fall on a crowded place was a dreadful whinny of contempt for everyone present.

The place exploded as if a whistle had roused a pack of sleeping dogs. People flew at each other without the slightest provocation. The American was struck by a massive sailor and Rosie seized Dick's hand, pulling him through the flailing figures, colliding with the visitors who were being dragged from the tavern by their police escort. Women dressed in greasy muslin tore at each other, cheeks smeared with blood and tears of laughter, for they were crying drunk.

Escape was made more difficult by a swarm of ragged children, attracted by the uproar, surging in from outside. Dick found himself pressed against the police sergeant, and, for a moment, their eyes met.

'Come on!' yelled Rosie, and the next moment they were outside. Dick raced ahead, for he knew that the tell-tale track on his face could alert the policeman, while the weals on his legs would convict him instantly if he was searched.

They ran down Swan Street, turning into the alley which led to Bell Wharf, and stopped at last in the shadows of a warehouse, pressing themselves against the wall as they listened for footsteps in pursuit. All was silent. When they regained their breath, they started to laugh. Rosie kissed Dick so passionately that he remembered the waiting attic room and started running again without a care in the world.

The tide was high, so they crossed the narrow footbridge over the canal, and Dick saw the sign of the Two Brewers beckoning ahead.

'We're here!' he called to Rosie, who was trailing behind.

A hand stretched out and seized his collar, while several shapes emerged from the shadows.

— 8 —

A London merry-go-round

Entering London from the west, the travellers from Raxleigh House were spared the worst of those far from
slumbrous slums which heralded the city. Even so, they
recoiled. Everything pulsated with life after the Devon
backwaters where ripples were caused if someone as much
as stirred. Here, no one cared if you thrashed the water.

After stopping at Chiswick Green, a waterside suburb
five miles west of Hyde Park Corner where they sipped
cool lemonade and watched the bobbing boats on the
Thames, they continued to the Mall at Hammersmith,
where the houses became more modern and less pleasing
to the eye; through a sooty density of working-class dwellings to the elegant squares of Kensington; onwards down
fashionable Piccadilly towards St James's Palace with the
scarlet sentries outside; into Pall Mall, crowded with
riders who wanted to see and be seen; and alighting at
last outside the old-established family hotel behind the
Strand called the Arundel.

Instead of putting up at a poorer establishment on the
fringes of town, Gussie had insisted on reservations in
the heart of the metropolis. The poignancy of this new
extravagance did not escape his wife, but she suppressed
her sighs, knowing that Gussie was trying to atone for
their departure. When he indulged his family in order to
make amends, not one of them protested.

Roly received an envelope, with promissory notes
which entitled him to draw money from their London

bank, while Sally and Matilda were taken to be fitted out with a number of fine creations as if they were embarking on the Grand Tour of Europe.

'A bit late, isn't it?' said Roly, regarding his wife's excitement with a look that was close to resentment. 'Still, the savages might fancy you. There's a lot of you to fancy . . .'

'Why do you have to say things like that all the time?' she protested, with new-found courage. 'You grudge me nice things, you really do. Why are you so selfish?'

It was the excuse he needed. Looking at her grimly, he walked out of the hotel on one of his daily prowls. No one knew where he went, but his family would have been surprised to learn how innocently he used his time. Instead of the taverns and gambling dens of their imagination, he ventured east.

Roly allowed himself to drift with the currents as he joined the flow of humanity beyond the Strand. Far from disgusting him, the stench from the sewers of the Fleet, the refuse which had been trampled into the cobbles to form a wet sort of mud so deep that sheep might well imagine themselves in the countryside were it not for the din, enthralled him in their novelty. He heard languages which he failed to recognise, and was startled by the sight of thickly bearded men dressed in black with curious turban-like hats on their heads. Children ran everywhere, darting in and out between the dense horse-drawn traffic, and Roly noticed that even the most tattered had a sort of merriment. They may have been hungry, but the resilience of the young was dominant even here. At first he scattered the coins they begged for, but by the third day he was impatient with playing the piper to the hordes which followed him and pushed the children away, their pleading smiles instantly replaced by obscenities. Beggars of all ages were everywhere, but Roly was more distressed by the pathetic efforts of those who tried to rise above their condition, the elderly men who struggled to keep up former appearances, though their cuffs were frayed and the soles of their shoes replaced by paper, with hats as worn and battered as their owners. Roly wondered if a man could recover once he descended below a certain level in such a merciless society, or whether he was submerged for ever.

Apart from the jostling markets, people held out objects for sale which were ludicrous in their paucity: three small cucumbers; shoelaces; matches; a second-hand dress; the metal discs for heels of ladies' shoes; and one adventurous fish which had been plucked from the River Thames.

Roly began to harden. Confronted by a youth who asked for the price of a pint, he remarked that he shouldn't be drinking on an empty stomach. To his surprise, the youth gave a hollow chuckle, and Roly gave him the money. Usually he reserved his charity for those who were unable to help themselves. It seemed to him that London must contain more cripples than any other place in the world. On impulse he gave a crown to a creature so hideously maimed that he had to press the coin between the stumps of former fingers. Looking backwards as he walked on, Roly realised that the man was blind, for he had taken up the coin with his toothless mouth and was rolling it with his tongue to make certain of his amazing fortune, twisting his head from side to side as if searching for his benefactor, or, more likely, alerting himself to the scent of thieves who would not hesitate to rob him.

Sometimes people spoke to Roly from friendly curiosity, more often to beg, sensing an innocent from the country. After the fourth day he waved a hand in polite acknowledgement and moved on without pausing.

With no destination in mind, he entered the darker alleys as if he wanted to be absorbed. The porter at the Arundel warned him that this was a dangerous part of town, where strangers were attacked, but the people seemed kind enough. Every hour or two, Roly stopped at one of the taverns, stepping back against a wall as a tremor exploded into a flailing mass, until larger men pulled the antagonists apart and Roly could return to the

97

counter, while a whistling boy swept up the broken glass as nonchalantly as if it was torn-up paper. Fights were a regular diversion, and gin the cause. They were not amusing. There was no beauty in the ugliness, no charm in the uproar, yet Roly was envious.

The plight of animals saddened him more than that of humanity, a sympathy he shared with his uncle. He was pained by the sight of blinkered, breathless ponies, or older horses covered in sores, beaten savagely as they pulled loads many times their weight. Cats scavenged openly, for they were more agile at escaping retribution than the lack-lustre dogs who slunk against the walls, glancing around them with nervous, hungry eyes. Once, looking up on a sudden impulse, Roly was disconcerted by the sight of an army of cats squatting on a roof above him, staring down malevolently as if they could see inside his soul.

On his sixth day in London, when Roly knew that his departure was near, he noticed a puppy marching with determination across a narrow lane, missing wheels and hooves with astonishing sagacity or luck. Reaching the other side, the tiny animal was knocked sideways by a running man who did not even see it underfoot, but the puppy shook itself indignantly and started off again. Roly followed, wanting to see where such a resolute spirit was heading. He followed it for half an hour or so before he realised that the expedition was aimless. The dog was simply going somewhere; anywhere.

It began to stop more often, bewildered, and it was obvious that it was becoming weaker, and so desperate for water that it lapped the spillage running between the cobbles.

With ample chance to observe, for the animal was either unaware of or indifferent to his observer, Roly suspected that the brown, bedraggled puppy, no larger than a shoe, was really black beneath the mud and filth. At last, it sat down on its haunches, scratched itself feebly, and gave a single squawk of despondency. Roly stepped out of the shadows and whistled, but the dog ran off.

Roly followed until they passed a stall selling saveloys and trotters, where he paused.

A few minutes later, reaching a deserted, litter-strewn alley, he unwrapped a pig's trotter. Placing it near his feet, he leant against a wall and waited. The puppy stopped and sniffed. The smell made it shiver with excitement. Temptation overcame fear, and the dog approached cautiously, made a swift lunge, and retreated with the trotter in its mouth, uttering a low, warning growl. Like the blind beggar with his coin, the dog could hardly believe its luck. It stared at the trotter for a disbelieving moment after laying it delicately on the ground. Then it began to eat, each taste enhancing and surpassing the last: the crisp crackling; the warm nourishing fat; the melting, tender pork; and finally the crunch of bones. There was so much to separate that the dog, whose teeth were hardly formed, tugged and tore, chewed and devoured, for several ecstatic minutes. Roly watched, silent and smiling.

When the banquet was over, the contented animal gave a sigh of pleasure and looked up. When Roly walked away, the dog followed.

Regretting his impulsive generosity, Roly tried to shake the dog off, but it haunted him like a shadow. At last, tired and hungry himself, he asked a stranger where he could buy some food. The man pointed at an archway further down the street, and muttered: 'Flowersellers' Alley.' That might have been the name of the place but there were no flowers in sight, nor any other splash of colour. The alley was lined with tables and benches with a narrow pathway in the middle, overcast by wooden boards to save the customers from falling debris; hundreds of men were talking, eating, and drinking with abandon. Most of them were drunk. There were no partitions, but each cluster of tables belonged to a separate shop and was served by a scurrying waiter. The dog had disappeared at last.

It was the wildest place Roly had come across in his walks across London, and the atmosphere grew wilder.

Each shop boasted its own violinist, apart from the street musicians who strolled up and down, stopping hopefully at each table until thrust away or paid a pittance. Many were foreign, playing weird-looking instruments Roly had never seen before, shining contraptions like gigantic cooking pots. Two Russians started to dance, their legs kicking out dangerously. At the end of the alley, Roly could see acrobats balancing on the tables and tumblers juggling with plates.

Suddenly, a roar rose above the din and Roly looked up to see an avalanche of people rushing towards him from a barrage of flying tables and stools. Two men, their faces covered in blood, pushed past him as he pressed back. Yet a moment later everyone was smiling as before: an accordionist upturned a fallen chair beside him and started to play, while a passing waiter held out a basket of oysters.

Roly started as he felt a movement at his foot, and looked down expecting to see a rat. It was little bigger; the puppy stared up reassuringly to show that he was Roly's, and Roly his.

That evening Roly returned to the hotel early for once, and stunned his parents – who were leaving for the theatre in Drury Lane – with the announcement that the dog was going with them on the voyage.

'It can't!' cried his father.

'If Raxleigh doesn't go, nor do I,' said Roly.

'Raxleigh?' For a moment his father was confused.

'To remind me of what I've lost.'

'Oh, my God!' moaned his father, while his mother peered anxiously at the motionless body clutched inside Roly's overcoat.

'Are you sure it's still alive?'

'Come on.' Gussie propelled her through the front door of the hotel. 'Or we'll be late for the play.' Once outside he gave an hysterical laugh. 'Your son's mad. Quite, quite mad!'

That night, after an enthusiastic bath, a glistening black puppy with unexpected splashes of white slept contentedly at the foot of Roly's bed in spite of Matilda's protests. At least Roly seemed happier. She was thankful for that.

Matilda woke Roly at dawn as the grey light crept round the heavy velvet curtains, and the early clatter of carts could be heard from the Victoria Embankment.

'Make me a lady,' she whispered. 'Treat me like one of your ladies.'

It was Matilda's fantasy to imagine she was one of the gentlewomen whose pursuit of her husband had not concluded with his marriage. Outwardly so confident, Matilda ached from a feeling of inferiority compared to those haughty young women. Where they were dainty, she was clumsy, and she longed to be otherwise.

It was a game she played so passionately that Roly sometimes found it embarrassing, but this morning he was prepared to share it. The dog was woken by the human combat, the strangled gasps of delight, and, not used to such sounds, jumped in alarm from the bed and cowered in a corner. However, when the last loud cries were followed by soft, affectionate sighs, Raxleigh jumped back again and fell asleep with a faint, contented sigh of his own.

'Was I as good as them?' she asked.

'As good as any lady in the land,' he assured her, staring at the ceiling, momentarily defeated, hoping she would leave it at that.

London was proving a delicious torment for Matilda. The smart establishments they visited, discussing the latest vagaries of fashion, dressing and undressing, slandering the titled patrons, gossiping and giggling, constituted an orgy of gentility that any Bideford lady, however supercilious, would have envied. Without Sarah to guide her or Sally to push her forward, Matilda would have been lost in the maze of snobbery. Everything was French, even the corsets, with names like *Corset Amazone* – 'a triumph of elastic lacing' – and the *Corset à la nourrice* for those who expected a happy event but did not wish to show it. The current controversy over tight-lacing raged even more strongly now that the newly invented metal eyelets meant that the victim could be squeezed even tighter than before, and actually trying on one of these contraptions gave Matilda a thrill which was almost sexual.

Sarah realised that their expeditions were more than fun to Matilda. The clothes were irresistible precisely because of their impracticality in Van Diemen's Land; and the intricate undergarments, with all the hem-stitching that would be involved in the future, were all the more desirable because no one would ever see them apart from Roly. But when the moment arrived for their final purchases, Matilda's rustic common sense replaced the dream. Instead of the *Corset cordiale* she chose 'Mrs Geary's Newly Invented Anatomical Stay', tried and trusted, and composed the following list after careful deliberation: 4 chemises; 4 nightdresses; 2 petticoats; 6 drawers; 2 camisoles; 6 vests; 5 flannel petticoats.

One glorious extravagance remained, which she could not bring herself to abandon, holding it so tenderly in an agony of indecision that Sarah, on a sudden impulse, insisted she should have it too. Matilda's protest faded, replaced by a look of absolute joy, and she was so radiant when she tried it on in the hotel that evening that no one had the heart to comment on the unsuitability of a crinoline in darkest Van Diemen's Land.

There were moments when Gussie forgot Raxleigh House. There was so much to enjoy in London; certainly a mass of business to attend to. Sir Anthony Payne introduced him to the illustrious Secretary for the Colonies, Lord Bathurst, who greeted Gussie with the breezy informality which he reserved for men of no importance. However, he was good enough to write a letter of introduction to Sir John Franklin at Government House, though he indulged in his particular brand of sardonic humour.

'May I recommend Augustus Stowe, Esquire, late of Raxleigh Manor in Devonshire, with the hope that you will ease his arrival in your . . .' he sought for the right word and found the wrong one '. . . your turbulent island. I am encouraging his passage to Van Diemen's Land in the knowledge that you will welcome a settler of his experience and offer him your protection against the wilder elements you have to contend with . . .'

Gussie waited, smiling brightly, his fingers drumming a soft tattoo on the elbow of the oak chair, and thanked the Secretary for his patronage when the letter was finally sealed and handed over.

'I think you'll find this letter more than satisfactory,' said Lord Bathurst complacently. 'I admire your spirit. Hope you get there safely.'

While the women did their shopping, Gussie made his lists. These grew alarmingly, not only with necessary items but also with luxuries to make the voyage more bearable: bottled water; potted meats; assorted biscuits; and jams and honey to supplement the ship's diet. Fresh fruit and dairy produce could be collected at the last moment at Gravesend. He enjoyed calculating their expenditure, cross-checking the lines of figures with meticulous care, determined to prove, to himself at least, that he was an excellent book-keeper, in spite of everything.

The entries were recorded in an imposing leather-bound account book bought for the purpose, itemised in his neat, legible hand, but it was typical of Gussie that his economy was based on pennies rather than pounds. Roly had been given promissory notes amounting to ten guineas, to use as he liked, yet Gussie accounted for every farthing he spent himself.

London was proving 'wildly expensive', but Gussie was more than satisfied with the Arundel Hotel. It was close to the theatre and shops, their rooms overlooked the River Gardens and the Embankment Promenade, yet it was quiet and the servants were deferential, which made a welcome change at a time when manners were deteriorating around them. He did not enjoy all the little embarrassments of sharing a bedroom again with Sarah, but realised this was part of his new life which he had to accept. He knew the sacrifice she had made without complaint in parting with her maid, and tried to help in every way he could.

Gussie was fonder of his wife than ever, deeply moved by her support throughout the loss of Raxleigh, but the intimate side of their life was over. He regarded the physical act as so absurd that he was not prepared to insult his wife by inflicting it upon her any longer. It would have startled his family and friends considerably to know that he was preoccupied with brothels, which he saw as admirable institutions for men like himself who regarded love and intercourse as incompatible. His love was reserved for his wife, but a man needed a sexual outlet, if only to return to his family in a relaxed state of mind. Paradoxically, for such a guilt-prone man, Gussie felt no shame in searching for such pleasure in London. Lord knows what chances he would find *over there* for good old-fashioned sin. This could be his final fling!

The stern-faced individual behind the hotel desk recommended a number of diversions which sounded extremely tedious, but the sly hall porter, sensing the banked-up energy behind the staid façade, had a word with Gussie outside.

'If you don't mind my saying so, sir, if you fancy something a bit frisky I might know just the place.'

Gussie disliked the man's familiar manner and walked past him with a curt nod of acknowledgement. In fact he possessed two vital handbooks – *Hints to Men About Town* and the spicy *Man of Pleasure's Pocket Book* – which he had bought in a surge of well-being after his interview with the Secretary for the Colonies and studied surreptitiously in the privacy of the hotel bathroom. They proved invaluable guides to the cream of the hundred thousand prostitutes in London.

The first was a directory of the 'seraglios' – the high-flown Turkish euphemism for the brothels of London, devoted to 'wit, pleasure, and wine' – with advice to men from the country, like Gussie himself, to prevent them from being 'kidded, flabbergasted, or eased of their tin'. The second handbook had detailed descriptions of the ladies for sale, complete with their addresses: Miss Tibby Leighton, a red-haired whore of middling stature; Miss Merton, with the advantage of 'sister hills that were prominent, firm and elastic', whose services cost a guinea, the average price. Gussie liked the sound of Miss Jane Fowler – 'tall, slender, with luscious orbs and a beautiful leg' – but he had no intention of going to a private address, where some accomplice might be waiting behind the door to rob him. He preferred the comfort of the brothel, with its wider choice of girls.

Leaving the hotel, Gussie went to a *cigar divan* in the Strand and paid a shilling for a first-rate cigar and an excellent cup of coffee. After a look at some of the newspapers and periodicals, he wandered into the games room where he was invited to play backgammon with a red-faced, ebullient character to whom he took an instant dislike. At the same time, he sensed that this was exactly the confidant he was looking for. Explaining in a whisper that he wanted a night on the town 'with no holds barred', Gussie sought his advice.

The man burst into song:

> 'Oh! dearest girls, I love you more than honey,
> London is a funny place,
> But costs a lot of money.
> Yes, London is a funny place
> Where rummy things are done,
> In London Town you will have to go
> The whole hog – or none.'

He concluded with a roar of ribald laughter, and Gussie was thankful that the room was deserted apart from a couple in the corner who were wholly absorbed in their game of chess. His embarrassment increased when the man opened his case and produced some pictures of women doing the most extraordinary things to each other. Gussie flinched as he took a closer look.

'That sort of thing interest you, watching them at it?' asked his mentor.

'Not really,' said Gussie, suppressing the disapproval in his voice with a bright, knowing smile. 'I'm not interested in watching.'

The man regarded his upright, bald companion more closely; he certainly looked the schoolmaster type. You never could tell these days. 'Backgammon, is it?' he asked with a twinkle.

'Excuse me?' said Gussie, confused, looking down at the board between them.

'Backgammon – you know!' To Gussie's horror, he rose from his seat, placed his fingers under the tail of his coat and waggled them about. '*Backgammon*!' Gussie looked so bewildered that the man added: 'Margeries – *boys*!'

'Certainly not,' said Gussie indignantly, flushing at such a suggestion.

'Nor me,' said the man indifferently. 'I suspect you're like myself – prefer your meat dressed to your own liking, more demi-mondaine than moth. I know just the flock for you, in prime condition and ready for sticking.' Gussie winced but expressed his interest, and was given the address of a 'high-class' brothel in York Street. Gussie ordered a large cigar for his benefactor and left the *divan*.

He wondered if he had made a mistake when he was shown into a charming drawing-room furnished in perfect taste, and was greeted by the formidable Madam. Mrs Emerson had been a beauty herself, a long time ago. Now she was heavily powdered, and the lines around her neck were obscured by ropes of pearls which must have cost someone dearly.

Her welcome was guarded. 'You can count on my discretion, my dear, but in view of my reputation I always like to have some sort of reference. Any name you care to give me will be treated in confidence.'

'Of course. If I may say so, I respect your caution. One cannot be too careful these days.' He gave the name of his acquaintance of the *divan* and she nodded, unimpressed. 'And you, sir, are . . .?'

'I am Lord Cleveland, of Kane House, near Bideford.' It gave him enormous pleasure to traduce the name of the man who had destroyed him, and Mrs Emerson was suddenly cordial, respectfully inclining her head, and making the astonishing request that he should call her 'mother'. Then she rang a bell and ordered champagne, which he feared he would pay for later.

'And now, my dear,' she said confidingly, 'what can I do for you?'

This was the moment he had been dreading, when he would have to tell the truth. Then he remembered that he was using Henry Cleveland's name and felt he had nothing to lose in coming to the point at once. 'I am a great believer in discipline,' he declared.

'Ah, ha!' she cried naughtily. 'Whacky-whack-whack. It animates the circulation wonderfully.' His interest held no surprise; many of her clients had been to public school where they learned the lesson of the cane, if little else.

'I know just the girl for you, my lord.'

Miss Woodruff looked too gentle for his liking, though there was a weariness about the eyes which suggested that she had seen her share of hardship. Once inside their scarlet bedroom, however, she revealed that she was far from gentle in the art of love. Choosing her rod deliberately, she ordered him to undress. After a preliminary romp she decided he should be punished.

'Well swished?' she asked when it was over. He nodded his agreement. It had proved deliciously painful, and this encouraged her to fuss over him attentively. Her sudden transformation from strict governess to solicitous nanny was so successful that Gussie pulled down his breeches again and threw himself on top of her in the usual position. He mistook her protests for play-acting, although in fact they were entirely genuine, for he had forgotten the precaution of a French letter. Like all the girls, she had no objection to flagellation, for this avoided the two fears of her profession, pregnancy and disease. Straightforward intercourse was another matter altogether. 'Mother' was none too pleased, either, for pregnancy was the last thing she wanted in her well-run establishment. There was little point in complaining after the event, but she took his money with an ill grace.

'Lord Cleveland' stepped into York Street feeling twice the man he had been and hailed a hackney-coach to drive him back to the Arundel Hotel. Tonight he was prepared to indulge himself.

When the carriage was held up by the press of traffic as it neared the bottom of Regent Street, he looked out and was certain he saw Lionel on the pavement, waiting to cross. He was about to call out and offer him a lift, but something about his brother-in-law, and something about the person he was with, made him sink back into the shadows of the hackney-coach instead.

Lionel Raxleigh disliked the Arundel Hotel. He considered it stuffy and old-fashioned, without the grandeur of the past or the smartness of the present – and the carpets reeked of cat – but he relished every second of his stay in London. His relief at leaving his tarnished reputation in Bideford was infinite. No whispered gossip would pursue him here. Even the loss of Raxleigh House was forgotten in all the distractions that London had to offer as the centre of the literary world.

He found that he was able to regain some of the dignity he had lost in Devon, and wondered if he would be able to retain it in the new land they were heading for. Yet there was no question of failing to accompany his sister, and he planned for the future with the passion of a shipwrecked survivor who has to seize a few vital possessions to carry with him to his desert island.

Determined to become a serious writer at last, he gathered the tools of his profession: books to write in, books to read, for words would be his lifeline from now on. His choice of fiction had to be limited and he passed happy hours in the bookshops lingering over his selection.

A resolve was forming in his mind to write about their life in Van Diemen's Land, so he bought the books which had been written about the island already. These proved remarkably few, though the narrative just published by James Backhouse, *A Visit to the Australian Colonies*, looked promising, with the first half of the hefty volume devoted to Van Diemen's Land. To learn how someone else had recorded his impressions of a foreign country, he bought the *American Notes* of the young writer Charles Dickens, as well as a copy of his latest novel *Martin Chuzzlewit*.

On a sudden surge of optimism he decided to invade the stronghold of *The Times* and seek an appointment with the new editor, John Thadeus Delane. Without a formal introduction, he braced himself for an ignominious rejection as he approached the low building surrounded by railings in Printing House Square, with the newspaper's coat of arms above the front door. A porter took his letter as if it was an incriminating document, holding it at arm's length as he went upstairs, but Lionel's audacity was rewarded fifteen minutes later by an interview.

Delane was a pleasant-looking man with a broad, good-humoured mouth, an imposing forehead, long side-boards and kindly but penetrating eyes which scrutinized Lionel closely. He sensed that Delane did not tolerate fools, but would prove the best of friends to those he trusted.

'You've caught me at a fortunate moment, Mr Raxleigh,' he said, holding out his hand. 'So you're off to Van Diemen's Land and wish to write for us? It's a subject that interests me. I'll have a word with our controller, Mr Walter, but I know he shares my concern over the treatment of our convicts. It seems unduly harsh. I should have thought transportation was punishment enough, without the cruelties of the penal settlement. Would you care for a spot of luncheon, Mr Raxleigh? My own appointment has been cancelled.'

Lionel replied that he would be delighted, as indeed he was.

'Capital. We shall go to my club.'

Lionel did his utmost not to drink too heavily while they consumed a dish of lamb cutlets in the Reform Club. Indeed, Delane's conversation was sufficient intoxication in itself, and it was thrilling for Lionel to find himself listening to the most powerful editor in England. Delane surprised him with his knowledge of the penal system; in particular he wanted a full report on the settlement of Port Arthur at the south of the island.

'Capital, Mr Raxleigh,' he said when they parted outside the club. 'Let me commission you to send back four articles on the condition of the convicts, and we'll see how we proceed from there. Keep your despatches simple, but give us plenty of detail. I'll send a messenger to your hotel with a letter of confirmation which you can show the authorities. Doubtless they will do everything they can to place obstacles in your way – they always do – but they'll be afraid to go too far with a representative of *The Times*. If your report is unfavourable, so be it. It's the duty of *The Times* to speak the truth always and on all topics – especially one as overlooked as this. Glad to have met you, Mr Raxleigh. I like what I've seen. Good day to you!'

Lionel floated to the Lamb and Flag. Generous terms had been mentioned, but money was unimportant compared to his new role in life – special correspondent for the London *Times*. It was a stupendous step forward, and deserved a celebration.

As the light faded outside the tavern he savoured his good luck like a wine-taster surprised with a rare vintage, and blessed the impulse which had made him act so boldly. It was out of character. Usually he was shy, confirming the hesitancy that showed in the boyish face with the thatch of light-coloured hair that fell across his forehead, the absence of beard or moustache, and the pale blue eyes which constantly crinkled as if he was short-sighted. But now he was expansive. This was the chance he needed to prove himself. It was *justification*, for lacking wife or children his life was pointless without achievement. The weight of the last few months lifted as he realised he was looking forward to the adventures ahead. He had been unaware of the extreme brutality meted out by the British to the convicts in Van Diemen's Land, but if that was what Delane wanted him to investigate that would be his new objective. The drink suffused him with an inner glow . . .

Several hours later, in a tavern he had never been in before, he had reached the stage of absolute certainty in himself, a vaulting self-confidence, that made him smile broadly at everyone in sight, aching to burst into conversation.

All his life he had wanted friendship, and, though this had escaped him in a deeper sense, he had known moments of great sympathy with passing strangers in taverns. Drink had the advantage of loosening tongues as well as wetting them. As for physical satisfaction, he had failed to experience it on the few occasions he had been with women. He knew the failure had not been with them, and could not suppress suspicions which surfaced though he preferred to ignore them. Certainly that aspect of life was not discussed in polite society, but there had been times, when he received a particular look, or came unexpectedly on two men who broke apart embarrassed, when Lionel wondered if such behaviour was so alien after all. Perhaps his own celibacy was the more unnatural? How he detested the whispered suggestion cultivated by Gussie that 'Lionel had been disappointed in romance', as if marriage was a moral necessity. 'Normality' was the curse of the English provinces. Thank God he had put that behind him.

As for London, it was so immense that there was room for every taste, as he had discovered already. He had been shocked on his first evening, when he entered the Coal Hole in an alley off the Strand, surprisingly close to the Arundel, to find that the supper-room was the scene of a mock trial, complete with judge and jury, examining cases of rape and breach of promise. It was several minutes before it dawned on him that the female witnesses were men dressed up as women, and he wondered at the

111

chance which led him there. The heckling grew louder, and the ribaldry so indecent that Lionel had left in alarm. He had returned three nights later to test his own reaction further. On his second visit he enjoyed himself more.

But tonight he wanted companionship, not entertainment. Startled to find how quickly time had passed, he moved on to a cheerful tavern in Coventry Street, where he sat down at a table next to a thick-set young man who looked so agreeable that Lionel offered him a drink when he made his order.

The young man introduced himself as Mick, divulging no surname, and was a merchant seaman from a village in the north of Ireland. He was the sort of man Lionel admired: a straightforward working man without a hint of artifice, and good-looking too, with black curly hair and thick moustaches. But it was his humour which appealed to Lionel most of all, the good-natured laughter and the smile which seemed to find fun in everything. The perfect companion.

Mick spoke of his recent voyage to Egypt, and Lionel told him of his own journey in a few days' time to Van Diemen's Land. He was disconcerted by the young man's terse reaction – 'Rather you than me.'

Lionel lost his shyness and found himself talking with a frankness that bordered on indiscretion. He told the young man everything about himself, including the loss of Raxleigh House.

When Mick mentioned that he needed to find lodgings for the night, Lionel was so reluctant to see him go that he wondered for a wild moment if he should take him back to the Arundel. Fortunately, he had the sense instead to speak to the barman, who wrote down a couple of addresses.

It was nearly midnight when they left, lurching up the road towards Soho, Mick holding Lionel's arm firmly though he was none too steady himself. A hard-faced woman in curlers complained that they had disturbed her when she had just fallen asleep, but she took Lionel's money nevertheless and showed them to a bleak and icy room. The two men undressed silently and drew close to each other in bed to keep warm.

Lionel woke suddenly. There was daylight outside and it was several seconds before he knew where he was. Then he remembered the sailor who must have left to catch his ship from Tilbury. For a moment, the image of his nakedness – then the shock of alarm as he scrambled out of bed. Everything had gone. He searched his pockets again, and yet again, he opened the drawers in the ugly solitary wardrobe, but nothing remained.

Oh, God, he thought, sitting on the edge of the bed. Why did it have to be like this? It was pointless to go to the police, or return to the tavern where he had spent the evening; and what would he do if he did find the man again? Fight him – or appeal to his better nature?

He gained one bitter, perverse satisfaction from the incident: if this was what London held in store for him, then he was lucky to be leaving it.

He did not even ask the landlady if she had seen the Irishman go. Returning to the Arundel, which seemed welcoming by comparison, he ordered a deep, hot bath to help him purge the shame.

PART 3

— 9 —

The last farewell

A strange assortment of people had been converging on Gravesend for the last few days, though their progress was scarcely noticed by the passers-by.

They came in various forms of transport from all over Britain. Many of them were unable to speak the English language, let alone write it: Scottish Highlanders, strong, dark men who had been evicted from their cottages to make way for sheep; taciturn farm labourers from the west country, where they earned five shillings a week and seldom tasted meat; Irish emigrants fleeing from impending famine, who would have preferred free America but were forced by necessity to make the long voyage to Australia instead. Some of them trudged on foot, others jolted by cart or covered waggon, and most were hungry. All had decided that there must be a better life than the one they knew.

In reaching their momentous decision they had been helped by a government eager to be rid of them. Billboards showed drawings of a family *Here* and *There*, like the miraculous *Before* and *After* cures in various medical advertisements. The family pictured at home was starving, the destitute father holding a sick child in front of a poster which proclaimed in bold letters: CAUTION TO ALL VAGRANTS. That was *here*. But *there*, on the far side of the world, the father was transformed into an upright, jolly man carving a large joint of beef while his wife and children watched him with delight. Their

115

number had increased on the voyage, proving that a good time was had by all, with a baby in a crib and a dog beside it to complete the happy scene.

Unlike the medical advertisements, where *before* is frequently more attractive than *after*, the degradation of *here* was undeniable. No one needed to be convinced of that. It may seem pointless to encourage a man to cross the world when he cannot afford a decent meal for his family at home, but the government was prepared to help the poorest pauper on his way with an assisted passage in order to populate the distant colonies. As this disposed of the most unfortunate elements in society, it was hard to say if Britain's loss was Australia's gain.

Though most were forced to emigrate by wretched circumstances, a few optimists looked forward to the adventure, believing that they would start afresh and earn enough money for their families to join them. Single women relished the prospect of seizing a husband in Van Diemen's Land, where men outnumbered women by ten to one. Indeed, so many applied that a special committee had been set up 'promoting the Emigration of Single Women and Widows of good character', with the stipulation that they were respectable and between fifteen and thirty years of age. The difficulty of proving either respectability or youth caused such embarrassment that many were accepted when a closer look at their faces would have denied the claim of 'twenty-nine' and confirmed that their profession was even older than themselves.

The whole procedure was perfunctory. Though *Female Emigration to Australia* was granted *on payment of Five Pounds only*, the smaller print revealed:

Those who are unable to raise even that sum here, may, when approved by the Committee, go *without any Money Payment* whatever as their notes of hand will be taken payable in the Colony within a reasonable time after their arrival when they have acquired the means to do so: in both cases the parties will have the advantage of the Government Grant in aid of their passage.

The idea of giving anything back to the government caused much merriment in the covered waggons which lurched on their way to Kent.

At least the women had freedom to look forward to. Less fortunate were the silent men who marched with gyves upon their wrists – convicts sentenced to transportation for life.

As for the Stowes, the enormity of the decision which Gussie had taken so impulsively on their behalf was now upon them, and the sweet melancholy of their departure made them unusually subdued as their carriage travelled the twenty-four miles from London. Gussie was checking his lists; Sarah was adding to hers; while Lionel turned over the pages of two documents he had bought for the journey but ignored till now. One was called *The Guide to Prospective Settlers*, the other *The Emigrant Voyager's Manual*, and he read them with growing alarm. Every type of person was encouraged to emigrate except for gentlefolk of good breeding, and the Guide offered one piece of advice which might have been written with the Stowes in mind:

> Gentlemen with large capital ought not to emigrate at all – England is the paradise of the rich – a man with capital can command many profitable ways of applying it without subjecting himself to the barbarians of the bush.

They were no longer rich, they had lost Raxleigh House and all the distinction which went with it, but they had the capital from the estate and they were certainly gentlemen. The Guide implied that a gentleman would be mad to think of emigrating, and Lionel wondered why Gussie's cousin had been so eager to help them. Would they be alien in Van Diemen's Land? Had Gussie been duped into going there? His eye caught that phrase again – *barbarians of the bush* – and he turned the page quickly in case it caught Gussie's eye. His brother-in-law looked glum enough already.

In fact, Gussie was cold with apprehension as he indulged in that deadliest of vices, putting the clock back – too late. If only he could start again. If only they still had Raxleigh House. If only . . . He tried to concentrate on his lists, but his mind kept returning to everything they had lost.

The carriage, piled with pyramids of luggage on top, had left the Arundel Hotel early so as to arrive in Gravesend while it was still light. Sarah had insisted on ample time to stock up with fresh provisions at the stores on the docks before the *Countess of Bath* sailed with the tide the following afternoon. Gussie had had sudden doubts about these stores. 'After all,' he pointed out with undeniable if unconvincing logic, 'their customers are hardly likely to lodge a complaint from the other side of the world. They could sell the most inferior goods with impunity.' As a precaution, he had insisted that Sarah buy half their provisions from a reputable shop in Jermyn Street, including two black hams and a side of bacon, which accounted for the quantities of extra luggage. This was the reason for hiring a carriage instead of taking the new express train from Charing Cross, which took little more than an hour to reach Gravesend.

Also, he was worried about the eggs. Eggs could be bought in Gravesend too, but Gussie felt easier with eggs of his own acquaintance. That was the trouble with eggs – until you opened them, they were ageless. Those at Gravesend might be rotten, so they had collected their own from trustworthy hens at Raxleigh, dipped them in goose fat, and rolled them gently in sawdust before packing them on end.

'Even with our stay in London,' Gussie explained, 'they'll be fresher than anything we could buy in town. They should last us for a good part of the voyage.' He took two of their best-laying hens as well. 'Whatever happens,' he declared, 'we shall not be short of eggs for breakfast.'

After his personal supervision that morning, a crate containing two hundred and forty eggs packed in sawdust was strapped firmly to the roof of the carriage. Gussie winced at every lurch over the cobbles, looking up anxiously as if he expected a quantity of whites and yolks to seep through the wood and canvas like the ingredients for a giant omelette.

Roly frowned. 'It's too bad that we have to go all this way to Gravesend when the ship was round the corner in the East India Docks.'

'I entirely agree with you,' said his father. 'I asked the same question myself when I called on the agents to check on our livestock. Apparently the boat has to make several calls after being loaded at the docks, and it takes some time, you know. She has to be towed down river, catching the tide. In fact she sailed three days ago. It's a bigger operation than I realised; four hundred and fifty passengers altogether . . .'

'Four hundred and fifty!' echoed Roly, astounded. 'I thought it was more like fifty.'

'The steerage emigrants.' Gussie gave a nervous cough. 'They were due to board her yesterday.'

'Four hundred,' exclaimed Sarah weakly. 'I had no idea there'd be as many as that.'

Neither had Gussie. Until now he had spared them the worst of it. Because so much had been arranged by Sir Anthony Payne he had not investigated the conditions as he should have done until he visited the offices of Marshall and Eldridge in Fenchurch Street. The agent had looked up from his papers and smiled over the top of his spectacles.

'The ship, as you may have been informed, is the *Countess of Bath*.'

'Yes,' replied Gussie agreeably, 'and the name pleases me greatly.'

The agent blinked, but he had little time to pursue the quirks of conversation and continued swiftly: 'Your captain is Joseph Peppiatt. An excellent man.'

'He sounds so indeed,' said Gussie. 'Might I enquire

119

how many fellow passengers we may expect to join us?'

The agent examined his lists intently. 'A total complement of four hundred and fifty – including the crew. Approximately.'

This had been the moment of dreadful truth. 'Excuse me,' Gussie murmured faintly, thinking he had heard incorrectly. The man repeated the number, but Gussie assumed he must still be mistaken. 'Surely,' he protested, 'there cannot be accommodation for as many as that?'

The man smirked at such innocence. 'You have no idea! That's empty compared to some we sail out of London. You're one of the lucky gentlemen with a cabin to yourself, and a good stern cabin at that. There are eleven first-class cabins all told. That accounts for thirty-six of you; then we have the intermediates who are paying their way with smaller cabins at twenty pounds or so, that's another eighty-four; but it's the steerage that make up the numbers. Packed into every inch of space like peas in a pod, they are – there's more than three hundred steerage.' He counted these off his list, for Gussie still looked incredulous: 'Sixty-one single men; fifty-eight married; forty-nine single women; thirty-one half-adults – that's children under ten – twenty-three soldiers and twenty-two crew . . .'

'Soldiers,' Gussie interrupted. 'I thought this was a government ship?'

'And so it is! The soldiers are there to look after the convicts. We have ninety-six convicts as well.'

'*Convicts!*' exclaimed Gussie, appalled.

'It's unusual, I admit. But you won't set eyes on them. They're kept in irons from start to finish, so they'll be no nuisance.'

'I should think not,' said Gussie icily. 'That's hardly the point, is it? If I'd known that my family would be cheek by jowl with the criminal classes I should have changed my passage.'

The agent sighed, having met with similar complaints during the last few days. 'You do realise,' he exclaimed patiently, 'that the *Countess of Bath* is a new vessel?'

'So I gathered, but I can't see what difference that makes.'

'She is a *clipper*.' The agent waited for some response.

'That only means she's fast, doesn't it? What on earth has that to do with convicts? Unless . . .' A new thought appalled him. 'Unless you mean that people are frightened to sail on her?'

'Not at all,' said the agent hastily. 'Just that she's been placed in commission too recently for people to have heard of her. When the government asked us to carry some transportees, odds and sods who don't belong to any regular consignment, we were obliged to agree.'

'But my cousin . . .' Gussie started to protest, hoping that the name of his illustrious patron would influence the man, but the agent turned it instantly to his advantage.

'Yes,' he agreed brightly, 'I *am* conversant with all the facts pertaining to yourself and your family. Sir Anthony has instructed us to accommodate you in the chief cabins at only half our usual charge of fifty pounds per passenger. As the cabins are newly furnished, I'm sure you will appreciate such a concession.'

'Very well,' he had replied stiffly. 'We shall have to make the best of it.'

'It's too bad,' said Gussie now, as they alighted outside the Falcon Hotel. 'I sent word that we'd arrive by four and it's nearly five. If the agents have sent a man to meet us, I hope he's waited.'

Disgruntled and cold they entered the Falcon with their overnight luggage, Raxleigh's collar held tightly by Roly. To Gussie's relief the third officer of the *Countess of Bath* was waiting to greet them personally, but he informed them that there was no chance of going on board that evening to unload their luggage. He explained that the steerage passengers had been boarding the vessel all day, after two nights in the Gravesend depots. Taking Gussie aside, he added that many of the emigrants were seizing this last chance for a drink on shore and he expected trouble. 'Not only the men, but the women too.

They're in a shocking state already. I advise you to keep your distance.'

Gussie gave a heartfelt sigh. 'Oh, lord! I suppose I should have expected as much. Tell me, are they a very bad lot?'

'All sorts, sir,' said the third officer diplomatically. 'I've known worse on other ships.' Because the passenger looked a reasonable man, the officer added: 'I can see why they wish to break loose on their last run ashore. They may never see England again.'

Gussie thought this a tactless remark, for it applied to himself as well.

'Yes,' he replied, 'it *is* an emotional moment, no doubt of that.'

'Those with least to worry about cause the most trouble,' the officer continued. 'The young men and women can't cope with the boredom at sea and turn to drink if they can get it; but pregnant women, and the old folk, you never hear a word of complaint from them.' Gussie sensed a hint that complaints were a tiresome self-indulgence.

'I gather the vessel is unproved,' he ventured. 'Can we expect a smooth voyage?'

'Certainly,' said the third officer quickly. 'She's A1 at Lloyds.'

'And what about our captain?'

The third officer hesitated, as if it seemed indecent to introduce such a deity into their conversation. 'Captain Peppiatt is an exceptional navigator, sir,' he said at last. 'He will get you to Van Diemen's Land faster than you might expect. In fact the company is taking a special interest in our maiden voyage. With a fine new vessel like the *Countess*, we could even break a record.'

'Then there's nothing we can do tonight?'

'Not on board, sir. But if you come with me to the custom house in Harmer Street there are forms you have to sign, and I daresay your ladies will wish to visit the stores.'

'Indeed!' Gussie brightened. 'My wife is looking after

the provisions, and I know she's concerned about the meals provided by the ship's cook. Perhaps you could have a word with her?'

'I shall be delighted, sir,' said the young man, who had sailed with emigrants before and knew the overwhelming importance of food on board ship. 'Though all meals are provided in the cabin dining-room, it's best to supplement them with little treats for yourselves. Now, sir, if you don't mind, they're waiting for us at the custom house.'

'Forgive me.' Gussie straightened his back. 'A quick word with my wife and I'm at your disposal.'

When Gussie had left, Sarah, Matilda and Sally were led by one of the hotel porters, a small boy in a vast collar, to the depot store where they could order provisions to be delivered to the ship the next morning. At this final stage, their choice was crucial: top of the list were raspberry-vinegar and ginger-beer powder to make the drinking water more palatable as it grew stale. It had come as a shock to Sarah to learn there would be no landing, even at the Cape of Good Hope, to provide the opportunity to take on fresh supplies and stretch their legs on shore. The non-stop journey was one of the alleged gains of sailing on the fast new clipper, but she regarded it as a penalty as well.

'Candles,' Matilda reminded her. 'We need dozens of candles and matchboxes.' Matilda's common sense was invaluable, but Sally remained indifferent and listless. Sarah was too busy to protest.

'Apples,' said Matilda. 'We'll need a barrel, and I want to see it filled, so they can't put a few good on top of a lot of rotten.' When the barrel was sealed, she had it marked with chalk to make sure they delivered the same one on board. Fresh fruit and vegetables were the immediate concern, but Sarah was becoming worried about the last part of the voyage when fresh food would be scarce.

The more she heard about the clipper and her captain, and the glimpses she had of the stumbling humanity streaming up and down the gangplank on to the *Countess*, revealed by a few flickering oil-lamps further down the quay, the more she realised that nothing would be as she had expected. She had been told that the voyage would take four to six months, but now it was rumoured that Captain Peppiatt was out to break all records by reaching Van Diemen's Land in less than a hundred days. Then there was the contrariness of the weather, for it seemed that winter would travel with them all the way. When they arrived in Hobart in April or May, it would be the start of autumn instead of the beginning of spring. So she bought lentils for soup, and large quantities of treacle and oatmeal for porridge.

'Blankets,' said Matilda. 'An extra blanket each. Even if we don't need them on board they'll be useful over there.' This was hardly true of the land of wool, but it was a point to bear in mind.

'Soluble cocoa,' Matilda declared, confronting a new label. 'This sounds a good one – "Guaranteed Pure Soluble anti-dyspeptic cocoa or chocolate powder, made Instantaneously with Boiling Water – Keeps for years in all climates – Palatable without milk. A teaspoon to a breakfast cup costing less than one halfpenny."' She repeated the words with effort.

'That sounds just what we need,' Sarah agreed, reading the endorsement. '"Highly commended by the entire Medical Press." Well, they would say that, wouldn't they? What do you think, Matilda? We've stocked up with tea and coffee already . . . shall we say five tins?'

'Could we make it more?' asked Matilda, who loved the taste of chocolate. 'As the tins are airtight, we could use them over there.'

She looked so wistful that Sarah laughed and gave her order to the hovering assistant. 'All right. Ten tins of Schweitzer's Cocoatina.' This was to prove the most popular purchase of the evening.

The overhanging threat of snow lifted on the day of their departure. It was one of those rare days when winter grows bored with greyness and decides to present a cheerful face, but the sudden radiance was out of tune with the sombre scene at the dockside, crowded with human merchandise.

All sailings seem chaotic to the uninitiated, but this departure was fraught in its permanence. The flow of humanity glimpsed by Sarah the night before was a torrent now, swarming up the broad planks with bundles on their backs; children struggling to keep up with their families, clutching any familiar coat-tail or sleeve; mothers with babies in their arms; mothers with babies swelling visibly inside them. The women kept warm with caps and shawls, though touches of coloured ribbon round their bonnets showed they were trying to look their best; the men were encased in black travelling ulsters or great-coats, and large black broad-brimmed hats. There was a momentary lull when the steerage passengers assembled on the poop deck for roll-call, their names shouted out as proof of their existence. They stood alert and apprehensive at this sign of regimentation, but the moment it was over turmoil burst out.

The poop deck was reserved for cabin passengers only, but the officers did not attempt to enforce the rule until they sailed. It would have been useless in such a free-for-all. The unfairness of the system would rankle soon enough – the most space for the fewest passengers – but this was the nature of first-class travel.

Though most of the emigrants had sailing papers, and cabin passengers had dealt directly with the agents, runners were still touting for custom, taking advantage of anyone heard to make enquiries, seizing hold of their luggage with the excuse of coming to their assistance. The runners were brokers' men, speculators who did not own any steerage space themselves but sold it on commission from the provision merchants and the agents. Because they recruited emigrants they were tolerated by the government, but they were parasites, feeding on the gullible. At this late hour they were desperate for a final catch among a few undecided visitors.

Then it was the turn of the privileged cabin passengers

to be fetched from their hotels or waiting carriages. The quay was packed and the porters had to force their way through the shouting mob, making way for the Stowe family behind them. Their luggage had been loaded on to handcarts, with special instructions regarding the crate of eggs, and the porters negotiated an obstacle course of buckets and barrels and large wicker chests scattered around their owners.

A few isolated figures stood in their way impassively, uninvolved: a watchful policeman; a glum black man, the new ship's cook; and an old woman who looked so close to death that Lionel wondered why she was making the journey at all. A group of young men, sharing 'intermediate' cabins 'tween decks, gave a carefully calculated impression of seasoned travellers, with sturdy boots, elaborate scarves, and binoculars in new leather cases.

When the Stowes reached the broad gangplank, the blackbeetles with bundles on their backs were ordered aside to let the ladies climb on board. Nervously, they did so, running a gauntlet of stares from the steerage women who regarded their frills with cries of envious contempt: 'Airs and graces won't be no use where you're going,' and other, saucier comments, lost in the uproar.

The malice was light-hearted, but it revealed a new self-confidence, a quickening hope that life would be different out there, where no man would be superior to his neighbour. Only the day before, the Commissioners for the Selection of Emigrants had supplied them with basic provisions, cooking utensils, mattresses, bolsters, blankets and drinking mugs, and for many it was the first time they had been given anything. It impressed them greatly with a sense of their new importance.

Sally nearly lost her balance as she stepped on deck. She looked up timidly as an arm swept round her protectively, and saw a young man with chestnut hair and light brown eyes who bowed politely before disappearing into the maelstrom. The Stowes were guided through the jostling crowd towards the door between the stairs leading up to the poop deck.

'You're lucky, ma'am,' said the third officer quickly to Sarah, who was shaken by the uproar. 'You're spared the stench of wool, and that's the first thing most passengers complain of. Until you smell it you can't imagine it. The stink, if you'll pardon my language, penetrates everywhere.'

'I didn't realise wool had a smell,' said Sarah, raising her voice in order to be heard at all. The officer laughed.

'I expect you're thinking of the knitting-needle variety, ma'am. The stench of the untreated wool the ships bring back on the journey home lingers all the way out again. You *never* get rid of it. As this is our maiden voyage you're saved all that. You couldn't find a cleaner vessel than the *Countess*.'

He was a kind-hearted young man, with more time for the passengers than the rest of the crew. He led them along the corridor to their cabins, anticipating their dismay when they saw the cramped conditions. Space was a vital commodity on board, and emigrants had been known to fight for it in their desperate need to move and breathe. The cabin passengers were more privileged than they realised: six feet by six for Roly and Matilda, and one of the two best stern cabins measuring a massive nine by ten feet for Gussie and Sarah, to be shared with Sally. Lionel was sharing with another bachelor, yet to arrive, and was quick to claim the bunk nearer the window.

There were nine cabins altogether, arranged in a horseshoe around the passageways, with a separate dining-room in the middle. Meals were to be taken in three sittings of twelve, enabling families and friends to stick together, or assume responsibility for anyone who might be travelling alone.

The Stowes absorbed all this silently, and the third officer recognised their bewilderment as they wondered how they would survive in such a space for such a length of time. But human nature is resilient and he knew enough to wait. In a few moments he was smiling as Sarah returned to her cabin to decide what should go where, advising the steward to lash their brass-bound sea-chest to the floor. Opening her canvas bag, she placed the family Bible on the shelf between the bunks, and set about the task of turning this cupboard into a home.

There was such a thundering overhead that Gussie went outside to see what was happening. An extraordinary scene confronted him. The emigrants were there as before, but as the moment of departure approached emotions veered from grief to wild celebration, or both simultaneously. Several of the Irish emigrants danced a drunken jig to a scraping fiddle, while a group of elderly chapel-goers sang mournful psalms on the other side of the deck to which the sailors responded with bawdy ballads of their own. This blend of revelry and religious fever was enhanced by the tall, saturnine figure of a clergyman dressed in a black surtout, who had been distributing tracts and now started to hold a religious service of his own. It may have been intended to comfort, but only succeeded in instilling a chilling fear in those who heard him. 'May God have mercy on these His unfortunate children, lost souls at home, now to seek a new life as strangers in a strange land . . .' The voice continued ominously while children played marbles between the feet of his dwindling congregation.

'I'll be damned!' exclaimed Gussie, forgetting himself. He elbowed his way through the swell until he reached the man who stood by the rails.

'Stanton! My dear old friend! This is good of you, to come all this way to see us off.'

His former clerk looked up, astonished. 'Mr Stowe!'

'To see a friendly face from home! I cannot tell you how touched and pleased I am . . .' He broke off as Stanton seized his hand and shook it violently.

'Mr Stowe! I'm blessed at seeing you.' Gussie was embarrassed to see that the man had tears streaming down his face. Not knowing what to say in the face of such emotion, surely excessive in spite of the years of faithful service, he shook the clerk's hand with equal warmth.

128

'Please don't distress yourself, painful though this is for all of us.'

William Stanton stared at him and shook his head in disbelief. 'I've been so out of touch, had so much to cope with, I didn't realise . . . I thought you were sailing next month. I had no idea.'

Now it was Gussie's turn to look confused. 'Then why are you here?'

'My son, Dick. I couldn't let him go without a last God-speed, poor boy. I've just left him. At least they allowed me that. But you should see the place he's in . . .' Stanton was so distressed he found it difficult to say the words. 'So dark and wet down there. Oh, can't they ruin a life!' He started to weep again. 'Chained hand and foot like a common criminal.' He whispered the last word in anguish. 'I caught a glimpse of hell, but now, thank God, I find you here.'

'Do I gather,' Gussie asked him gently, 'that young Dick is one of the transportees?'

'Why do you imagine I'm here?' Stanton asked impatiently. 'I implore you, do what you can for the boy. He's one of the best-natured lads you could wish for. He deserves better than this. *You* know that.'

Stanton stared at him so oddly as he said this that Gussie had the uneasy feeling he was being imposed on.

'My dear Stanton, of course I shall do whatever I can . . .'

'You *must!*'

Gussie winced from the rudeness the clerk had never shown before. He frowned, trying to control his temper.

'I'm sure Dick is still the good boy I knew in spite of his misfortunes. If I find the opportunity to assist him, I shall do so. Now, before you leave, let me fetch my wife from our cabin. I know she'd never forgive me if she missed you.'

As he left him, he was aware once more of the curious look on the man's face, as if Stanton was on the point of making some confession which he would rather not hear. By the time he reached the cabin he was wondering if it would be wise to tell his wife that Stanton was on board. He allowed the minutes to pass until it was Sarah herself who expressed the wish to go out on deck to witness their departure. When they reached the rails, Stanton had gone.

Gussie experienced an infinite relief, as if he had averted something unpleasant. He knew how much his wife would have liked to say goodbye to their old clerk, but the emotion of such a farewell could only upset her. As for that unfortunate youth below, it was a dreadful business, but he had been found guilty by a court martial. There was nothing they could do, so he decided it would be kinder not to mention either of the Stantons to Sarah.

By now the round, red winter sun was descending and the sky exploding with glorious flashes of crimson and silver, like a firework display to honour their departure. Every rope and spar was thrown into sharp relief against this final glow, and the *Countess* shivered and shifted as ropes were cast adrift, so slowly at first that the movement was hardly perceptible. The emigrants surged towards the bulwarks; those left behind ran alongside, shouting and waving, while the oarsmen in the tugs pulled with all their strength and turned the *Countess* into the river. Suddenly the gap between the boat and the shore had widened so much that the running figures lost their identity, but this did not prevent the emigrants from waving their hats above their heads and hoisting children on to their shoulders for a last look at the land they were leaving behind. When the military band played 'Rule Britannia' at the quayside the music was drowned in the cheering, but now the strains of 'Home Sweet Home' followed them across the stillness of the water with a bitter irony. A fleet of smaller boats escorted them into the middle of the channel; the passengers on the passing Gravesend ferry crowded the decks to give the emigrants three resounding cheers, which were answered by those on board the clipper with a frantic activity of flags and hats.

Lionel found himself shaking convulsively, tears streaming down his cheeks, and thought that his heart would break. Everywhere, grief was open and unashamed. Husbands and wives consoled each other, arms flung around shoulders, while bewildered but trusting children pressed closer. A young woman, plainly pregnant, looked so pale that she was helped towards a chest where she could rest; strangers introduced themselves, forging an immediate intimacy. A Cornish miner bent down to kiss his son's forehead, tilting the boy's straw hat to do so. Children shouted with excitement as a gun was fired from New Tavern Fort on shore, and an answering boom from the cannon on the *Countess* frightened Raxleigh into terrified silence at last.

Another surge to the bulwarks, and a hush as the emigrants looked over the rail to watch the arrival of the pilot boat and Captain Peppiatt, who left the business of departure to the mate until the last possible moment. A man who was lost on land, he was little less than a god on board, and the passengers studied him respectfully as he climbed the rope ladder. The estuary pilot was the last man on board. Sticking out of the captain's pocket was the day's newspaper wrapped in oilskin, to prove the authenticity of the sailing date in his log should he claim a record. With a dark cap pulled over his forehead, and a grey beard covering the lower part of his face, he gave nothing away in his appearance.

Seeing him, the sailors sprang to with new efficiency. They answered the cries of command from the mate in a ritual that was only intelligible to the crew.

'Raise tacks and sheets.'

'Helms a-lee, all clear for'ard?'

The answer was a shout of 'Ay, ay, sir' and a great clattering as canvas, ropes and blocks heaved above them like a second sky. The sun had set by now and a slight breeze filled the sails. The ship was alive!

'Steady your helm, keep her full!'

The sailors sang as they heaved and the clipper gathered speed:

'Fare you well my lovely gal,
Heave I-ho, heave I-ho,
I'm a-leaving of old England
So I pray you let me go.'

The Thames narrows at Gravesend to a width of half a mile. The *Countess* turned towards the straits of Dover and the open sea, the gap between the opposing shores widening all the time. Everyone who worked on the river knew where she was heading and sympathised with those on board: jaunty tugs and clumsy hay-barges hooted their sirens in respect as the graceful clipper sailed by. Past the custom house, Terrace Pier and the harbour master's office, towards the Isle of Grain and the low, interminable marshes. The light was fading quickly and the steerage emigrants were sent below, but a few of the cabin passengers lingered by the rails, the young looking eagerly ahead while the old gazed back wistfully towards the receding land. Joe Peppiatt eyed them with his usual curiosity, frowning as he remembered the social ritual ahead. He had to introduce himself to the cabin passengers and make himself agreeable. One family was connected with the Secretary for the Colonies and he expected trouble from them, but that was nothing new.

Roly stood by himself, Raxleigh asleep in his arms. Now that they were under way he was bereft. Until this moment he had clung to an inner certainty that something would save them, but now all hope had faded. When Matilda joined him and started to link her arm through his he pushed her roughly aside as if she was the last person in the world entitled to touch him.

The captain watched as she moved away, plainly hurt, and thought: There's a bitter young man. Sally, talking coquettishly to the young doctor, he put down as a beauty who knew it.

Gussie and Sarah bent over the rails, desolate with the fear that they might never see England again.

'Oh, my dearest,' Gussie whispered. 'I'm heartbroken. What have I done?'

She replied with false conviction: 'We had to go. After all that happened we had no choice. You mustn't blame yourself.'

He had to persist. 'Can you ever forgive me?'

Sarah suppressed a sigh of irritation and replied with fabricated anger: 'Never say that again. Never. There's no question of forgiveness, so forget all that. We're together and that's the only thing that matters. We must think of the future from now on.'

The pent-up strain of the last few months was released as he kissed her passionately on the lips. Then he sobbed quietly, pressing his head against her breasts. How strange, thought Captain Peppiatt as he watched them. He looks such a dry stick yet he cares deeply.

Darkness had fallen. He had a word with the first officer, promised the estuary pilot a hot drink, and went below to prepare himself for the ordeal of being civil.

In contrast to the golden day, it was growing cold. Roly was soon the only passenger left on deck, his broad-brimmed hat bent back by the breeze, staring sightlessly ahead with Raxleigh asleep in his arms.

The only sounds were the stirring of the sails in the freshening wind and the creak of the timbers groaning softly in the darkness as if, like muscles stiff from lack of practice, they were thankful to be stretched at last.

PART 4

— 10 —

The privileged few

Once under way, the pain of departure eased as the travellers adjusted to their new surroundings. There was much to distract them.

Everyone complained and most had reason to. The mass of steerage passengers were dismayed by the space allotted to them – or, rather, by the lack of it. Privacy had been abandoned for the voyage, but there were still those who dreaded the ordeal of undressing in front of strangers. The men were better off. They could lie on their bunks and wriggle out of their trousers, but this manoeuvre was denied to the women.

Seeing the density of the bunks in double tiers, with no more than eighteen inches of headroom and even less between tiers, married couples wondered how the sexual act could be performed without becoming a public entertainment. One couple, who had married the week before, paid the ship's carpenter to rig up a partition which gave them a few feet of blessed isolation.

Catering for those needs which do not take kindly to postponement was one of the nastiest prospects. Again, it was better for the men, who could relieve themselves on deck, but this was impossible at night when the hatches were battened down. There was a rough water-closet for the women, but many did not know how to use it and the pipe was choked already. Only a few had taken the precaution of bringing chamber-pots. The rest had to use jugs and dishes, even if these had been intended for food.

The Highlanders were prepared to use them for both functions with a perfunctory wipe in between.

Any hope that their new equality would start on board was shattered. As soon as the *Countess* got under way, the steerage passengers were banished from the poop deck with instructions never to return. Two young girls dared to linger and were scolded for their impudence by the mate, Emlyn Conway, an ill-tempered fellow with eyes like blackcurrants who thought himself important and used his power with the exaggeration of a little man. His uniform was immaculate, the grey hair trim, and he walked with the stiffness of a ramrod. He talked with an odd lilt, emphasising the wrong word in a sentence – 'Thank yew, *very* much!' – which he thought was humorous but amused no one. During his frequent inspections he wore a pair of white gloves and like most martinets he was a bully, especially towards defenceless victims like the two girls on the poop deck.

'You,' he called out as he trotted towards them.

'Us?' asked one of the girls, giggling.

'Don't try to *be* clever with me,' he snapped. 'Get back where you belong, below, and keep your place *in* future. This deck is out of bounds to the likes of you.'

The girls, determined not to be intimidated so easily, – though they might have been less brazen on their own – continued to giggle. It was partly due to nervousness, but Conway took it personally, as he did everything.

'I'll remember you *two*,' he threatened.

As the girls started to run down the stairs to the main deck one of them saw Matilda leaning over the rail. 'Tilly! Tilly!' she cried, and Matilda turned instinctively at hearing her old nickname, flushing with pleasure as she recognised a schoolfriend from Bideford.

'Harriet! Fancy! You of all people!' But in the next second her joy was marred by the realisation that Harriet must know the scandal which had forced the Stowes to leave Raxleigh, must know everything she had put behind her.

Harriet Baker mistook Matilda's expression and asked more shyly: 'You still remember me?'

'Get on with you, of course I do . . .' Matilda was about to join her when Conway seized his opportunity.

'I've warned you girls. Stop molesting this young lady and get below where you belong before I put you in charge.'

Matilda was about to protest that they were her friends when Harriet dropped her a mocking curtsey. 'Sorry, m'lady,' she said, and Matilda stood there miserably, longing to call them back. Instead she said nothing as she watched the girls disappear down the hatchway, thinking how awful it would be if Harriet talked. News of her own lack of quality would seep through every level of the ship, and she was beginning to suspect that background mattered as much at sea as it had on shore.

In this she was correct. A large vessel depended on her pecking order. Each deck looked down on the one below. Regardless of his social standing on land, the master dominated the pile. He was the absolute ruler of his kingdom, with the power to administer any punishment he considered necessary, even unto death. Like a king surrounded by his court, the master was flanked by the martinetish mate, the first, second and third officers and the purser. The only man who came near him in authority was the surgeon superintendent who was responsible for the welfare of the passengers. In that capacity, he and he alone was entitled to question the captain's divine right of decision should he dare to. Occasionally this led to rivalry and conflict, but more often the surgeons were elderly men who had failed on land and had little wish to assert themselves.

The doctor on this voyage remained an unknown quantity, a last-minute substitute for an old man from the midlands who had taken one look at the brawling mass of emigrants in Gravesend and gone straight home again. His replacement, young Timothy Blake, was hardly out of his teens. He was too pretty, with his chestnut hair and arrogance: a blend of saint and sinner, was the

137

captain's first impression. But the captain had broken young doctors before.

Next in this elaborate hierarchy came the privileged cabin passengers. The charge for a cabin passenger was fifty pounds, and this ensured every comfort the stewards could provide, including fresh milk from the solitary cow, and an excellent water-closet with a special protective flap.

From the poop deck, the cabin passengers looked down on the intermediates, passengers who had paid twenty pounds for their smaller cabins on the gun deck. And they considered themselves superior to the three hundred steerage passengers further along, who endured a state of incessant uproar and over-crowding. But even their conditions were luxurious compared to the horror of the level below, in the long, narrow orlop deck. Here were separate quarters for single men and women, with married couples between them for the sake of decency, none of whom had contributed a penny towards the cost of their passage. These were the true emigrants, as opposed to those on the levels above who liked to think of themselves as settlers.

Yet even the orlop emigrants, with neither influence nor money, looked down on a lower level. This was the small space underneath the fo'c'sle, known accurately enough as the black hole, where the convicts were locked in cages and guarded by soldiers whose conditions were little better. This was the lowest level of all.

Knowing how closely they would be confined together, the Stowes scrutinised every face on the poop deck. A few cabin passengers stood out from the others at this early stage: a severe-looking lady called Mrs Chant, who was sometimes described as 'handsome'; three kindly, middle-aged sisters who were travelling to join their brother, a chaplain in Hobart; and a shy girl of twelve, going to her parents in Launceston, who had been placed in the care of the three maiden ladies for the voyage.

George Flanagan attracted attention because he had been to Australia before, so successful in the goldfields north of Melbourne that he had returned home with enough money to buy himself a pretty little wife and was now setting out again to make a new fortune. Gussie knew at a glance that Mr Flanagan was not a gentleman, even if he could afford to travel like one, and disapproved of the way he fondled his little wife in public. But he had to admit that when the clipper left the quayside the Flanagans were the most radiant couple on board.

Typically, Roly took an immediate liking to Flanagan when they met in the saloon that evening. At least, Gussie thought, it meant that Roly was talking to someone, even if hardly a word was surrendered to his own family.

Like everyone else, the Stowes had taken a particular interest in the odd-looking person who made a breathless dash up the gangplank as it was being pulled on board, shouldering such a massive bundle that when he was half way up the weight of it almost pulled him back, leaving him teetering precariously as he struggled to regain his balance. His efforts were rewarded with rousing cheers from everyone around him, thankful for distraction at the painful moment of farewell.

Tony Plunkett's role in life was to be the jester even when he meant to be serious. For this his appearance was largely responsible, for while the bundle on his back gave him a snail-like look, he was transformed to an owl once it was removed. His round, elastic face was half concealed by a pudding-basin fringe of hair, and his rather protruding eyes were hidden behind a massive pair of spectacles. His mouth was exceptionally wide and turned upwards at the edges, but the most surprising feature was the absence of any sign of a neck, giving the impression that his head rested on his torso like a ventriloquist's dummy's. This was partly due to the high wing collar, which like the rest of his clothes was far too large and emphasised, rather than disguised, the fact that he was not only an odd-looking person, but a very small one too.

The Stowes paid special attention to this odd, small

young man because he was sharing Lionel's cabin on the voyage. As soon as he stumbled in, wriggled out of his harness and let his bundle fall to the floor, he straightened up and stared at Lionel with surprise. 'I say,' he exclaimed, 'I expected someone younger.'

'Really?' said Lionel, crinkling his nose. 'And how old are you?'

'Twenty-one.'

'I wouldn't have guessed.'

'The specs – they don't fit, do they? I went to this place in Regent Street – "spectacles to fit the face" – but nothing seems to fit mine. These aren't my own clothes, you know. All given me by my friends. I'm a sort of hand-me-down person.'

'He's a queer fish, but I rather like him,' Lionel told Gussie later. 'The only trouble is that he suffers from a disastrous compulsion to tell the truth.'

'I see nothing wrong in that.'

'You will. I can feel my hackles rising already.'

Baffled, Gussie turned his attention to the other privileged passengers in the cabin class. He had an impression, in the blur of introductions, of gentlefolk who were impoverished but proud, still clinging to their former pretensions. They treated him with respect – for news of his patronage had spread quickly – and Gussie was gratified when the third officer knocked on their cabin door shortly after sailing with the news that Captain Peppiatt requested the pleasure of Mr and Mrs Stowe, and Lionel Raxleigh, at his table that evening.

Sarah was busy unpacking for Sally and herself: cotton dresses, petticoats, sixteen chemises – which Gussie found excessive – nightdresses and shoes; and his own fustian jackets, shirts and canvas trousers. Gussie dressed quickly for dinner, thankful to escape.

By now he was determined to see good in everything. Their cabin with the stern window was known as the great cabin, more spacious than it seemed at first in spite of the sprawl of unpacking. When he stepped into the corridor he found it longer than he remembered, more than six feet wide, shaped like a horseshoe with the dining-room and adjacent drawing-room in the centre running the length of the poop. The cabins of the captain, ship's surgeon, and purser were ranged on the other side. Gussie peered in and found three tables in the dining-room: a long one for the passengers; and a smaller for the captain, which occupied the best position and was well laid out with silver cutlery and glass. The third table in the opposite corner was less well-dressed, reserved for the ship's officers who used it in rotation.

The steward approached Gussie with a glass of madeira on a silver tray and asked him to wait in the drawing-room where the other cabin passengers were assembling.

When Captain Peppiatt made his entrance, he revealed a startling feature without the covering of his peaked cap. A mane of prematurely grey hair, the shade of old silver, gave him an added distinction. Gussie was proud of his family. Even Roly thanked the captain for his permission to allow Raxleigh on board, which had been obtained by messenger that morning after the mate had forbidden it.

Matilda gave her best curtsey, but in doing so remembered Harriet's mocking movement earlier and was overcome with confusion. The captain saved her from further embarrassment by taking her hand firmly to lift her up again. 'I am delighted to see such a cheerful and attractive face on board my ship,' he assured her, and she flushed with pleasure.

Even Sally looked radiant, and of course Sarah could be depended on to be gracious. But it was Lionel who surprised Gussie the most, with his new confidence as correspondent for *The Times*. Until now there had been something almost disgruntled about his brother-in-law, but Lionel seemed completely at ease as he spoke to the captain. It was only too apparent that Peppiatt would have preferred to continue their conversation instead of leading his guests into the dining-room, taking Sarah's arm.

For this night at least, Captain Peppiatt made an effort

141

to be pleasant to everyone. The ladies relaxed, assuming he would remain like this for the rest of the voyage. Mrs Chant – who believed in being outspoken – dared to ask if he was married, and he joked that he had six wives at sea – the ships under his command. For reasons of his own he made no mention of his invalid wife in Chatham, and he was so charming that he gained the reputation of being 'a man for the ladies'. In fact this was far from the truth. He regarded women as a nuisance on board, especially 'tween decks where they managed to squeeze their way into the quarters of the crew or single men, making the segregation act unworkable.

The stewards served them with a series of courses which brought murmurs of approval. Apart from enjoying the fresh produce while it lasted, it was the captain's deliberate policy to satiate his passengers with quantities of rich food from the beginning, so that by the time it ran out they were thankful to accept a more spartan diet of salt beef and biscuit. The fattening up started with a warming broth, followed by poached salmon which would have been garnished with Gravesend shrimps later in the year; duckling with crisp, succulent skin and a sage and onion stuffing; boiled ham with redcurrant jelly and pickles; roast beef and winter vegetables including leeks and cauliflower; a sorbet; plum pudding; an excellent stilton and biscuits; and a large plate of almonds and raisins. Anxious not to appear impolite by discussing the food too openly, the passengers were plainly astonished by the excellence of the dinner, unaware that most of it had been prepared at the Falcon Hotel earlier that day, to be reheated in the ship's ovens. The wines were *bona fide*, followed by excellent port and French brandy, and Gussie watched apprehensively as his brother-in-law consumed them with alarming relish, though he appeared to remain sober.

In spite of his wish to swell the livers of his passengers like so many Strasbourg geese, Captain Peppiatt was a generous host, genuinely pleased by the success of his first dinner-party of the voyage. The new third officer was proving invaluable. His skilful manipulation of the seating ensured a lively flow of conversation, without those sudden awkward silences which can fall upon strangers. The sole error was the unfortunate decision to place Mrs Orbison Chant next to Tony Plunkett, for it seemed to Gussie, who sat opposite, that they took an instant aversion to each other, as cat to dog. She was brusque, and he was tactless, stepping off on the wrong foot with his opening remark.

'I see you're to have the pleasure of my company from now on.'

Mrs Chant lifted her pince-nez and studied the young man closely, as she would an offensive object. Gussie had to admit that Plunkett did look unusual. His sleeves were so large that his hands only appeared when he brought them out in order to eat.

'The pleasure of your company?' she repeated. 'That remains to be seen.'

Gussie found it impossible not to overhear this opening skirmish, for Mrs Chant projected her voice as if she was addressing a public meeting.

'I shouldn't worry,' Tony Plunkett assured her complacently. 'I know we'll get on famously.'

'I'm not in the least bit worried. As we're cheek by jowl, we'll have to make the best of it. You're Mr Stowe, aren't you?' she informed Gussie. 'The friend of the Secretary of State? But who are you?' She turned back to Tony Plunkett. 'I failed to catch your name. People will mumble when they introduce themselves, as if they're ashamed.'

'I'm not in the least ashamed. My name is Tony Plunkett.'

She remained unimpressed and peered at him again. 'Really? I am Mabel Orbison Chant.'

'Of course you are,' he agreed. 'Miss Mabel Orbison Chant. A formidable name!'

'There's no need to be impertinent. You know perfectly well that I am Mrs Chant.'

Gussie felt obliged to say something and murmured

politely, 'I have not had the pleasure of meeting your husband.' He looked around the table enquiringly.

'It would be most surprising if you had. He has been dead for the last nine months. I am on my way to Hobart Town to stay with my brother and his wife, and possibly make my home there. Why are you going?' she asked abruptly. Gussie began to outline his plan to buy a property and farm it, but she interrupted him by turning to her companion instead. 'And why are you going, Mr Plunkett? I do not wish to appear curious, but you don't look rich enough to be travelling cabin class.' She eyed his clothes with interest rather than criticism.

'I'm as poor as a church mouse. My passage has been paid for by the government.'

'Ah,' she exclaimed, satisfied. 'The government seems to have money to throw away nowadays. Might I ask why you deserve such patronage?'

'I'm a teacher,' he told her with evident pride.

'A teacher! You don't look like a teacher. My husband was the principal at the Clifton Academy for Young Ladies near Bristol, and I assisted him. So I know what's what.'

'But that's splendid!' he cried. 'You can assist me with my lectures.'

Surprisingly, this presumption did not seem to offend her. 'What do you intend to teach the poor things?'

'Everything I can about the land they're going to. They have a craving for knowledge.'

Mrs Chant looked at him sharply. 'Opening the minds of the ignorant is a great responsibility. Perhaps it is my duty to help you.'

'You admit it's a splendid opportunity?' he insisted. 'A school with pupils of all ages, waiting to be taught.'

'Who can't escape, you mean. What qualifications do you possess? You're not telling me you've been out there yourself.'

'I've done my studies and I know my facts, which is more than I can say for most people. Can you tell me who Van Diemen was, Mr Stowe?'

Gussie had been dreading such a question. 'A Dutch explorer?' he hazarded.

Mrs Chant gave her superior smile. 'Anton Van Diemen,' she declared, giving the name a Dutch inflexion, 'was born in 1593 and discovered the island in 1636.'

'Bravo!' cried Tony Plunkett. 'You've proved my point. Totally incorrect. He became the Governor General of the Dutch East India Company in 1636. The island was named after him by Abel Tasman who discovered it six years later. *He* was the explorer.'

'If it was discovered by a Dutchman,' asked Gussie, 'why is it British?'

'Captain Cook anchored there in 1777, nearly a hundred and fifty years later, though he thought it was part of New Holland. It was only at the start of this century, when Napoleon seemed interested, that we started a settlement of our own. Since then we've held on to it.' Tony Plunkett smiled proprietorially.

'I see.' Gussie nodded his head. 'How right you are to say that we should learn as much as possible about the place we're going to. I know my brother-in-law, whose cabin you're sharing, will be particularly interested in any information you can give him. He's a writer, you know, for the London *Times*.' Having scored this point, he turned his attention to the passengers' table where his daughter was looking more lively than she had done for months. Much relieved, he wondered why this transformation had taken place, attributing it naively to the fresh sea air.

The reason was romance. There is nothing more calculated to lift the spirits, especially on board ship, and Sally felt the prickling of a new sensation as she listened to the young doctor beside her. She had discarded her sullen 'gooseberry face', as Gussie called it, and her newly-recovered youthful bloom was not wasted on Timothy Blake, who counted himself fortunate to be placed next to her at dinner.

While the doctor talked, Sally was content to watch him, admiring the curve of his curly moustaches and the sheen of the chestnut hair as he told her of his excitement at finding himself on board after the last-minute message from the Society of Apothecaries.

'I suppose they chose me because I'm not tied down by families and things,' he said modestly. 'Probably they were glad to get rid of me. After they approved my appointment, I raced back to the London Hospital and left a note at my digs for the landlady saying "Gone away for a year to Van Diemen's Land". She won't have the faintest idea where that is!'

'The London Hospital! It sounds very grand.'

'Not really,' he smiled. 'You should see it – or rather you shouldn't. It's a dreadful place right in the heart of Whitechapel, in the East End of London where they're fearfully poor, almost starving. Still, I learnt a thing or two watching the other medics at work. I only qualified recently. Anyhow, I dashed back to my locker to pick up my bag of tricks, which is all I have with me. Talk of panic!'

'Bag of tricks?' asked Sally.

'My box of tools from Arnold and Sons, the grisly instruments of my profession: knives and scalpels and circular saws.'

'Circular saws!'

'Well, not really circular, I was joking, but amputation-saws in case I have to cut someone's leg off . . . sorry, I didn't mean to alarm you.'

'No, that's all right,' she assured him. 'I must get used to such things.' But she paled becomingly.

'So must I,' he laughed, 'for I must admit I had no idea what I was letting myself in for. The man at the Apothecaries said it was just a case of sick-bay and a few pills, but I'm finding out it's a lot more than that. To tell you the truth,' he leant forward confidentially, 'I'm scared stiff. Do you know, I'm a sort of guardian angel to the emigrants, responsible for their conduct as well as their health.'

'How important!'

'That's what I thought. I've got to make sure they're

146

clean and check the rations to see they get a fair share, and settle their quarrels. As for discipline, all my life people have been telling me that's what I need myself! And now I'm put in charge of four hundred passengers. I've got a medical inspection tomorrow. The old duffer who did the vanishing act was supposed to cope with that in the Gravesend depot, but now it's up to me. Frankly, I'm dreading it.'

'But you're glad you accepted the post?'

'Oh, yes. If I do well, it will stand me in good stead when I'm home again.'

That was not the answer she expected, and she felt a pang of regret at the mention of 'home'. 'You said you had no ties, but you must have a family?'

'No, they're all dead. There's only a sister.'

'*Only a sister*! That's rather hurtful. It's what I am to Roly.'

'She's not a real sister, like you. She's a stepsister and she's old and gnarled and lives in Rhyl and washed her hands of me years ago. I get a card at Christmas, without an enclosure, and that's all. No, I'm alone in the world.'

He said this with a mocking self-pity which she pretended to take seriously, protesting, 'Oh, don't say that, please. We'll adopt you for the voyage. I insist on it.'

'Then I shall be your honorary brother, if your own brother permits.' He looked at her intently, for there was genuine feeling behind the banter, and for a moment he rested his hand on hers underneath the tablecloth. Then they started to devour the duck, sharing their secret understanding with an elation that almost shivered in the air until she felt that everyone else must sense it too.

When the lengthy dinner was over, Captain Peppiatt invited a few of the gentlemen to join him in his cabin for further brandy and cigars, explaining that lack of space prevented him from including everyone as he would like. This provided the excuse to invite whom he pleased. The privileged guests were Lionel Raxleigh, Tony Plunkett, Augustus Stowe and Timothy Blake.

'Gentlemen,' Captain Peppiatt declared, waving the

steward away and filling the glasses on the tray himself, 'I should warn you that you'll find I have no time for the niceties of society once we're at sea. I spend most of my time on deck or locked in my cabin, but if I feel the need for intelligent companionship I know where to find it. Let us drink to a speedy voyage!'

They raised their glasses.

Lionel opened the conversation. 'Captain Peppiatt, I should be grateful if you could tell us how you hope to break the record. It could form the basis for my first despatch to *The Times*, and I am sure it would interest my readers.'

My readers! Even kind-hearted Gussie blinked to hear how readily his brother-in-law used the phrase when not a word from his pen had yet been published, but the irony escaped the captain. He was only too pleased to find a correspondent able to testify to every entry in his log and give him maximum publicity should he succeed. Apart from this, he had taken a liking to Lionel, plainly a man's man who enjoyed his drink.

'To tell you the truth,' said Lionel with becoming honesty, 'I know nothing about the choice of routes involved.'

Timothy Blake was bold enough to remark that it seemed a pity they were not stopping to take on fresh water and supplies.

'No need,' said the captain abruptly. 'Wastes time and upsets the migrants. Once they taste the delights of the Cape they go wild on shore and come back dissatisfied, if they come back at all. They prefer to get the voyage over as quickly as possible. Ask them, Dr Blake,' he smiled, noting the doctor's hesitation, 'and you'll find I'm right. Speed is the rule on board the *Countess*.' He relaxed. 'I can see that none of you are experienced navigators, so let me try to explain. We have to catch the right winds to carry us forward, and this means finding the best latitude. Most people think it's a question of sailing on a straight line, but it's not as simple as it looks on the map.' He pointed to a chart pinned on the cabin wall. 'Once we get far south, the curve of the world dips, as I could show you on the globe if I had one, and *that* is the shortest distance.'

'How far south?' asked the teacher, who knew more than the captain suspected.

'As close to Antarctica as safety permits. Then we can pick up the roaring forties to carry us across two and a half thousand miles of emptiness.' He picked up a book from the table. 'This is my Bible – Towson's *Tables to Facilitate the Practice of Great Circle Sailing*. This is an advance copy – it's not been published yet, so I doubt if you've heard of it, but I can promise you, Mr Raxleigh, that this will change everything. I reckon I'm one of the first who dares to sail his ship according to the Towson rules.'

'If we sail so close to the ice floes, what about the cold?' asked the doctor.

'What about it?'

'The passengers?'

'Wrap 'em up and feed 'em soup. Cold's better than hot.'

'How many days will this save?' asked Lionel, suppressing a belch, for he had eaten prodigiously in order to stay sober.

'In the old days merchantmen were used for convicts and cargo. They were dumpy things like hermetically sealed boxes, floating along like corks with little sail aloft. They were slow but speed didn't matter. Until eight years ago, few ships made it under a hundred days. Now the company have heard things which make them believe the gold regions are about to take off in a big way, and every day will matter then. That's why they are watching this voyage so closely. They want to be prepared, and this is the vessel to show them how.' The captain listed the qualities of the *Countess* as if she were a lover: her slender lines and sheer curves, her sharp-raked prow and sloping stern. 'This is a speed machine. I reckon it will become possible to make the voyage to Hobart Town in eighty days.'

149

The young doctor was going to say 'That's impossible', but changed it to 'That's astonishing! I'm beginning to understand why we haven't got time to stop at the Cape!'

'We have another advantage; our destination is Van Diemen's Land, the southernmost point in the colonies, so the curve of the world favours us with the shortest distance.'

'I've heard a rumour of a sensational prize if you break the record,' said Lionel.

'That's correct. The company have offered me five hundred pounds if I break the record, plus twenty pounds for every day under that. As the standing record's ninety-four days, it could prove most lucrative.'

'An excellent incentive, and you sound confident.'

'Of course,' smiled the captain. 'She's a fine vessel.'

'What is the point of getting there so quickly?' asked Tony Plunkett.

'The point!' The captain's bellow of laughter was not good-humoured. 'What's the point of doing anything, except to be first? Where is your sense of challenge, Mr Plunkett? A hundred things can go wrong on the voyage, and I would not insult you by pretending otherwise. The *Countess of Bath* is unlike any ship I have sailed in, but therein lies the excitement. She sails untested and untried.

'I believe it is possible to reach a speed of twenty knots if we spread her sail to the utmost – nearly ten thousand square yards – but I have no means of knowing if she can withstand such pressure. If not, she will fall apart. Of course there are risks in sailing so close to Antarctica. I know that endless stretch of water, the storms and freezing cold, and I can promise you it won't be fun.'

'Then why . . .?'

'*Why*, Mr Plunkett? Because it is the nature of man to stretch himself to the limit. Think of the glory if we sail from Gravesend to Hobart Town, a distance of sixteen thousand miles, in less than ninety days. Then I can claim a new record. That's *why*, Mr Plunkett. That's the point of it.'

The captain refilled his glass, flushed and trembling.

The others glanced at each other briefly as he did so, with looks of alarm.

'My word,' said Gussie, breaking the silence politely. 'It sounds as if we're embarking on a most remarkable voyage. I had no idea.'

The others murmured their assent, uneasily.

Simultaneously, over a glass of port in the ship's dining-room, the chaplain warned Roly of further dangers once they reached their destination: 'I fear you must expect adultery, fornication, theft, drunkenness and violence.'

'Hm,' said Roly, 'sounds promising.'

The Reverend Silas Guard stared at him, then turned away in disgust.

— 11 —

A hideous day for Dr Blake

Lionel woke with a splitting head, but he was comforted by the sound of lapping water and the feel of the ship's movement.

Tony Plunkett looked over, blinking short-sightedly without his glasses. 'You look terrible. Must have been the brandy.'

'Those nuts and raisins,' said Lionel decidedly. 'They're the ones that did me in!' They chuckled with the rapport of drinkers.

Their frivolous attitude would have been out of place in the captain's cabin. Joseph Peppiatt received his new doctor brusquely at the stroke of nine. Neither showed the slightest strain from the night before, but the cordiality was gone.

'Dr Blake, it's good of you to come aboard at such short notice. I warn you to be firm with the migrants from the outset. Otherwise they'll make your life hell. Be on your guard against everyone and everything. Half your hospital cases will prove a sham, but they'll recover soon enough if you cut their rations. Now, first things first. Thanks to the misconduct of your colleague, the migrants came on board without the proper medical examination in the depots. What do you propose to do?'

'I intend to hold it today, sir.'

'Good. Sooner the better. Trouble is, now they're safely on board they'll kick up one hell of a fuss, so you'll need to be tough with 'em. Have you had the time to meet our matron?'

'No,' the doctor admitted. Everything was such a rush. I tried to find her yesterday, but she escaped me.' He smiled. 'From all I've heard, Miss Gissing is a tough old bird.'

'Be thankful she is,' the captain rebuked. 'Don't take against Miss Gissing because of her appearance. You'll be glad to have her on your side, especially today. You'll need all the help you can get. If I were you, I'd bribe one or two of the female migrants. Bribery works wonders. Officially, drink and dice are forbidden, but I suggest you issue them with five fluid ounces of spirit a day if they behave themselves. You can buy goodwill if you're liberal with the wine to your favourites. Don't look so alarmed, Dr Blake, it's only wine.'

'It's just that you've reminded me of the water, sir.'

'What about the water? Is there anything wrong with it?'

'I understand they took it from the Thames.'

'That's usual.'

'It's not healthy.'

'Then you'll have to dilute it with lime-juice. We have barrels of the stuff.'

'I was wondering if we could refill at Deal?'

Captain Peppiatt stared at the young doctor incredulously. 'Do you realise how long that would take?'

'Several hours?'

'It would take at least one day, docking, emptying the tanks, arranging to have them refilled. Could be two days, plus the risk of the migrants getting ashore and losing themselves just as they've settled down.'

'Not a chance, then?'

'None,' said the captain emphatically. 'You've got a distilling apparatus, haven't you?' Dr Blake nodded unhappily, knowing how ineffective this would be. 'Then use that. You can always keep the water fresh by pouring it out on deck from one container to another, so the air gets to it. Water goes stale wherever it comes from after a week or two, but wine keeps its freshness. As for me, I drink nothing else, apart from French brandy.'

'I see,' said the doctor doubtfully.

'I'm glad, because we'd better get this straight from the start. Under the new Passenger Act I'm obliged to have you on board, and of course you are employed by the government so you have the right to complain to the naval authorities once we land. But while you're on my ship you're under my command . . .'

'I do understand that, sir,' said the doctor quickly.

'Of course you do,' said Captain Peppiatt. 'Now, attend to your sick parade, and be sure to establish your authority at once, for they won't respect you otherwise.' He studied the doctor closely, wondering how far he could trust him. He continued, 'I'll appreciate it if you do not repeat my plans to any of the migrants. Doubtless they'll ask you, but they won't understand and you'll only upset them with imaginary fears if you so much as whisper the word Antarctica. Otherwise, feel free to call on me when it's a matter of real importance as far as the safety of the ship is concerned.'

'I shall indeed, sir. Thank you.'

Dr Blake went below in search of Miss Gissing. From the fierceness of her reputation he expected a large woman, but she was tiny. She stood outside the ship's surgery, small and scowling, and scrutinised him without a word of welcome, not even removing the small clay pipe which was clenched in her tight-lipped mouth, for she was the exception to the rule that smoking was forbidden 'tween decks. But he remembered the captain's advice and resolved to be agreeable.

'Well, matron,' he said brightly, refusing to be intimidated, 'are you ready for the sick parade?'

'I've been waiting for you, haven't I? Since yesterday,' she snapped. She had the grace to remove the pipe as she added: 'And sick parade is right, judging by the look of 'em.'

'Looks can be deceptive,' he ventured.

'Come to the orlop, doctor, and you'll see what I mean. Lice!'

'Lice. Oh, lord, I saw enough of those in Whitechapel.'

'Then you'll feel at home. You'll find them head to toe on the orlop deck; mostly head.'

Dr Blake followed her down to the third deck and was shocked by the turmoil which confronted him. Possessions were strewn everywhere and though he was not a tall man there was so little headroom that he had to bend down as he made his way along the narrow space between the bunks and the line of tables in the middle, avoiding the swinging lanterns, trying hard to smile as he stopped himself from retching. Already the air was foul with the stench of urine and excrement, impressing him with the need for ventilation.

Miss Gissing had unlocked the separate quarters earlier to allow the mess captains to collect the daily rations, but no single woman was permitted to enter the married or the single men's section unless she said so. Any woman caught talking to a man on deck, or to one of the crew, was punished by being kept below for a week.

Understandably, the single women watched their arrival suspiciously. They glared at Miss Gissing with sullen resentment, but received the handsome young doctor with smiles and a few curtseys. In spite of his curly moustaches, he looked so young and innocent that they hoped to win him over to their side, against the matron.

He approached them cautiously, stopping at one bunk to explain about the medical examination to a young woman with long red hair.

'Do you mind?' he asked, taking her head between his hands as he did so. 'Ah! How long have you had these?'

'Long as I remember,' she replied indifferently.

He looked at the small pillow tacked to the blanket and saw that it was crawling with lice as well.

'Right!' he exclaimed cheerfully. 'I'll see you later when I examine you.'

'Yes, doctor,' she replied coyly. 'I'll look forward to that.'

Acquisitive eyes followed him all the way but he nodded tersely to those who tried to stop him with their problems, explaining that he would see them later too.

Back in the surgery, he wondered what to do.

'I suppose we'd better get a move on, matron, or we'll never be finished.'

'That's right.'

'So I'll be grateful if you'll send one of your women to fetch them.' Miss Gissing chose her 'staff' from among the emigrants and bribed them accordingly. 'Will you stay with me while they undress? To be on the safe side, you know.'

'That stands to reason. Otherwise they'd take advantage.'

'Right. I'll get one of the crew to help me when I do the men . . .'

'Why?' she interrupted. 'I can do both.'

'Well . . .' He felt embarrassed. 'I'll have to examine them in the most private places.'

'Oh, *that*!' she scowled. 'Don't you worry about that. I've seen enough of them things, and most of them well-nigh invisible, to last me a lifetime. Even shaved them 'tween decks, not that I've had the benefit.'

He looked at her with surprise, beginning to suspect that in spite of the permanent scowl Miss Gissing was a humorist. He sensed that she had years of experience, too, judging by her warning of typhus spread by lice. He wondered if she could be as old as her prune-like face and meagre hair suggested.

He decided to be honest. 'Frankly, matron, I have no idea of the ropes. What do *you* suggest?'

Plainly this was the right approach. The scowl was replaced by a smile which could hardly be described as 'flashing' in view of the discoloured teeth, and Miss Gissing gave her advice without hesitation. 'Start from the bottom up, and I mean the decks. The orlop's all we've time for today, but that's the bad 'un. I always say it's best to get the worst over first.' She replaced the pipe with an air of anticipation.

'Should I appeal to those with any form of vermin to come forward voluntarily?'

'Certainly not!' she replied indignantly. 'You might as well appeal to the better nature of the lice themselves. Most of 'em have been bred among animals, so it's no surprise to the women if animals breed on *them*. They won't come forward.'

'You mean we'll have to force them?' The prospect alarmed him.

'We might have to try. Whether we can is another matter. I'm tough but I can't fight more than half a dozen at a time, even with my helpers.'

'Goodness!' Dr Blake exclaimed. 'I wasn't thinking of fighting them. What should we do?'

'Trick 'em, like we do with sheep. Give 'em a good whack when they step out of line.'

The young man considered the matron's advice and surprised her by shaking her hand enthusiastically. 'Matron,' he cried, 'you've given me an idea!' He led her into the adjacent hospital where no one could overhear them and outlined his plan.

Word was sent below that the compulsory medical examination would start at once and continue throughout the day in strict order according to the number of their bunks, to be called at intervals of five minutes. This was the ordeal which the emigrants had dreaded at Gravesend, and hoped they had been spared when they were allowed on board without it. But though they feared the examination and jeered at the boyish surgeon behind his back, they knew it was a ritual which could never be avoided. The single women went first, one by one, leaving their section when their number was called and the door unlocked, escorted by one of the 'staff'.

Flanked by Miss Gissing and her assistants, Dr Blake greeted each woman as she entered the inner hospital, naked and shivering, to be scrutinised by the matron who shouted out her name and wrote it in a book, robbing her of anonymity.

Doctor and matron played their respective roles: she

was intimidating, he was courteous, and between them they shattered the women's resistance.

They kept to a simple formula: if the girl suffered from parasites the doctor told her so, using so many Latin names that he scared her into thinking something terrible was going to happen. Then he became reasonable instead.

'I'm sure you realise your good luck, sailing in a new vessel like this. The timbers are not yet infested with vermin and that's the way to keep it, but *you* are so it's best to get rid of that trouble right away. It's for your own good,' he added persuasively. 'So we're going to cut your hair off' – a howl of anguish – 'and you can either fight us or agree. I have four ladies to help me, so have it your own way.'

The four ladies were towering Amazons selected by Miss Gissing, married women with such experience of life that nothing was left to surprise them. They had been conscripted with the promise of special rations and had been at the wine already. One out of every four women had lice and if she dared to protest they swooped on her in a pack and held her rigidly while the ship's barber hacked her hair off, lathered the scalp and shaved it rapidly – a risky business for all concerned. As the final humiliation, the woman was submerged in a tub concealed behind a curtain and scrubbed vigorously with sea-water.

For most of these women it was the only bath they would have during the voyage; an unfamiliar, terrifying experience with the alarming sting of dilute chloride of lime as a disinfectant.

While she was being scrubbed her clothes were soaked in a stronger mixture of carbolic, and when the torture was over the spluttering woman shook herself like a dog and was handed a coarse damp towel to wipe off the rest of the water.

Each emigrant was then issued with a new set of clothing and a tot of rum to keep her warm. Invariably the rum was knocked back in a single gulp, and the doctor was quick to refill the glass – 'A small reward,' he explained gallantly, surprised at first to receive no answering smile. Then the woman was handed her bundle of wet clothes and taken on deck to dry off.

When the shaven-headed women appeared on deck they were greeted with laughter and ribald remarks and they never forgave Dr Blake. Because they were let out on deck one by one, instead of being returned to their quarters, they were unable to warn the others. The rest of the women continued to report at the hospital unaware of the humiliation ahead. In this way, doctor and matron prevented a panic by a process of isolation.

Timothy Blake's admiration for Miss Gissing grew throughout that dreadful day as the procession of women, men and children continued. Her knowledge of human nature made up for her ignorance of the latest medical techniques. She supplied him with an all-purpose powder which had no qualities whatever but satisfied the hypochondriacs, and faithful standbys like castor oil to free the works and ground chalk to seize them up.

When a woman fought back, Miss Gissing threw herself into the mêlée with the courage of a guardsman, pinning the victim to the deck. Yet she revealed a compassion which Dr Blake had not expected, arranging mugs of hot chocolate for the children and tobacco for the men to ease their mortification. Most of them accepted their shaven heads as a joke, realising they would run the risk of greater derision if they objected.

Huddled on the main deck like so many bedraggled chicks, many of the women sobbed for shame. The blankets had been taken from their bunks, fumigated, sprinkled with vinegar and strung out around them to dry, and this was the bizarre scene that confronted the captain when he left his cabin.

He sent for the doctor, and when he heard the full explanation he gave a great bellow of laughter. 'My lord, Blake, I admire your nerve! No man will fancy them now, and that's a blessing!'

He took another look and roared again. 'Good God, man, how did you make the orlop girls submit?'

'When matron advised me to treat them like sheep, I remembered the sheep-dips when I was a boy. Once through the fight goes out of 'em.'

But these sheep were wildcats now, scrawny and spitting as they whispered bitterly among themselves. Nothing could have emphasised their degradation more than their shaven heads, proof of their uncleanliness, of their wretchedness as government-granted passengers with no rights of their own. There was nowhere for them to hide on the main deck, and scant material to cover their hairless skulls. They looked so pitiful that the laughter gradually faded and those on the poop deck looked down with a compassion which the women found even more detestable.

Matilda felt a pang of anguish when she recognised her schoolfriend, Harriet. She ran down impulsively to comfort her.

Deprived of her dignity, the girl shrank away, and it took all Matilda's guile to save the situation. She threw her arms around her. 'Harriet,' she whispered, 'it's so good to see you, to have a *real* friend on board. What a lot I have to tell you, and such a lot to hear! We must meet every day. But what have they done to your lovely hair? How dare anyone do such a wicked thing?' Overwhelmed, the girl did not resist when Matilda pulled off her prized new London bonnet and placed it on Harriet's head instead. She stepped back to study the effect, clapping her hands with delight. 'Oh, you look lovely. But you always were so pretty. Of all the girls I envied you the most . . .'

Harriet, who had kept control of herself throughout the examination, was broken by such kindness. She burst into tears and wept on Matilda's shoulder. Matilda sobbed as well, thankful for the chance which had brought them together again; slightly sad about the bonnet, too.

It was true that concealing that awful, bristly head it made Harriet beautiful once more. The other women crowded round. Such was the emotion of the moment that Sally raced down from the upper deck to give her own bonnet to the first woman who grabbed it. Sarah followed, throwing hers from the rail, and so did several others, including the three pale sisters. Though their bonnets were less attractive, they covered heads just as effectively.

Emerging from her cabin with a quantity of shawls, Mrs Chant handed them out like prayer books to a congregation, and before long all of the shaven women were covered. Thirty-seven had been forced to submit, the rest found free from parasites.

Dr Blake was bewildered by the hostile reception from Matilda, who seemed as accusing as the shaven girls themselves.

'Their hair will grow again by the end of the voyage,' he protested.

'But you let everyone see them, don't you understand?' asked Matilda angrily.

Sarah came over to stop Matilda saying too much. She had seen the faces of the women, and knew the doctor had made too many enemies too quickly.

'It's always so difficult,' she smiled, trying to make light of it while making her point at the same time. 'People never understand when you do something for their own good.'

'But it *is* for their own good,' the doctor insisted, smarting at the unfairness of it. 'And your good, for that matter. If we had a typhus epidemic the lice would cause it to spread like wildfire in the conditions below.'

'Of course you're right,' said Sarah tactfully. 'But we must think of ways to restore their pride.' She kissed her daughter-in-law on the forehead, remembering the spontaneous gesture with her precious bonnet. 'Now, let's have a glass of madeira. I'm sure you need one after all your hard work, Dr Blake.' But the young man declined sulkily. Feeling unjustly treated, he walked to the stern and leant over the rail to stare at the wake below.

What a hideous day it had been – the saddest he had ever known. The lice were revolting enough, though so far no more than a nuisance, but the overall condition of the women was tragic. Many had sores and inflammation which would not improve. Others, soon to be confined in childbirth, were so weak that he doubted if they or their babies would survive. There were men plainly suffering from syphilis for whom he could do little, except a course of mercury later on. Many cases of dysentery. The children were the most vulnerable of all. Already he had suspected a case of scarlet fever, probably caught in the depot, where the blankets were seldom changed and were used by scores of different families.

Outside the day had been a halcyon one. An early haze had floated off the distant marshes, pierced by a pale sun which cast silver rays on the calm water and revealed the shapes of small boats and even distant villages. And then the mist had cleared, yielding to a peerless blue, as the graceful clipper glided over the rippling water.

Now the sun was starting to fall again, casting reflections which were golden at this time of day. They were making good progress, and passengers started to assemble once again on the starboard side after they turned south at Foreness Point and sailed into the straits of Dover.

They skirted the treacherous Goodwin Sands and hove to when they saw Deal Castle against the skyline, Walmer and the Downs beyond. One coastline looks much like any other once you leave harbour, but this would be their final view of England.

A longboat which had been lying off in readiness was rowed swiftly towards the clipper to take off the estuary pilot. He descended a few minutes later, the massive pockets of his oilskins bulging with the passengers' farewell letters, followed by several other figures who climbed precariously down the rope-ladder thrown over the side of the *Countess of Bath*.

It was a harrowing scene as the boat pulled away. It held a steerage couple who were leaving of their own accord, shocked by what they had seen 'tween decks, holding hands defiantly as they turned their backs on the future. Their sorrow, however, was nothing to the grief of the family who would have given all they possessed to stay on board. They had been rejected by Dr Blake after a further examination of the red spots and swollen glands of the small girl had confirmed the case of scarlet fever.

When the stricken parents caught sight of the young doctor leaning over the rail, their bitterness broke out in a stream of abuse.

'Murderer!' screamed the mother irrationally. 'What's to become of us now?' She clutched the frightened child as if to protect her.

'You bastard!' cried the father, a young man who had been living in expectation of the new life ahead. 'I'll swing for you if I set eyes on you again.'

The mother shouted her support, though the sound was fading now. 'May you die yourself before the voyage is out.'

Their cries echoed as the longboat slid into the darkness.

– 12 –

South to the 50th

It was a voyage like any other voyage, but for most of the emigrants it was the strangest experience they had ever known.

Life at sea was still governed by the three deciding factors – food, weather and sex. The passengers who placed intercourse first when they were on land found it came a furtive third in the cramped conditions on board, though that did not prevent them from fantasising.

Food was the justification of the day and the preparations started at five o'clock when the fires were lit in the galleys. At this ghastly hour, far too premature considering that no one was going anywhere, ghostly figures scrubbed the decks while men with buckets emerged from hatchways like animals from underground holes to wash themselves at the bulwarks on either side.

The messes started to mix their stirabout puddings at six; at seven the mess captains and their assistants were issued with tin plates and frying pans to cook their bacon and eggs. At half past seven, the mess captains received their allocation of boiled coffee, and the stewards came down with pails and the rousing cry of 'Tea-water!'

Cabin passengers rose at the kinder hour of eight and toyed with a breakfast of fresh tea and coffee which had not been stewed, salmon simmered in butter, ham, rice, and rolls. The Stowe family contributed their Raxleigh eggs, which they shared with the others in their circle: the talkative Tony Plunkett, locked in verbal combat with his adversary, Mrs Chant; and Mr and Mrs Flanagan, included on Roly's insistence, bringing the Stowes' party to a complement of ten. 'At this rate,' sighed Gussie, 'the Raxleigh hens will have to rally.'

No sooner had breakfast been disposed of than people thought of lunch, and the extra treat of pea soup ladled out on deck four times a week at eleven. It had been the tradition since the days of the first transport ships that convicts should be given two-thirds of the naval ration, and the emigrants received no less.

Each mess of six people received a weekly issue of bread, flour, and butter, with eight ounces of rice and the same of suet, and six pints of oatmeal, though the Scots demanded more. By contrast, the Irish were so unused to tea that they pressed the leaves into their pipes and smoked them.

Fresh meat, supervised by Dr Blake, was taken from a cask twice a week and ringed with a metal disc which could be identified by the individual messes after it was cooked in the boiler. For those emigrants who had seldom tasted beef before, this was luxury indeed.

Food was temporarily forgotten when they sailed into the Bay of Biscay, replaced as the main topic of conversation by the weather. On land the emigrants shut out the elements with the simple closing of a door, but there was no hearth to retreat to here. The weather travelled with them and there was no escaping its moods and eccentricities. It changed abruptly as the *Countess* reached the French coast at Brest, worsening near Belle Isle. This was a shock for those who had assumed it would become warmer as they sailed south. The pale blue sky grew overcast, the air bitterly cold, and the wind started to create a swell until the entire sea was flecked with low but conflicting waves. This was when the *Countess* began to roll with an alarming heaving motion which soon had the emigrants heaving too.

Dr Blake was summoned to give assistance, but the moment he descended to the orlop deck he felt sick himself from the lack of air. The acrid stench had started a chain

165

reaction and with few utensils to be sick into – most were filled with excrement – the emigrants were vomiting straight on to the planks. His hand clamped over his mouth to stop himself from retching too, Dr Blake ordered members of the crew to go below and swab the decks. This distasteful duty, which they called 'sickers', was undertaken with understandable scowls of resentment, but the young doctor was relieved to find that the men were prepared to obey him.

Sea-sickness was bad enough, but at least there would be a reprieve when they entered calmer water. There was no escape from the crowded conditions in which emigrants were literally hurled together as the ship tossed and heaved. Many raged that they would give a hundred pounds, if they possessed such a fortune, to be safely back in England, and envied the couple who had dared turn back. Yet such is the resilience of the human spirit that they seized every opportunity to turn their situation to advantage. If people had to share a bunk which was only three feet wide, it meant that they had someone to cling to for comfort in their distress. If the air was suffocating, at least they were warm.

If some were too sick to eat their rations, there was more for the others.

If life was vile, it had not been much better on land. And they had prospects now.

They imposed a discipline upon themselves, and welcomed it. A captain was elected for each mess and though it was a chore to fetch the rations and dole them out fairly it broke the monotony, and the mess captain could be certain that he or she would have the benefit of the strongest brew and the choicest portion.

There was one problem that could not be overcome, and that was damp. The eager emigrants who seized the bunks below the hatchways, with their promise of a breath of air and a glimmer of light, were disillusioned the moment they entered Biscay. Whenever the clipper rolled too far, torrents of sea-water rushed down before there was time to close the hatches and the decks below were flooded. As usual, the orlop deck had the worst of it, objects floating about like a crazy armada. The water drained away soon enough, but bedding and piles of clothing were left sodden.

There were casualties, too. A swinging boom hit a young sailor like a bat striking a ball, knocking him into the sea. There was an instant cry of 'Man overboard', but a retaliatory wave hurled him back against the side of the ship with such a crack that it must have broken his spine. Though the thrown lifebelt landed within his grasp, he lost consciousness and sank below the surface. Sarah had been watching, horrified by the speed of events and the failure of the captain to stop his ship, but the sympathetic third officer assured her that there would have been no point in doing so. 'His oilskins and sea-boots, ma'am – so heavy, they'd have dragged him down long before we could have turned and reached him. A pity.'

It was the boy's first voyage, at the age of sixteen, and his brand new sea-chest was opened on deck so that his belongings could be auctioned and the proceeds sent to the family whose portraits inside the lid were his most treasured possessions. His father's final instructions were pasted there as well: 'Honour, truth, dependence on God, diligence and docility, will carry you through all danger and difficulties. Remember that your father would welcome your dead body if you died in honour, and spit on you living if you returned in disgrace. Lay these things to thy heart, and God protect thee.' The words had such a terrible poignancy now that no one felt like making a bid for something so personal, and the chest with its contents remained unsold, to be cast overboard.

The other casualty was a simple Irish girl who startled everyone, her bunk-mate in particular, by a pregnancy which no one had suspected. Even the girl herself was woefully ignorant of her condition, which was only discovered when she complained of sharp pains in her stomach. Her labour had been brought on prematurely by her physical weakness, and she was carried to a top

167

bunk in the hospital, away from the swirling water of the flooded deck. This did not make Dr Blake's task any easier as he struggled to help the delivery, holding the girl down while she screamed and twisted in pain. Her screams ceased after the birth of her tiny son, replaced by low moans drowned by the creaking timbers and the storm outside. The last flicker of the mother's life went out an hour later, and the baby was brought to a married couple. Dr Blake returned to his cabin, deeply ashamed of having failed to notice her condition during the medical examination, though she was one of those with a shaven head. God, what a lot he had to learn! Yet he fell asleep the moment he stretched out in his bunk.

As for sex, behaviour which would have been unmentionable on land became acceptable on board. It was as unavoidable as a prevailing wind, for the captain's sole obsession was speed and he had no interest in the morals of his crew or passengers – though the mate did his best to make up for this by prowling around in the hope of catching someone 'at it'.

There were rules in abundance, but these were so strict that they asked to be broken. Single women were forbidden to leave their quarters without permission, and even the mess captains were supposed to be escorted by one of Miss Gissing's assistants when they went to the galley in case they spoke to a man on the way. On deck they were threatened with a week's detention if they so much as fluttered their eyelashes at a member of the crew. Consequently, there was a thrill in flouting these laws; there is something about the motion of a ship which lends an added zest to immorality.

In a society which depends on the granting of favours, prostitution is a natural form of currency. It prospered on the *Countess* in spite of all the regulations.

A girl of twelve showed great ingenuity in escaping from her quarters to spend most of her time with the crew. Plainly she had seduced the young sailor with whom she spent her nights, though no doubt he had succumbed readily enough. A number of the single women were shocked at first, but they dared not complain about her behaviour, in case it reflected on themselves, and the girl thrived on the extra rations provided by her lover.

There was undeniable coupling in the single men's quarters as well. Certainly something was happening under several heaving blankets, to the disgust of the others. But, like the single women, the virtuous decided that their own welfare was paramount and left the others to their vices.

If unnatural behaviour flourished, natural affection flowered too, though it had to fight for survival in such cynical surroundings. Sally's infatuation for the young doctor was transparent. The two of them behaved as if they were alone, impervious to the smiles of the cabin passengers and the sniggers of the emigrants. Their problem was privacy, so Matilda and Roly found excuses to leave the couple alone in their cabin while they exercised Raxleigh on deck. By now the puppy had reached the ungainly stage, all spindly legs and floppy body, relieving himself at every opportunity on every available object. Acutely embarrassed, Matilda followed him with cries of 'Stop it!', trying to conceal his tracks with a damp cloth and sheets of rough paper. Harriet had seen the mate aim a kick at Raxleigh when no one else was looking, and though the puppy had dodged in time Matilda knew that Emlyn Conway was looking for an opportunity to have the dog punished.

Early one morning a wave shook the clipper so unexpectedly that one of the crew slipped from a yard-arm, falling on to the deck with such force that his back was broken and his skull fractured. At dusk another simple ship's burial service was held on the swaying deck, attended by the captain and the crew, with the body stitched inside a canvas bag weighted at the feet and covered with the flag like the young mother before him.

'God's will be done . . .' concluded the ship's chaplain after the brief ritual, and the flag was removed as the dead man was tipped into the sea. The crew set about their work as before, but the few emigrants on deck who had watched the ceremony began to wonder how many more would die in the weeks ahead. This was the second funeral so far, and the third death.

The *Countess* sailed on, dipping, tossing, heaving, shuddering, and then suddenly the torture was over – the calm they craved had arrived.

Radiant day followed radiant day, and dolphins escorted the *Countess* like underwater rainbows. Cape pigeons flew overhead, but the passengers' exclamations of joy turned to groans when Conway appeared, armed with a gun. The mate gave the impression of a sportsman, but he was a poor shot and several of the birds fell, flapping, into the water, to drown.

Turning to fishing in the afternoon, he hauled a dolphin on board. The animal died slowly, gasping as its iridescent colours faded in the sun.

'I'd like to kill that man,' muttered Roly to Matilda beside him. 'When you think of such a noble creature landing up at the feet of someone like *that* – what an end!' He turned away, finding the eyes of the dying dolphin too painful to meet.

The damp discomfort of Biscay was forgotten as if it had never been. It was astonishing what a difference the sun made to everyone's temper. Even the animals seemed pleased. Gallant, the Stowes' beloved stallion, quivered with joy as he was led around the deck to exercise his aching joints. No one thought of the wretched Merino sheep, hidden in the darkness of the hold, nor of the convicts in their similar condition.

The decks were crowded from dawn to dusk and the scene had a carefree gaiety as parents read aloud to their children, laughed with new-found friends and smoked their clay pipes, or hung out their washing to dry. At night there was music and dancing, supervised by the ship's special constables, who saw that the crew did not join in. In charge of the ship's morals and hygiene, such as they were, the constables were instructed by Conway to keep a constant lookout for any single girl who tried to wander – which did not prevent them from taking advantage of such an opportunity themselves.

The entertainments varied according to the level of the deck: meticulous quadrilles on the poop; polkas and country dances on the gun deck; a scraping of fiddles and Irish jigs on the orlop in the depths.

'It's odd,' Tony Plunkett remarked to Lionel, 'how the songs reflect their characters. The Welsh are always singing of home; the Scots play their dreadful bagpipes and fight; and the Irish dance about and curse.'

'What do the English do?'

'The English? They listen and think themselves superior, which we *are*, of course!'

Plunkett held classes for those who wanted to learn the history of the land they were going to, though he had the sense to admit from the outset that he was as ignorant about present conditions as they were and only knew of the past from documents. He was pleased to discover how hungry they were for facts, listening intently as he told them of the First Fleet which sailed to Botany Bay in 1786: 'Even though their ships were smaller than our own, overcrowded with people and animals, only twenty-four convicts died out of a total of seven hundred and fifty-nine.' He did not reveal that two hundred and sixty-seven died on the second voyage, and four hundred and fifty needed medical treatment when they docked in Sydney.

'Everything has improved since those early days,' he continued, 'but this is still a great adventure. I urge you to keep diaries to show your children and grandchildren in years to come.'

The ship's chaplain, the Reverend Silas Guard, held daily services on deck which people enjoyed for the singing, and Sundays became fashion shows of ladies' finery.

The physical instructor organised ball-games and boxing; better educated passengers started a library, exchanging their precious books; Lionel made copious notes; Roly discussed the prospect of gold with Mr Flanagan; and Sally floated in a world of her own, on neither land nor sea, with the realisation that she was in love with Dr Blake.

The fine weather changed the appearance of the passengers, too. The young blades who shared the steerage cabins disported themselves on deck in their best regatta shirts and straw hats, and the girls competed in cotton dresses. Even without such plumage, the orlop girls looked healthier than before, with new colour in their faces – though some had gone from ivory to bright brick-red. There was the odd exception, like the lanky Irish youth called Murphy, who had never been known to wash. Even his eyes looked dusty. One morning, unable to stand the smell any longer, his nearest bunk-mates carried him on deck, stripped him, doused him with sea-water and scrubbed him violently; all of which he accepted without protest, putting on his filthy clothes afterwards so that the smell was no sweeter than before.

So the *Countess* sailed south and the emigrants had no reason to think that the fine conditions would ever change. Past the Azores, past the Canary Islands, past Santiago off Cape Verde where the winds became more variable. When they woke the next morning they wondered what had happened. It was not the noise, but the lack of it; not the wind, but the total absence of wind that sounded strange. They had sailed into the doldrums. Trapped in a pocket between the North East Trade winds and the South East Trades, they had entered a state of limbo, airless and devoid of colour. White clouds, tantalisingly low on the horizon, never advanced. Nor did the *Countess*. She inched her way slowly forward as if the water was indeed the molten lead it resembled. The flat grey sky enclosed them like a lid.

Though the *Countess* had every sail unfurled, these hung listlessly even when dipped in sea-water to make them taut. The emigrants doused themselves with sea-water too, emptying buckets on the decks to make them bearable to stand on.

To vent his frustration, the captain lowered a rowboat and swam furiously alongside his ship. Although a few of the emigrants laughed and cheered at first, they soon stopped when they sensed his anger. Lighter relief was granted when the boat was lowered again for the benefit of the male cabin passengers, including Lionel, and Roly who insisted taking Raxleigh for a swim as well. Some of the passengers cheered him on, but a few of the women cried out in alarm as they saw Roly drop the puppy into the water, to sink or swim on his own. However, when it looked as if the dog would sink, Roly jumped in to save him.

Some of the younger men from steerage watched enviously and asked permission to use one of the other lifeboats. Conway refused abruptly, explaining that they were full of livestock. This was unanswerable, but when a couple of the braver boys lowered a rope and swung merrily in the gentle, rippling wake of the clipper, the mate found fault with this as well.

'You *had* no right to swing like that.'

'Why not?' asked a young Cockney defiantly.

'Because I say so.'

'But the gentlemen there had a go.' He pointed to the group of cabin passengers who were drying themselves on the poop deck. Tony Plunkett came forward to listen. 'If it's all right for them, why not for us?'

'Because they're cabined.'

'Cribbed and confined,' laughed the teacher, which earned him a mystified glare. 'I can't see what harm they were doing,' he added in the boys' defence.

'They might have come to harm,' said the mate tightly.

'That's their look-out . . .'

The mate cut him off sharply, furious at this interruption from a teacher; not even a fare-paying passenger.

'I am not standing *here* to take argument with you, sir, thank-yew-very-much!'

'Oh yes you are, old chap, that's just what you're doing, thank *you* very much!' cried Tony Plunkett. 'Why shouldn't these fellows have a splash if they feel like it? You hate to see anyone have a good time – even that poor dolphin you slaughtered to prove you're a man.'

The words carried in the stifling afternoon, entertaining the emigrants who watched the scene with amusement from a safe distance. Roly joined in with a nastier smile. He had been sipping chilled wine since the early morning and the dip in the clammy water had done nothing to freshen him. He stood stripped to the waist, glistening with new perspiration as he abused the mate with the venom of a fish-wife and the insolence of a schoolboy.

'You think you're so important, don't you? Telling everyone what to do like a tinpot Napoleon . . . mincing up and down as if you're wearing one of those new-fangled corsets, and I shouldn't be surprised if you *are*! But let me tell you this. If you dare to touch my dog again I'll kill you . . .'

The mate stood still, erect and expressionless. The jibe about the corset hurt and he wondered how Roly had discovered that. Otherwise the young man had been hoist by his own invective. No one spoke to the mate of a ship like that.

Realising that Roly had gone too far, Tony Plunkett pulled him away, incriminating himself with his parting shot: 'Come on, he's not worth it . . .'

That evening, Captain Peppiatt sent word to Lionel Raxleigh that he wished to see him in his cabin. 'Sorry about this,' he explained, 'but your nephew's stirred things up a bit. Frankly I don't blame him for having a go at Conway. I was planning to replace him anyway, though this makes it more difficult. He's the sort of man who comes to me whining about the crew, and goes back to them complaining about me. But your nephew was out of order and I'd be grateful if you'd tell him to spare us such behaviour in the future – especially in public. That's where he let himself down.'

Lionel was about to protest that the captain should speak to Roly himself when he remembered that Peppiatt had more pressing problems to worry about than a passenger's tantrums.

'Of course,' he replied instead. 'I'll see that my nephew is warned off.'

'Thank you.' The captain mopped his brow. 'It's this infernal calm. The doldrums bring everyone down.'

'Have you any idea how long this might last?'

Captain Peppiatt sighed. 'They've held us three days now. Tomorrow I'm going to empty the boats of livestock and use the oars. With luck we might catch a cross-current. If we don't, we've lost the record.'

The animals were pitiful in their sweltering confinement. They seemed to welcome the touch of human beings, and while Roly stifled in his bunk, overcast with gloom, Matilda made her visits of the day. The lugubrious horse accepted the gift of an apple, but when she brought the two Raxleigh hens some slices of stale cake she heard a noise behind her and looked up at two small boys who watched her so hungrily that she gave them a warm smile in case they ran off. Telling them to stay there, she went away, reappearing a minute later with two slices of fresh cake which they clutched suspiciously, running off without a word.

At lunchtime she scraped the left-overs from their plates and returned to feed the Raxleigh piglet. He looked alarmingly thin, though he was supposed to be fed with an all-purpose mash prepared by the stewards. Piglet seemed overjoyed to see her, grunting with such delight that she laughed aloud. A few minutes later she brought him a bowl of water when no one was looking. She was unaware that the stewards had been watching her all the time and no longer bothered to feed the piglet themselves.

Matilda did not visit the Merino sheep because she had promised Sarah not to venture below decks, so she did not know that three of the animals had suffocated during the night.

Lionel was leaning over the side, staring at the lifeless ocean, when Dr Blake came up to him. 'You're supposed to be a writer; there's something you should see.'

He led Lionel down hatchways and passages unknown to most of the passengers, for even a small ship has a labyrinthine underworld. The *Countess* was larger than most vessels and Lionel lost all sense of direction as he followed the young man into depths where the air was fetid and it was so dark that he had to feel his way. At one point the doctor stopped and pulled an orange from his pocket, cutting it in half with a penknife. 'Take this,' he told Lionel, handing him one of the segments, 'in case you choke.'

A soldier unlocked an iron grille and they entered an area which seemed sombre and still, but as Lionel's eyes adjusted he realised with a shiver of apprehension that it was full of crouching people.

'Oh, lord,' he murmured. 'Oh, God, Timothy, I'd no idea.'

'I know,' the doctor whispered. 'They might be dead for all anyone cares, and they're not far off it.'

The convicts were still chained, though there was little need for it down here. Most of them were too weak to move. In a louder voice, which embarrassed Lionel because they must be overheard, the doctor continued as if describing livestock: 'They shite where they sit. It's not their fault; they can't do much else. There are some buckets in the corner but they've hardly got the energy to use them. Food is shoved through the grille and the strongest get to it first, so the weak are growing weaker. But it's the air that's the danger – or the lack of it. They're suffocating, and Peppiatt won't do a damned thing about it. Says it'll upset the passengers if they know such things are going on below. That's why I need your help, with the power of the press behind you. I'm going to fight him on this one – indeed, I blame myself bitterly for letting it go on so long.'

At the end of the cage lay another, with fewer occupants; these were the women. It was several moments before Lionel could tell, for their heads were shaven and their clothes indistinguishable in the murk. They studied the visitors intently, looks of appeal on their faces. The doctor managed to control his emotion, and spoke through the bars in a low but encouraging tone. 'Good

176

day to you, ladies. I think you know who I am – the ship's doctor. My friend is a writer for the London *Times* . . .' Lionel nodded, the orange, hidden in the palm of his hand, pressed to his nose. 'We hope to bring you some relief.'

There was a moment of absolute silence as his words sank in, and then a surprisingly forceful clamour as the women shouted their grievances.

As they returned through the larger cage, one man stretched out a hand to Lionel as he passed. Fighting the impulse to draw back in revulsion, Lionel steeled himself to hold it briefly in his, looking into the convict's eyes as he did so. He bent closer when he realised the man was trying to tell him something.

'You don't remember me, sir?' Lionel shook his head. 'Stanton, sir, Dick Stanton . . . Bideford . . . my father . . .'

One of the soldiers came up to kick the convict away, swearing at him for his impudence, but Lionel stopped him. 'No, I know this man. He comes from my home. His father worked for us.'

He stared helplessly at the man with the scar across his face, remembering the boy whose father had introduced him so proudly at Raxleigh House. There was no trace of that boy in the creature before him now.

'Richard . . . how grieved I am to see you like this . . .' Lionel touched him on the shoulder. 'I'll be back.'

He followed Timothy Blake up the tortuous route until they emerged on to the main deck. Even in the doldrums, the atmosphere was fresh compared to the fetid air below.

The two men leant over the rail, breathing deeply. 'Well?' asked the doctor. 'Now you've seen it for yourself. If I go to the captain, will you back me up?'

'To the hilt.'

'Fine. I depend on that. If only there were others we could rely on.'

'The chaplain?' Lionel suggested.

The doctor laughed contemptuously. 'Silas Guard is utterly useless. He cares more about the convicts' morals than their health. Anyhow, he's washed his hands of them since he went below with his issue of tracts and Books of Common Prayer.' The doctor chuckled. 'Unfortunately the convicts tore them up to make packs of playing cards – rather a good idea, I thought – but he hasn't been back since. I had a stand-up row with him when he threatened to report them for gambling. I suggested that God would be delighted if His book gave them some harmless amusement, so he's threatened to report me for blasphemy as well. No good calling on the Reverend Silas Guard to help us.'

'What about Tony Plunkett?'

'He's rather outspoken – but so am I, for that matter. Good idea.'

In fact it was a bad idea, for Captain Peppiatt had little time for the teacher. Neither was it a good moment to confront the captain, in a rage of frustration as his ship lay stranded in the doldrums. Two boats had been lowered and members of the crew were pulling the *Countess* forward: a welcome chance of exercise but little more than a snub to the elements. Peppiatt saw his chance of the prize-money receding, so he was in no mood to listen to Plunkett talking about the convicts' rights.

'Rights?' he exclaimed sharply. 'What rights? They've forfeited their rights. That's why we're transporting them.'

The schoolmaster assumed they were having a reasonable argument and blundered on accordingly. 'Then they're being punished without the chance for reformation?'

'You could say that.'

'But surely they've paid for their crimes by being sentenced to Van Diemen's Land? Isn't that punishment enough? It isn't justice to punish them further.'

'Look . . .' said the captain, controlling himself with effort, 'I don't know if you're drunk, which would explain your interference in the running of my ship, but I don't wish to hear another word from you on this subject – or any other, for that matter. You use words like justice and reformation which are meaningless on board my ship where I am justice. I never wanted the convicts on my ship. It's not my fault if they're overcrowded. And you seem to forget you're pleading for hardened criminals who *have done wrong*.'

'They're human beings too,' said Lionel Raxleigh, making an effort to sound calm. 'I've seen them for myself, Captain Peppiatt; and I had no idea that men could sink as low as that.'

'Ah well, Mr Raxleigh, something for you to write about.'

'No,' said Lionel firmly, 'not unless I have to . . .' He left the sentence hanging in the air. 'But the place they're in, it's little better than an animal's cage.'

'The iron bars, Mr Raxleigh, are not only there to *cage* them in. They allow currents of air to pass through. Better than walls.'

'There *is* no air, sir,' the doctor protested. 'The atmosphere is so heavy no currents can move it. I must be allowed to construct a ventilation chute down to their quarters before they are poisoned.'

'It's these accursed doldrums. We're all the same.'

'No, sir, *their* conditions are hellish. If we don't do something now they'll die. *At least half of them will die.*'

The captain looked at him with a cynical smile. 'I thought you registered them fit after you came on board?'

'They were fit then. Not now. You may not realise it, sir, but it's suffocating down there. I ask you, sir, to give your consent: let me bring them on deck each day, while their cages are hosed down and fumigated.'

'Oh no,' said the captain softly. 'Oh no, that won't do at all. Have you any idea what's involved in bringing them up from below?'

'I'll manage that,' said the doctor quickly, 'with the help of my friends. These men are my responsibility. Two thousand pounds have been lodged by your company with the government as security for their welfare, which rests with me as ship's surgeon. I have to report to the Governor on my arrival, and the bond is not released until he signs a certificate in receipt of the convicts. I doubt if he will do so if most of them are dead.'

'Now we have it! Out in the open at last. So you threaten to report me to the Governor, or the Home Office on your return?'

The three men were silent.

'Well, sir,' said the captain suddenly, remembering the progress of his ship, 'you can threaten all you like, but the answer is "no". Your responsibility lies with the passengers, not the convicts. They find it bad enough travelling in the same ship, without having to *see* any of them. I cannot have the passengers upset.'

'A darned sight better to upset them than let the convicts die,' said Tony Plunkett rashly.

'Better still, sir, to let me run my ship. Her security is all that matters to me, and that's my last word on the subject. Good day to you.'

Everyone suffered that day as the air grew hotter. Gussie was feverish, and Sarah stayed in the cabin with him, heavy-eyed. At one point the passengers were terrified by a glow surrounding the top of the mainmast, and although the crew assured them that this was a common phenomenon known as St Elmo's Fire, the majority of the emigrants were convinced it was a warning of impending tragedy.

The storm struck that night, but there was no accompanying wind to push the ship forward, only an electrical display of lightning streaking across the sky. At one terrifying moment a flash of fire plunged towards the *Countess*, spreading widespread fingers into the sea a few yards ahead, with a hiss of steam and a lingering, acrid smell. Captain Peppiatt gave orders for all sail to be hoisted to take advantage of every breath in the short-lived squalls which followed, but the rain fell like iron railings and the airlessness remained.

Battened down below, the emigrants heard the rainfall with longing. Many of the cabin passengers ran from their quarters under the poop deck in their night-clothes to catch the precious water in any containers they could lay their hands on. Fresh water was vital for themselves, for animals, for the numerous plants. When Sarah heard the rain she struggled from her bunk and made her way unsteadily to the poop deck. The plants she had lifted from the Raxleigh gardens were stored there, and she wanted to remove the tarpaulin from the boxes.

It was a strange sort of light which confronted her, the sea so phosphorescent it was brighter than the ship itself, except when those brief flashes of lightning revealed everything for an instant. There was uproar, apart from the battering rain: Captain Peppiatt was shouting orders at the mate, who bellowed at the crew, and in one burst of illumination Sarah looked up and saw the rigging alive with sailors entwined along the yard-arms. But it was the scene immediately below her that caused her to clutch the rail with disbelief. In that second she was convinced that the fever had unhinged her senses. Then darkness fell again like a blanket, obscuring the ghostly procession of grey figures, naked except for rags round their waists and clanking irons on their feet. Another flash of lightning, and one of the faces looked up towards her.

'Mother, are you all right?' Sarah found herself being supported by Sally, who was stroking her forehead anxiously.

'Are you all right, mama? What happened?'

Sarah clutched the rail and struggled to her feet again, forcing herself to look below. Nothing. Then another flash of lightning. It had not been an illusion after all, nor were the figures an apparition.

'Are those the convicts?' she asked in a tremulous whisper. 'Poor souls.'

'Tim has been so brave, ma. He's standing up to that awful Peppiatt, who wouldn't allow them on deck, and Uncle Li is helping him. We're all helping him. He thought it would be best in the darkness, but the rain has brought everyone out. What about you, mama? You'll be drenched. You shouldn't be here at all.'

'The rain is glorious,' Sarah assured her. 'I'm better now.'

The convicts below raised their faces to drink the precious water and let it pour over their bodies. When Timothy Blake had made the decision to allow them on deck, he knew that darkness would be no cover. Nor could he attempt such an upheaval in secrecy, for the soldiers resented his orders however much they approved his action. At least the convicts were taken up while the emigrants were battened down. The captain would not be able to complain that the steerage and orlop passengers had been upset. The doctor had spoken in advance to the cabin passengers, who were flattered at being taken into his confidence and promised their support, but any hope of further concealment had been dashed by the lightning, which exposed the convicts on the main deck as effectively as the footlights on a stage.

The doctor was dismayed by the first, revealing zig-zag streak, but then he welcomed the rain as an unexpected blessing and called for soap and towels to be brought for the men. He was helped by Lionel, Roly, Mr Flanagan and Tony Plunkett, while Miss Gissing and her staff shooed the female convicts behind a hastily rigged tarpaulin, ordering them to undress and wash themselves, a rare experience altogether.

'Get your clothes off, you lot,' the matron cried with her odd brand of bossiness and mercy. 'Don't play modesty with me. Get a move on. There's another shift when we've done with you.' She helped to unfasten buttons and laces, pulling down the dresses of those too weak to help themselves.

Rightly or wrongly, the captain believed that the steerage passengers were so like the convicts in their own squalor that they would find such a confrontation deeply upsetting, but the favoured cabin passengers felt an instinctive sympathy for those with whom there could be no comparison. Sarah gave a heartfelt sob as she recognised the reality of her 'ghosts', and heard the murmuring of the convicts below.

'Come on,' she told her daughter. 'Let's see if we can give a hand.'

'Good show!' cried a vigorous voice. Mrs Chant joined them, incongruously dressed in a thin white evening dress which might have been suitable for the earlier oppressive heat. Now it was damp and dishevelled, but its owner looked ready for the fray. 'Up guards and at 'em!' she exclaimed.

Sally suffered from the conventionality of girls her age, but she was anxious to prove herself to the young doctor and followed her mother and Mrs Chant down the steps to the main deck. Conway blocked their way. In this strange, luminous light, his white gloves seemed grotesquely out of place.

'No further, ladies, *if* you please! There's naked men washing themselves on my deck. And *no* ladies allowed on deck after ten unless accompanied by husbands.'

'Don't be ridiculous,' Mrs Chant told him impatiently. 'My husband's dead!'

They were interrupted by a roar from above as Captain Peppiatt saw the group in another flash of lightning. '*Mr Conway!* Get back to your post and stop gossiping with women. You have your duties to attend to.'

The luminosity surrounded them again as they crossed the slippery deck.

'Mother!' Sally whispered, clutching Sarah's dressing-gown to pull her back. 'It's Mr Stanton's son, Dick Stanton, he's one of the convicts.'

Sarah turned and recognised the face she had seen in her 'apparition'.

'Mrs Stowe,' he muttered, wrapping his cloth around him, embarrassed by their meeting, as Sarah was quick to realise.

'Dick. My dear boy,' she cried, overwhelmed by the extraordinary coincidence which had cast them together. 'My dear, dear boy.' She embraced him emotionally.

'Mother!' cried Sally, shocked by her mother's impulsiveness.

Dick found Sarah Stowe's gentleness more upsetting

than any of the hardships he had endured. Feeling the need to say something, he told her, 'I saw Mr Lionel this morning.'

'No!' Sarah exclaimed, her hand to her mouth. 'Why didn't he tell me?'

'We didn't want to upset you,' Sally broke in quickly. 'We thought you were worried, looking after father.'

'Sally, go back to our cabin and find something for Dick to eat, will you?'

'What is there?' Sally was flustered.

'I have no idea. Use your imagination.'

Sally returned with a paper bag filled with two hard-boiled eggs, several slices of ham, an apple and some barley-sugar.

'It's all I could find,' she apologised.

Dick looked around him guiltily. 'I dare not take them below.' Clutching his rags in one hand and the bag in the other, he stepped back into the shadows. Sarah and Sally hurried forward to join the group around the female prisoners. There was much to be done.

Hunger had made Dick light-headed. He thought he was imagining the voice at first.

'Raxleigh . . . here, Raxleigh . . .' Dick froze in his hiding-place, wondering why anyone should call that familiar name. A moment later the mongrel pup appeared, whining for his master.

'Raxleigh . . . good dog . . .' Raxleigh turned his head suspiciously. 'Raxleigh. Here, blast you. Come here, you bloody little nuisance. Raxleigh . . .' The words were uttered in a wheedling, ingratiating tone. 'Don't be afraid of me . . .'

In a ragged burst of lightning Dick saw the shape of the man who was calling the dog. There was the glint of white gloves as the man moved like lightning himself, seized the puppy by a back leg and swung him over the side of the ship. Darkness enveloped them again. There was nothing, not even a cry from the dog. The man with the white gloves had gone.

There was no logic in what Dick did next. It was impulse which prompted him to jump across the deck in his irons and haul himself over the side. Only when he found himself struggling in the water as he tried to reach the animal did he realise the insanity of his action. Inexorably, the irons dragged him under the phosphorescence.

'Man overboard!' A cry from above. Dick felt the terror of finality as the *Countess* seemed to pull away from him. Then the instinct for survival overwhelmed him as he sank below the surface and forced him to rise again, choking as he swallowed sea-water. He could hear the dog struggling inches away and reached out to grab him, but Raxleigh in his terror resisted so wildly that Dick abandoned the attempt – his own survival was all that mattered now. He felt himself sinking again . . . a glimpse of faces peering over the rail . . . a vague impression that they were almost overhead, so the *Countess* could not have drawn away after all . . . a splash beside him and a lifebelt tied to a rope came so near that he was able to grasp it . . . the dog, amazingly, still beside him and too weak to fight him further. A few moments later, Stanton lay on the deck, gasping.

For the last hour Captain Peppiatt had needed all his self-control as the curious procession of grey figures emerged from the depths below. A man who believed that discipline was essential at sea, he was physically pained by the lack of it. This was not an exaggerated obsession but a compelling sense of duty towards the ship under his command; anyone who placed her in jeopardy was regarded as hostile towards himself.

Ever since he had caught sight of the convicts in the strange electrical light he had been raging inwardly. He had succeeded in containing his anger, for he was a fair man and knew that the doctor was within his rights as the medical superintendent in charge of the convicts' welfare; there was the consolation also that the doctor had taken this action entirely on himself, so would bear the blame should anything go wrong. Peppiatt was more concerned with the possibility of wind, and returned to the rails to assess the likelihood of further squalls. The electrical storm had, if anything, gained in strength, and a particularly vivid flash revealed a grotesque tableau to his startled gaze: a naked, and possibly dead, young man, surrounded by women who should have shown more modesty, and in the background the spectres of convicts shepherded by the doctor and tiny Miss Gissing. The captain's patience broke and he bounded down the steps from the poop deck to the main. 'What in Christ's name is going on?' he demanded.

The rain stopped on the instant, as if to listen to the answer, and every word was audible in the sudden silence.

Roly surprised everyone by stepping forward to accept the blame. 'My fault, sir. My dog fell overboard. This man risked his life to save it.'

'Really!' Captain Peppiatt exclaimed sarcastically. 'No doubt the animal jumped over the rail?'

'He was thrown,' whispered Dick Stanton, regaining his breath.

'*Thrown?*' The word reverberated around the deck, echoed by several voices.

'By whom?' the captain demanded.

'I did not see his face, sir,' said Dick, who was regretting his outspokenness, 'but he wore white gloves.'

'White gloves!' echoed Peppiatt.

'Ah!' The sound shivered among the spectators like a sigh of recognition.

When Roly and Lionel reported to the captain's cabin the following morning they found him surprisingly composed. The reason for his good humour was simple: a slight but gathering breeze had lifted the *Countess* out of the doldrums and the ship was moving. The chance of a record was not lost. Peppiatt barely listened to Lionel's explanation of the night's disturbance, but showed some interest at the mention of the convict who had dared to speak to him.

'So you know the man? A strange coincidence!'

'His father worked as our head clerk at Raxleigh House.'

'Well, it was a damn fool thing to do, jumping into the water when he was chained. He'd have drowned except for the doldrums, and serve him right.'

'He saved my dog,' Roly pointed out.

'What is the man's crime?'

Roly looked to his uncle, who answered for him. 'It sounds a curious sort of offence – he fell against a midshipman when Her Majesty inspected the Fleet at Plymouth. He swore it was an accident.'

'Hah!' Captain Peppiatt exclaimed. 'They all say that!' He remembered the scar across the man's cheek, and frowned. Stanton might be a trouble-maker, but he had behaved courageously and that was in his favour. He remembered his charts and calculations. 'The man can be allowed on deck for an hour each morning, as long as you accept full responsibility. I'll tell the master-at-arms to remove his leg-irons when he's with you.'

'Thank you, Captain Peppiatt,' said Roly with real pleasure. They rose to leave, but the captain had a further word of warning.

'This dratted dog of yours – keep it tied up, or it'll meet with another accident. Mr Conway has been demoted, so he's not in the friendliest of moods. Anyhow, the dog's a damned nuisance. Keep it out of my way, at least.'

It was only later that Lionel realised he had not referred to Dr Blake throughout their conversation. This was to be Peppiatt's policy from now on. He ignored the doctor, refusing to see him and walking straight past him when they happened to meet. Blake continued to exercise his convicts on the main deck at night, but the captain's silence alarmed him.

'I can't make Peppiatt out,' he said, when Lionel

187

described their conversation. 'He didn't mention me at all, not even to blackguard me?'

Lionel shook his head: 'Not a word.'

Freed from the doldrums, the graceful clipper sailed south once again. The oppressive days were forgotten in the solace of a constant breeze. Only the more perceptive noticed the captain's increasing isolation and the steady fall of the barometer, until the day when the truth had to be faced – it was cold, and growing colder every day.

As the Roaring Forties pushed them onward, the name of 'Antarctica' was whispered by those who knew.

Past the Colony of Good Hope, over latitude 40 towards the Crozets and the icy waters of the Antarctic Convergency, with a drastic drop in temperature and a darkening sky. No longer was the weather merely cold. It was freezing now and so consistently vile that it was barely a topic for conversation; food was stale and musty, not to be looked forward to with any pleasure, fresh beef replaced by salt-pork boiled in sea-water; and sex was either a memory or something to be snatched when the opportunity was there, desperately, in the knowledge that the relief was bound to be short-lived.

Even so, the daily routine continued with surprising regularity. Even the cabin passengers had taken on small duties of their own. Matilda discovered she had assumed the entire responsibility for the Raxleigh hens and piglet. One morning she arrived to find the pigsty empty, and was brusquely informed by one of the stewards that the animal had died of cold in the night.

She could well believe this, but could not bring herself to eat the succulent roast pork served in the cabin dining-room that evening. Remembering the piglet's eyes, she left the room in tears.

People made allowances on board ship. Stripped of their pretensions, they forged friendships which they would not have contemplated on land. Hardly a day passed by when Lionel did not bless his good fortune in sharing a cabin with Tony Plunkett. He was an invaluable source of information as he prepared his lectures on Van Diemen's Land.

One morning, as they lounged on their bunks, Plunkett took Lionel by surprise. 'Tim's sweet on your niece, ain't he?'

Lionel crinkled his nose, embarrassed. 'I suppose he is.'

'Marvellous feeling,' his companion murmured rapturously, 'being sweet on someone. You realise I'm head-over myself?'

'No!' Lionel was puzzled. 'Not with Sally too?'

'Don't be silly.' Plunkett laughed. 'She's far too young. I like a more substantial woman. Mabel Orbison Chant – there's a woman for you. More like a man.'

Lionel was surprised into silence, but Plunkett was right about Timothy Blake and his 'sweetness' for Sally. Weighed down by his responsibilities, receiving little thanks for his attempts to cope in sickening conditions, Tim would have been disheartened had it not been for her. He was entranced by Sally's innocence, finding a tranquillity in the simple act of watching her, absorbing every detail.

When his running conflict with Captain Peppiatt erupted over a punishment he found too harsh, like that of the steerage passenger lashed to the rigging for not paying his fine of a shilling for striking the baker, he sought her assurance that he was right to send a formal protest. When a single man died after breaking a leg, and his body was thrown overboard without a proper funeral because the captain could not spare the time for the ceremony, it was Sally who consoled him.

One evening he whispered his decision to stay in Van Diemen's Land in order to be near her; on the next evening he proposed and she accepted, though they decided that in view of his position on board as the Crown's surgeon superintendent it would be best to keep their engagement a secret until they landed in Hobart Town.

One afternoon they risked detection and slipped into the doctor's cabin, locking the door behind them. They emerged later, elated and amazed by the passion engendered by an excess of cuddling and kissing. Sarah misinterpreted her daughter's flushed silence at dinner as impending illness. 'I do hope you're not going down with something,' she sighed. 'None of us feel at all well in this terrible sea.'

'No,' said Sally, 'I'm all right.' She lowered her eyes, but raised them to smile at Dr Blake opposite. 'I've never felt better.'

It was the giddy, carefree stage of love – all innocence and promise.

That was the last dinner in the cabin dining-room which was tolerably pleasant. Thereafter meals became increasingly agitated as the *Countess* heaved and twisted her way through the mounting seas. The cabin passengers lost their appetites and the captain stayed away, intent on seizing every advantage from the violent winds which propelled his 'speed machine' forward at a startling speed of 14 knots. One astonishing day the *Countess* achieved a record 17 knots, and though her timbers trembled from the constant shock she covered 411 miles in that single day.

For Captain Peppiatt there was sheer exhilaration as the rigging whistled in the wind and the icy spray burned his cheeks, but the passengers spoke bitterly of the dangers of sailing ever further south. It was the Howling Fifties which sped them now across thousands of miles of the emptiest ocean in the world. One joyous day they sighted land, the islands of St Paul's and Amsterdam, but they were no more than barren rocks more melancholy than the sea itself. Another time they narrowly avoided a fatal collision with an iceberg, slithering past with barely a bump, though for a terrifying moment 700 feet of grey-blue mountain soared out of the mist and towered above them. The clipper looked like a toy boat by comparison. Even Captain Peppiatt breathed a sigh of relief when they were clear. He reckoned that the iceberg was two miles wide, and a jagged peak below the surface could have ripped his ship apart.

In spite of such hazards, the *Countess* raced across this frozen eternity with no mishap. The captain tempted fate by veering towards the 51st latitude, but the next morning the deck was covered with five inches of snow and the sails were frozen stiff so he steered northwards again on his bouncing course. Alarmed by these unexpected conditions, forbidden to go on deck and throw snowballs, the passengers defied the ship's regulations and pressed the crew for information, but Conway's replacement, Mr Herring, gave strict instructions that his sailors should reveal nothing. 'Don't even mention such things as the forty-ninth or fiftieth parallels!' the captain had ordered. 'They wouldn't understand. Nor would their lordships in the Admiralty if they got to hear of it; they'd stick to the thirty-ninth if they ever put to sea, but I sail by Towson's forty-ninth and my own instinct.'

But the sea grew more violent than he expected, until the appalling day when every fear was confirmed as the elements closed in on top of the tiny ship, forty-foot waves striking her with such an awesome crack that it seemed the hull must split apart. As passengers prayed, rats driven mad by the scraping chains ran from their holes. Contents leapt from shelves and rolled backwards and forwards, for it was pointless to replace them, and water seeped everywhere though all the hatches were battened down.

'The master's mad!' Everyone blamed the captain for risking his ship. 'No wonder they call him "Devil" Peppiatt!'

Anxious for his wife, who was about to give birth, Flanagan went to the mate to ask why the captain refused to slacken sail in such conditions. 'Instead, he's putting it on. Has he lost his senses?'

Mr Herring shook his head, but said nothing.

The afternoon was so overcast that little could be seen through the haze of spray. Timothy Blake inched his way across the tilting deck, exhausted by the difficult delivery of Mrs Flanagan's baby girl, stricken with guilt over the loss of mother and child. Nearing the stairs to the poop deck, he looked up in time to see the main topsail torn to shreds in a sudden ferocious blast which submerged the *Countess* in an avalanche of water. When the clipper rose again the mate realised that the doctor was gone. He glimpsed the rag-doll body a moment later, hoisted by another mountainous wave, and then the doctor disappeared.

Tied to his safety-line, the mate forced his way along the rail until he reached the captain at the wheel.

'Man overboard,' he screamed. 'Dr Blake, sir, *overboard*!' He gestured wildly behind them, but the captain merely nodded and looked ahead.

For a moment the mate stared at him, aghast; then he shook his head and staggered back to the main deck. The waves continued to break above them, shutting out the sky as they fell.

By evening everyone knew what had happened.

It was still dangerous to move on deck, and food and drink were forgotten as passengers stayed in their bunks, fully dressed. On every level Captain Peppiatt was denounced as callous. Even the women who used to spit in the doctor's path as he passed by mourned him now.

'How could anyone do such a thing?' wept Harriet. 'The cap'n didn't even try to save the poor doctor, didn't turn back . . .' The sentiment was echoed everywhere. The Stowes were devastated, feeling a personal loss. Sarah never forgot her daughter's reaction when she broke the news in their cabin.

'Tim's missing,' she said foolishly, trying to cushion the impact.

'You mean they can't find him?' Sally shook her head, confused.

'They fear he might have been washed overboard . . .'

'What do you mean?'

'Oh, my darling, they think Tim must have drowned.'

'Must have drowned . . .?' Sally repeated the words emptily.

Sarah whispered, 'Don't you understand, Sally? Tim's gone.'

Sally's grief broke in the middle of the night, and then it was so abandoned that Gussie and Sarah had to hold her down in the swaying cabin. Finally Sally collapsed, sobbing, against her mother. 'Why did he do this to me?' she cried out once. 'He made me fall in love with him and now he's left me alone.'

She confronted Captain Peppiatt three nights later, when the storm abated and he visited the cabin dining-room for the first time in weeks. It was a rash gesture on his part, unless he sought the opportunity to present his case. These days there was little conversation except for mere formalities as people sat down. Passengers had difficulty in eating, and though everything possible was fastened down objects still rolled backwards and forwards, adding to the constant din of sea, wind and sliding shutters. Empty seats told different stories: the three pale sisters confined themselves to their cabin and a diet of dry biscuit, praying even more intensely than before. Tony Plunkett and Mrs Chant had taken their places consistently, regardless of doldrums or gale. 'If no one else feels up to it, *we* must show the flag,' she instructed him.

Flanagan stayed in his cabin, grieving for his wife and still-born baby daughter. Mother and child were granted the courtesy of burial in spite of the storm, and a few giddy figures had gathered on the quarter-deck as Captain Peppiatt committed the remains to the ocean. That was the last time the captain had been seen in public.

When he sat down any murmur of conversation ceased, leaving only the sounds of the storm: the creaking timbers, the harsh rattling of the chains above, and the raging wind outside – the language of this melancholy ocean. Captain Peppiatt nodded to the passengers, apparently unconcerned by their silence, consuming his food with agility gained from long experience. A few looked up from their plates to stare at him with unconcealed dislike. Lionel glanced at his niece and saw the colour rising to her cheeks until she could bear the proximity no longer. Slipping out of her tethered chair, she hurried towards the door. As she passed the captain's table the ship lurched violently and she fell against him. Struggling to right herself, she seized a pewter mug and threw the claret in his face. Then she ran from the room, sobbing. Sarah followed her without a word, but Gussie retained enough respect for authority to blurt out: 'Please forgive her. She's distraught . . .' The apology was intended for the entire company, but the captain took it on himself to reply as he wiped the wine from his face.

'I quite understand, Mr Stowe. She's not herself. I forgive the girl.'

'*You* forgive her!' The shout came from Roly, but other voices followed.

'Why didn't you go back to look for him?' from Tony Plunkett.

'You didn't try,' cried Matilda, 'and that was rotten!'

'Or did you *want* him dead?' asked Roly. 'You'd had it in for Tim ever since he stuck up for the convicts.'

Even Mrs Chant joined in the prosecution. 'Have you nothing to say in your defence, Captain Peppiatt?'

'*Defence?*' he repeated, as if the word were new to him. 'Defence? I have no need to defend my actions. You've had your say and I hope you're satisfied. I shall not tolerate such accusations again. Have *you* any experience of changing course in a sea like that? It would be several minutes before I could even attempt to turn. Do you know how long a man survives in these waters? Sixty seconds. In two minutes he'd be frozen stiff.'

'There's the rub!' cried Tony Plunkett with an advocate's glee. 'We wouldn't be sailing in these waters were it not for your obsession with speed. The doctor drowned because you sailed too far south.'

'If you believe I wanted Dr Blake dead,' said Captain Peppiatt so softly that they had to strain to hear him above the noise, 'then you mistake my responsibility as master of the *Countess of Bath*. My motivation in everything I do is our survival. Dr Blake's death was tragic, no less

194

so than Mrs Flanagan's or her new-born child's, but unimportant compared to the survival of my ship and the hundreds of passengers on board who may be less popular than Dr Blake but are human beings nevertheless. If you can't see that, there is no point in my saying anything further.'

But Captain Peppiatt had been forced to defend himself, and was found guilty. He left the room and was not seen until eighteen days later when an urgent message brought him running to the masthead. Within minutes the *Countess of Bath* echoed with the long-awaited cry of '*Land!*'. The passengers had survived the voyage of sixteen thousand miles. No one thanked the man who had brought them safely through.

PART 5

— 13 —

Far from home in Hobart Town

'It's a rum old life,' gasped Tony Plunkett, lying on his bunk puffing away at a vast cigar which filled their tiny space with fumes.

'In what way?' asked Lionel, waving the irritating smoke away. He never touched the weed himself.

'In spite of everything, all that cold and discomfort, and the death of poor old Tim Blake, against all the odds I've enjoyed the voyage. They warned me it would strengthen my character if I went abroad, and, dash it, I think they were right.'

'I know what you mean,' Lionel agreed. 'I've never known any experience like it.'

'So much the better for you – as a would-be writer.'

Though the qualification hurt, Lionel knew that Tony Plunkett spoke the truth. He was learning that any experience, however distasteful, was grist to his mill. Some writers are born with the gift inside themselves, but he was not one of them. He needed to observe the hurly-burly of life in order to write about it, and the voyage on the *Countess* had provided him with a wealth of material. With luck, Van Diemen's Land might prove equally rewarding.

'Of course I'm madly . . .' Tony Plunkett began, and broke off in a fit of coughing.

'Madly what?'

'Madly in love, of course. With my betrothed.' Seeing Lionel's expression of bewilderment, he burst into laughter. 'Didn't I tell you last night? I've proposed and

197

she's accepted. Mabel and I intend to be wed in Hobart Town and want you to be our best man.'

Lionel transformed his smile of astonishment into one of congratulation.

'My dear fellow,' he cried. 'I *am* pleased, for you both. At least something good has come of this voyage.'

'And you'll be our best man?'

'Of course I'd be delighted,' Lionel agreed, dreading the prospect.

At the final muster most of the passengers were sickly creatures, so weakened by their confinement that many had to be supported by the few who were healthy. Their appearance belied their perseverance, however, and a startling transformation took place with the sighting of land. Even the weakest revived when they saw Port Davey in the distance, and sailed round the South West Cape with its empty shores and virgin forests and the quartz mountains beyond. A few expressed their disappointment that the land looked brown instead of green, but most were thankful for any relief after the endless, freezing sea.

The colour of the water began to change from olive to a deep, dark blue as the ship neared land and the infinite depths began to lessen; the crew caught a six-foot shark on a hook baited with pork, and placed the heart in a bucket of salt-water where it continued to beat for several minutes to the amazement of children and the consternation of others. Soon they were able to take soundings.

Now that the end was literally in sight, everyone recovered a measure of conceit. The young blades in their fancy waistcoats trimmed each other's sideboards like monkeys delousing their young, and even the orlop girls produced the fineries they had guarded so carefully throughout the voyage. It might be assumed that the female convicts were beyond vanity, all traces of femininity crushed for ever, but this was not the case. On the contrary, they had every reason to show themselves to the best advantage, for it could mean the difference between a tolerable life and abject misery. If they were claimed by a relative on their arrival, they would be granted parole on the spot. They knew from word of mouth that men would assemble on the quayside and cry out greetings to any 'sister', 'cousin' or even 'aunt' whom they happened to fancy. If the authorities suspected a deception, they turned a Nelsonian eye.

The prospect of a home and freedom galvanised the female convicts on board, and desperate attempts were made to improve themselves in the final days. The few teeth that were left, black, brown and broken, were scraped with brushes; hair, shaved during Dr Blake's inspection at the start of the voyage, was now long enough for curling with hot iron bars; and the rouge formerly obtained by soaking the dye off scarlet-covered Bibles was now the genuine article, contributed by sympathetic orlop girls. If the result was grotesque, it was highly provocative too. Attach a tempting label and the product starts to tempt. In this case, the travesty of beauty was desirable in itself.

The orlop girls were little better off than the convicts. Their cases varied: some were joining husbands who had fallen 'under the frown of justice' but had since been paroled, making their families eligible for free passage. Others, like Harriet, had no one waiting for them. Destined for domestic service, it was vital that they should make a good impression too. Consequently, the quarters of the single women were plunged into activity – sewing, and stitching, and all the wiles of titivation.

Harriet had lost the zest which had been her priceless quality. She was sweet and trusting as before, but fearful for the future and desperate for reassurance. She never recovered the slight touch of defiance which had made her strong, though Matilda tried to cheer her with the promise that she should join the Stowes the moment they were settled. Matilda's distress was genuine, for the two had grown closer as the voyage progressed until they agreed that they were each other's 'best and dearest friend'. Now they were about to be separated, and they embraced each other tearfully as they said goodbye.

In contrast, Dick Stanton regained his youthful relish for life, largely due to the influence of Lionel Raxleigh, who saw him daily. At Lionel's behest, the mate had signed a statement testifying to the courage of convict Stanton in rescuing the dog, name of Raxleigh, which he did with pleasure as his predecessor had fallen from grace because of it. Unfortunately he diminished the effect by adding: 'For all the good it will do him. Once on land convicts tend to disappear.' The danger remained that the wheels of officialdom would roll on inexorably, taking Dick with them. Both men dreaded the possibility of losing touch. Lionel promised Dick he would make a personal plea to the Governor to have him assigned to the Stowes, and tears came to his eyes as he embraced the young man for the first time, in the guise of a fond farewell.

A strong south-easterly brought them round the south of the island and almost drove them into Bad Bay after passing dangerously close to Acteon Reef. Then they steadied and sailed past Whale Head and Tasman's Head on the east coast of Bruny Island. A member of the crew who had crossed these waters before pointed out the landmarks: Adventure Bay, One Tree Point, Trumpeter's Bluff and finally Storm Bay, at the north of the estuary where the ship stood off overnight. Early the next morning the *Countess* entered the River Derwent. The passengers crowded the rails to absorb this foreign shore, where woods ran down to the water's edge and hardly a human habitation was seen. The tranquillity was impressive, but the sense of isolation was undeniable.

A few cheers rose as the pilot boat came towards them, and the medical superintendent of Hobart Town boarded the clipper.

Cries of interest echoed as the passengers spotted the first signs of civilisation, a cluster of jaunty, white-washed cottages and a solitary figure waving a welcome from a distance.

Several groans were heard as the clergyman made one of his rare appearances on deck. As a sort of farewell performance Silas Guard offered thanks to 'the Great Preserver of Man' for His mercy in landing them safely, but the service was scarcely attended now that the danger was over.

A hush fell as they neared Hobarton or Hobart Town: a windmill to one side, the cupola of a church rising on the other; white houses, green hills, and the vast, dark, snow-capped mound of Mount Wellington soaring 4,000 feet beyond.

Couples drew closer to each other, pointing out the details.

'At last, at last,' murmured Gussie, stroking his wife's arm. 'Thank the lord it's over.'

'It's beautiful,' said Sarah, but her voice faltered as she turned to Sally beside them. Then she rallied. 'So beautiful . . . I know we're going to love it here.'

Matilda waved merrily further along the rail, mouthing her excitement. Even Roly smiled at seeing her unaffected happiness.

There was a cheer as they heard the good news: the medical superintendent was not going to place the *Countess* under quarantine but declared her free to land. The last few yards seemed unnecessarily slow, but they came to rest at last in Sullivan's Cove, where the graceful clipper was lassooed by ropes and tied fast to the quayside like a captured Gulliver.

Captain Peppiatt was the first to disembark, as he had been the last to climb on board at Gravesend. He carried the London newspaper wrapped in oilskins whose date would establish his claim to a record voyage of 84 days. He walked down the gangway as soon as it was placed in position without a word of farewell or a single backward glance. To those on shore who saluted his arrival, what they could see of his face beneath his peaked hat looked stern and impassive.

There seemed an interminable delay before the passengers were allowed ashore. The Stowes were the first of the cabin class to land, as befitted their position, but this time they did not run the gauntlet of jeers which had

201

greeted their arrival. Instead they were touched by the cries of 'good luck' from the friends they had made on board. Matilda flushed with pleasure as she received a special cheer, for she was universally popular, but when she reached the quayside and waved back she was saddened to glimpse Harriet's face in the crowd, pale and frightened. Of all the orlop girls, she was the only one who had not bothered about her appearance, apart from the green shawl, Matilda's farewell present, draped around her shoulders. Even so, she was still the prettiest on board.

Gussie was dismayed to find that no one was there to greet them. This was hardly surprising, for they had no personal friends in Van Diemen's Land and carried the precious letter from the Secretary of State for the Colonies with them. Even so, it was a hurtful reminder that they were strangers in a strange land, of no account to anyone.

Yet first impressions were comforting. Hobart Town was a young town, less than fifty years old, but already there were spacious streets, attractive gardens, and a number of impressive buildings which gave an air of distinction. The situation on the Derwent could hardly have been improved upon.

Gussie took Sarah aside. 'If you and Lionel can look after the luggage, my dear, I'll proceed straight to Government House and make myself known.'

'Surely there's plenty of time for that!' she exclaimed. 'Let's get settled in first.'

'But that's the whole point,' he explained impatiently. 'If I deliver my letter now, I have no doubt that we shall be asked to stay at Government House.'

'But there are so many of us,' protested Sarah, unconvinced.

Undeterred, Gussie hurried off, determined not to lose the advantage of being the first to disembark. A boy directed him to Government House – 'Just round the corner.' He might have enjoyed the walk in less breathless circumstances, but the corner was a good mile away through gardens and trees to a low white building on the water's edge with its own private jetty. The house had a long, overlapping verandah supported by columns in true colonial style. The effect was pleasing, but Gussie's exasperation grew when he was informed by a lackadaisical secretary that the Governor was away on business. Gussie emphasised the urgency of his visit, referring to the letter from the Secretary of State, 'who has commended myself and my family to the protection of the Governor'.

In spite of such patronage, the secretary was surprisingly unconcerned and asked him to sign his name in the Visitors' Book with an address where he could be contacted.

'I *have* no address, as yet,' Gussie protested. 'Don't you understand? We've just arrived on the *Countess of Bath* and there's no one to help us.'

'I'll tell the Governor,' said the secretary, unmoved by Gussie's agitation, 'and here's the name of a hotel where you can put up.' He scribbled on a piece of paper and looked up with an automatic smile that held no humour. 'It's not far from the government domain, in Liverpool Street. I'm sure they'll make you comfortable.'

Gussie hurried back to the quayside, to find his wife in conversation with a lady in an open carriage drawn by two horses with a liveried man in front.

'There you are! At last!' cried Sarah cheerfully, and introduced him to Lady Franklin, the Governor's wife. He knew it was stupid, but he resented the way Sarah had established the relationship without him. He was quick to make amends.

'Lady Franklin.' He bowed respectfully. 'What a coincidence! I have just come from Government House.'

'So have I.' She smiled prettily, and Gussie had to join in the laughter, though he was impatient to introduce himself formally.

'I am Augustus Stowe,' he managed to blurt out at last, 'late of Raxleigh House in North Devon. And this is my wife, Sarah . . .'

'Of course she is!' Lady Franklin interrupted merrily. 'We are old friends by now.'

Gussie looked at the two women suspiciously. Had they known each other in England, or was she being arch? Noticing his expression, Lady Franklin leant forward conspiratorially. 'We took to each other at once. You have no idea how I crave for feminine company and a friendly face from home. Ladies are rare here, so you must forgive me if I take your wife under my wing.'

Sarah squeezed her gloved hand. 'What a lovely idea! I couldn't have hoped for a kinder welcome.'

Gussie remembered his mission. 'I have a letter, Lady Franklin, for the Governor . . .'

'I know you have,' said Lady Franklin, with her annoying habit of forestalling him before he could finish. 'Such a shame you missed him. He was here to collect his letters – he can't bear to wait for the post. You missed him by seconds. But if you give it to me I'll deliver it personally.' Before Gussie could prevent her, Lady Franklin had plucked the letter from his hand. This was not what he had in mind at all. He was looking forward to presenting it formally to the Governor himself; surely that was the proper procedure? Yet he could hardly ask for the letter back without seeming discourteous.

'How kind of you,' he conceded stiffly. 'And may I hope to see the Governor shortly?'

'But of course.' She smiled wickedly. 'That's all arranged.' She looked towards Sarah as if they shared a secret. 'You're all coming to dinner at Government House tomorrow. I wish I could invite you to stay, but we have the builders in.' She sighed, thinking what an unfailing excuse this had been on countless similar occasions. 'So you will see my husband then.'

With a merry wave to those around her, she nodded to the driver and the carriage drove away.

'Damn!' said Gussie. He sounded so indignant that Sarah laughed, though she did so with deepest affection.

'Oh, Goosie,' she said, using a long-ago name, 'never mind. You'll be seeing the Governor tomorrow night.'

He shook his head sadly, realising that she did not

understand. He had been looking forward to handing the letter to the Governor throughout the voyage and now he had been robbed of his triumph. A minor triumph, perhaps, but his alone.

Sarah tried to distract his attention by pointing out that half their luggage seemed to be missing.

'That's all I need!' he cried. 'Why does everyone take advantage of me?'

'Thank goodness you're back to put things in order,' she said tactfully.

He was gratified but determined not to show it, and went off muttering to himself.

As he climbed on board the *Countess* he saw that the animals were being prepared for shore, though it was obvious at a glance that landfall had come too late for many of the wretched beasts. The hens had been hurled overboard in their hen-house by the monstrous wave which had smashed one of the lifeboats. The piglet had been eaten. The rest of the animals, crowded together in cages, were piteous in their resignation. Less than half had survived the ordeal.

Gussie had never liked his sheep, finding them the most foolish animals on earth, but his heart went out to them now as they were hoisted in nets from the hold, blinded by the sudden daylight, so weak they could hardly utter a 'baa' of complaint, unable to stand upright without support from the others pressed against them.

'Madness to have brought them,' he thought. 'How could my cousin have urged me to do so?' He looked at their sores and wasted bodies with dismay, but his thoughts were interrupted by a cheer from the passengers and crew as an old friend was led down the gangplank: Gallant, the horse who lived up to his name. Gallant had endured the worst of the voyage enclosed in his box and was so emaciated that you could see the skeleton beneath the skin, but as he felt the earth again he quivered in recognition and tossed his head with pleasure. At first they walked him slowly forward but when he passed the ship a few minutes later he did so at a canter. The passengers laughed and waved, delighted by such an omen.

By afternoon the cabin class passengers and most of the livestock were safely on land and it was the turn of the respectable steerage passengers who had paid the cost of their transportation. The first thrill of arrival had faded and they hurried on to the quayside impatiently, hardly recognisable in their best clothes, clutching their baggage in one hand and scraps of identification in the other. They looked around them anxiously, asking directions from anyone with time to stop. A few hired the carriages plying for custom and drove off, not bothering to look back at the ship which had been their home for the last three months. That part of their life was over.

It was dark when the assisted single men and women were finally allowed to follow, though they had protested angrily throughout the afternoon that they should be free to go where and when they liked. Apparently this was not the case and the uneasy suspicion began to dawn that they were being treated no better than the convicts still held below. Far from the welcome they had been looking forward to, no proper preparations had been made to receive them. Incredibly, nobody cared.

Any remaining optimism faded when they learnt that because of some official 'oversight' no accommodation had been organised. They were being marched to the Factory instead.

The girl beside Harriet shook her head sadly as they looked down at the bustling quayside. 'I don't understand. Isn't the Factory the place where they put the convicts? We're being treated as if we're criminals. Why?'

'I don't understand either,' said Harriet to the girl. 'I thought they wanted us here.'

Orders were shouted along the quayside and the women told to fall in line and follow one of the superintendents to the Factory half a mile away. Afterwards people asked why they had been sent there instead of assigned immediately as servants. Obviously someone had blundered. It was not a deliberate act of callousness, merely incompetence, but it proved as bad in the end.

The Factory was not intended as a reception centre for arriving migrants. Its function was that of a house of correction for female convicts. Harriet expected a single building but it was more of a village, with several wards and separate apartments for the supervisors. They were woefully short-staffed considering the demands on their time – only five free officers looked after a convict population of around 400. Normally the wards housed the female prisoners on their arrival or served as a place of transition from one servitude to another. If a prisoner misbehaved during her domestic service, she was returned here for punishment and a stay in one of the solitary cells. The Factory fulfilled many purposes, but it was not a reformatory. The same was to prove true of Van Diemen's Land itself.

To complete the effect of a village there was a chapel, a hospital, and a school for orphans. Harriet caught sight of the convicts dressed in prison garb; at least the orlop girls were spared this particular ignominy.

Their ward was supposed to be better than the others, with beds instead of hammocks, but was little more than a barn with thick stone walls and high, narrow windows. The atmosphere was as dank as the orlop deck Harriet had escaped from, and she still felt as if the earth were swaying beneath her. At least there was space to stand upright, but it took several moments before she absorbed the details – or the lack of them, for the barn was sparsely furnished with beds and trellis-tables and little else. Plainly the washing facilities must be elsewhere, though the familiar smell of urine was overpowering. Oil lamps flickered in a breeze from the rafters above, casting eerie, distorted shadows, and she shivered. The moment she stepped inside she felt the impulse to draw back, but she was powerless, pushed forward by the others. Anyhow, she had nowhere else to go.

'Dear God, have mercy upon my soul,' she prayed inwardly, but she tried to make a joke of it. 'Not much of a new life, is it?'

Her friend laughed. 'If I'd known it was going to be like this, I'd have turned to crime back home. Better an English gaol!'

Another girl, overhearing them, did not find this amusing. 'Stop moaning. The party hasn't started yet.'

Party? Harriet wondered if there was going to be a proper reception after all, and her hopes rose a few minutes later, after she had succeeded in claiming a bunk for herself, when the heavy doors burst open and a crowd of men surged in clutching bottles of spirits, shouting and laughing. Some had brought provisions which they slammed on to the tables, and the rough-and-ready celebration began.

Harriet recognised several members of the *Countess*'s crew, looking different in these surroundings, and a number of strange men who must be Hobartians. Occasionally she glimpsed men in uniform, red jackets and white trousers, soldiers or guards, who stood outside the door allowing the men to come in after a whispered word of recognition and a handshake. It seemed that everything had been planned.

Unsure of herself, yet anxious not to appear stand-offish, Harriet smiled at the unshaven man who plunked himself beside her and offered her a drink from his bottle. She sipped reluctantly. Another man lurched over and tried to embrace her, spilling red wine over her dress, but he was shoved away angrily by her companion. 'Manners, you drunken bastard!' he cried, as the intruder sprawled on his back. 'Clear off and wait your turn, can't yer?' He swivelled round and attempted a smile as he touched his discoloured hat with a grimy finger. Harriet tried to smile back, though the leer of yellowish teeth and the smell of his sweat sickened her. How strange and primitive it was, though they were doing their best to be friendly. Or . . . but she tried not to think of that.

Suddenly, as if a shot had been fired or a clock had

chimed, the meal came to an end. Someone started to scrape a fiddle, a few attempted to dance, and men and women leapt on each other greedily, unbuttoning trousers, tearing down skirts, without the slightest shame. Soon, a number were copulating violently with screams of pain and pleasure, while several of the orlop girls plunged their heads downwards hungrily, their eyes closed, their mouths open. To Harriet, the scene in the flickering lamp-light resembled Hades.

The man pulled her towards him and kissed her roughly. 'Come on,' he whispered, sensing her fear. 'No need to be afraid a'me. I'll look after thee.'

His skin looked like mud cracked by the sun, but he was not unpleasant compared to the others. In other circumstances she might have liked him, but she had not saved herself for this. The thought of being intimate with any man except the one she intended to marry had always been repugnant to Harriet.

Her treasured bridal dress had been stained by seawater on the ship, a loss far beyond material possession. The others called her daft for bringing it and jeered obscenities about her wedding night, half scornful and half envious that she would go to it a virgin.

So she struggled to break free. Her resistance excited him, and he called for help. Some of the orlop girls broke free from their own embraces and swooped on her gleefully, pulling down her petticoats, lifting up her dress, while the man removed his trousers and clambered on top of her.

'Don't listen to 'er!' they screamed as they urged him on. 'When 'Arriet says no, she means yes. We know 'er. Give it 'er!'

Harriet moaned as the man straddled her. She knew in her heart that there was no point in fighting further.

'Oh, God,' she thought as she clenched her teeth against the pain, 'why have You sent us here to be destroyed?'

— 14 —

The human auction

Lionel Raxleigh did not mean to go missing. If Gussie had stayed on the quayside instead of wandering off to Government House on some fool's errand they would have been able to discuss the storage of their baggage. He was assured by the third officer that the porters had everything under control and there was nothing to worry about.

'Feel like a jar?' said the voice of temptation behind him. He turned round to find Flanagan, smartly dressed and ready for fun.

'Why not!' Lionel exclaimed with relief. 'We deserve it.' Then he felt a twinge of guilt as he remembered the man's loss.

'I haven't had the chance to tell you . . .'

Flanagan stopped him. 'Don't bother. Sympathy won't bring her back. Let's get down to the serious business of drinking.'

The Irishman had been to Hobart before so Lionel followed him willingly. He was depressed by the sense of emptiness, though Flanagan saw it differently. 'Hardly recognise the place,' he said. 'It's growing all the time. Ten years ago when I came here first the population of Hobart Town was less than nine thousand, but it must be twice that by now. A metropolis, wouldn't you say?'

Lionel would not have said so, but he nodded his agreement as they walked up the spacious street, which was lined with brick houses covered with slate-like shingles, each standing separately in a small garden. Certainly it was a gentle place, but Lionel was relieved when they turned into the main street. He observed the details with interest: a covered arcade with a Bootmart and a store which advertised Berlin Wools. On the other side a D & J Room and a sign outside a grocer's which proclaimed *Pepper & Perrin*. But the pavements were not crowded and there was ample space for the few horses and carts in between.

Lionel's enthusiasm began to evaporate, overtaken by a sense of guilt at leaving the others to cope with the luggage and the chore of finding a temporary hotel. He was tempted to turn back.

'Do we need a cab?' he asked.

'Not much call for them,' said Flanagan. 'And they wouldn't drop us where we're going.'

'Why's that?' asked Lionel innocently.

'Because they're afraid, that's why.'

A few moments later they turned a corner and Lionel saw the poorer face of Hobart, though the narrower streets were still uncrowded.

'You'll like it at Ma Sloper's,' Flanagan promised, noticing his companion's bleak expression. 'Ruby is the proverbial Madam with a heart of gold.'

'You mean it's a brothel?' asked Lionel uneasily.

'You could say that,' Flanagan replied enigmatically, 'but then you could say that of Hobart Town as a whole. Anyhow, she's a great character.'

Their route had taken a horseshoe turn and the waterfront lay ahead at the end of the cobbled street. Lionel heard a hubbub of noise coming from a whitewashed house but he was unprepared for the blast which struck him the moment he stepped inside. His instant impression was of pigs swilling at the trough. When Ruby Sloper was introduced, a large and heavily painted Jew, she eyed him suspiciously. She had forgotten Flanagan in spite of his warm embrace, which she tolerated glumly. Lionel was unimpressed. Two hours later, his conscience

211

dulled by drink, he had warmed to Ruby and was finding the place more congenial.

The room in which he woke looked clean. Plainly it did not belong to Ma Sloper's, an impression which was confirmed when he looked from the window and realised it overlooked an impressive building across the road which seemed curiously familiar. For a split second Lionel imagined he was back in London. There was no sign of Flanagan.

Going downstairs, he entered a saloon, new and pristine compared to Ma Sloper's, though a group of men were already swilling at the bar. Sunlight filtered reproachfully through the window. The few who looked up did so with neither welcome nor recognition. Thirsting for a drink to revive him, he sorted the coins from his pockets and found he had spent surprisingly little the night before. He ordered himself a beer.

'Where from?' asked the barman laconically.

'Off the *Countess of Bath* yesterday.'

'Thought as much.' A silence fell between them like a shutter.

'Excuse me,' said Lionel, anxious to penetrate it, 'but where am I?'

This time several of them turned for a closer look, surprised by the question and the accent which marked him out as 'different'.

'Flash spark,' one of them muttered audibly.

The barman revealed his whereabouts grudgingly. 'Custom house.' He nodded towards the impressive white building with the royal coat of arms across the road, and Lionel realised why it was so familiar. It was modelled on the custom house in London.

'That explains why I thought I was home when I woke up.' Lionel smiled, crinkling his nose with embarrassment.

'Cor, mate!' exclaimed the barman. 'You are in a bad way if you thought that. This is the corner of Morrison and Murray, if that means anything to you.'

The names meant nothing. He wondered where he should go in search of the others. Overwhelmed with guilt over his sister and the rest of the family, he got up to leave.

'Here! Forgotten something, haven't yer?' called the barman as he turned towards the door.

'Have I?'

'Too true! The guvner, Charlie Taylor, let you crash upstairs but your friend swore you'd settle up.'

'How much do I owe?' The barman handed him a slip covered with figures and calculations, reaching a total which devoured his change. Obviously he had spent lavishly the night before after all, but had put it 'on the slate'.

The barman grasped the coins. 'Good on yer.' He volunteered a smile at last.

Lionel turned right into Morrison Street and was thinking of asking at the ship chandlers next door how he could reach Government House when a piercing voice ricocheted across the street. 'Mr Raxleigh! Can I have a word?' Miss Gissing hurried towards him, hoisting her skirts out of reach of the mud.

'Mr Raxleigh,' she said excitedly, 'could you buy me a drink?'

He hesitated, wondering if women were allowed in the custom house. She answered for him. 'There's a snuggery in the back.'

Preferring ale to wine, she drank it thirstily, and declared: 'It's been a wretched business.'

'What's that?'

'Some girl found floating near the ship this morning, her poor, pale face among the cabbage leaves and corpses of cats, and I *knew* her. One of the girls from the orlop deck. Think of it, her first night on shore.'

'An accident?'

'Likely she saw herself as a no-hoper and did herself in. They took her with the rest of the girls to a hall in the Factory that's used by the convicts, and I daren't think

213

what happened to her there. Well, you can imagine! And she must have broken free in the night. They didn't give her a chance.' Miss Gissing rocked backwards and forwards in her chair in genuine grief.

'The whole wretched system is wrong. Treating these girls like criminals just because the government pays their passage, assigning them as servants so they're doomed from the start. I tell you, Mr Raxleigh, you'll be shocked by things you see in this place. One day, perhaps, enough free men like yourself and your dear family will settle here and tilt the balance. Till then it's convict island and *you're* the interloper, the dickey-toff from poor old England.' Tears ran down her pitted cheeks, and she wiped them away with the back of her hand.

'I wish there was something I could do.' Lionel used the cliché automatically.

'There *is*,' Miss Gissing replied emphatically. 'Tell them back home in your newspaper what happens to those girls when they get here, treated little better than the convict women. Tell them about that poor girl I seen this morning. Oh, the waste of it, the waste, to travel all this way and end like that. What's the point in paying their passage if they don't get a kind word or a helping hand once they're here? You have such power, Mr Raxleigh, though you don't seem to realise it. Even in this godforsaken place the name of the London *Times* counts for something.'

'Miss Gissing,' he began, but she interrupted him with a gap-toothed smile as she removed the clay pipe from her mouth.

'Call me Jacobina,' she declared surprisingly. He had never thought of her as possessing a Christian name.

'I shall be delighted to do so,' he replied courteously, though he thought it would be difficult. 'Well, Jacobina . . .' He paused, thinking how inappropriate the fulsome name was for such a small person. 'I know that Dr Blake was concerned about the future of those girls on the orlop deck, and what would become of them. He asked me to write about them.'

'I know that,' she said impatiently. 'Why do you think I sought you out? Write the truth about the things you see; let them know at home what transportation means. Tell the truth. Encourage people back home to come here, qualified people, free settlers like yourselves. Which reminds me, your sister's worried about you. Better go and put her mind at rest.' She gave him the name of the hotel where Gussie and Sarah were staying, and they parted.

Arriving at the Adelphi Hotel in Liverpool Street – which was less imposing than the name suggested – Lionel Raxleigh found a note from his sister:

Dearest, So concerned. Hope no mishap has befallen
you. Waited all morning for word and have left
with Sally for a promenade towards a place called
Battery Point. Should we not meet, please see us
at luncheon. There is much to discuss.
Yours Most Affty, Sarah

Instead of setting out to find them, he washed and changed into his best clothes in order to present himself to the Lieutenant-Governor, Sir John Franklin, at Government House. He was concerned about Dick Stanton's future.

Slightly alarmed by the engraved calling-card of the 'Special Correspondent for the London *Times*' presented by his secretary, the Governor received Lionel without the usual delay. Each man assessed the other cautiously, like the circling of dogs which decides if a stranger is friend or foe.

Sir John's appearance was rotund and affable, the perfect counterpart to his wife. With a bald scalp and a broad chin, his head would have looked much the same upside down, but he was sharper than this jovial impression suggested.

Lionel knew from enquiries made in London that John Franklin was an explorer of considerable reputation, having led two expeditions into the Arctic regions of North-West America before he was appointed

Lieutenant-Governor of Van Diemen's Land in 1836. These were his final months in Government House before his successor was appointed, after which Sir John intended to set out yet again to northern Canada in the hope of fulfilling his life's ambition by discovering a North-West passage.

Sir John was anxious to leave his domain in as prosperous a state as he could, and he welcomed the chance to offset the adverse publicity spread by a former private secretary back home. Now it might be possible to confound the libel through the pages of *The Times*, and he greeted his visitor with genuine if calculated warmth.

Just as his wife had welcomed a new friend in Sarah, he was glad to meet a true gentleman. For his part, Lionel was relieved to find a friendly face. Most of those he had seen in Hobart Town reminded him of the granite surliness of Cornishmen back in England.

'You'll have a glass of madeira wine?' said Sir John, waving Lionel to a chair which faced the light. His own was turned against it. Lionel accepted the glass goblet with pleasure but was devastated by the Governor's next remark. 'So what do you make of our community? I gather you've met our notorious Mrs Sloper; I'm told she's quite a character!'

Oh, lord, thought Lionel, is Hobart Town a place where everyone knows everyone's business in a matter of hours? Apparently so, for the Governor continued: 'We've had trouble from her in the past; that's why we keep an eye on the place. She has a fondness for deserters and convicts on the run. Can be useful to us when we're looking for someone in particular, but it's best to keep your wits about you in such places!'

Sir John leant back in his chair and smiled. With this word of advice he had managed to establish his superiority by revealing that he knew of Lionel's behaviour the night before while remaining sympathetic.

'I'm afraid I acted impetuously,' Lionel explained, defending himself instinctively.

'Don't apologise, for heaven's sake,' said Sir John. 'As

a writer you need to see every stratum of life over here.'

'It was partly relief at being on dry land again.'

'Captain Peppiatt told me about the storms of Antarctica. It must have been alarming for you.'

'You've seen the captain?'

'Of course. Every captain from home makes his report in person. I know Peppiatt of old, a keen navigator. It seems he's established a new record.'

Lionel came to the point of his visit – the welfare of Dick Stanton. To his surprise, Sir John Franklin knew the name.

'The convict who saved the dog, eh? Peppiatt recommended him for parole.'

'He did!' Lionel exclaimed.

'Captain P. is nothing if not meticulous. I told him I could not let the man go free, but I am prepared to assign him to your family as a servant, which I presume is what you wish. Then you can keep an eye on him. He will become a free man before the year is out if you wish to make such an application.'

'That's exceptionally good of you, sir,' said Lionel with a feeling of immense relief. 'I realise it's a big responsibility.'

'Not much. You don't have to pay them and the moment they step out of line you can send 'em back. The cost of upkeep is little more than twenty pounds a year per convict, and they do what you tell them. Always remember that they're criminals.'

He held out his hand to say goodbye. 'A word of advice, Mr Raxleigh, which could prove useful. This place is like a prison. It depends on barter – one good turn justifies another, if you know what I mean. To put it more bluntly, if you like us, we'll like you.'

At that very moment, Dick Stanton and the other convicts were enduring the full weight of officialdom. First there was a muster before the superintendent of police, who listed their names and ages in a large book before adding his own assessment of the man's character, influenced by any recommendation from the ship's master-at-arms or Miss Gissing, in the absence of Dr Blake. A few questions elicited the type of work for which the prisoner was best qualified. It was not a bad system, though perfunctory. In this way the superintendent of the convicts was supplied with enough information for a just assignment, though the concept of justice ultimately depended on the character of the particular superintendent. In this case, Mr Hitchens was a former convict himself, but far from making him tolerant towards the convicts brought before him it had the opposite effect. Mr Hitchens was renowned for his harshness, as if he was trying to distance himself from the men who reminded him of his past. With the outraged zeal of the reformed drunkard, the ex-convict became a devil of respectability once he was granted a free pardon, and the convicts preferred to be tried by anyone rather than one of their own kind.

Consequently, instead of understanding the individual needs of each prisoner and making allowances accordingly, Mr Hitchens took pride in his arbitrary decisions in which compassion played no part at all.

When Dick Stanton was brought forward the former convict studied the scar across the young man's cheek and reached his decision. 'Well, then, Stanton,' he concluded. 'You're not second transportation. Even so, I can see you're a trouble-maker, so you're assigned to the chain-gang at New Norfolk. Building roads and clearing land should cool you down. If you behave yourself, you will be assigned to private service after the appropriate time. Next.'

As Dick was led away he knew that his childhood scar had singled him out for tougher treatment than he deserved, yet he was not dismayed. He had faith in Lionel Raxleigh's word, and the excitement of landing was overwhelming. Far from being cowed by their experience in the depths of the *Countess*, the convicts were so thankful to leave that dungeon that some were almost mischievous in their whispers as they shuffled down the gangplank in their irons. All were dressed in the new suits of clothing issued on their arrival, a drab colour to distinguish them from the free settlers and make it easier for the soldiers to shoot them should they have the nerve to make a run for it.

In contrast, the soldiers who lined the wharf were colourful in their red and white uniforms. After a roll on the drums, the convicts stood rigidly to attention and the Governor, who had come straight from his interview with Lionel, started his inspection, accompanied by Mr Hitchens and Captain Forster, the chief police magistrate. He stopped every few yards to speak to one of the men, enquiring after his health and assignment, receiving sub-servient replies which inevitably denied the man's real feelings. When this formality was over, Sir John Franklin mounted some steps and began the conventional address which he used to welcome the convicts to Van Diemen's Land.

'You have brought yourselves here through the crimes you have committed. Now is the time and place to start again, so let me give you some words of warning which will be useful in the future. If you fall under the influence of bad company and drink you will only be punishing yourselves, for once you take the wrong turning in Van Diemen's Land you are doomed. If you yield to temptation you will be sent to the chain-gang, the penal settlement, and that ultimate destination – the scaffold. I should not need to warn you of the special danger of drink, for many of you know from bitter experience that the door to the public house can be the entrance to a gaol.

'However, let me assure you that if you behave well, and labour for your masters cheerfully, you will be re-warded in due course with a ticket of leave. Then you will be your own masters, reaping your own profits which will be considerably more than you could hope for at home. A conditional pardon gives you the liberty of the colony, and a free pardon offers you the chance to return to England should you wish to do so. But by then I hope you will think of this place as home. So the choice is yours. Behave badly and suffer; work hard and prosper. I shall not insult your intelligence by telling you which course to take. Welcome to Van Diemen's Land, and may God have mercy on you.'

The men listened to the homily with varying emotions, though their faces gave little away. Some felt contempt, others the instinctive resentment of authority bred from bitter experience; most were fatalistic, suspecting that their future depended on the luck of the draw; but a few were eager for a new life, and Dick Stanton was among them.

Having finished his address, the Governor descended the steps. He caught sight of Lionel among the onlookers who had come to see the convicts disembark, and beckoned him to come forward.

'Mr Raxleigh – Captain Peppiatt, master of the *Countess of Bath*, has made a special recommendation due to an act of heroism during the voyage.'

Lionel bowed his acknowledgment. 'That is correct, Your Excellency. The convict, Richard Stanton, is known to myself and my family through his father who was employed by us back home. The act of bravery was on our behalf.' He hesitated to mention that it involved the rescue of a mongrel pup called Raxleigh.

'So I gather,' said the Governor. 'Captain Forster, will you bring the man forward?'

Sir John studied the young man who caused such concern. He looked abject enough, apart from the scar across his cheek.

'Has this man received his assignment?' The Governor turned to Mr Hitchens who was standing like a ramrod beside him.

'Sir. Assigned to the chain-gang . . .' He stopped, noticing the Governor's frown. 'Light duties only,' he added quickly. 'Clearing land at New Norfolk.'

'Even so, it seems excessive for a first offender. Alter that to a new assignment as servant to Mr Raxleigh, will you? The man is to be kept in custody until Mr Raxleigh is ready to claim him.'

Mr Hitchens gave a sharp salute in acquiescence. Dick glanced at Lionel with a look of relief before he was returned to the ranks. Uncertain of the proper procedure, Lionel stayed where he was.

'On your head be it!'

Lionel turned round and recognised Mr Sloley, the Governor's languid private secretary, who had taken his card to the Governor an hour before.

'What are you talking about?'

'Your young friend,' said Mr Sloley, a wealth of meaning in his sepulchral voice. 'The convict Stanton. A word of caution, Mr Raxleigh.' His Adam's apple quivered. 'Beware of pity. By all means give him the food and bedding he's entitled to, but don't spoil the man and never expect gratitude. The slave resents the master to whom he is indebted.' He gave a pained and sickly smile.

Though he was seething inwardly, Lionel managed to laugh. 'I would hardly describe the relationship in those terms.'

'Wouldn't you?' Mr Sloley inclined his head like an inquisitive hen. 'You give him his food and bedding in return for his servitude. I don't see much difference.'

'Do I detect a note of bitterness?'

'More than a note. A concerto which has been composed since I came here.'

Lionel looked at Mr Sloley with new interest. 'It isn't that bad, surely?'

'You have no idea of the degradation you will meet here, Mr Raxleigh. If you wait a minute you will see how they treat the female convicts, the last to leave the *Countess of Bath*. Most people find the spectacle entertaining, but I do not. Look at them,' Mr Sloley continued sourly, with a disdainful wave towards the men gathering on the quayside. 'Like animals around a bitch on heat. We've had guards posted on board for the last twenty-four hours to stop the men climbing on deck. We even have a government boat patrolling the water on the other side.'

Lionel was puzzled, unaware of the ritual during which

female convicts were 'recognised' by their new-found 'relatives' as they stepped on land.

'I don't understand what's going on,' he said. 'It reminds me of market day back home.'

Mr Sloley shook with a paroxysm of silent mirth. 'You have little idea how correct you are – except that we call it the auction.'

'The auction? I don't understand.'

Mr Sloley giggled and raised his eyes to heaven. 'Judge for yourself, Mr Raxleigh. The auction is starting.'

Someone blew a trumpet, followed by a clatter on the drums drunkenly performed by one of the waiting men. A momentary hush fell on the quayside, broken by a thunder of raucous cheers as the female convicts appeared. The women had achieved an extraordinary transformation, disguising their drab uniforms with outrageous borrowed plumes: dazzling dresses, bonnets à la mode, ear pendants, shawls and veils. Some wore new silk stockings, saved throughout the voyage for this display; several held hand-made parasols in their kid-gloved hands; and their perfume was of such a violent nature that it set the crowd's numerous noses twitching. Sensing their moment, they took their time, pausing at the top of the gangplank to look down disdainfully on the men below as if they were about to make the bids themselves. They stood there, hands on hips, with an arrogance which struck Lionel as magnificent in the circumstances. A shrug of the shoulders, a pout of the lips, and then, chins tilted high, they began their descent. If the settlers expected servants, they were faced with princesses. In the Haymarket or Leicester Square they might have been scorned for their grotesque maquillage and tattered finery, but here they were the real thing, greeted after the initial cheering by another awe-struck, wistful silence which was almost reverential. Then the men surged forward as one.

Names were called at random: 'I'm your brother, Pete.' 'Come here, cousin. Here!' 'Nellie! Good on yer, Nell. It's me, Dave. Over here.' 'Jeez, don't you remember me? It's Bill! Hell, I can't have changed that much.' 'Let me get at you, my beauty. It's yer old man!'

The auction was over in minutes. Twenty of the younger women were claimed, and now the old and sick were allowed to land as well. The men gave a final rousing cheer and started to move away. Within a minute the quayside was as quiet as before, the *Countess of Bath* tethered to the bollards like a great, dead whale.

'I shall accompany you to your hotel,' announced Mr Sloley, turning to Lionel. 'Might I ask, Mr Raxleigh, if you intend to write about that charade for *The Times*?'

Lionel laughed: 'Somehow, Mr Sloley, I don't think my readers would appreciate the gusto.'

— 15 —

The dinner party

When Lionel strolled into the Adelphi Hotel he found his sister's patience had been stretched too far. 'Where have you been, Lionel?' she demanded. 'We needed you.'

Intending to impress her, he described his visit to Sir John Franklin, but this made matters wose.

'You mean you've been to Government House already?' Gussie exclaimed.

'I was anxious about Dick Stanton,' Lionel replied defensively. 'I've procured his assignment as a servant as soon as we're settled.'

Gussie left the room and went downstairs to the saloon. Ordering a glass of cognac, he raised it to his mouth with trembling fingers. It was intolerable the way his family let him down on every occasion. Bad enough that Lionel and Roly vanished from the quayside just when they were needed, but they had to complicate everything as well. Already shattered by a confrontation with his son, Gussie leaned back in his armchair and tried to compose himself. Roly had burst into the hotel in the early hours, banging and shouting, waking everyone up, and had not surfaced again until the late afternoon.

'What is the matter with you?' Gussie had asked, when Roly came to his room. 'You're making your mother ill. You seem to take some perverse delight in flouting me. You've been in this country less than twenty-four hours and you've upset people already, bursting into the hotel like that, shouting obscenities. As for your dear little wife, it breaks my heart to see her poor eyes so red from crying. For pity's sake, Roly, pull yourself together – make an effort.'

Roly gave a groan. 'Father, do stop it. It's time I got dressed for this bloody dinner.'

That was an hour ago. Not a single member of his family had made the effort to join him, so he ordered another glass of cognac. This was uncharacteristic, but after his disturbed night Gussie was not feeling well. He was dreading the evening ahead.

As he dressed for dinner in Government House, His Excellency was not in raptures either, though his wife was trying to deflect his bad temper. Like her husband, whose pussy-cat appearance belied the lion underneath, Jane, Lady Franklin was more formidable than the bright-eyed kitten who peeped playfully out from beneath the tight little curls. Certainly there was mischief in her nature, but she took genuine interest in everything she saw. Her instinctive liking for Sarah Stowe was not superficial but genuine delight at finding a friend of her own age who had seen a play and read a book and listened to a concert, achievements which were rare in Van Diemen's Land. Sarah did not give herself airs, unlike many of their visitors from England. Consequently, she defended Sarah's husband vigorously as the Governor inveighed against Lord Bathurst's letter.

'I've never read such insulting nonsense in my life.' He seized the letter from the dressing-table and repeated the phrases which he found so offensive: '". . . your *turbulent island . . . wilder elements . . .*"'! It shows that the Minister hasn't the faintest idea of life over here. Far from encouraging settlers, he tries to put them off.'

'He doesn't understand what you have to contend with.'

'But he should understand. That's what angers me. After all, he's Secretary for the Colonies, so he should know something about them.'

'From all I've heard,' she said reassuringly, 'Lord Bathurst has a peculiar sense of humour. I'm anxious everything should go well tonight. I like that woman, so I want you to be especially nice to her funny husband.' Before he could protest, she continued quickly: 'How do I look? Do I pass muster?' She looked towards him archly.

He smiled at her proudly. The low-cut gown from Paris was most becoming, and a silk shawl covered her shoulders.

'You look lovely, my dear. A credit as always.'

She curtsied demurely, relieved that his good humour was restored.

A visit to Government House was a privilege in a country where social graces were so rare that they were almost considered bad form. New arrivals were eager to learn everything they could about Van Diemen's Land, while they were welcomed for the latest news from home. Consequently, conversation was never a problem. In addition, the Franklins were known for their excellent table, and Lady Franklin was famous for her skill in mixing her guests dangerously – the art of a born hostess.

As she checked the fires in every room – a necessity now that the evenings were growing cold – she felt the familiar excitement of the lull before the conflict. The Stowes were top-drawer, even if they lacked a title, and a correspondent from the London *Times* could prove a useful ally. When they were shown into the drawing-room she met them with a beaming smile, but after the usual formalities of greeting Sir John drew Gussie aside.

'I have read your letter from the Secretary of State,' he said, 'and I must say I take exception to it.'

'You do?' asked Gussie in alarm.

'It reveals the usual paucity of knowledge of our situation. I'm surprised you decided to risk it here.' The Governor beckoned to Lionel to join them, thereby rubbing salt in the wound. Gussie was still smarting from his brother-in-law's presumption in seeking an audience with the Governor before himself, and seeing them on friendly terms while he was regarded as the harbinger of bad news was painful in the extreme.

'Mr Stowe?' Gussie's thoughts were interrupted by a hand resting on his shoulder. 'Will you escort me in to dinner?' He looked around. To his surprise the room was almost empty.

'I shall be delighted, Lady Franklin. Please forgive me.' He struggled giddily to his feet, trying to conceal his confusion, while she regarded him with amusement.

The evening started well, though the Stowes were startled to find the clergyman, Silas Guard, among the guests – 'an old friend, I'm sure'. Also present were a local merchant and his wife who lived in 'the most beautiful house in Hobart Town'; Mr Sloley; a single lady devoted to good works, called Miss Dowling; and Miss Williamson, governess to the Franklins' daughter, Eleanor – a party of fourteen altogether.

Conversation adapted to the courses: niceties over soup, with Sarah's account of the latest success on the London stage and Lionel's comments on the current popularity of the government. Local scallops in a delicate white sauce with a piping of mashed potato created an interest in the geography of the country and its place-names.

'I'm confused,' Sarah admitted. 'Should I say Hobart or Hobart Town? And why do some people say Tasmania instead of Van Diemen's Land?'

'You have touched on a very sore point,' laughed the Governor. 'My wife prefers Hobart Town, but if I am honest I must declare myself in favour of Hobart, plain and simple. Hobart Town sounds as old-fashioned as London Town. As for Van Diemen Land, as it should be called, I suppose it's a bit of a mouthful. At least Tasmania is better than *Diemenia*, which sounds like a nervous disorder. More and more of our friends are calling it Tasmania.'

'And Abel Tasman did discover the island, after all,' said his wife. 'Personally, I think it has a nice ring to it

– Tasmania – shorter and simpler too. You'll find the derivation of our names fascinating.' She turned to Sarah. 'Did you know that Maria Island was named after Van Diemen's daughter?'

'I am sorry to correct you, my dear,' the Governor interrupted, 'but it was his wife, not his daughter.'

'Are you sure?'

'Positive. Remember, I have been there.'

Noticing Lady Franklin's embarrassment at being corrected in public, Sarah broke in quickly: 'What astonishes me are all the English names – Ramsgate and Norfolk and Swansea. Whenever they speak of Launceston, which is not that far from Bideford, I feel at home.'

Everyone laughed, as she intended, and Lady Franklin recovered her composure. 'But you *are* at home, with us.'

'No one could have made us more welcome than your husband and yourself, and we are deeply grateful,' said Sarah warmly.

'Hear, hear,' said Gussie. At least Sarah could be relied on.

The talk became tougher after the fish-plates had been removed and the servants brought on the mutton.

'The scourge of the colonies, as you may have heard,' declared the Governor, 'is the blacks. You'll be startled to discover that our legislation exists to protect the blacks at the expense of the whites. The balance has tipped against ourselves, which is madness. Our own convicts are treated worse than the blacks. None of these facts are properly known back home, Mr Raxleigh, and you'll do us no harm if you tell the truth.'

'What about the treatment of the convicts in Port Arthur?' Lionel asked him. 'They tell me it's a brutal place.'

'Then I hope they told you that Port Arthur is intended for the worst sort of criminal. It's their final chance of correction.'

'And if it fails, Sir John?'

'Then they've reached the end of the road, Mr Raxleigh. There's no hope left.'

'I would say, Your Excellency,' Mr Sloley volunteered with one of his sideways smiles, 'that the moment a man arrives in Port Arthur he's dead to the world.'

'Don't they try to escape?' asked Roly.

Sir John and Lady Franklin laughed at such naivety. 'They try,' said the Governor, 'but they don't succeed.'

'Is the prison so impregnable?'

'It's the lie of the land, as you'll see for yourself if you travel there. To escape, the convicts have to cross a narrow isthmus called Eagle Hawk Neck where hounds are tethered every few yards. Meat is thrown 'em once a day, but never quite enough. They hurl the rest of it into the sea.'

'The sea?'

'For the sharks!' cried Lady Franklin, delighted by their consternation. 'So any convict who's brave enough to make a run for it has to pass either the dogs or the sharks.'

'Do you mean they are eaten alive?' Sarah sounded so distressed that the Governor hastened to reassure her.

'Shot, more likely. The hounds set up such a barking that they bring the guards running from the sentry post. No, there's not much point in trying to escape. Few of the convicts can swim.'

'Have any of them made it?' asked Lionel, determined to visit Port Arthur and see the conditions for himself.

'Two or three, as far as I remember – maybe a couple more who were never found. Even if they do get away there's not much hope for survival in the land beyond. If the natives don't get 'em, the tigers will. It's fearful wild.'

'If the commandant was on one of his visits to Hobart Town, I'd have invited him to join us tonight,' said Lady Franklin. 'He'd have told you things to make your flesh creep, though I doubt if he realises the effect he has on us. O'Hara Booth is so immersed in violence that he takes it for granted.'

'Then I'm rather glad,' said Sarah, 'that he isn't with us tonight.'

'I don't want to say a word against Booth,' said the

Governor, intending to do exactly that, 'for he's a tough man in a tough job, but my wife is right: he does seem to take a sadistic pleasure in his work.'

'That frightful smile of his.' Lady Franklin started to giggle. 'No, I shouldn't . . .'

'His smile?' asked Lionel, hoping to lead her on.

'It seems so unfair to judge a man by his appearance, but you'll understand when you see him. There's something almost albino in his looks, with his pale eyes and white lashes.' She touched her lips, wondering if she should go further. 'And he's had a set of ivory teeth made by one of the convicts from the tusk of some animal and they're so white! You've never seen whiter teeth. Absolutely perfect, without a single blemish. They're dazzling! And to make it worse, though he's no sense of humour whatsoever, he smiles all the time!'

Lady Franklin leant back in her chair, shaking with such infectious laughter that everyone else started laughing too, in spite of the malice in her description.

'Oh dear.' She caught her breath at last. 'Whatever you do, please don't repeat a word I've said. But there's one thing I can say for certain: I'd hate to be married to the man.'

Lionel made a mental note that O'Hara Booth was a name to remember. He turned to his sister. 'By the way, I saw Miss Gissing this morning.'

'Jacobina Gissing!' cried Lady Franklin, overhearing the name. 'I love that woman. Such a shame we can never invite her here.'

'Why not?' Sarah asked instinctively.

'Because,' said Mr Sloley with one of his smiles, 'Miss Gissing happens to have been a convict. Convicts are persona non grata in government domain.'

'I cannot imagine that her crime was very serious,' Sarah ventured. She was unprepared for Lady Franklin's startling reply.

'That depends whether you consider attempted murder a serious business.'

'Murder!'

'The very nicest type of murder,' Lady Franklin explained. 'In France they would call it a crime of passion; they say her husband left Jacobina for another woman, so she shot him. She missed his heart, but he was no longer the man the other woman had bargained for. At times I can't help wondering if Miss Gissing was such a bad shot after all!'

'My dear,' protested the Governor. 'You are too indiscreet. And you don't know the real truth of the story. All that is hearsay, and probably an outrageous slander on the poor soul.'

'Of course, my dear,' she said submissively. 'And I wouldn't be surprised if the real story isn't deadly dull. Anyhow, I won't hear a word against Miss Gissing. She's a marvellous organiser and I want to enlist her help to sort out these single women on their arrival. She understands them better than anyone.'

'That's certainly true,' Lionel agreed. 'She was dreadfully upset over that poor girl who drowned last night.' As this was news to most of the people present, he started to describe the tragedy. Even as he did so, he *knew* with a sudden, sickening clarity that the dead girl was Matilda's friend.

Matilda stopped eating and stared at him appalled, sensing the truth as well.

'Do you know her name?' she whispered.

'Baker,' answered the Governor. 'Yes, I'm sure that was it. Harriet Baker.'

Matilda gripped the tablecloth, her eyes wide with shock. Then she turned towards Roly, but he was too late to catch her as she slid to the floor.

In the confusion that followed, Sally ran from the room, clasping her hand to her mouth.

The Governor rose as Matilda began to recover consciousness and turned to Gussie. 'I think it would be helpful if we reversed the usual procedure and let the ladies stay here while we take our cigars in the drawing-room. Is that agreeable?'

'Excellent,' said his wife. 'We can look after the poor

231

dear far better if you all go away and leave us alone.'

In the drawing-room Gussie started to apologise, but the Governor stopped him quickly.

'On the contrary, Mr Stowe, it was my fault for blurting out the girl's name like that, though of course I had no idea that your daughter-in-law knew her.'

'She was a close friend,' Roly explained, 'and I know she was worried about her. In fact, Sir John, I should like to ask you a favour. I know it would distress my wife if the girl was buried in a pauper's grave, and I should like to avoid that at any cost to myself.'

Gussie looked startled by his son's concern, but pleased nevertheless. That was the redeeming factor: Roly's constant capacity to astound.

'Good,' said the Governor. 'I'll order a church service and burial, and keep you informed. And now let us turn to the vital subject which no one has yet referred to. Eh, Mr Stowe?'

'What is that?' Gussie asked nervously, holding on to the back of the chair for support.

'Your future! I've been waiting for you to outline your plans.'

'I thought that should wait until we were alone, Your Excellency.'

'No time like the present, Stowe. After all, we're among friends and can do with their advice. Please sit down, won't you? What do you have in mind?'

Yet again, the unfortunate Gussie was caught on the wrong foot. He had been expecting the Governor to come forward with a specific suggestion.

'I was under the impression,' he admitted, 'from what my cousin told me, that we would receive a grant of land, with your welcome advice on how best to use it.'

The Governor regarded him quizzically. 'Your cousin told you that? My God, they have no idea in London of what goes on.'

'I'm afraid I don't understand,' said Gussie anxiously. 'You mean that is not the case?'

'No, it isn't,' said Mr Sloley. 'Free grants were abolished some time back, as the Secretary of State for the Colonies should know . . .'

'But I am empowered to sell you the best government land,' Sir John interrupted more sympathetically, 'for as little as five pounds an acre. You are perfectly correct in thinking we need free settlers with a sense of responsibility like yourself and your family. At the same time, there's no point in playing the gentleman farmer here. So what do you have in mind, Stowe? Oxen, cultivation, horses? Our crops are promising well.'

Gussie wilted under this inquisition, longing for the ladies to join them, but he did his best to rally. 'I was hoping for the benefit of your valuable experience, so I thought it would be premature to fix my mind in advance. I have my sheep, of course, though I fear . . .'

'Do you mean,' Roly's voice broke in like the rasping of a saw, 'that you've brought us to this wilderness with nothing in mind? Can't you do anything right?'

Acutely embarrassed at being spoken to in such a way in public, and aghast at Roly's reference to a 'wilderness' in front of the Governor, Gussie turned on his son angrily. 'There was no point in making plans on paper. We had to see the lie of the land.'

'Then we might as well give up,' said Roly in disgust. 'I think I'll go to New South Wales and look for gold.'

'Oh, *do*!' Gussie shouted, exasperated beyond endurance. 'I wish to God you would.'

At this moment the ladies entered the room and were startled by the warmth of their reception. Matilda had recovered and Sally had returned. Lady Franklin noticed the expression on her husband's face and looked forward to hearing all the details when they were alone. Sarah was shocked to see Gussie was on the verge of breaking down, and hurried to him. She was disturbed to find that he was shaking uncontrollably.

Like the argument which helps cement a friendship, the dinner party at Government House was not as disastrous as everybody feared.

'At least it was different,' said Lady Franklin when the last guest had gone. 'That poor country girl fainting, and the other, silent one running into the garden to be sick.'

'And the son turning on Stowe,' added the Governor. 'If I'd spoken like that to my father he'd have killed me.'

'Even so,' his wife declared, 'I do like them.'

'Yes,' her husband agreed. 'I feel I was rather hard on poor old Stowe. I'll ask him to call on me alone, which is plainly what he wanted, and get this question of their land sorted out. Though I wish the settlers wouldn't use me as a wet nurse. How can they cross the world without a definite objective in mind?'

There was a bitter frost a few nights later, but the day of Harriet's funeral was radiant. The service was to be held in St Andrews, a simple stone Presbyterian church, the oldest in Van Diemen's Land.

The Stowes waited outside to welcome the Governor and his wife. Matilda found herself the centre of attention.

'She was so proud of you, Matilda,' said Sarah. 'So proud to be your friend.'

Even Roly squeezed her hand reassuringly, and she looked up, flushing with pleasure. Since their arrival she had waited up for him every night, aching to see him return safely, yet dreading the manic energy which was likely to burst into violence unless she skilfully diverted it; the recriminations, and the filthy outpouring of bile that tore him and her apart; the threats of suicide which poured out incoherently. In her naivety, the girl had looked forward to a new life with Roly, but now she realised that the new life was a sham – Roly had brought his discontent with him. If hearts can be broken, hers came close to cracking then. Yet the nights' outbursts seemed so insignificant in the sunlight; especially now, as he looked down at her so protectively. Suddenly, she began to weep.

'For God's sake,' Roly whispered crossly, reverting to his usual temper, 'stop making a display of yourself.'

'No,' she told him tearfully. 'Don't you see . . . it's so kind of them.'

People were coming round the corner, an awkward procession of men and women dressed as soberly as possible, approaching the church uneasily. They were the people who had known Harriet on board ship: Miss Gissing in a large black bonnet that dwarfed her tiny figure; several of the convict women who had been declared 'freed' and clutched the arms of their new-found 'relatives'. They had come to pay last respects to a girl who had been less fortunate. But the greater part of the company consisted of the orlop girls. Even those who had taunted Harriet and jeered about her bridal dress while she was alive knew remorse now that she was out of reach.

After the service they filed out of the church, shielding their eyes against the sudden sunlight, and there were cries of interest as they noticed a dark shape on the shimmering water below – the *Countess of Bath*, ready for the homeward-bound voyage the following day. Few noticed Sally slipping away towards the gravestones. When Sarah found her there, her first reaction was one of dismay – how could she clean up the grave? Then her maternal instinct brushed such considerations aside as the girl started retching again, gasping as she leaned on the tombstone. 'Oh, my poor darling,' she said softly, putting an arm around her daughter to comfort her. 'You shouldn't have come here today. It was too distressing for you.' The girl looked terrible, her skin lack-lustre, spots of vomit staining her white shawl.

Sally was unable to answer, or disinclined to do so, but Sarah heard a voice behind her and was startled to see Lady Franklin.

'You dear, dear woman,' whispered Lady Franklin as they walked a few yards away. 'Didn't you realise? I guessed the other evening.' Sarah shook her head, confused, and Lady Franklin gave a knowing little smile. 'My dear, don't look so worried! It's wonderful news – you're going to be a grandmother. Why on earth didn't you tell me the girl was married? Who is he, and what's he like? You must tell me all about him!' Lady Franklin laughed aloud and hugged her warmly.

When Sarah broke the news in the privacy of their bedroom, Gussie leant forward as if a weight had been laid on his shoulders. Sarah's immediate reaction had been appalled but practical – What are we going to *do*? What are we going to *say*? – but Gussie remained bowed down by their disgrace.

'Why does God always punish the virtuous?' he demanded. 'What have we done to deserve this endless catalogue of disaster? Our beautiful home – *lost* – and now our reputation – or the shreds that are left. To think I condemned that poor child Matilda when I thought she was with child. Even if she had been, Roly intended to do the decent thing.'

'Tim would have married Sally.'

'To seduce an innocent child and then abandon her . . .'

'Hardly that!' exclaimed Sarah impatiently. 'I'm sure his intentions were honourable. Tragically, he was never able to fulfil them.'

'I'm *glad*,' snapped Gussie, his voice like the crack of a whip. 'I'm glad the seducer drowned.'

'What a terrible thing to say! Apart from anything else, it's left Sally without a husband.'

Gussie did not need reminding. 'At least we're spared the disgrace at home, among our friends.'

'It will be quite bad enough here,' Sarah replied sternly, on the verge of losing her self-control. 'Now we've talked long enough about ourselves. We must think of Sally.'

'How is she?' Gussie asked indifferently.

'Stunned.'

'Did she suspect?'

'No.'

'And you're certain you haven't jumped to the wrong conclusion?' He clung to a last glimmering of hope.

'There's no mistake. She simply did not understand. I

blame myself for not telling her more about the seasons of a woman. I could hardly believe it myself at first, it's happened so quickly. But I've checked the dates.'

'And what did you say to Lady Franklin? Did you confess that Sally is without a husband?'

'I didn't know what to say. I expect she knows the truth.'

'Everyone will know soon enough.'

'Unless we can find some man to marry her immediately.'

'Sarah!' Gussie was genuinely shocked. 'What a wicked suggestion. Anyhow,' he continued bitterly, 'no decent man would marry a girl who's carrying another man's bastard. No, I have a better idea than that.'

It was well after midnight when Gussie returned to the hotel, exhausted but triumphant. 'Here.' He handed Sarah an official-looking envelope. 'It's a certificate testifying to the marriage of Sally Stowe and Timothy Blake, performed on the *Countess of Bath* several weeks ago. It bears Peppiatt's signature. I have witnessed it, and so must you.'

Sarah looked up with wonder, searching his face for further information.

'Why did Peppiatt agree?' she asked timidly.

'He's a decent man at heart. I was sure he felt badly over the doctor's death so I told him the plain, unpalatable truth. As a man of honour he saw this was the only course we could take.'

'I bless him,' said Sarah fervently.

'It means that the wretched infant will bear a father's name, and we must be thankful for that at least.' Gussie started to sob silently. Sarah clasped him to her.

'You've done a noble thing,' she said. 'How wise of you to think of it. And how good of Captain Peppiatt.'

'In two hours' time,' he said, trying to compose himself, 'he'll be at sea and no one will be able to question him. With any luck there's a possibility that no one will find out, as long as you can stop Lady Franklin from indulging in gossip. I find that woman too perspicacious for my liking.'

'Shall you tell Sally now? It will come as such a comfort.'

He recoiled. 'I couldn't bear to see her.'

'Very well.'

Sarah slipped into her dressing-gown, took a lighted candle and knocked on Sally's door further up the corridor. As she expected, her daughter was awake. She listened to the news without expression and without comment. Sarah asked her anxiously: 'You are pleased, aren't you? It makes everything so much easier, doesn't it?'

'Doesn't it?' Sally echoed sarcastically.

'Very well, my darling, I'll leave you to sleep. You can do so more easily now.' She kissed her listless daughter on the forehead and softly left the room.

Now that Sally no longer needed to maintain the pretence of a hard indifference she clasped the bolster for comfort, remembering every detail of that appalling day on board ship. She could never share her secret with anyone.

Tim had been such a boy that afternoon when she led him into Matilda's cabin, with the excitement of the storm raging outside. When she had undressed impulsively in front of him, he had not been able to restrain himself, and had thrown off his clothes as well.

'Stop . . . oh, God! . . . no, please stop.' Her protests were ignored in Tim's need to satisfy himself. Plunging in a spurt of energy, he achieved the release he craved and rolled over, gasping. She was sobbing on the pillow beside him, the sound penetrating the creaking, cracking noises in the cabin as the ship bucked and tossed in the wild sea.

'Did I hurt you?' he asked anxiously.

A muffled reply told him that he had and Sally sensed that he was cursing himself for taking her virginity against her will.

'Why did you?' she said. 'Now it can never be the same between us again.'

'But I thought you wanted it?'

'Not like that. How could you believe such a thing?

238

Does every man think that, after he has had his way? Do you think I wanted to . . .'

Then had come the knock on the cabin door.

'Tim.' Matilda had to pitch her voice against the whistling wind. 'I'm sorry, but I had to let you know. They're looking for you everywhere. It's Mrs Flanagan.'

'Oh, God!' Tim groaned, shocked to realise he had forgotten his patient. Dressing in seconds, he had scrambled below, arriving too late to save the child or the mother whose moans were a hideous mockery of the earlier, ecstatic pain and pleasure. He left the sick-bay appalled and desperate for air. Sally had never seen him again.

— 16 —

Strangers in a strange land

After the excitement of the Stowes' arrival in Hobart Town their fortunes went into reverse, as fortunes tend to do. The unfamiliarity of everything new, without the solace of the old civilisation, the physical discomfort compared to the luxury of Raxleigh House, were bad enough, but the anguish caused by Sally's pregnancy was harder to endure.

The first shock of her condition was followed by the second: in spite of the bluff of the wedding certificate, it seemed that people *knew*. Though Lady Franklin remained a devoted friend, she had guessed the truth, and of course she gossiped, exactly as Gussie had feared. In such a tight community suspicion spread like bushfire and, though Sarah accepted curiosity as inevitable in Hobart Town, where new arrivals were bound to be the object of attention, she was dismayed to discover what a narrow-minded lot the Hobartians were. Considering that the population was largely composed of people who had been rejected by 'polite society' she had expected tolerance, but met the opposite. The citizens seized on any laxity in their so-called 'betters', and spread the gleeful word that the Stowes had no greater claim to morality than themselves.

Meanwhile, to make things worse, Sally expressed no regret, displayed no shame. Just as a child grows up to discover that his parent is fallible, Sarah realised with a sadness which was never to leave her that she

240

loved her daughter still but no longer liked her.

Sarah would have welcomed sympathy from the other members of her family, but only Matilda offered it. Lionel was too busy making notes for the despatches which had yet to be despatched; Roly confirmed her belief that he was the laziest young man in the world by emerging at noon from his hotel bedroom to complain that he needed a 'livener'. At night he explored the taverns of the capital with Flanagan, who at least had a reason for drowning his sorrow; Roly's wife was left on her own. She was company for Sarah, but Sarah felt, nevertheless, that it was hard on Matilda, who needed friends of her own age.

Gussie caused her the greatest anxiety. All his life he had idealised his 'little girl', refusing to recognise Sally's selfishness. Until now he had yielded happily to the blackmail of her petulance, but there was no longer any contact between them. If this was retribution, Gussie was paying heavily for having spoilt the girl, but that was no consolation for Sarah. She was puzzled by the swiftness of the physical change in him. The tall man who had been so upright walked with a shuffle now, depending on his stout walking stick to keep his balance, a bent figure with eyes cast down to avoid the glances of those around him. His eyesight seemed to be deteriorating rapidly too. Was it possible, Sarah wondered miserably, that the shock of Sally's pregnancy could have taken such an immediate toll?

She looked forward to her visits to Government House as a welcome distraction, in spite of Lady Franklin's propensity to slander. Apart from realising that the Franklins' goodwill was vital to their future, she relaxed in the peaceful atmosphere; the gleaming silver and glass, the white-gloved servants, the piles of English books and papers, the bowls of flowers which reminded her so wistfully of home. And Lady Franklin was not the fool she seemed.

Sarah was anxious to learn as much about her new country as possible, and Lady Franklin bubbled over with anecdotes and odd scraps of information.

'The natives had no idea that people existed outside their island. When one of Napoleon's sailors took off a pair of fur gloves a native female fainted. She thought they were his skin!'

Lady Franklin told Sarah of the aborigines' attacks on the settlers and the line of thousands of soldiers and civilians which had stretched 120 miles in an attempt to corner the blacks in the Tasman Peninsula as they swept forward, but somehow the natives had faded into the landscape and only one old man and a boy were captured. She spoke of the terrible Risdon Massacre when some harmless aborigines were fired on unnecessarily, triggering fear and hostility which had never abated.

A keen explorer, like her husband, Lady Franklin had seen New Zealand and crossed Van Diemen's Land to visit the first penal settlement of Macquarie Harbour on the west coast, long since abandoned because of the difficulty of access, even by boat. 'It was so wild that the guards hardly bothered to stop the convicts from escaping, for they knew they wouldn't survive. A couple called Cox and Pearce managed to dodge the soldiers sent after them, but soon they were overcome with hunger and waited for the other to fall asleep. Finally Cox gave way, and Pearce killed him with an axe. He lived on the remains of his friend for several days, until he was so overwhelmed with horror that he made his way back to Macquarie and gave himself up.'

'You don't mean it!' Sarah exclaimed, absorbed but aghast.

'Indeed I do,' Lady Franklin replied with obvious relish. 'You have no idea what goes on over here.' She liked to astound her new companion. She spoke of the great rain forests which had been impenetrable until the convicts built canoes out of Huon pine; the mutton birds which flew in from Alaska in the spring; the striped tiger, six feet long, with the face of a dog; and the cuddly wombat and kangaroo, previously unknown to the white man.

Sarah began to comprehend the peculiarities of Van Diemen's Land and the resentment towards the settlers which stemmed partly from the attitude of John Franklin's predecessor, Sir George Arthur. 'He saw it as his duty to govern this place like a prison, resisting any attempts to bring the settlers and the convicts together. His sympathies lay with the criminals, whom he hoped to reform, and he had no time for the settlers. He discouraged emigration, so while thousands of convicts are still sent here the only emigrants who've arrived this year came with you on the *Countess of Bath*. Arthur made things very difficult for John. Now they've ended transportation to New South Wales he says we're the last "refuse" of the British Empire – the final dustbin for the criminal classes!'

While Sarah enjoyed her tête-à-têtes with Lady Franklin, her brother had talks of a more official nature with Sir John, though these were strictly 'off the record'. Hovering throughout was the enigmatic figure of Mr Sloley. If he had a Christian name, no one used it.

Lady Franklin spoke of him with mixed feelings, referring to the time when she was lost on the west coast and feared attack by her convict guards. They defended her party instead, receiving their freedom afterwards.

'I suppose I owe my life to their initiative in getting us back safely,' she admitted. 'Sloley insists that the convicts are basically good people who have met with bad luck, and though I detest the liberals back home who sympathise with the criminal and forget the victim I suppose I have to concede some truth in Sloley's point of view.' She gave a slight frown. 'Once I took Sloley's word as gospel. Now I'm not so sure. Nothing is what it seems over here – that's something you'll find out for yourself. I know your family can make a fine life here if they're prepared to work at it, but you must accept things as they are, not as they ought to be.'

Lionel was amused by the Governor's obvious embarrassment in dealing with his secretary.

'You wish me to stay, Your Excellency?' It was hard to tell if this was a question or a statement.

'Well, no,' said Sir John unhappily. 'I feel it might be best if I assume the entire responsibility for my interview.'

'Of course, Your Excellency,' said Mr Sloley, giving a sinuous bow in Lionel's direction. 'As you please.'

'An interesting man,' Sir John assured his visitor when the door was shut. 'Be sure you never underrate him. Sloley has friends at court – not literally, but close enough. He sends back secret reports to people in high places. They tend to be indiscreet, as I'm beginning to find out.' The Governor looked uneasy, uncertain how much he should say. 'I tell you this in confidence,' he ventured, 'but letters I have just received from home suggest that he has criticised the penal system in a report which has been taken up by an English newspaper. This places me in a difficult position: either his views are taken to be my own, which they are not, or I provoke a controversy by denying them. I've had trouble like this before, with my previous secretary, but at least he was open about it. Sloley is sly. And the irony of it is that I rather agree with him in principle, but I have to govern this awkward island, while Sloley – whom I trusted implicitly – goes behind my back.

'He reflects the new ideas back home. The Reform Act has created a growing opposition to punishment by transportation. People fail to realise that Van Diemen's Land is less than fifty years old, and it would be absurd to import liberal laws into a community totally unfitted to adopt them. Do you realise that more convicts have been sent out here than all the thousands transported to New South Wales since 1788? They must give us time to breathe. We are an infant society.'

'But you would like to see an end to transportation yourself?'

'Of course. Who wouldn't?' The Governor sighed. 'When the time is right. My hope is to leave this island as a colony in its own right, rather than an echo of standards set at home. Meanwhile, I'm caught in the middle, trying to appease the Colonial Office and the cauldron of personal animosities here. Something has got to be done quickly. As an old Navy man, I can feel the swell of resentment. I can recognise the smell of mutiny.'

'Mutiny!' Lionel exclaimed, experiencing the thrill of the journalist who has arrived at the right place at the right time. The Governor withdrew instantly, like a snail touched on its antennae.

'I did not mean that literally,' he declared with finality, 'and of course that's confidential.'

When Lionel left Government House, Mr Sloley insisted on walking him back to the Adelphi Hotel.

'I trust you had a fruitful talk with His Excellency,' he remarked casually.

'Most interesting,' Lionel assured him.

'Good. I'm glad of that. He has a difficult job and people do not always understand him. He needs others to speak on his behalf. I, too, send despatches home, to the Colonial Society in London. If it would help you, I should be delighted to invite you to dinner and offer you the benefit of my experience. As you will have gathered from our little talk at the auction, I find the present system intolerable. We cannot treat prisoners in our penal settlements as we do without fear of repercussion. Instead of investing in the future of this island, we are stoking a fire which could destroy us all.'

'Is the treatment in the settlements so cruel, Mr Sloley?'

'You have no conception, Mr Raxleigh. You will dine, so that I can supply you with the facts?'

'Thank you, Mr Sloley. I am sure your knowledge would prove invaluable. What would you say to Thursday next?'

Mr Sloley chuckled. 'I should say no, Mr Raxleigh. You must be the only man on the island who has forgotten that Thursday is the Queen's birthday. No doubt I shall have the pleasure of talking to you at the Governor's ball, and we can suggest an alternative time.'

Mr Sloley gave a formal bow and Lionel smiled when he looked back and saw him positively gliding on his way to Government House. 'What an odd man you are,' he thought. 'I wonder what fires are banked behind that cold façade?' He was uncertain how far he could trust the man, and whether he wished to become his confidant, for he had been impressed by Governor Franklin's honesty and regarded him as a decent man – not that decency counted for much in Van Diemen's Land.

'My God!' Roly exclaimed that evening over a dinner of greasy lamb stew. 'What a disgruntled lot they are! It's one of the few places where people actually scowl.'

Lionel agreed. 'And no one likes to take the responsibility for anything, so nothing gets done. Every chance I get to purchase land ends in frustration.' Since Gussie's decline, Lionel had tried to negotiate on his behalf.

'That happens back home as well,' Sarah pointed out gently, remembering Lady Franklin's advice – accept things as they are.

'But they're so rude,' said Sally. 'They don't bother to serve me in the shops. They simply stare at me as if *they* were superior, and I don't belong.'

'They do that to me,' said Matilda hastily. 'Yesterday I went to see the public buildings in Murray Street and lost my way. I found myself in a side street lined with little wattle cottages, and all the women came out and watched me as I went by. I felt so embarrassed, I'm sure I turned scarlet. They just looked and smoked their pipes and stood at their garden gates with their arms akimbo – I didn't dare to ask the way. I thought they'd spit at me! Mind you, I remember I felt much the same when I walked down Irsha Street in Appledore when I was a young maid. I suppose the women are quite nice, really.'

The laughter was cut off abruptly as Sally cried out: 'What did you all expect? None of this would be happening if we'd stayed at Raxleigh.' She burst into sobs and ran from the room. The other residents paused in the middle of mouthfuls and turned round to stare, but Roly stared back so fiercely that they turned away.

'Well,' he sighed, 'that's another nail in our coffin. I'm surprised she doesn't advertise her condition in the *Courier*.'

'That's enough,' Gussie told him sharply, and Sarah shook her head so sadly that Roly hesitated to go further. He had surprised everyone by his deeply puritanical reaction to his sister's condition.

'Well,' he continued lamely, 'she hasn't made it easy for the rest of us, has she? You should hear the comments made for my benefit. Frankly, I'm amazed that she's been invited to the ball. I think it's very brave of Lady Franklin.'

'Of course Sally's been invited,' said Sarah soothingly. She was unaware that this had been a close-run decision, only reached when Lady Franklin sought the advice of Mr Sloley, who assured her that it would cause even more talk if Sally Stowe was excluded.

On the morning of the Queen's birthday, the Stowes were summoned to the empty dining-room of the Adelphi. There Lionel read them his long-awaited despatch, which was to be carried by the captain of a clipper sailing with the afternoon tide.

'I'm not too sure of the title,' he began with sudden hesitancy. 'I think I'll leave that to the editor. For the time being, I've called it *Notes from a Forgotten Country*.' He started to read aloud:

'People over here describe this place as "The land that God forgot". And since my own arrival in Hobart Town a few weeks ago there have been occasions when I have wondered if people back home care about Van Diemen's Land or remember that such a country exists. A year ago I myself had only a vague idea of a far-away island on the other side of the world, but of all the outposts in the British Empire this must be the most extraordinary: the final refuge for those we have rejected from

247

English society. Yet it must be said that many of the thousands of convicts transported here in the last few years have been sent for reasons of colonisation rather than punishment, and it must be doubted whether their treatment will lead to the reform of either the hardened criminals or those who have been unlucky in life. They are treated the same. Reform should be the aim of transportation, and reform seems to have no place in Van Diemen's Land. The question must be asked: Has the time arrived to put an end to a system which future generations will condemn as barbaric? . . .'

Lionel flushed with pleasure when the family praised him. It did not occur to him that they were hugely prejudiced.

'Mr Delane should be delighted,' said Sarah affectionately.

'Well done,' said Roly. 'Wish I could write.'

'Excellent stuff,' said Gussie, genuinely impressed, for he was a man who could make a list but found it hard to compose a letter. 'That should shake them up at home.'

There was only one regret: the months that must pass before Lionel could see his name in print. But that was a moment worth waiting for.

Mr Sloley was correct in stating that everyone on the island was aware of the Queen's birthday on 24 May. The ball at Government House, the vexed question of who was invited and who was not, had been the only topic of conversation in Hobart for the last few weeks. The occasion meant more in this outpost of Empire than it ever could at home, giving the expatriate emigrants the chance to reaffirm their allegiance to the Crown. The free settlers were all too aware that patriotism meant little in a country where most of the population consisted of people on the wrong side of the law, and they prized their invitations to Government House as proof of their respectability.

Nine hundred and sixty gold-embossed cards had been sent throughout the island, but Lady Franklin did not realise that the symbol on the mantelpiece was all that mattered; attendance was secondary.

As she moved among the first arrivals in the Government House gardens, her eyes flickered anxiously in the hope that the trickle would soon turn into a flood. The Stowes arrived by carriage, slightly self-conscious in their finery, and she hurried across the lawn to welcome them.

'My dears,' she cried. 'I'm so thankful you came early.' She kissed her friend warmly on the cheek, genuinely glad to see Sarah's careworn, kindly face. 'We're off to a dreadful start. Mr Sloley's in disgrace and though I must have sent a thousand invitations it doesn't look as if half of the wretches are turning up.'

'The distances are so great,' Sarah reminded her. 'Surely it would take days to get here if the people lived in the north?'

'With the state of our roads,' Lady Franklin agreed, 'and those barbarous bushrangers who frighten everyone away. No, it's not surprising if the settlers want to stay and protect their estates.' She laughed as she repeated a daring phrase that she had used several times already: 'And Her Majesty might have chosen a birthday at a better time of year!'

'It's spring in England,' said Lionel, shivering.

'Well, it's autumn here, and decidedly chilly, so let me take you inside as my very special guests. First of all, let me look at you.' She stood back and clapped her hands in affected delight. 'My word,' she cried, 'Matilda, you'll be the belle of the ball!' Matilda blushed with pleasure, acutely aware of how conspicuous she looked in her crinoline.

'Van Diemen's Land has never seen anything like it,' Lady Franklin declared truthfully.

'And you, Mr Raxleigh.' She whirled on Lionel alarmingly. 'I hope you'll be kind to us in print. And Sally, how are you, my dear?' She frowned slightly as she studied the girl's figure and turned her eyes away: 'Roly,

I declare you're the handsomest man in Hobart. Augustus, I have a nice surprise for you, as you'll discover later. Now, everyone, come along for French champagne inside. Lovely fizz!'

Lady Franklin linked her arm in Sarah's and led her towards the closed verandah which ran the length of Government House. The less privileged guests watched resentfully as the Stowes followed.

'It's the prettiest table I've ever seen,' Sarah gasped as she saw the banks of flowers and the shimmering glass.

'I know,' agreed Lady Franklin. 'These are the top tables. You, Gussie and Lionel will sit with us here.' She pointed to a particularly fine spread of silver and cutlery.

'All the plate is our own, brought from home. The plate on the other tables belongs to the military mess, and the tables in the marquee make do with odds and ends. Now let me show you the *pièce de résistance*.' Guiding Sarah into the house through banks of flowers and greenery, she pointed to two massive gilt chandeliers which had not been there before.

'But they're magnificent. Where did you find them?'

'They were shipped out to the Scotch church but as they're far too expensive to run they were sold to the lampseller in town, who makes a fortune letting them out. They cost me twenty pounds. He wouldn't take a penny less, though he never charges so much when he hires them out for public balls. It's always the same with poor old Government House. Even the most scrupulous tradespeople don't bother to deny it. They're bleeding us to death.'

'I've never seen anything so fine. I long to see them lit.'

'And so you shall. It takes an age for the man to finish. He has to be so careful.' Lady Franklin called for a servant, and the great chandeliers were lowered by pulley. There were cries of admiration when they were pulled up again, ablaze with candles in their glass containers. Lady Franklin introduced Sarah to the clergyman sent out by Dr Arnold of Rugby to run the local college, and hurried off to welcome the latest arrivals.

Remembering Lady Franklin's startling allusion to Mr Sloley, Sarah turned conspiratorially to the genial Mr Gibbett. She suspected, rightly, that the reverend gentleman was a gossip, as most reverend gentlemen are.

'Why is poor Mr Sloley in disgrace?'

'Ah, you've heard, have you!' His small eyes beamed behind their glasses. 'Well, I expect everyone knows by now. Little is secret in Hobart Town. I assume you have not seen this week's *Courier*?'

'I thought it was published tomorrow?'

'So it is, in theory, but pages escape in advance. Poor Mr Sloley, as you call him – though poor Sir John might be more accurate – has been terribly imprudent. He wrote something to friends back home which the *Courier* has republished. As the editor owes his appointment to Mr Sloley's patronage you can imagine how he came by it. Anyway, "poor" Mr Sloley is accused of making inflammatory statements about the treatment of our criminals, coupled with libellous condemnation of the free population. You can imagine how popular he will be tonight.' The clergyman giggled. 'All this must be a terrible embarrassment for Lady Franklin. She has always championed Mr Sloley's lost causes. Now he has repaid her by comparing our laws to Scottish justice – "hang them first and try them afterwards".'

'Oh dear!' Sarah could not prevent herself from smiling.

'I know it's funny,' said the Reverend Gibbett with a schoolboy's glee, 'but it's unbecoming in the Governor's private secretary, who, *ex officio*, is presumed to echo Sir John's own sentiments.'

'And what will happen to him now, do you think?' asked Sarah.

Mr Gibbett looked serious. 'As a man of honour, he should resign. He has betrayed Sir John's trust by kowtowing to his influential friends back home. Whether Mr Sloley *will* resign is another matter. He's a born trouble-maker, I fear.'

'Yet he looks incapable of giving offence to anyone.'

By now the room was crowded, but Sarah could see the troublesome man in question making his way to a less congested corner. To her surprise he stopped in front of Sally, and Sarah realised with a shock that until then Sally had been sitting there alone. She hoped it had not been for long; what could the others have been thinking of?

In fact Sally had endured several minutes of humiliation. Roly and Matilda had gone in search of Gussie, assuming that Sally would have plenty of admirers to keep her company. They were woefully mistaken. The older women studied her censoriously, without looking at her directly, while several young officers eyed her with interest but dared not approach for fear of being compromised. Even those who knew about the young doctor's death and felt for her because of it could not be seen to condone her sin by talking to her.

Sally did her best to look unconcerned, furiously studying the picture closest to her while she was scrutinised herself, her chin tilted defiantly above the high collar of the white lace dress and the single string of pearls. She wondered if her virginal appearance aggravated her offence in the eyes of those who guessed her secret and studied her behind the safety of their fans.

'Miss Stowe?'

She looked up in surprise, not having heard Sloley approach.

'May I have the honour of joining you?' His voice sounded strangely forlorn. He coughed, raising a hand politely to his mouth. 'Miss Stowe, may I have the pleasure of your company? Lady Franklin has asked me to escort you in to supper.'

'I suppose so,' she replied unenthusiastically, for he was not a man who appealed to her, but her acceptance seemed to please him and he gave a sigh of relief.

'I appreciate that.'

She looked at him again, suspecting irony or pity, but she found neither and was suddenly ashamed of her lack of warmth. He, of all the men present, had approached her with respect and saved her further embarrassment.

'Then that is settled,' she said vivaciously. 'I'm dreadfully hot in here, Mr Sloley. Do you think we could have a stroll through the gardens to help me lose some of the colour in my cheeks?'

He offered her his arm. 'I should like that. I find it crowded here myself. Indeed, I find the present company as tiresome as I expect you do yourself. I must warn you that I am under a temporary cloud.'

Her indifference was replaced by curiosity. 'What sort of a cloud? I do hope you've done something awful which has upset everyone terribly!'

'Not too awful.' His smile was genuinely humorous. 'My crime is simply that I spoke my mind.' He paused on the gravel path to look at her intently in the fading light. 'This must be a strange place for someone so young and lively as yourself.'

Sally returned his gaze with a new awareness of the man. She often played a game in which she listed people under an initial; until now Sloley had been a definite D: dry, desiccated, dull. He must be dreadfully old, well over thirty, almost Dead, and there was something Dank about him too. But now there was something else – could it be Desperation?

'What's the matter?' she asked him suspiciously. 'What are you getting at, Mr Sloley?'

'I'm not getting *at* anything,' he replied with some asperity. 'I thought you of all people would understand why I welcome the chance to talk freely. There is a lack of neighbourly feeling in this island which can lead to extreme loneliness.'

'Yes,' she agreed, disliking the drift of their conversation. It was presumptuous on his part to hint at her innermost feelings, yet there was truth in what he said. 'I admit I do find it rather primitive over here.'

He turned to her with an extraordinary expression, so contorted it was almost Devilish. 'Would you consider returning to England, Miss Stowe, if I should be recalled by the government? I am, of course, aware of your unhappy predicament . . .' Sally tried to stop him, but the words poured out, brooking no interruption. 'I have admired you since our first meeting and would dearly like to make you happy. If you did me the honour of accepting my proposal we might return together. Your child could be born at home, and become our child. No one need ever know what happened on the *Countess of Bath*.' He stopped at last, his mouth still open, as she stared at him. The thought of marriage to Sloley was preposterous.

'Have you lost your senses?' she demanded. 'I scarcely know you.'

'I thought you might welcome such a solution . . .'

'Do not pity me, Mr Sloley. I warn you, do not presume so far.'

He was surprised, for the girl had spoken like a grown woman. 'If I have been tactless, spoken too rashly . . .'

'You have been impertinent, Mr Sloley, even to think of such an arrangement.'

He winced at the rejection, but answered with spirit: 'If you regard my concern for your happiness as impertinence, I must indeed apologise. I may be inexperienced in matters of the heart, but I am fully aware that people can be narrow-minded and cruel. I was offering you my protection. There is no cause to mock me for that.'

Again she was prompted to study him afresh. He was hardly the suitor of her imagination. She tried to imagine what it would be like to sleep with him. Was it conceivable that an ardent lover lay behind the dry exterior, that he would look completely different without his clothes? Would he be able to satisfy her? There was one way of finding out, though she was not certain if it was safe at such a stage in her pregnancy. It was hardly a question she could ask her mother; even Matilda would have been shocked.

'I spoke too hastily,' she said more graciously. 'You took me by surprise.'

'I blame myself for being clumsy . . .'

She interrupted him: 'Would you see me back to my

hotel, Mr Sloley? I have no heart for tonight's celebration.' It was perfectly true that she dreaded the shal-
low conversation during dinner, the ordeal of dances
afterwards.

'I shall be delighted,' he replied, taking this as a sign
that he had been forgiven. Far from taking offence at her
initial rejection, he admired the strength of will which
prompted it. Most girls would have accepted his offer
without another thought. It was plain that she was giving
it consideration. There is no deceiver like a self-deceiver
in love.

'I assume her ladyship is near at hand,' he said.

'Lady Franklin?' asked Sally, surprised.

'You will wish to make your excuses, some apology for
leaving so soon. A headache, perhaps?'

'No,' said Sally firmly, knowing that Lady Franklin
would insist on her staying. 'No, much better to leave
without upsetting anyone. I can send a letter tomorrow.'

'Entirely as you wish.' Sloley knew that Lady Franklin
would be offended, when she saw their empty places at
the second table, and he, at least, would have to hurry
back as quickly as possible. Their minds bent in different
directions, he helped collect her cloak and they walked
together through the gardens towards the Adelphi. After
the initial shock of her rejection, Sloley felt new confidence, and held her arm in a firm grasp which she
interpreted as an indication of his rising passion. Now
she was excited by his proximity, imagining his lean body
when he undressed. Was it true what the girls had claimed
about the size of noses, when they examined the crew of
the *Countess of Bath*? Sloley's nose was formidably aquiline.
So Sally asked him to escort her upstairs to her bedroom,
risking the censure of the usually languid clerk. She
handed the lighted candle to Sloley as she opened the
door and closed it quickly behind them. For a moment
he stood there disconcerted, before she moved forward
and pressed herself against him, asking him to remove
her cloak. He responded, surprised by the sudden change

255

in her attitude. But he stared as she hurried to the bed, threw the counterpane aside and started to undress.

'What are you doing?'

She scarcely heard him. The light was low and flickering, and she whispered, 'Hurry up!', standing there in her chemise, waiting for him to take the initiative. But he stayed where he was.

'What's the matter?' She was still unaware that she had mistaken his intentions. 'Don't you want me?'

'Of course I want you,' he whispered, 'but not like this, not here, as if you were a woman I'd picked off the street . . .'

'*Get out!*' she said, trembling with mortification.

'I think perhaps I should.' For once he was momentarily lost for words. 'My proposal was genuine. I did not intend to take advantage of you.'

She rushed at him, pushing him into the corridor, and slammed the door shut. After locking it from the inside she crept into the solace of the bed, biting her lip with anguish as she realised she had presumed too much.

Sarah made her excuses to the Reverend Gibbett and went in search of Gussie. She found him in the crowded arcade, conversing with several military men of his own age, and smiled in relief. She had no idea what they were talking about, but Gussie was plainly at ease and that was all that mattered. She hoped his new friends would prove helpful in his efforts to find land. The best had gone already, especially within easy reach of Hobart, but these officers must know the entire country and should be able to advise him. He was looking happier than he had done since the news of Sally's pregnancy; it is remarkable what a little happiness can do for the appearance. In recent days Gussie had been suffering from the 'clumsies', a word originally invented by Roly to laugh away his habit of dropping things when his hands were trembling after the night before, but now Sarah realised, sadly, how well it fitted Gussie. No sooner had he picked something up than he dropped it; if she handed him his stick he let it fall; glasses slipped through his fingers like melting butter. Tonight he was apparently sure-footed and sure-tongued. Suddenly he looked across as if he sensed her presence. Their eyes met and he beckoned her over, introducing his wife to his new friends with unconcealed pride.

In spite of her earlier fears, Lady Franklin's ball was proving a success. Sarah was particularly pleased when she caught a glimpse of Matilda, Roly leading her firmly by the hand. Guests made way for the massive width of the crinoline as they hurried through the hall, leaving a ripple of comment behind them. But it seemed good-natured, and Sarah smiled when she heard the echo of Roly's raucous laughter in the next room. How good, she thought, that they are making friends and settling in at last. There was no denying the sensation caused by the extravagant crinoline. Rarely had Matilda been so thrilled: her expression shone with transparent pleasure. People smiled back instinctively, reflecting her own good humour.

As Roly entertained a group with a scandalous account of their voyage on the *Countess of Bath*, Lady Franklin felt she had underrated Sarah's son and his unaffected wife. Nothing helps a party so much as laughter, and she paused impulsively to give Matilda a swift kiss on the cheek. 'You look so lovely in your Paris gown,' she whispered graciously, before moving on.

A silence fell, and Matilda reddened. Roly squeezed her hand affectionately: 'Quite the toast of the ball. Not bad for a Devon dumpling.' The others laughed, assuming this was a joke, and Matilda joined in, for she could tell that he was pleased.

Lady Franklin continued her progress, smiling, waving, stopping briefly to welcome her guests; when she spotted Augustus Stowe she darted towards him triumphantly. The champagne had improved his temper so greatly that he greeted his hostess with more warmth than he had ever shown before.

'I should like to congratulate you on an excellent occasion,' he said with a slight bow. 'Most enjoyable, indeed.'

'Thank you, Augustus. I hope to make it still more enjoyable with the surprise I mentioned earlier.'

'Surprise?'

'There's a lady I want you to escort into supper. She's the most wonderful character and knew you back in Devon. Anyhow, I know you're going to adore her.'

Ill-advised words. The moment Gussie set eyes on Lynda Wynette, he winced. If there was one quality he detested it was self-satisfaction, and it oozed from Miss Wynette like cream from a shop meringue. Her clothes advanced before her like a warning, a flounce of pleats and lace and neat little ruffles, all in an artificial shade of blue. Her hair, which was plainly a wig, rose to the occasion in a cluster of curls and ringlets. Her cheeks were heavily rouged, creating the effect of some gigantic doll, and her voice, when she spoke, had the squeal of a ventriloquist's dummy. In Gussie's eyes she was a monstrous artifice, and in spite of her insistence he had not the faintest recollection of having met her before.

'I envy your capacity, Raxleigh!' The words penetrated Lionel's abstraction, making him aware that time had passed without his being aware of it. A few minutes earlier he thought he had drunk himself sober. Now he was not so sure.

'What's that?' He turned to the man beside him, who was smiling as if they had enjoyed a conversation.

'You're drinking as if there's a hole in your glass!' The man was a stranger, but in Van Diemen's Land everyone either cut you dead or slapped you on the back.

'I think that's my business,' said Lionel. The man moved on, muttering to himself about stuck-up dickeytoffs who came from England and thought they owned the place as soon as they landed.

Lionel thanked the servant who arrived at that moment

with a tray and refilled his glass. 'I believe, sir, that dinner is about to be served.'

Lionel joined the crowd swelling into the covered arcade. It was insufferably hot, and he wiped his brow with a handkerchief as a red-coated band struck up a deafening military march. He was surprised to see his brother-in-law unhappily arm-in-arm with an over-dressed woman, while Sarah was escorted by the Reverend Gibbett not far behind.

There was a clattering and scraping of chairs. Lionel found himself among a group of settlers.

'I hope you'll be lucky in your servants once you settle down,' said his neighbour, a middle-aged woman determined to be agreeable. 'It's pot luck, but we've been frightfully lucky with ours. They're almost part of the family.'

'You mean they eat with you?' asked Lionel.

'Hardly that!' She looked to her husband for support.

'They are servants and know their place,' he explained, leaning across. 'Anyway, it's against the law to mingle with 'em and they'd hate it if we did.'

'So when you say they're part of the family,' Lionel persisted, 'you mean the relationship is that of slave and master?'

'Servant, yes, and they're glad of it.'

'And dare to answer back?'

The farmer sensed Lionel's antagonism. 'I don't know if you're trying to be offensive, but you're new here. Of course they don't answer back. They'd be whipped if they did.'

'For their own good, I suppose.' Lionel tried to smile sarcastically, but it was more of a grimace. He could feel the anger rising inside him. 'A crack of the whip and everyone's happy.'

'Come on,' said the farmer to his wife. 'We'll find somewhere to sit where the company is more polite.' Another couple followed them, to the unconcealed dismay of Lady Franklin.

Slightly ashamed of his outburst, Lionel tried to catch

his sister's eye, but Sarah was looking at Gussie, who was visibly distressed by the chatter pouring from Lynda Wynette. She had taken trouble over her appearance, but Gussie was so close that he could see the jaded skin beneath the rouged cheeks, the folds in the jowls, and the wrinkles not quite concealed by the frills adorning her turkey's neck. None of this would have been offensive in a woman who admitted her age, but he found it odious in someone as skittish as Lynda Wynette. Even so, he could have forgiven it if she had not insisted on their close acquaintanceship with an archness which implied they had been close friends.

'I *know* you remember me, Mr Stowe,' she declared, 'so there's no point in pretending otherwise. Bideford?' she added mischievously.

'Yes, I lived near Bideford. But I regret you have the advantage over me. If we met there I cannot remember it.'

'You silly man. All your secrets are safe with me. I used to be Lynda Lashwood. Does that jog your memory?'

He shook his head.

'And you told me you lived in a lovely home which overlooked the river. It was called Raxleigh House . . .'

'Everyone in the district knew that.'

'I have always wondered how you could bring yourself to leave such an idyllic spot. Of course I've heard about . . .' she looked at him pityingly, 'the circumstances of your departure, and you have my sympathy. Life can be very hard, as I know from my own experience, but your family skeletons are safe with me. I have heard of your daughter's pregnancy . . .'

'Kindly lower your voice!' he ordered in a furious whisper which would have alarmed a lesser woman than Lynda Wynette. 'That is not a word to be used in public.'

'Of course,' she agreed, unruffled. 'You will be pleased to hear my good news.'

Gussie remained silent, so she continued: 'I have just received a letter from home, brought out on the *Cressy*, and my sister tells me that Lord Cleveland lives at

Raxleigh now – either Lord Cleveland or his son, I'm not sure. I thought you'd be pleased to hear it's a happy place these days. It must be some consolation to know that your old home is in such capable hands, but what I still want to know, Augustus, is how you could bear to sell it?'

She interrupted the torrent to thrust a large portion of lobster into her mouth, and then made the mistake of wagging her finger in front of his face. The offending hand was draped in a white lace mitten to hide the large brown liver spots, but to Gussie it was a flag provoking him beyond endurance. Pushing back his chair, he addressed the people near him. 'I wish you to know that I have never set eyes on this lady. She presumes an acquaintance that I wish to dispel at once and for ever . . .'

Lynda Wynette was taken aback, but cried out merrily: 'I don't know what's the matter with the man. We're the closest of friends, whatever he says.'

Gussie stared at her, realising how absurd he must appear. He tried to speak but lost the thread of what he intended to say; desperately he turned towards Sarah, who was looking at him imploringly, willing him to sit down. Lady Franklin sat tight-lipped, observing every nuance of the scene.

'My dearest Gussie,' Sarah said, summoning a smile from some reserve inside her. 'You know what our memories are like. We have difficulty remembering the names of our children! I'm sure we must have met this lady somewhere. So all's forgiven.'

'Hear, hear,' cried Lady Franklin, clapping her hands, and the others laughed dutifully as if Sarah had made a witty remark. The band struck up another deafening march. Gussie rose from his chair, stared at Lynda Wynette as if he was going to hit her, mumbled his excuses, and disappeared. A few moments later, Sarah caught up with him hurrying through the illuminated gardens, a bent, limping figure with tears streaming down his cheeks. He clutched her and they stood motionless for

261

several seconds. Then she ran to collect her cloak and led him slowly back to their hotel.

Matilda burst into their bedroom several hours later. Sarah whispered angrily that Gussie was asleep at last and should not be woken, but in the faint light of the breaking dawn her daughter-in-law was plainly distraught.

'Have you seen Roly?'

'No, of course not. What's happened to him?'

'He went mad, he did, for no reason at all, except I said we might be happy here.' Matilda burst into strangled sobs. 'I was so happy, and the ball was such fun. I said it was good to see him settling down and he just went mad. He threw me on the floor and put his hands around my neck until people pulled him off. And he tore my dress . . .' She could not continue. Sarah saw that the crinoline was torn and dirty.

'Oh, my dear, I am sorry,' she said softly. 'You're not hurt?' She slipped out of bed to take the girl in her arms.

Matilda reassured her, but she sounded heartbroken. 'I don't know how long I can carry on like this. What could these people have thought? And Lady Franklin looked so angry . . .'

'They don't matter,' Sarah insisted. 'If you're all right and no harm has come to Roly, that's all that matters.'

She meant to comfort, but she realised how damaging the incident could be to their future in Van Diemen's Land. 'Settling down' was just the phrase to provoke Roly, who had obviously indulged in one of his tantrums.

Next morning, Sarah received a letter from Government House.

Dear Mrs Stowe,

Never in all my life have I been so mortified as I was by your husband last night. Not only did he upset one of my dearest friends, but he did so in public, mortifying me and mine, and left the table without a word of explanation. I can understand that you felt it your duty to follow him, but you did not consider it necessary to bid me goodbye. As your daughter, for reasons of her own, retired before the dinner had begun, three vacant seats thus spoiled the appearance I had striven for throughout the day. Your brother insulted four of my guests who were obliged to seek another table. I did not expect such rudeness from a gentleman of *The Times*. As for your son, I shall make no comment on his shocking conduct, for I assume he was under the influence of alcohol and did not know what he was doing. In the circumstances I feel it would be better if you refrained from calling at Government House for the time being. My husband shares my distress in the implicit insult to Her Majesty in such behaviour on an occasion which means a great deal to people over here. In due course I should be grateful if you would return the various books I lent you.

Jane Franklin

— 17 —

The finding of Swansdowne

Two days after the ball the Stowes decided it was time to leave the Adelphi.

A ray of comfort was offered by Mr Sloley, who heard of their departure as soon as they thought of it themselves. He came to pay his respects, leaving a confidential letter for Sally assuring her of his devotion should she ever need him. Perhaps it was that glimmer of hope, or his own disgrace, which made him appear in a giddy mood.

'Frankly, I find myself in an impossible position,' he confided to Lionel. 'Officially I am attached to Sir John, but in my unofficial capacity as emissary of the societies back home I have my duty to myself. I am in a position to condemn the whole system of penal discipline, but of course that would enrage everyone here. The people are blinded by habit; Sir John is not a bad man, but he is weak and accepts the status quo, and that is just as dangerous.'

'I begin to suspect that you are a champion of humanity.'

'All of us are human.'

When Sarah entered the hotel drawing-room, he bowed politely and cheered her considerably with his verdict on Miss Wynette. 'A truly dreadful woman. I have every sympathy with your husband. She's been pursuing me for weeks. Her ladyship has some very odd friends, but of course Miss Wynette agrees with every word she says.'

Economy was the main reason for leaving the Adelphi. Far from being cheaper than home, the cost of shipment to Van Diemen's Land made most things more expensive. Worst of all, it was becoming clear that the purchase of land was fraught with obstacles of every kind, and when the Adelphi announced an increase in charges to coincide with the arrival of two passenger ships from New South Wales Gussie and Lionel agreed it was time to move into a temporary home while they sorted out the future. It would be a relief to be on their own in any case.

The winter had closed in and the side streets were ankle-deep in mud. People were apt to fall headlong unless they trod cautiously. It rained steadily, and the prospect of a log fire in their own parlour became increasingly attractive to the Stowes.

Lionel and Roly set off optimistically, expecting to find a simple cottage on the verge of the countryside, away from the alien town but still within reach of the shops. The countryside proved no problem. It was all around them: when the Hobartians needed firewood they simply axed the gum trees, which had to be felled anyway as the town boundaries advanced. The country cottage, however, was an arcadian dream. They tramped through the mud in their leather boots and London-made coats, the target for stares of suspicion and muttered sneers, looking at huts which were little more than shacks. At dusk they returned to the hotel tired and disconsolate.

'You'll have to find something,' Sarah pointed out. 'The hotel wants our rooms by the end of the week.'

So they hired a 'cottage' with two apartments for a rent of twenty-five shillings a week. 'Apartment' turned out to be a fulsome name for a room, and it was all the space they had – two rooms and an outhouse, no bigger than a pigsty, where Dick Stanton lived and slept. Nor were the two rooms luxurious. They had no proper floor, and the earth was damp due to the rain which fell through the gum tree shingles that pretended to serve as a roof. Each room boasted a window, but the glass was glazed and hard to see through. There was a fireplace in the room shared by the three women and a small front door.

'It can't have cost twenty-five shillings to *build*!' Sally exclaimed with disgust when she saw the hut for the first time. It was their lowest moment.

Their anxiety to find a proper site to settle on became an obsession. There were times when Lionel wondered whether the officials were being deliberately obstructive on the instructions of the Governor himself, but he suspected the delays were simply due to incompetence, which was just as discouraging. 'I thought you wanted free men to settle here!' he cried when he was told that a likely plot of land was being held for the government. The man behind the desk merely gave an enigmatic smile and said nothing.

The only brightness in this overcast period was the cheerfulness of the convict Stanton. The change in him was as marked as that in Gussie, except that Dick Stanton had recovered the zest of youth while Gussie was moving rapidly into old age.

It was hardly surprising that Dick was happy after the prison-cage on the voyage, for he was a man who welcomed activity and the chance to stretch himself. He was pleased to be able to help his benefactors, as he regarded Lionel Raxleigh and the Stowes, collecting their furniture from the stores – chairs, tables, mattresses and tarpaulins – arranging for a cart to bring them to the hut a mile away; even carrying some of their smaller possessions on his back.

Sarah had developed a habit of looking into the distance as if she was scanning some vague horizon, but she felt at ease with the convict and watched him with pleasure as he performed his duties. There were times when she ached to embrace him as a true member of the family, but she knew she had to suppress the instinct. The reaction to Sally's pregnancy had confirmed the necessity of keeping Dick's illegitimacy her life-long secret.

Without being servile, Dick knew his place – that of an assigned servant. He nodded respectfully when Sarah sent him on errands as she and Matilda struggled to make some sort of a home in these abject surroundings. They worked him hard. No sooner did he return with provisions than he was sent off again for china, and then someone remembered some forgotten thing which they 'could not live without'.

He remained good-humoured, which meant as much as all his repairs to the roof and floor, and it could be said that all the family loved him in their different ways.

Increasingly dismayed by the provincialism of Hobart Town, Lionel found relief in the young man's company, resting a hand on his shoulder as he outlined their future and promised that the convict would receive his pardon.

'He dotes on Dick as if he were his son,' Roly complained to Matilda, who turned away with a smile, recognising the twinge of jealousy, for Roly doted on Dick like a favourite brother. Ever since the night when Dick had thrown himself overboard Roly had offered the convict his friendship. Now that they were on land the two were inseparable. The faults which exasperated everyone else in Roly – his selfishness, his tantrums, his surrender when life went wrong – did not exist as far as Dick was concerned. He could see no wrong in Roly, and this had an astonishing effect on his hero. Anxious to set a good example to the younger man, Roly began to curb his outbursts and was positively jovial as he strode through the streets of Hobart Town in his crimson waistcoat and high hat, waving his silver-topped cane of zebra wood, with his convict and his dog beside him.

As for Raxleigh, the dog adored his saviour, leaping up hysterically when Dick reported for work each morning. But Raxleigh adored everyone. Now that he had the earth at his paws after those tiresome months on deck, Raxleigh lived in a state of ecstasy.

The whole family was grateful to Dick for sustaining them at such a difficult moment, yet it was a bitter relationship. He was assigned to them as a servant, but it was against the law to treat a convict with familiarity.

Longing for land of their own, they made excursions into the countryside in search of a new home. Richmond was only twenty miles away, but even such a modest distance proved an expedition in Van Diemen's Land. First they had to cross the Derwent River in an open whale boat with three powerful men at the sweeps pulling two oars each. As the family waited at Ferry Wharf to board her on a chilly morning, they recoiled from the stench of whale oil and rotting carcases which mingled sickeningly with the reek of the town's notorious cess pits.

'Oh my!' Matilda exclaimed, wrinkling her nose.

'Oh fie!' echoed Sally, clasping a lace handkerchief to hers.

If Hobart Town was a convict town, it was also a whaling port. Sometimes whales were chased along the estuary, to the cheers of the townspeople who watched the spectacle. Sailors swarmed and staggered everywhere, their bare, tattooed arms clasped around their female companions. One man lay in the gutter, face-down. It was impossible to tell whether he had passed out, unable to find his ship, or had been attacked, robbed and left for dead.

There was no concealment, no shame, even at this respectable time of day, and Gussie regarded the scene with growing dismay. He had never envisaged such mass drunkenness as he had experienced during his short stay in Van Diemen's Land. The women were as uncontrolled as the men. Several jostled past them with insolent stares, dressed in dirty blouses and long, ragged skirts of some heavy material, though their feet were bare. Others lay incapable in the road, petticoats hoisted around their waists, everything on display for those who cared to look. Gussie turned away, outraged by the open prostitution. Two shillings and sixpence was the going rate, according to a woman who had accosted him two nights earlier. He gathered his family around him like a goose with her goslings as they faced the oily water.

They shared the ferry with seven other passengers, including a red-coated sergeant of the 63rd in charge of three convicts, two of whom were tough-looking men with pockmarked faces while the third was a frightened boy of thirteen. None of them spoke.

When they were seated, the oarsmen bent to their oars and swung the ferry into the estuary. It rose and dipped immediately in the strong currents. When the oars missed a wave the passengers were drenched in spray, and the soldier motioned to the convicts to bail out the water with their round leather caps. Lionel was surprised that they obeyed instinctively, as if the fight had long since left them. Sarah and the girls gripped their seats anxiously until the ferry reached Kangaroo Point, where they stepped ashore with smiles of relief. Only the three convicts remained morose. Two soldiers greeted the red-coat, who declared loudly that he had brought two men 'for the drop'. Gussie hoped that Sarah had not overheard, and escorted his family smartly to the post where a dray should have been waiting to take them the rest of their journey. No one was there.

'Where is the dratted man?' he exclaimed impatiently. He was beginning to suspect that the excursion was not such a good idea after all. Nothing in Van Diemen's Land was what he had expected: the drunkenness, the prostitution, and the constant incivility which distressed him even more. When a rough-looking character finally arrived, driving a dray drawn by two horses, he insulted Gussie by demanding his money in advance.

'I'm hardly likely to cheat you, am I?' Gussie said sternly.

'Could be,' replied the man impassively. 'I don't know you, do I?'

Gussie sorted out the alien currency with trembling fingers – Spanish ring dollars, with a hole punched in the middle, which were worth five shillings; and the pieces which had been punched out, known as dumps or Spanish rupees, worth one shilling and threepence.

'A most confusing system,' Gussie muttered, peering at the coins with dislike.

'Get a move on, can't yer,' muttered the man. At that moment the cart was surrounded by several drunken women who held on to the sides and started to shake it until a soldier ran up and prodded them away with his musket.

'Thank you, sergeant,' said Gussie, presenting the man with a dump. 'I wish you could escort us all the way to Richmond,' he added hopefully.

'There's no need to worry, sir,' said the soldier respectfully. 'We're working the road all the way from Kanga Point to Richmond. The chain-gangs are patrolled, so there's no risk of trouble. I wish you a good journey, sir.' He saluted, and told the driver to start without delay.

'Thank heavens the military's here,' Gussie said in a loud voice as the cart rattled off. 'You can always rely on a military man.' The driver gawped at such naivety, and spat.

Though Richmond was the centre of the wheat-growing district and the third largest town in Van Diemen's Land, they were in no mood to be impressed when they arrived late in the afternoon. Gussie's temper did not improve when he was told the tariff at the Lennox Arms.

'Can you credit it?' he muttered to Lionel. 'The charges are actually higher than they are in London.'

'Shocking,' Lionel agreed, secretly thankful to have reached the inn regardless of the cost.

When Gussie and the ladies retired, Lionel and Roly stayed at the bar below talking to the landlord and his solitary customer.

'Richmond looks elegant, I grant you,' said the stranger pontifically.

'It does?' asked Roly, stony-faced, having taken against the place.

'Of course it does,' Lionel said hastily, before his nephew gave offence. 'Some fine shop-fronts.'

'Very nice if you like shop-fronts,' said Roly.

'True,' said the man, who revealed himself as Mr John, butcher and local magistrate. 'But that's all it is – a shop-front. It *looks* a peaceable community in the eyes of a stranger, but the young people have no respect. No respect for the law, and certainly no respect for their elders. They do nothing but fart and sing flash songs.'

'That's the trouble with young men today,' the landlord agreed. 'Sole aim in life for most of them is shooting kangas.'

'Mind you,' said the magistrate, deciding it was time to recommend the place as well, 'we've a better type of settler now that the free-grants have stopped. In the old days any drunken discharged prisoner could have a piece of land until he sold it to satisfy his thirst. Today we landowners are more select.'

With a few drinks the magistrate became bluffer and the landlord cajoled him into revealing his passion in life – apples. Like any man who is an expert on his subject, his enthusiasm was infectious as he described the fruit trees he had stowed in the hold of the ship which brought him from England. 'They all survived the voyage, unlike the passengers, and now I have some of the finest young trees you ever did see. With the climate here, they shoot up in a year or two and bear fruit in less than six. I've Ribstone Pippin and Golden Harvey and French Crab, and they taste even better than they did in England. They call this district the granary, but it's an orchard too. Everything seems to do well over here. Oaks, ashes and sycamores grow two or three feet in their first year. Extraordinary!'

The next morning the family felt more kindly disposed towards Richmond. They walked through the town, which boasted thirty houses including three inns, to inspect the court house. Standing near an inlet known as Sweet Water, it was also used as a place of worship by the Episcopalians and the Wesleyans. Further down they stopped at the bridge spanning the River Coal, built by convicts in 1823 and already a famous landmark in Van Diemen's Land. Gussie examined it closely and tried to make up for his bad temper the night before.

'Excellent craftsmanship, marvellous work! Look at the spaces between the arches – and the parapet.'

'Looks like any bridge back home to me,' said Roly, who hated these family outings.

Sarah turned away. It *did* look like the stone bridges she had known in the west country. Compared to the friendly fields of Devon, the previous day's journey had brought her through a hostile landscape of white skeletal trees which she found forbidding in their immensity. Yet, paradoxically, she had preferred it to this gentle, familiar scene, with the Catholic church glimpsed through the spans of the convict bridge, for she knew that no place in Van Diemen's Land could provide the happiness she had known at home.

Suppressing a sigh of despair, she remembered Roly's cynical remark and gave a gasp of resigned amusement instead. 'Oh, Roly, you're quite impossible.' She did not deceive her husband, who decided against Richmond. It reminded him of home as well.

Their next journey was happier. Tempted by reports of areas covering two or three thousand acres where only a hundred had been tilled, and of hills which were too rocky or wooded to be ploughed but were excellent for sheep, they set out to explore the land beyond Elizabeth Town, recently renamed New Norfolk after the number of settlers who came there from Norfolk Island.

Lionel, much to his satisfaction, managed to obtain a permit allowing Dick to travel with them.

Roly insisted on making the first stage of the journey on horseback, riding the faithful Gallant. In a country where horses fetched as much as £50 compared to £20 back home, he was of some importance, and the journey provided his first testing exercise.

Roly set out at daybreak, skirting the foot of the mountain range that loomed behind Hobart Town. The others walked down to the wharf and took a cutter twenty-two miles up the river to Bridgewater. There they were met by a chaise.

Meanwhile, Roly rode contentedly through the villages of New Town, O'Brien's Bridge and Glenorchy – flat pastureland beside the river which resembled a chain of picturesque lakes – stopping at the Speckled Snake inn for a tankard of ale in the middle of the day. He enjoyed his own company, for life was claustrophobic in the shack and he hated confinement. As it grew dark he heard the unfamiliar sounds of frogs and lizards and the shriek of strange wild birds. He joined the others at the Bush Inn in New Norfolk in time for dinner, finding Gussie in one of his more expansive moods.

'This is more like it, Roly. At least the hostelry has two storeys. Lady Franklin planted a pear tree in the garden which looks decidedly ill to me!' he added with grim satisfaction. 'Red fingers, no doubt!'

Though it was one of the oldest inns in the country, noted for the cheerful management of Mrs Bridges, Gussie found the prices far more reasonable than in Richmond: two shillings a night for a bed, and the same for a meal. 'Good value,' he declared. 'I've confirmed our bookings for the next two nights.'

The following morning, after a visit to Willow Court to see the red-coats standing in the stone sentry-boxes, they met their guide and bullock-cart and left the main road which continued north to Bothwell, setting out in a westerly direction to explore the Derwent Valley. The driver protested that it was quicker to continue on the main road and branch off when they neared Baghdad, but Gussie was heartily sick of 'uppity' servants and told him to follow his instructions. The command was received with an ill grace, but Gussie did not realise that the man's surliness masked unease: familiar with the road to Launceston, he had little knowledge of the jigsaw of valleys beyond New Norfolk.

Unaware of this, his passengers had set out in high spirits, enjoying the cold but crisp and sunny weather. The town of New Norfolk had grown to more than fifty houses, but the buildings thinned out after a few minutes. They paused to exchange formalities with the Episcopalian chaplain, who informed them that he was on his way to visit a nearby chain-gang to provide the convicts with 'much-needed Bibles and tracts on temperance, righteousness, and the aweful judgement to come'. He raised his wide-brimmed hat and rode off, upright and righteous.

'Convicts and churches seem to go together here,' said Lionel. 'The first places they build are a church and a gaol. I suppose the one takes the curse off the other, but I doubt if that gloomy individual will spread much joy.'

Later they passed a solitary prisoner splitting wood from a peppermint tree, but it did not occur to them to ask if they were heading in the right direction until it was too late. Soon they had left all sign of habitation, and were travelling into the wilderness along a track lined by blazed gum trees, their white, ghostly pillars blackened at the base by the fire which had burnt off the dense undergrowth to make the passage easier. Strips of bark hung from the branches, and regiments of rotten trees had fallen on top of each other across the forest. Green parrots darted from tree to tree.

'We might be in the African jungle!' Roly cried gleefully, riding up beside them on Gallant. To endorse Roly's comparison, a flock of black cockatoos which had been tearing the bark from the tall eucalyptus trees to feed on the grubs underneath startled them by rising with angry, piercing screams. Roly fell back to explore the 'jungle' more carefully. Matilda, excited, jumped off the cart and strode ahead, followed by Dick and the dog. Suddenly, Raxleigh came to a stop, barking fearfully as he backed away.

Three men stepped out of the bush. Grinning broadly, one of them opened his blood-stained bag and pulled out a human head.

Matilda was to remember it as the most frightening moment of her life. She raised a hand to her mouth to stop herself screaming as the man held up the bloody head by its hair and waved it in front of her. Alerted by Raxleigh's frenzied barking, Roly had ridden up to see what was happening. He cursed himself for having left his rifle in the cart. The men were plainly outlaws, and it was possible that more were hiding in the bush waiting to rob and kill them. Sensing their alarm, the man laughed and threw the head back in the bag.

''Tis the head of Michael Howe,' he announced triumphantly.

Howe was a notorious bushranger for whom a large reward had been offered – dead or alive. 'We found him shot in the back after escaping from some military. But they said the money was on his head and here it is, so we're on our way to Hobart Town to claim it. Good day to you, sirs, and be careful of living villains like 'e.' He slapped his bloody bag with satisfaction, doffed his hat to Matilda, and after a whistle to his friend continued his journey, keeping a close watch in case they were ambushed and robbed of their grisly prize.

The cart had been straggling far behind. When the others caught sight of Matilda in tears and the men looking about them nervously, the guide sprang out, ready to turn back if there was danger ahead. Sarah and Sally scrambled out after him and comforted Matilda.

Roly was still shocked, but recovered his authority. 'It wasn't just the sight of the head that upset her,' he explained, 'but the way the man waved it around in front of poor Tilly's phiz. They call the blacks savages, but the whites are just as bad. From now on I'll have my gun beside me, just in case.' He put his arm around Matilda, who clutched him gratefully.

After some discussion, they overruled the advice of the guide and decided to continue.

It was three hours before they realised they had lost their way. Finally they emerged on the ridge of a peaceful valley, which stretched for miles ahead to the mountains in the distance.

'Gussie!' said Sarah excitedly, tugging at his sleeve in the hope that he would take some interest. 'Do get out and look. It's so beautiful.'

Gussie smiled wearily. 'Is it, my dear? Then let us stop for our luncheon.'

Sarah had prepared a splendid picnic, including a bone

for Raxleigh. Sally broke her silence at last, but she did so to aggravate. 'It's just like Devon,' she declared as she peeled a boiled egg. Sally compared everything with home, frequently asking, 'What are the things you miss most of all?' The immensity of the virgin landscape which stretched before them had no resemblance to Devon whatsoever.

The relief of finding themselves in open country encouraged them to leave the cart and explore the countryside. Time slipped by until they realised with a shock that the light was fading.

'Lord knows what we'll do now,' said the driver. 'I warned you.'

The problem was solved a moment later when they turned a bend on the river bank and saw a low building, half-hidden in the trees, surrounded by a log fence.

'Thank God!' said Sarah. 'Now we can find out where we are.'

She approached the low building with interest, having wondered about the sort of home settlers would make for themselves in the wilderness. As she drew closer she saw that the weatherboard house had an unpretentious dignity. It was built on a wooden platform a foot or two above the earth, with an outside verandah from which pillars supported the red tin roof. She stepped over the narrow border that might have looked bright with flowers in the summer but was scrawny now, and listened for a sign that people were inside. Nothing. Roly ventured round the side, past a vast water butt, but he could see no one. Perhaps the occupants were hiding, deliberately.

The silence was broken by the guide's loud knock on the door. Shocking in the quiet surroundings, the noise echoed back accusingly from a far distance. A few birds flapped away, and Sarah was beginning to fear that the place was deserted when the door opened slightly and a woman holding a baby peered out suspiciously. When she saw Sarah's kindly face she opened it further, revealing two grubby-cheeked children of indeterminate sex who clung to her apron, half-hidden among the folds, and peeped out to study the intruders doubtfully.

'We're sorry to trouble you,' Sarah explained, 'but we've lost our way and hoped you could tell us where we are.'

'You'd better come inside, then,' said the woman with obvious reluctance, pushing back her straggling hair with her free hand. She looked pale and tired, as if she had been weeping, and made a hopeless attempt to tidy up the room, removing a pair of boots from a chair, brushing crumbs from the table, picking up a toy from the floor. Embarrassed in front of strangers, she gestured Sarah towards the old cane chair and apologised for the untidiness.

'We seldom have callers here. Please forgive the mess.'

Roly burst into laughter and the woman reddened. Sarah was quick to explain. 'My dear, we're laughing because this seems like a palace after the place we're living in.' She looked around admiringly. 'You've made it so nice.' She continued with a description of the shack in Hobart Town, and the woman began to lose her suspicion. But when Sarah said how lucky she was to live in such a place she burst into tears again.

'I like it here myself, and now we're leaving, just when it felt like home. And it's breaking my heart . . . I'm sorry.' She sniffed, wiping her nose with the edge of the apron.

'Oh, my dear,' said Sarah. 'What has happened?'

''Tis my husband's father and his two brothers, all gone. We've had word from the Old Country. Cornwall.'

'I don't understand.'

'Happened a year ago. They're fishermen, you see, and they never came back. And now there's a smallholding back home and no one to look after what's left of the family. I say let 'em look after themselves, but there's children, you see, and no man to care for them, and that's why we have to go back. But you haven't come here to listen to all that. Where is it you're heading for? You say you've lost your way?'

When the guide explained that they were due back in Norfolk Plains it was the woman's turn to laugh. The children looked up with sudden pleasure at this unfamiliar sound and smiled as well.

'If you've lost your way getting here, you'll certainly lose it going back in the dark. No, you're staying here, if you don't mind the lack of comfort. There's two rooms at the back, once I clear them out.'

At first they were undecided, but the danger of running into natives, bushrangers or wild tigers convinced them. Gussie in particular was thankful to stay. He doubted if he could have made the return journey without a night's rest in between.

One disturbing problem remained. The bullocks were likely to be attacked by wild animals if they were left unprotected. Eventually, the scowling guide was sent back to feed them and spend the night in the cart, armed with Roly's rifle. He asked for Dick to go with him, but Lionel refused, saying he might need his services.

'What happens if he does a bunk?' Sally asked as the man departed, his face blacker than ever.

'He won't,' said Lionel. 'He hasn't been paid.'

'And what if he does!' Roly exclaimed. 'We'll find our own way back. Let's enjoy ourselves and stop worrying!' He produced a bottle of brandy from Gallant's saddle bag and brandished it triumphantly.

The woman introduced herself as Minnie Tucker. Charlie Tucker returned an hour later, a lean man who had shouldered too many responsibilities in his life. He brightened a bit when he understood what had happened, especially when Roly filled his glass with cognac and he saw that Matilda and Dick were helping his wife with all the work involved. After two glasses of brandy he started to enjoy the novelty of people to talk to.

The smoke and noise grew too overwhelming for Sarah. Yearning for solitude, she left the room quietly and walked down past the hawthorn hedge to the swirling river. She stood there a long time in contemplation, soothed by the sound of the water.

'Are you all right, my dear?' She turned round, startled to see Gussie. 'I was worried about you,' he said. 'You do so much.'

'If only I was useful in some way,' she sighed despairingly. 'When I watched Matilda just now, coping with everything so efficiently, I felt such a failure.'

Gussie turned her towards him, smiling behind the drooping moustache. 'You are a funny old thing,' he told her affectionately. 'Don't you realise? We depend on you. You're our mainspring.'

'Do you mean that?'

'We couldn't manage without you. I know I couldn't. I've been wanting to tell you that.' He paused. 'I haven't been myself these last few weeks, though I'm feeling better now . . .'

'The air is wonderfully fresh, isn't it?' She gave a slight shiver. As he linked his arm around her to keep her warm, the same thought came to them both.

'You don't think . . .?' Sarah began.

'This is the place we've been looking for? I think it might be.'

'I believe we could be happy here,' she said wistfully. 'Oh, Gussie, how wonderful if Sally's child could be born here.'

'My dear, don't count on it, please. I'll speak to the man when we get back. Not a word to the others before I do. I've raised enough hopes.'

They stood there, closer than they had been for months, absorbing the graceful scene as the river meandered through the valley, golden in the last days of autumn. Suddenly she stiffened and squeezed his hand. 'Look!' she whispered. They watched breathlessly as two swans whiffled down to the opposite side with a booming of wings and a splash as their feet hit the water and braked. Then the birds advanced against the current with effortless ease and immense power.

'Aren't they magnificent!' she gasped. 'I still can't get used to them.'

The swans were black.

*

After the weeks of negative negotiation in which deals fell through or Gussie selected land only to discover it had been marked out by someone else, they had found their home by accident.

Fearing an immediate refusal, Gussie was taken aback when Charlie Tucker gave a beaming smile, removed the pipe from his broken teeth, scratched his head and declared: 'This could save a heap of trouble for both of us.'

Surprises were still in store. Tucker was not the simple farmer he seemed but an intelligent man who had earned a fortune trading in Hobart Town after his arrival ten years earlier. Not only did he know the value of his land as it stood at present, but he was also aware of its future potential. And his land was far more extensive than Gussie had imagined, stretching as far as the eye could see. To buy it would use up all his resources, but by now Gussie felt that this was destined.

Tucker listed the advantages. 'There's water all year round. All you have to do is sink a well in the lower land or clear a pool from one of the mountain streams. You'll find a number of small lagoons – real nice they are – further down the river, with arable land behind the sand-banks good for oats, barley and wheat. There's sixty head of cattle and a hundred and sixty Merino sheep, and a couple of hundred more which are leggy but large, with good coarse wool. There's the house, the barn and the outhouse, and an old log cabin further down which settlers built a long time ago before they moved on. Then there's implements and things, and a lot more to be reckoned up. I've been going into this, of course, planning to sell up and go back to the Old Country, so you can take my word for it, though no doubt you'll be calling in a surveyor if you decide to go ahead. I reckon that apart from the buildings, which must be worth eight hundred pounds, there's close on a thousand acres all told. There was a sale of uncultivated Crown land some time back not far from here. It was knocked down for twenty-eight shillings an acre, *but* . . .' Tucker added quickly, 'that was at public auction six months ago and the price is rising all the time. I've made up my mind that I'll not sell for less than two pounds an acre. That's roughly two thousand pounds for the land; eight hundred pounds for the property; with stock and cattle . . . say three thousand five hundred pounds. Take my word for it, that's fair.'

Gussie nodded. 'You'll want to put this in the hands of your agents in Hobart Town?'

'Why?' Charlie Tucker smiled. 'You'd rob me less than they will. You strike me as an honest man, but once you let those vultures in they'll never stop picking until they see our bones. You know my circumstances, the bad luck that's forcing us out of here – a quick sale suits me fine.'

'And myself,' gasped Gussie, hardly able to believe this rare stroke of good fortune. 'The sooner we can get matters settled, the better I'll be pleased.'

'Then we'll shake on the principle of the thing,' said Tucker, holding out his hand. The others sensed what had happened when the two men joined them for a dish of steamer.

This was a tasty mash with bacon, which they ate ravenously after their day's journey in the open air. The meat tasted like mutton or beef, until Mrs Tucker told them it was made from the tails of kangaroo, when Sarah lost her appetite. Afterwards they talked long into the night. The fire of gum tree logs gave out a fragrant scent, and a kettle was kept on the boil to refill the teapot, while Roly poured out the last of the brandy. Raxleigh crunched the bones of the kangaroo tails contentedly, pausing from time to time to thump his own tail on the floor and look up at Roly, who bent down and scratched behind the dog's ears affectionately. 'Raxleigh will love it here,' he smiled, and Lionel cast a quick look at Gussie, alarmed that everyone was taking it for granted that this time the plans would go through without a hitch.

Sarah had taken a liking to the shy little wife, sympathising with the problems she was having to face in shifting her roots again. 'I've planted a few things,' said Mrs

Tucker when Sarah spoke of a garden. 'The lupins look lovely in the summer. Just like home. Will you keep the name?'

'What *is* the name?' Lionel exclaimed. 'I don't think anyone told us.'

'We were going to call it Mousehole . . .' Charlie Tucker began.

'But we didn't call it that, after all,' Minnie Tucker finished. 'It's called Swansdowne.'

'Swansdowne!' There was an echo of surprise as the Stowes absorbed the name.

'That sounds homely,' said Dick, anxious to be agreeable.

'I'm not sure,' said Roly doubtfully, but Sarah had no doubts whatsoever.

'Swans live on the water here, don't they? We saw two of them earlier.'

'Did you?' exclaimed Charlie Tucker with interest. 'There used to be dozens when we first got here, but the trade in eggs has cut down the numbers until they're a rarity now. Minnie thinks they're beautiful. That's why she called it Swansdowne. But you call it whatever you like. It won't make any difference to us now we're leaving.'

Later, when it was quiet at last, Sarah lay in her corner wide awake, thinking of the future. She felt an overwhelming sense of peace, daring to hope that they had reached their destination at last. Then, in the distance, she heard the beat of wings, resembling the sound of a child's whirling top, followed by the plaintive cry of the swan like the echo of a harp. She sat up, alert and anxious, remembering the saying that swans only sing at the point of death.

They were out early the next morning, determined to see as much of Swansdowne as they could before their journey back to New Norfolk. Gussie had matters to discuss with Charlie Tucker. Minnie took Sarah to see the old oak tree whose massive branches offered welcome shade in summer.

'Lord alone knows how it got to a place like this,' said Minnie. 'Someone told me it came from the Old Country, but I don't see how.'

Sarah studied it with affection. If anything could have confirmed the rightness of Swansdowne, this was it, reminding her as it did of the even more ancient oaks above Raxleigh House.

'It is a fine tree, isn't it!' she said admiringly.

A shot rang out, piercing the optimistic moment and cutting it dead.

The two women saw a farm labourer walking back from the river with a broad smile across his face. Over his shoulder swung the limp, massive body of a black swan.

'Oh, no,' Sarah groaned. 'Why did he have to do such a thing? Why kill one of those beautiful creatures?'

'For their down, of course. Sells for eightpence a pound.'

Cruelty to any animal pained Sarah physically, but this was something she could not explain to Minnie Tucker. She felt she had to say something.

'It's *seeing* the swan that upset me. It seems such a crime to shoot it even for the down.'

'Better that,' said Minnie Tucker indignantly, as if she had been accused of something dishonest, 'than catching 'em and letting 'em starve to death.'

'Why should they do that?' Sarah's distress was so obvious that Minnie Tucker replied in a gentler tone.

'They do say it gets rid of the oiliness. Anyhow, the down is easier to pluck when the bird is lean. So you see, shooting them's not as bad as all that.' She smiled reassuringly, and Sarah managed a pale smile herself.

'No,' she sighed, 'I suppose not. Well, it's time for us to leave.'

But the image of the black swan, its neck swinging near the ground, stayed with her for days. She knew that swans mate for life, and she felt instinctively that the female was left. The pen had sung her swansong the night before, sensing that she would pine to death in the weeks to come.

Sarah said nothing about the swan to the others, who were too excited to notice the change of mood. They had found their new home at last.

PART 6

— 18 —

The provocation of Dick Stanton

They took possession in August, at the end of winter, setting out from Hobart Town with two bullock teams of eight animals each, pulling two English red-wheeled drays piled high with their belongings. Sally's son was born three months later.

Now, in the spring of 1848, little Timothy was just a couple of months short of his second birthday, and as she walked through her new garden Sarah Stowe was able, momentarily, to forget her overwhelming sense of apprehension. Scarcely two years old, it was a mockery of Raxleigh, but roots had taken and green buds appeared on the driest wood. In some cases the shrubs were little more than twigs, but against all the odds they were still alive and she marvelled at the resilience of nature. The sun was shining, spring was in the air, birds sang and leaves unfolded. She examined everything, gaining particular consolation from the shoots on the rose cuttings brought from Bideford which had adapted to the new climate with a speed she envied. If only she was blessed with such a gift for recovery. She sighed as she remembered the trials of the last two years.

In the first year the distraction of settling in had preoccupied her. There was much to do, and Matilda and Dick working in harness had done most of it – installing the furniture, helping their convict gang to build a new room at the back – while she added the final touches which were so important: installing the luxury of scented mutton-leather beds; helping the convict Martha to polish the mil-

dewed furniture; hanging pictures and displaying orna-
ments, until Swansdowne resembled a home. But it
remained a parody of Raxleigh House, their possessions ill
at ease in their new stark setting, aliens in strange rooms,
reminding Sarah of the house where they belonged.

Sally had refused to help. The organ had been assembled but she refused to play it. Books were aired and
arranged on shelves but she refused to read them. Most
depressing of all, she refused her son.

Sally's indifference to her child was painful to watch.
She did not bother to conceal it. The first faltering steps
of young Timothy delighted the others, but Sally stared
at the baby without expression.

Gussie was unable to express affection for the boy
either. Once Sarah had entered the room silently and
been shocked to see her husband recoil as the child
crawled up to him, craving attention. She had lost any
hope that the birth of the child would bring about a
reconciliation between Sally and her father, whose health
had deteriorated steadily. With shaving now a difficulty,
his straggly white beard had the sadness of an abandoned
bird's nest.

'Don't you mind that your father's ill?' she complained
to Roly one day, exasperated by his remoteness.

'What's the point?' he replied. 'If he's ill, he's ill.
There's nothing I can do about it.'

'You can show you *care*!'

'You take things too seriously, ma,' Roly protested. 'I
know he's a bit deaf these days, but that's part of growing
old.'

Sarah sighed and avoided the subject thereafter, but
she knew that Gussie's decline was not so simple. He was
ageing before his time.

She derived comfort from the land. To plant a tree and
see it grow was the most rewarding experience of her
new life, but besides herself only Dick Stanton found
satisfaction in planting for the future. Roly assumed the
role of overseer of the gang of convicts, ten men to begin
with, quarrying stone for the new extension behind the

house. Sarah despaired of these men. Either the Stowes had been unlucky or the convicts had been selected for their laziness. Most of the time they did not even pretend to be busy, idling the hours away, drowsing in the summer sun.

'I've never seen a lazier lot,' she complained to Roly, whose instructions they ignored. 'This system of "probation", as they call it, discourages those who want to work and rewards those who don't.'

'That's the vice of Van Diemen's Land,' Roly declared. 'With no incentive, it turns them into scroungers. Lord knows how we'd cope if it wasn't for Dick.'

Though Dick enjoyed his outdoor work, even in the first bitter winter when he strove from dawn till dusk and changed his clothes on Sunday, he lived an in-between existence. He belonged neither with the family nor with the other convicts, who had no interest in the future of Swansdowne and resented the privileges which Dick received from Lionel. Consequently, he worked on his own: building the brushwood fences and planting the pines and poplars given him by Sarah, steadily transforming the sandy soil above the house into a garden, enclosing it with a six-foot wall. Arduously he double-trenched and manured the virgin earth, and placed large stones at the roots of the espaliered fruit trees which grew against the wall.

Now, in their third year, they looked forward to the potatoes which they would fold into the lower ground in October, and had cleared six acres of land to sow the spring wheat. Gradually, however, they were realising that farming was something of a fallacy in Van Diemen's Land, in spite of all they had been led to believe. The reason was simple: however rich the harvest, there was little gain without the market to consume it. With the island's tiny population, wheat was sold at the nominal price of just a few shillings a bushel.

'It's fifty to one against keeping our heads above water,' Roly informed his father, 'unless we abandon the plough for cattle.'

287

Gussie nodded, but did nothing about it.

Raxleigh would have grown fat on the discarded, leaner parts of kanga meat were it not for the exercise and the days spent in the open air. Like most dogs, he had the ability and sagacity to adapt more readily than his human masters, and he relished his sense of usefulness as he ran with Roly, helping the working dogs to herd the sheep, acting as watchdog at night on his rug on the verandah, alert to the approach of strangers. Every fallen tree or boulder outside the settlement had been removed in case it offered cover to the few remaining bushrangers who still roamed Van Diemen's Land, notorious for the audacity of their raids. When the sun grew too hot, Roly took the dog down to the river to bathe, and Raxleigh, now in his prime, would lie in the shadow of the willows afterwards, his eyes seldom leaving his master, his tail thumping gently on the ground to signify contentment.

He was a much-loved dog; hence the consternation one morning when one of the convicts saw him snatch at the carcase of a sheep suspended from a tree. The carcase had been rubbed with strychnine, butter and sugar to lure the predatory native cats which stole into the folds at night, sometimes killing as many as eight sheep in less than twenty minutes. It was lucky that the servant noticed Raxleigh yielding to his ravenous appetite, and luckier still that he knew of the effect of cold water on prussic acid. Shouting to the others, he carried the prostrate and by now lifeless dog to the water butt and immersed him in the cold water until only his nose showed above the surface. As the family gathered in dismay, there was no sign of recovery. Then, after an interminable minute, the servant shouted triumphantly as Raxleigh's eyes regained some animation.

'Hold his head up!' cried Dick. In thirty seconds Raxleigh tried to stand of his own accord, fell, shook himself, and rose again. For the rest of that day he remained stupefied.

'I told you it was wrong to use poison,' said Sarah reproachfully.

'It's the way of things out here, ma,' said Roly. 'Even so, we've killed enough of the wild cats. We'll put an end to strychnine. Can't risk Raxleigh.'

'Thank the lord for that,' said Sarah.

She felt sometimes that they had landed in a territory determined to consume them. Just as everything seemed to be going right at last, the sheep went down with catarrh, a condition resembling human pneumonia, and the vile mucus wiped out an eighth of the stock. Neighbours told them they were fortunate to escape so lightly; that these were natural hazards to be accepted.

There was scant profit in livestock either, as they discovered when they sheared the surviving sheep. It was one of the happier times, with a strong sense of communal good-fellowship round the fires at night, but when Lionel and Roly added up the cost against the profit they were shocked by the narrow margin. The costs were never-ending: food for the shepherds, hut-keepers and carters; the added expense of six men to wash the sheep over three weeks; and then the five shearers and the cost of their grog – a formidable item in itself. Three men were needed to roll and press the wool, and the bales had to be transported to Hobart. After the government levy, the wages for all the men, and the sundry expenses of the station, the total came close to £1,500. The sale of the wool yielded approximately £60 more.

After the catarrh, they were left with 3,000 sheep – 2,000 ewes and 1,000 dry. The cost of another epidemic could prove devastating. As it was, their reserve of funds was stretched to the limit.

So the first two years, which should have been so satisfying, with all the adventures of building a new life in a new land, were overshadowed. And though many would have envied their existence, an irrational malaise settled on the family. Only Dick and Matilda rejoiced in their new surroundings, ending each day in blissful exhaustion, he in his convict quarters, she in the house. Roly led an isolated life, riding for miles to inspect the post-and-nail fences, Raxleigh running behind. As for

Sarah, she was unable to forget the past and accept the present. Even on this fine spring morning she sighed as she remembered the greater splendour of Raxleigh House, and the tall trees which overlooked the Torridge.

'It's not the same. It never can be.'

She turned quickly, startled to hear her thoughts echoed behind her. Lionel had come up silently, and now put his arm around his sister.

'I know you yearn for home,' he told her gently, 'but don't make this a substitute. Think of it as something new for Roly and Matilda, and the baby. Don't try to recreate Raxleigh here. It's not possible.'

'I know you're right,' she said vaguely. 'It's lucky that so many of the roses have survived. They won't send me anything from Hobart.'

Lionel found it hard to be sympathetic. He felt it was worse for him than for the others to be stuck out here in the wilderness with so little to stimulate his mind. It had been eight months before he received Delane's reaction to the first despatch. Secretly he had been hoping for a letter of unreserved congratulation and the offer of a regular job, but Delane thanked him courteously, advised him not to make his writing too personal, and added that he was pleasantly surprised by the favourable reception of the published article which he enclosed. Lionel read the printed page again and again, admiring the skill with which it had been edited, but mourning every sentence which had been cut.

'What more do you want?' Roly asked him, annoyed by his ultimate dejection. 'The bloody thing's published and Delane liked it. I suppose you thought he'd ask you to join his staff?'

'No, of course not,' Lionel lied. 'It's just that I'm not too sure where to go from here.' He knew that he was stifling his chances by staying at Swansdowne, yet he stayed for the sake of his sister now that Gussie was increasingly helpless.

'Make the best of it,' he told her. 'We're together, and that's what you wanted.' He prided himself that he had

290

never reproached her for his sacrifice when he might be enjoying life in England. He had forgotten how glad he was to turn his back on Bideford.

'What about Gussie?' she asked. 'What are we going to do with him?'

He was tempted to reply that this was her responsibility, but he told her what she wanted to hear. 'He's with you. That's all he cares about.'

'You don't understand, any of you. I believe he's dying. His eyesight is so bad he can hardly see where he's going. He can't read without his magnifying glass . . .' She stopped, on the point of tears. Lionel hated to see her so unhappy, but resented it too.

'God knows what we'd do without Dick,' he said. 'He's coming on well, isn't he? Of course, the other convicts despise him because he spends his spare time reading, but it's easier now that most of them have gone.'

'How do you think Sally is?' she asked, changing the subject, feeling guilty as always at concealing Dick's parentage from her brother.

'Sally?' He frowned, reluctant to reveal his true feelings. He was constantly appalled by Sally's lack-lustre attitude to life, the perpetual grievance she suffered, expecting them to suffer too. 'The baby keeps her busy,' he said evasively.

'Does he?' she asked with a new note of bitterness. 'Matilda shows more interest in the child than she does.'

'Well,' he sighed, finding the conversation depressing, 'Matilda's marvellous. But be fair to Sally. She's far too young for such responsibilities.'

'She doesn't seem young to me any more.' It was true: the peach-bloom of adolescence which had prompted Tim to fall in love with her had been replaced by a harder look, her hair swept back severely, exposing the high cheek-bones, the staring eyes and open petulant lips. But if the delicacy had faded, there was no denying Sally's attraction now. Beauty was too easy a label; it was something different, an animal magnetism, a musk.

'She's very popular,' said Lionel tactlessly, thinking of

the young men who came to the house whenever possible to feast their eyes, lingering after their business.

'Yes.' Sarah gave a particularly long sigh. 'I know what you mean, though popular is hardly the word. Those young men . . . even the convicts . . . at times she's like a bitch on heat, provoking them.'

Lionel was shocked to hear his sister use such a phrase, although it described the situation exactly. How strange, he thought, that dear, foolish old Gussie and his upright sister should produce children like Roly and Sally.

'It will be all right,' he told her reassuringly. 'Sally will get over it, and at least we're all together. Family. Now, show me your garden. Tell me what we'll see here in the years to come. Your gorse is running wild already.'

'I want you to see my favourite honeysuckle,' she said, smiling. 'I believe it is going to flower.'

Dick Stanton was content with life, though still awaiting his pardon.

> Dear father, (*he wrote*)
> This comes with my kind love to you, hoping to find you in good health as, thank God, it leaves me at present very comfortable indeed. I have my own place near the farmhouse, and I have plenty to eat and drink, thank God for it. I am allowed 2 ounces of tea, 1 pound of sugar, 12 pounds of meat, 10½ flour, and 2 ounces of tobacco each week, but the family see I get a bit extra. The government gives me 3 pairs of shoes, 4 shirts, and 2 suits of clothes a year. You will be happy to hear that I am still assigned to Mr Lionel Raxleigh and the rest of his family who treat me well. Some masters are a great deal worse than others and I count myself lucky. All a man has got to mind is to keep a still tongue in his head and do his master's duty, and then he is looked upon as if he were at home – as I am here; but if he don't he may as well be hung at once, for he would be

taken to the magistrate and get 100 lashes and then
get sent to a place called Port Arthur, if the master
makes complaint, to work in irons for 2 or 3 years,
and then he is disliked by everyone. But you will be
pleased to hear that this country is before England in
everything, both for work and money, even for the
likes of me. After work I have the chance to make
a few shillings by hunting or shooting kangaroo
which is the size of a sheep, or ducks, tigers,
tiger-cats or native cats. But there is nothing that
will hurt a man but a snake. They are about 5 to 6 ft
long but they get away if they can. When we first
came there was a swan gone mad which dragged
a lamb into the river and drowned it, which I shot
though did not tell Mrs Sarah for she is not keen about
hunting or shooting, so I do not discuss this with her
though everything else. She gives me a shilling each
week for my work in making her a special garden,
so I have money now for anything I want, thank God,
but I am far away from all beer shops, the nearest
20 miles away. Most of the other convicts have gone,
which is a good thing, but I still have a fellow
prisoner living with me, a shoemaker, and he is
learning me to make shoes which will be a great help
to me; in 2 years I shall be able to make a pair myself.
Mr Lionel is also training me with learning in the
event of my receiving a pardon, God willing, and Mr
Roly is always good to me ever since I rescued his
dog, now a fine animal who joins us if we go hunting
together. Then there is Mr Roly's wife, Matilda, and
Miss Sally who had a son born two years ago but I
wrote you about that at the time and it is not a
subject to speak of. So you can see that when all things
are considered, I am doing better than at home only
for the wanting of you with me, or me with you,
and that is all my discomfort in not being able to see
you. But I hope that time may come, dear father, and
that meantime you will gain pleasure in reading this
letter as I have had in writing it. So no more at present

from your loving though unfortunate son, hoping I
shall be hearing from you shortly,

Dick Stanton

Dick was in the best of spirits when Sally came into
the barn the next morning. Here Dick lived, worked and
slept, along with the three other convicts who had been
kept on, including the cobbler. Originally it had been
built by the first settlers as their home, with six shooting
holes in the wall on either side of the doorway, which was
so low you had to crouch to enter but was quick and easy
to shut once you were safely inside. It was still a stockade
in so far as it served as a storeroom for the precious sacks
of flour.

After the convicts shut the sheep in their folds at night
to protect them from the aborigines' spears, they took it
in turns to climb the oak tree to see if there was any sign
of fire. Once, by the light of a full moon, Dick had seen
a tribe two miles away, shapes dancing against the fire
as if performing a ritual. Another time, one of the convict
gang had gone missing, or so they thought until they
found him pinned to a tree with a spear embedded so
deeply in the wood that six inches broke off when they
pulled it out. Though fewer now, the blacks were an
ever-present peril, and Dick went around armed, even
carrying a gun in the tail of the plough, placing it on
the ground beside him when he was building, draining,
fencing, or preparing the twelve-acre orchard where the
young apple trees would be grown from the pips bought
from the butcher at Richmond. At night he slept on his
bark bed with musket and ammunition beside him, next
to the stack of flour. After one successful raid by the
aborigines, a vengeful neighbour planted a gin-trap inside
a flour bag and left it temptingly near an out-house.
Returning the next morning he found the bag still there,
but the trap held three black fingers in its vice.

Dick looked forward to the autumn, when they would
thrash and grind their own wheat with the mill brought
from home, and he could bake his own bread for supper.

Meanwhile it was his responsibility to guard the government flour and he had just carried the last bag of the latest delivery inside when Sally followed him through the low door. When she straightened up she smiled mischievously at finding him alone.

'Where are the others?'

'Preparing pockets of ash, Miss Sally, for the planting of the spring wheat tomorrow.'

Something about him annoyed her: the subservient way he touched his forehead; the wistful expression which resembled a dog staring at its master, appealing for affection. Even the shabby, ungainly clothes of the assigned servant irritated her.

How different men are, she thought, making him feel awkward as she looked him up and down. The scar suggested strength, yet there was something girlish about him with his falling curls and fresh complexion. If that was the role he wanted to play, she would let him play it.

'Anything I can do for you, Miss Sally?'

'Yes. I have a job for you. Wait here.' She gained a sadistic satisfaction from treating him like a servant rather than a friend of the family. A few minutes later she returned with a bundle of dirty clothing. 'There,' she ordered, 'these need to be washed. Make sure you take care of my undergarments. They have to be handled gently.' She flung the clothes on the ground at his feet. 'Well, hurry up.'

Dick looked at the intimate clothing, blushing from the shame of it.

'Here!' She snatched up a pair of silk drawers and threw them with such perfect aim that they landed across his face. He could smell the scent of her body until they fell back on the floor.

'Pick them up,' she ordered. She had teased him before in her playful way but he knew she was tantalising him now, leading him on in a way that was different altogether. He ached to embrace her, his youthful body on edge.

'I won't,' he whispered. 'I won't do none of that.'

'Oh, yes, you will,' she answered sternly. 'You do what you're told. You're a servant.' She took a step towards him, daring him to react, but when he stood rigid she picked up another of the garments and rubbed the silk against his mouth.

'No,' he repeated, though he dreaded the consequences.

'I might let you off, if you . . .' She reached up to whisper in his ear and he swung round instinctively, dreading discovery. What would happen if she accused him afterwards?

'We can't,' he warned her hoarsely. 'You know what would happen to me if we were found out.'

'What a coward you are,' she said scornfully. 'Who's going to find us here?' She stepped back towards the door, lifting the wooden latch into place, and then led him towards the hay stacked in the corner. As she started to fondle him he was unable to resist any longer. Heedless of danger, he began to kiss her passionately.

When it was over, he separated slowly, quivering with fulfilment. Sally was left with emptiness, and looked resentfully at the young, contented man whose body had the curious scent of honey.

'Sally?' He turned towards her, but his smile faded when she stared back as if he had been impertinent.

'Sally?' she echoed, frowning. At that moment she was ugly.

'Mrs Blake, I mean,' he whispered.

'And wash those clothes as I told you.'

'Wash them yourself!' He was stronger now.

'How dare you?' For a moment her anger was genuine as she struck him across the face.

Dick Stanton stood up without a word and fastened his clothing. With a queer smile he walked to the centre of the barn and picked her clothes off the dirt floor, tearing the pair of drawers apart as he turned to face her again. Then, with slow, precise gestures, he dropped the clothes, placed his hands on his hips and started to dance the hornpipe, his feet beating faster and faster, stamping the soiled clothes into the earth.

'How dare you?' she screamed. 'Do you realise I can have you flogged?'

Dick stopped dancing and went straight up to her, seizing her hands in his before she could strike him again. 'Sally,' he declared breathlessly, 'or Mrs Blake, or whatever you like to call yourself, you're mazed at times. If you think I'm here to wash your fancy things, you've made a sorry mistake. I'm not here to molly-coddle you.'

When she had run from the barn, Dick removed his secret shillings from their hiding place in the rafters, changed into his best clothes and boots, and left.

There was an angry argument in the house that night when they discovered he had gone. Roly had seen Sally as she ran back into the house, and suspected that she had something to do with Dick's departure.

'What happened between you?' he demanded, guessing the truth.

'What do you mean?' she asked guiltily. 'He wanted to leave, that's all. He was bored.'

'I don't believe you.' Roly looked at her coldly. 'Dick would never have left without a good reason. Not without telling me.'

'He's lost his chance of a pardon now,' Lionel added softly.

'Oh, God!' Roly seized the chair he was leaning on and crashed it down on the floor. 'See what you've done, Sally. You've thrown away everything Uncle Lionel's worked for.'

'Oh, don't bring him into it.' Sally spoke contemptuously. 'Everyone knows he's in love with Dick.' There was a shocked silence.

After a moment Lionel spoke.

'Of course I love him,' he said carefully, deflecting the accusation. 'I love him as if he was my own son. And I had the highest hopes for his future. If you cannot understand that, you don't understand a thing.'

'What will they do if they capture him?' Matilda asked tearfully.

'Flog him,' said Lionel savagely, tormented by the prospect, 'at the very least. More likely they'll send him to a penal settlement, if they catch him alive.'

'Oh, God!' said Roly. 'What have you done?' He turned to his sister, horrified. 'What have you done?'

'I'm sorry. I didn't realise . . .'

'That's just it,' said Roly with obvious disgust. 'You never do.'

Sally ran from the room.

Roly broke the silence. 'If anyone imagines I'm staying here without Dick, the only person whose company meant anything . . .' He could not finish the sentence. 'I'll go after him. If anyone asks about him you can say he's gone with me to Hobart Town. If they catch up with me, I'll think of something to say. But if I find him, I'll bring him back and no harm done.' He hurried out. Matilda followed him.

'Where will you go?' she asked desperately, as he packed by the light of a candle.

'None of your business.' Then, realising her distress, he turned to her and rested his head against her, exhausted. 'Forgive me. I know I've failed you . . .' She tried to reassure him, but he continued: 'It will be different when I come back, but I've got to give myself this chance as well as look for Dick – I must get away from all this, I must, I must.' He kissed her and she realised that his cheeks were wet.

'Come on, Raxleigh,' he said. The dog shifted himself instantly and followed his master to the stables. Matilda watched them leave in the darkness, clasping herself in sorrow.

— 19 —

Sentenced to Port Arthur

When Dick Stanton walked into Hobart Town three days later, he found that the town had grown in his absence. This time he kept to the darker back streets, where he was less likely to be noticed. Most of the people here had been convicts themselves and were ready to hide him at a price, unless a greater reward was offered for his capture. So far his name had not appeared on any list or billboard, and he was absorbed into this darker part of town, where the muddy roads were dimly lit by flickering oil-lamps from tiny windows.

Renting a bed in a dilapidated house, Dick began to hate the convict capital: the screams at night, the sight of a boy apprehended in a neighbouring street, taken away to be hanged; Mrs Buff, who lived in the tumble-down house next door, so poor that she survived on potatoes and scraps from the gutter. She was a disturbing sight, sitting on her doorstep and cutting off wisps of her dingy hair to shove in her mouth because someone had told her it would kill the worms that crept about her arms and neck. One evening she ran from her room with all her clothes on fire. Passers-by tried to put out the flames by beating her with sticks or whatever came to hand, but she died from her burns that night. Others Dick knew by sight were dying more slowly, eaten up with disease.

Dick regretted his departure from Swansdowne. By that rash decision he had lost his chance of security and betrayed the faith of Lionel Raxleigh. He haunted the waterfront taverns in the hope of meeting a sailor from the whaling fleets who might find him a job if bribed to do so.

Ma Sloper's became his favourite tavern. At first he thought her macabre, with her rouged cheeks and jet black hair, but when he knew her better he enjoyed her caustic wit. She befriended him, always sympathetic to young convicts on the run, who reminded her of a man she had known when she was young who had killed himself after a pitiless flogging in the old penal settlement at Macquarie Harbour. She employed runners to watch at the end of the street, and warned Dick whenever the police were heading in their direction. She bought him as many drinks as he paid for himself, overcharging the drunken foreign sailors to make up her profit.

One night, lonelier than usual, he looked round suspiciously when a stranger sat down at his table, a man plainly down on his luck. This was hardly a novelty, but there was something about the man which made Dick examine him more closely: he was filthy, his face ingrained with dirt, his hair and beard matted as if they had not been washed for months. Then Dick saw his shaking hands and the white gloves that were torn and no longer white.

'Conway,' he exclaimed, giving himself away.

'Who the hell are you?' The red-rimmed eyes studied him. 'Christ,' he whispered. 'It's the convict who went after that dog and cost me my job. I've been hoping to meet up with you. What became of you? You're a servant to that family, aren't you? That girl who had the bastard by the doctor who went missing.'

'She married him,' Dick broke in unwisely.

'Married? Never! You can't fool me. He drowned. I remember *that*. Fell overboard.'

'Captain Peppiatt married them in his cabin before that, secretly.'

'Secretly?' Conway gave a gap-toothed smile. 'Never! They spun you a yarn, my lad, and if Peppiatt says he did he's a liar. The girl's no better than a whore and the child's a bastard.'

'Never say that again,' Dick whispered.

'How would *you* know?' Conway demanded. A new thought occurred to him: 'Yes, how would you know unless you're still assigned to them? And if so, what are you doing here?' He laughed nastily. 'You're on the run!'

'He's with me.'

Dick looked up to see Roly standing over them, with Flanagan behind him. 'Thank God,' said Roly, holding out his hand. Dick clasped it firmly. 'I've been looking for you, Dick. Thank God I've found you.' He turned to Conway. 'You, whatever your name is, what were you saying about my sister?'

'I was saying the girl was never married to the doctor, if that's what you mean,' the mate replied with unexpected spirit. 'I know better than that fairy story.'

Roly leapt on the man, shaking him like a terrier with a rat. A seaman came to the mate's assistance, and in moments the inn was a tangle of brawling, shouting figures, bringing Ma Sloper hurrying from her room upstairs.

'Get out,' cried Roly, sensing the danger to Dick. 'I'll leave word for you here, but get out now before it's too late.' One of Ma Sloper's runners was thrown inside, followed by the police. With no chance for Roly and Dick to agree on their story, it was too late already.

When the line of shuffling, leg-ironed men reached the government brig, the *Tamar*, Dick turned his head to look back at Hobart Town. It might be the last time he would see it, yet he was not cast down. The doubts of the last few days had been settled, and though he had received the punishment he had been dreading he found consolation in knowing that his future was resolved. Dick was a fatalist; life had made him so. At this moment, the absolute novelty of everything around him, coupled with a powerful sense of his own destiny, excited him. The fatalist is usually an optimist. And a self-deceiver.

It was six in the morning and Hobart Town had never seemed so peaceful as the heat-mist started to lift, promising a perfect early summer's day. Even the stink of whale oil seemed less pungent. Shafts of light began to pierce the mist, picking out the green slopes on either side of the snug valley. Though he could not see it yet, Dick knew that behind the settlement and the wisps of smoke Mount Wellington rose darkly, devoid of snow in summer.

As he absorbed the scene, Dick felt elated. Then a shout and a shove and a pull on his leg-irons brought him down to earth as the men were led up the plank from the wooden wharf.

Apart from the captain of the *Tamar*, John Burn, and the mate and the carpenter, there were two passengers already on board: a Quaker missionary and a dandy young officer recently arrived from England, with an eye-glass and a bottle of black rum nestling beneath his pea-jacket. Sound travelled at that time of day, and Dick overheard the officer introducing himself to the captain in a languid voice. 'Name of Cool, Lieutenant Cool. Have a touch of this rum, Captain Burn. You'll find it remarkably good.' The captain accepted the offer reluctantly.

'Remarkably strong,' he spluttered, having swallowed more than he intended. Dick could believe it, for the tantalising fumes wafted across the deck, but at that moment the hatchway was opened and the convicts were pushed below. It was a small area containing a lot of people; ten soldiers and a sergeant were quartered in one part of the hold, with provisions, several sheep, two of the soldiers' wives and four children. Dick was one of eighteen prisoners sentenced to the penal settlement of Port Arthur on the south-east coast of Van Diemen's Land, and they were locked in the ship's gaol which was separated from the other side of the hold by strong wooden bars. The crew of twelve seamen, most of them former convicts, slept in shifts on hammocks which they strung up on the fo'c'sle. It was dark and stuffy, for the hatchway was fastened tight by brass bolts, guarded by one soldier in the hold and two on deck. Only two prisoners were allowed up for air at the same time, still in their chains, so there was little chance of diving overboard and little incentive to do so. Dick stretched out on the bed of stones which acted as ballast and fell asleep immediately, waking later to sense the motion of the sea as the *Tamar* sailed down the Derwent towards Storm Bay.

The missionary had observed the arrival of the convicts with concern. He produced his notebook and asked questions of Captain Burn with the eager innocence of a visitor seeing Van Diemen's Land for the first time. Having arrived on the same ship from England, Lieutenant Cool knew no more than the missionary, and he listened silently to the exchange.

'This year's transportation from the Old Country?' repeated Captain Burn. 'I'd say it'll come to four thousand male and six hundred female by the end of it. Far too many. They've increased the convict population by forty per cent in the last four years and don't know what to do with them.'

'They're not all sent to the settlements when they arrive, are they?'

'Lord, no! Just a few to Port Arthur – that's the only settlement now Macquarie's closed down, apart from a couple of distant islands. I reckon there's less than two thousand convicts in Arthur all told, and that's including the boys.'

'Poor souls, poor souls.' The missionary shook his head slowly. 'These criminals, are they very wicked? How can they be, if boys are sent there too?'

'Ah, there's the rub,' replied the captain, airing his unexpected Shakespeare. 'There's no rhyme or reason – luck of the draw stuff. Arthur was intended for double convicted felons, but hardened offenders can get a cushy number while some poor wretch who stole a chicken ends up in the settlement.'

They arrived at Port Arthur at eight the following morning. The infamous settlement was situated on the south of the Tasman Peninsula, which was linked by a narrow isthmus known as Eagle Hawk Neck to another 'island', the Forestier Peninsula, linked in turn by another strip to the mainland, like a two-tier earring. As the *Tamar* rounded Cape Raoul and sailed into Maignon Bay, the missionary and the officer came on deck. They were joined by the ship's carpenter, who knew the settlement well and pointed out the landmarks as they approached.

'That's Point Puer,' he told them sombrely, indicating some buildings on top of the cliffs.

'What's that?' asked Lieutenant Cool, desperately sober now that his rum had gone.

'That's where they send the boys, and that –' he pointed to the hummocks of rock rising from the sea, 'that's another Frenchified name, Eel dez Moorts.'

'I was wondering about that,' said the missionary, suppressing a smile at the odd pronunciation. 'Why are there so many French names on the map?' He produced a chart from his pocket and referred to it. 'Baie de l'Aventure – Baie Mauvaise – and that little dot over there, L'Isle des Morts, which you pointed out to us.'

'Frog navigators,' explained the lieutenant, pleased to exercise his knowledge. 'Admirals d'Entrecasteaux and Bruny – hence Bruny Island. Trust a frog to name a place after himself.'

'Surely Port Arthur was named after the last Governor?' the missionary pointed out. Receiving no smile in return, he asked more humbly if they knew why the rocks were known as the Island of the Dead.

'Don't know,' said Cool. 'Do you?' He turned to the carpenter, who nodded grimly.

'I do well enough. *Bones*.'

'Bones?' asked the missionary. 'What sort of bones?'

'Convict bones. Them what have gone beyond punishment and they want to be rid of. A whaleboat dumps them out there to starve, though some choose the other way and give themselves up to the sharks. More dignity in that, I suppose. Funny thing – because of all them bones they're making it a proper burial place now, with headstones and things. I make the coffins, so I know.'

'A special graveyard for the convicts?' asked the missionary.

'Not for convicts! A proper one, for soldiers and their wives and babes, and the constables. The convicts are thrown into mass graves and covered up with lime.'

The missionary said nothing, but he stared at the desolate spot with a sense of impending sadness. What sort of a place have I come to? he wondered. 'Life in Port Arthur must be brutal,' he murmured.

'Fit for brutes,' said the carpenter. 'But it looks a treat, don't it?'

They gazed at the settlement ahead, each man absorbing the scene in a different way. Captain Burn and the mate scarcely noticed the landscape, preoccupied as they were with currents, rocks and reefs and other nautical hazards. Cyril Cool was seldom impressed by anything, but he was startled by the size of the settlement, which had grown into the fourth largest town in the colony in the space of sixteen years. His eyes picked out the turrets of a guard house next to a parade ground with some officers' cottages to the side, one of which might well be consigned as quarters for himself. Joshua Claymore, the missionary, was surprised by the massive church topped by a tall tower, the ever-welcome landmark. Then, as he sensed the strength of the long, low prison buildings with the massive barracks behind, he felt overwhelmed by melancholy. Was it due to his knowledge of the ironed convicts, or had their presence blighted the land? He could not say – but he found himself shivering as if they were sailing under a sullen sky instead of the sunshine of another perfect day.

With skill gained from long experience, Captain Burn brought the *Tamar* neatly beside the stone jetty. It was a handsome structure, built by the convicts, some of whom were there at that moment waiting for the ship's arrival.

The colours of their uniforms identified their level of guilt: grey for 'good conduct'; yellow and black for prisoners serving life; plain yellow for those thought to be beyond redemption, the 'irreclaimables' as they were referred to officially, or the better-named 'no-hopers'.

The convicts on board were heaved on deck and led down the plank. The missionary studied them intently, and noticed Dick Stanton in particular because he was smiling. Apart from one strikingly cherubic youth, most of the other men in the shuffling line were older and resigned to their fate, but Dick looked about him with curiosity.

'Poor things,' Claymore whispered to Lieutenant Cool as they were led past. 'They must feel they've come to the end of the world.'

The lieutenant gave a surprising giggle. 'But that's exactly where they have come to!'

The armed soldiers who led the new arrivals to the reception block took little interest in them. If they had noticed Dick's smile they would have put it down to vacancy, or even madness, which was commonplace in Port Arthur with its resident asylum.

The line of men passed a new penitentiary which was nearing completion on the edge of the water, and were taken up the hill. They came to a halt in front of the guard tower, which Dick compared to the building he had seen when he was marched through the East End of London on his way to the hulk. The guard tower, however, was on a miniature scale compared to the great Tower of London.

Wild valerian grew round the base. The red flowers reminded him of the west country. He had picked them as a child to provoke a neighbour's cat into a frenzy of excitement. It was comforting to find it growing here; indeed the whole settlement gave a superficial appearance of peacefulness, with its wild flowers and avenues of young, newly planted trees from the Old Country. A stream sparkled on its way to the sea. Even the penitentiary looked attractive in the sunlight. The only hint of menace was the regular cracking sound from the old gaol, heard at five-second intervals when it was not obscured by the clanking and hammering from the workshops.

The missionary paused and wondered as he was led to a cottage on the other side of the harbour.

'What's that?' he asked his escorting officer.

'What?'

'That noise?' The officer was so used to the sound that he had to listen for a moment before he recognised the familiar echo from the punishment yard.

'Oh, that . . .' He was about to invent a lie when the truth was confirmed by a terrible cry of pain which pierced the air. 'The flagellator,' he explained hastily, and led the party on.

The screams continued. Dick heard them as he waited outside the 'office' where new arrivals were made ready for inspection. 'Thirty-five . . . thirty-six . . .' He counted the lashes as he stood there, naked, his clothes at his feet, his irons removed. One of the older convicts covered his genitals with his hands, but Dick had walked naked too often on the *Juniper* and the hulk to care about modesty – until the soldiers seized the opportunity for a medical examination of their own.

'Feet apart . . . wider . . . wider!' A stick struck him on the shins and he stretched his legs as wide apart as possible. 'Turn round . . .' Another blow, this time on his back. 'Bend down . . . down . . .' This time the blow fell on his neck and left his ears ringing. 'Straddle . . .' He heard a curious rustling sound as one of the soldiers pulled a rubber glove over his hand, and suddenly a shooting pain as a finger was thrust inside him and turned agonisingly in its search for gold or money concealed in a *plan*: a hollow cylinder three inches long, its two halves screwed together, usually made of ivory since metal would corrode.

'Stand up . . .' A blow of the stick to the calves. 'Raise your arms.' Dick obeyed, smarting from the pain, and the soldier looked between his legs and under his arms.

'Open your mouth . . .' The gloved finger smelling of his excrement explored his cheeks, hoping to find a ball of rolled tobacco. Nothing. 'All right. Clean.' The voice sounded disappointed, but there was no personal animosity. Dick was not a human being capable of feelings, but a newly arrived shipment with a number. He started to count the lashings again to obliterate the shame, starting from fifty: 'Fifty-one . . . two . . . three . . .' He wondered what the limit would be. Did a man have to faint before they stopped?

'Stanton 982?' A soldier came out of the guard tower, examining a list. 'In you go, and smart about it.'

Free of his irons, Dick walked inside quickly and was told to sit on a bench to wait his turn for the barber. To say the man 'cut' hair would be as true as to say a farmer 'cut' wheat, for he did so without resort to brush, comb or mirror, seizing the locks in one hand and slicing them off with a pair of rusty scissors clutched in the other. As they were blunt the process was as painful as the 'medical examination'. Dick was thankful when it was over and he was ordered outside, though his shaven head made him suddenly conscious of his nakedness. He was marched into another cell where an officer wrote down personal details and checked the information against his list. Out into the sunlight again, where the sound still echoed from the hollow: perhaps it was a different man, for there were no more screams. Then the prisoners waited for their inspection by the commandant of Port Arthur – Captain John O'Hara Booth.

It was Booth's fancy to keep the convicts naked while he addressed them. Sometimes his officers wondered about this instruction: did it establish his own superiority from the outset, did it express his contempt for the prisoners, or did he enjoy it? It was noted that his eyes glinted with pleasure when men begged him for leniency, even now when he was on the point of retirement because of ill-health. His gout was so crippling that he found it difficult to walk more than a few steps, and he arrived at the guard tower in a litter which bore such a close resemblance to a converted wheelbarrow that the effect was not only bizarre but comic.

By chance Dick was closest in line when the commandant was helped to his feet, so he was able to study this tyrant at close quarters. His smile expanded. The man looked as if some gigantic stone had been lifted up and O'Hara Booth had crawled out from under it. He was a large figure, almost bloated, on the point of exploding his tight-collared uniform with its heavy epaulettes. His colour, which was that of a slug, confirmed his aversion to the sun. His eyebrows were so pale that they were invisible, and his hair, as fine and silky as a child's, was pinkish rather than red.

When he stood upright, a cane was placed in one hand and a fan in the other. Dick could see the sweat pouring down his face and could smell his sickly-sweet odour. Suddenly, to the amazement of everyone present, Dick laughed. It was a dreadful sound at such a moment, and in such surroundings. O'Hara Booth swung round and stared at him. Hobbling a few steps until his face was inches away from Dick's, he looked the convict up and down uncertainly. 'I'll remember you,' he whispered. His voice was high, but the man's most alarming feature was his mouth. Dick's laughter had been a nervous reaction, for when O'Hara Booth opened it he resembled a shark. His teeth were sharp and gleaming, a brighter white than any human teeth could ever be, for these were polished ivory, carved from whalebone by a convict.

O'Hara Booth's smile had a hideous perfection.

The commandant stepped back and started his habitual speech of welcome in his shrill but penetrating voice. 'I have only a few words to say to you men, and these are words of warning. You'll find nothing funny in this place – nothing to laugh about, I can promise you that – but if you're sensible and do as you're told you'll receive excellent rations and fair treatment from your overseers, who are first-rate fellows with full responsibility to see that my orders are obeyed. But if anyone fails to carry out my orders, he'll be carried out of here in a box.' The muster officer awarded this little joke a dutiful smile, knowing the speech by heart. 'Anyone who is rash enough to try to escape will not only find that that is an impossibility here, but will be guilty of gross ingratitude and can expect no leniency from me.' He swung round with unexpected agility, and stared at Dick in particular. 'I swear I shall show you no mercy, so you'd best remember that. I'm a reasonable man, I do my best for everyone here, but if you have foolish ideas forget them now. There's only one way out of Port Arthur, and I have the key in my pocket. That's all.'

In the stores, six of the luckier men were told that their irons would not be replaced, but Dick was not among them. He was issued with a yellow suit – a 'no-hoper' – had the irons fastened again, and was marched off to the gaol. The only possessions the men were allowed to keep were their braces.

There are men who enjoy the company of other men and find life easier when it is stripped of all responsibility, reduced to a routine of simple acquiescence. There is a certain satisfaction in surrender. But Dick was not one of them. His natural instinct was for survival, and though he was still in his teens he had seen the worst of life already: in the hulk, and worst of all in the prison cage in the depths of the *Countess of Bath*.

His new companions in the long dormitory looked at him with interest – anything different relieved the tedium of life for those who resisted the prison mentality.

Dick had a number of advantages. The first was a mixed blessing: his youthful figure was stared at longingly by a number of the inmates in spite of his scar and shaven head. He had known of the practice whereby an older man becomes the protector of a younger and expects favours in return ever since he joined the *Juniper*, but the inmates here looked more desperate than men he had known before. Perhaps his other advantages would assist him: his gift for laughter, his saving grace, which had marked him out already, for news of his confrontation with O'Hara Booth had spread through the prison with astonishing speed; and his practical use in writing letters home for men who had never penned a word in their lives beyond their 'mark'. This asset was more precious than any cylinder concealed inside him.

As for his new companions, it would be hard to imagine a more disparate lot. Apart from a few blackguards whose faces revealed their relish for evil, their offences were hardly crimes at all but rather excuses to relieve the overcrowded prisons back home by populating a virgin colony. No gentleman of breeding would have been convicted, let alone transported, for similar crimes: theft of a few pence to buy food for a starving family; insubordination; possession of a rabbit caught in a snare; failure to repay a debt of five shillings. These were the crimes of the luckless prisoners, embittered by misfortune, the true 'no-hopers'. If they had resigned themselves to despair, who could blame them?

There were others who proclaimed their guilt with a pride that kept them buoyant: Silas, a Dorsetshire labourer, had set fire to a haystack during the Swing Riots of 1830 when farmers replaced their men with threshing machines. His single regret was the suffering of his family back home. Barney, a cheerful Scot, had struck a constable who came to evict him. Mick had been sentenced for treason but reprieved from the gallows at the last moment, and it was still his aim in life to free his country from English rule, though he held no rancour against individuals. In spite of his rough, red face, Mick was known as a 'gentleman convict', the term for all political prisoners. His inseparable companion was 'Rogue' Kavanagh, who boasted, 'We can survive better than any of you lot. We haven't been sent here for what we've done but for what we believe! That's why no one can break us.' And it was true that even the overseers treated the two Irishmen with respect. The same applied to Charles Smith, dubbed a 'Tolpuddle martyr', transported for his belief in trade unionism by a Dorchester court.

These were some of the people Dick noticed that first

day, when they piled into the long dormitory after work. A cheerful-looking man with a tuft of fair hair falling over his forehead walked with an odd gait, swinging one leg in front of him. Sensing Dick's attention, he turned round and smiled. Dick smiled back, and regretted it, hoping it would not be interpreted as a signal.

He was issued with a plate, a pannikin and a metal bowl and mug, all stamped with a prison number, and joined the others as they waited for the scavengers to come round with their baskets of rations. Each convict was allowed a daily ration of two ounces of flour, but as this was added to the common pool in the prison kitchen most of it went to the overseers and their families, for the cook was a prisoner himself and unlikely to refuse them. Now that it was summer and the convicts were out all day with the chain-gangs, the evening meal in the mess-room consisted of six ounces of salt pork, a couple of slices of brown bread and a pint of soup. The latter was no more than the water which had boiled the pork, but as some cabbage leaves and Swedish turnips had been thrown in as well it had a flavour in spite of its weak appearance. At a given signal, someone said grace and the prisoners sat down. Ten minutes later they were locked up for the night.

The dormitory reminded Dick of a ship, with a low platform along either side where the convicts lay on rough blankets a foot or so apart, their heads to the ship's side. A rail ran along the edge of the platform holding the convict in his place by a single leg-iron fastened by a ring. This had the advantage of making the overseers feel safe enough to leave the convicts alone, thus allowing them to talk in low voices long into the night, although this was against the rules. As the entire settlement depended on favouritism and bribery, it was possible, even here, to buy or barter from the overseers, and Dick saw a rolled cigarette passed from mouth to mouth until so little was left that the butt was stuck on to a pin. An oil-lamp glowed dimly from the centre of the long room, but a number of the prisoners had small tin lamps of their own, using the light for carving ivory, mending their trousers or playing cards. There were sixty men in his dormitory, and though the air was less humid at night it was still oppressive. At last the voices died down and the only sounds were the groans and snores of the men and the clicking of their leg-irons on the rail as they turned over.

The settlement bell which hung from a plinth in the yard outside pealed out at five o'clock, just before daylight. The constables unfastened the ankle-locks and escorted the prisoners in batches to the space where they could plunge their faces in buckets of murky water and relieve themselves. Five minutes later they had their leg-irons replaced and received their issue of brown bread and skilley, a kind of porridge made with two ounces of oatmeal and half of molasses. Soon after that Dick was told to report to one of the carrying gangs. These were graded: the strongest of the convicts carried planks or beams. Dick, as a new arrival, was assigned to the gang which carried shingles for roofing from a hill named Tongataboo, four miles away.

This was heavier work than it sounded, for the green wooden slats weighed twenty-five pounds or more when they were tied in bundles, but it was the character of the sub-overseer, Benjamin Hearn, that gave his gang a bad reputation. Sub-overseers typified the penal system: they had no legal authority but enjoyed the power to have a man flogged merely on their say-so. Selected from the gangs themselves, they fought for their position with their fists, and when they won they had all the authority they needed. They gave the places at the front of the gang to their favourites, receiving bribes and information in return. Benjamin Hearn took sadistic pleasure in encouraging informers to tell him if they discovered any member of the gang who possessed something of value.

This was how the settlement worked, each man set against another, each gang competing against a rival, and on this basis Port Arthur flourished. If a man had nothing to sell, he offered his support.

It was scarcely half-past five when they set out for Tongataboo and the early haze promised a sweltering day to come. After a mile or so they entered scrubland, which made for slower going, and Dick lifted the irons slightly from the chain which was tied round his waist. It was a shuffling process, depending on the speed of the man in front, for they were linked together like the vertebrae of a grass-snake. Two armed soldiers kept their distance, on hand in case of trouble. Ben Hearn walked beside the chain-gang with his stick and noticed Dick's braces, given him by Sarah the previous Christmas. When they arrived at the top of the hill they were given ten minutes' rest to pick the thorns and prickles from their skin and recover their breath. By now it was stifling and Dick had a terrible thirst.

'Nice.' Ben Hearn bent down and fingered the coveted braces. 'Very nice indeed. Feel like a tip-up?' This was his way of asking Dick to hand them over before they were taken by force.

Dick was wondering what he should do when another voice broke in. 'Leave him, Ben.' He looked up to see the prisoner who had smiled the night before.

Ben Hearn hesitated, then moved away. The prisoner sat down on the ground next to Dick, thrusting out his leg stiffly to expose a wooden stump as the trouser-leg lifted.

'Joseph,' he muttered. 'They call me Stumpy Joe because of this.' He hoisted the trousers higher to show that his right leg was amputated below the knee. The wooden stump was evidently a remarkable substitute, judging by the speed of Joe's ascent. Dick was to learn that he asked for no concessions because of his disability, nor did he receive any. Instead he commanded the respect which had made Ben Hearn turn away, for he was a man no one liked to tangle with, notorious for the strength of his arms and the wildness of his temper if he was crossed. He had been known to pull off his wooden leg and use it as a club, battering another man half to death before he was dragged away. None of this showed in his amiable

314

face, and he was one of the few popular men in the settlement. Dick had little idea how fortunate he was that this particular man had singled him out, but he took the outstretched hand gladly.

When the ten minutes were up Hearn blew a warning blast on his whistle. The prisoners scrambled to their feet and started to cut the trees and collect the slats. With the bundles trimmed and tied and hoisted on their shoulders, the journey back was harder going all round. If a man fell, he was dragged along the ground until he managed to rise again. If he let go of his bundle he was punished.

Shortly after their return, at a quarter to twelve, a ball was pulled up the flagstaff and the prisoners were sent to the mess-room for their meagre midday meal. Then it was back to work again. In the afternoon the heat was relieved by one of those strangely violent summer storms. Dick scarcely noticed the gradual loss of light until they reached the top of Tongataboo and he looked behind him to find the sky was black. The rumbles were distant at first, as if the sky was starting to crack under a great weight, and then it split apart with a crash of thunder and falling shafts of lightning like liquid fire. A few massive drops followed and then ceased. The atmosphere grew so dense that it was impossible to see more than a few yards ahead. Suddenly the rain poured down from the heavens in such a rush that they might have been standing under a waterfall, and this was followed by hailstones as large as farthings – in summer!

Though people in houses rush for cover in such a storm, or peer through windows in alarm, Dick welcomed the chance to raise his mouth to the sky, letting the water drench him all over and wash him clean, laughing at the hail which made the deluge cooler.

Then the sounds grew distant again and the force of the falling water slackened, as if the heavens had been emptied. The chain-gang returned to the settlement in a jollier mood, though the wet chains chafed the skin and made it raw.

A storm was a treat in Port Arthur.

Such was the routine. On the second night, taking a stroll by the water's edge with James Brownlow, the doctor in charge of the hospital, Joshua Claymore paused as he heard an unexpected peal of laughter echoing from the prison.

'Surely that can't be the convicts?'

'Yes. Sometimes you hear them singing. It's rather pleasant, but the commandant calls it their "hideous mirth".'

'How can mirth be hideous?' The missionary smiled. 'How silly.'

'I think he compares it to the jollification round the guillotine, or the mirth at a public hanging.'

Claymore reflected. 'I suppose that sort of mirth is hideous. It astonishes me that these poor wretches are able to laugh at all in a place like this.'

'They have to,' said the doctor, 'or go mad, as many of them do. I find their laughter admirable.' He spoke with such compassion that the missionary was happy to agree.

'Yes, I am starting to understand. For those without the solace of Christian faith, deprived of their families, still to be able to laugh ... the human spirit is truly amazing.'

But laughter was not common in Port Arthur, and Dick's confidence began to fade as he recognised the misery around him. The saddest cases were not the young men, who lived in hope, nor the very old who looked forward to death, but those in their thirties and forties who were so desperate to see their families again that they went to terrible lengths in their efforts to do so. A few had attempted to escape: the 'incos' or incorrigibles, rebels who remained unbroken in spite of their spells in solitary for 100 days or longer, whose backs bore the scars of countless lashings from the flagellator.

However, there was another way of leaving the settlement: through such a physical disability that Captain O'Hara Booth was happy to produce his 'key' and dispose of the useless man. Dick was woken one night by the panting of the convict beside him. He saw the movements by the faint glow from the oil-lamp and then, to his dismay, watched as the desperate man smeared the semen into his eyes.

The man turned, sensing that Dick was looking at him, and peered back through the whitish substance. Raising a finger to his lips, he whispered: 'To get an infection. Then they'll let me go.'

A few nights later the bunk was vacant, and Dick knew that the man had been successful. Word came back from the hospital that he was being discharged from the settlement. He had gained his wish – except that he was blind.

The incident had a sequel: far from acting as a warning, it encouraged one half-crazed convict who yearned to end his days in peace to regard blindness as a blessing rather than a curse. For several nights he approached the others with a needle, asking them to push it in his eyes. All refused, for he had nothing to give them in return. Finally he attempted to do it himself but the point was blunt and, to the horror of those who saw him, it failed to penetrate his eyeball when he tried to press it in. He was taken to hospital and returned in twenty-four hours with a partial loss of sight in the eye, which had turned blue-grey.

Dick tried to reconcile his feelings of shame by ignoring the worst of life around him. Each day he absorbed the landscape, studying every detail intently. One day he had a chance to see Eagle Hawk Neck. He was assigned with Stumpy Joe and an old convict, Charlie Worrell, to carry rations for the garrison of soldiers stationed on Mount Arthur, and when they were allowed an hour's rest, in deference to Joe who was obviously in pain though he made no complaint, Dick shuffled to the summit and looked down over the thin strip of land he had heard about so often. In the far distance he could see the faint line of East Bay Neck which joined Forestier's Peninsula to the mainland. These necks were the keys to freedom and Eagle Hawk was the first and the most dangerous, one hundred yards long but only twenty yards wide. Shielding his eyes, he could just make out the soldiers stationed across the sand. To make it more impassable, a pack of straining dogs were tethered at intervals, their chains just allowing them to touch. On the western side there was a signal-station and a look-out at One-Tree Point, while the Southern Ocean broke ferociously on Descent Beach in Pirate's Bay. Dick sighed. It was plain from this high vantage point that anyone trying to escape would be torn to pieces by the dogs if he was not shot by the soldiers. Charlie Worrell shuffled up beside him, his rat-like face screwed up with suspicion though he was eager to air his superior knowledge. He looked slyly at Dick.

'It's dogs or sharks, you takes your choice. They do say that Government Billy is the slyest shark in all the sea. Thinking of chancing your luck?'

Dick stared straight back. 'No, but *you* are.'

Charlie Worrell looked around him nervously and spat to conceal his embarrassment. 'Get along with you. No chance.'

Dick studied the cackling old convict and decided that the man could not be trusted. His impression was confirmed when he repeated the conversation to Joe, who told him: 'Trust no one. Least of all Charlie, who'd tell on any man. He's waiting to pounce on mugs like you and he has the ear of Ben Hearn. Remember – there's one hundred pounds, free pardon, and a passage home for anyone informing on an escaper.'

'You're right,' Dick admitted. 'Charlie says there's no chance of escape. Is he right?'

'There's always a chance,' said Joe, 'but leave me out of it. I'm bushed enough as it is. This is far enough for me.'

'Trust no one. Help no one.' Advice from Joe, born of experience. But Dick was tempted to help the young Scottish convict, Angus Steehouder, who had sailed with him on the *Tamar* and was now assigned to the same chain-gang. Angus had become the new recipient of Ben Hearn's sadism, after an informer swore he was 'holding' money, though Angus denied it.

The day after Dick's encounter with Charlie Worrell he rejoined Ben Hearn's gang and climbed the hill to Tongataboo. The day was tranquil and Dick dozed off in the ten-minute break. He was woken by a single scream. Later, Joe told him that Hearn had jumped on Angus Steehouder from behind and thrown the youth over his shoulder, while Charlie and another of his tame convicts seized his feet. They had manhandled the Scot out of sight behind the scrub so quickly that it was hardly noticed.

'I'll see if you're holding,' Hearn told him savagely – it had become an obsession by now – and when no ivory or wooden phial was found the overseer loosened his trousers and thrust himself inside the writhing convict in a rage of frustration. 'I'll give you something to hold,' he muttered in his ear. The penetration had caused the broken scream.

When it was over, Steehouder lay on the ground as if he was dead. The overseer emerged from the undergrowth and looked so guilty that it was possible to guess what had happened as he fastened his belt.

'Someone will swing for Hearn one of these days,' Joe whispered to Dick, 'and I'll cheer when it happens.' Dick caught a glimpse of the overseer's eyes, and turned his head away. They were sated.

Steehouder came out of the undergrowth with the two tame convicts, and to Dick's surprise looked as if the fight had gone out of him. The change over the next few days was more alarming. Whenever possible he kept close to his tormentor, wearing a hang-dog expression.

'Christ,' said Joe. 'I do believe the bastard liked it.'

Such behaviour was hardly rare in Port Arthur, where deviation was the norm, but it seemed a loathsome reversal in the case of the young Scot. He might have looked like an angel with his long lashes, but he had been a man in his earlier defiance. A change came over Ben Hearn too. He started to include his victim in his hand-outs of tobacco, and moved him from the back of the grass-snake to a favoured place in front, until it became obvious that the boy was the object of genuine affection rather than the lust that would have been easier for the others to understand.

'I'd never have thought it,' said Joe with disgust. 'He's become Ben's girl. He's got a taste for it now.'

Their disappearances into the scrub became routine, accepted and finally welcomed by the others as the ten-minute break lengthened into fifteen minutes, sometimes twenty.

Dick never forgot the howls of agony a month later, or the sight of Ben Hearn staggering into the open, shouting his head off. He gazed appalled as the overseer clasped and unclasped the stump that was left. When they pulled Steehouder from the scrub he was still gasping for breath and his neck was raw where Hearn had choked him as he tried to break the grip of those even teeth.

Having seen the overseer's agony, Dick was unable to laugh, but the news raced through the settlement and 'hideous mirth' echoed in every quarter. Even O'Hara Booth was heard to giggle as he signed the Scot's death warrant.

Dick never saw Steehouder again but was told that he smiled as he went to the gallows in Hobart Town.

— 20 —
Ravenous dogs or 'Government Billy'

In the days that followed, Dick took stock of his fellow men and began to find himself in the process. He had endured many ordeals in the last two years and looked a fully grown man, but he was scarcely twenty years old. If Port Arthur could break some men, it could strengthen the resolve of others, and in this respect Dick had several advantages. He did not possess academic knowledge, nor intellectual brilliance, but he had the absolute self-confidence that lives for the day. In the prison cage on board the *Countess of Bath*, with the daily battle for survival, this had been understandable; but even at Swansdowne he had found it hard to concentrate on plans for the future when the daily routine around the farm demanded all his attention.

In the settlement Dick had the chance to see himself in perspective. Like a lawyer preparing his case, he studied the evidence and reckoned his chances. The verdict was straightforward: there could be no thought of serving his time in Port Arthur. Endurance was not worthwhile if he emerged at the end of it no better than an 'assigned servant', without any rights of his own. Port Arthur had taught him to hate the role of servant, forgetting the kindness he had received at Swansdowne. Jumped-up publicans and junior officers were known to boast that they had 'a fresh servant every week', and if the servant was female she was likely to become the man's mistress. But if the servant was male, the 'mistress' had the right to marry him. The thought tantalised him: Sally as his wife, with the power to have him flogged if it suited her whim. There was a horrible fascination in his fantasy.

Even his return to 'society' as an assigned servant depended on his good behaviour, and in Port Arthur the smallest misdemeanour could double a sentence in seconds. He might be forty years old before he was released. At best he might be given the lighter duties of the officers' servants, performed by the 'educated convicts', but this meant perpetual submission. At worst, he would be sent to the coal mines west of Eagle Hawk Neck where sixty 'marked men' were stationed under guard, cut off from any contact with the outside world. Port Arthur itself was a natural fortress, surrounded by hills with semaphore signals at the top. When a prisoner was mad enough to bolt, the entire 'island' was alerted in less than twenty minutes. This was something to remember when he escaped, as escape he must.

Dick's resolve had been strengthened by a tragic incident involving two young convicts, inseparable companions until they were divided by a spell of solitary confinement after they were reported for 'dumb insolence' by their overseer. They were strangely silent following their release, speaking in whispers as if solitude in the granite cells had damaged their sense of sound. When they returned to the long dormitory Dick was puzzled by the gravity of their expressions as they played a game of cards one night by the light of a flickering candle as if their lives depended on it. When the younger man won he let out a great sigh and the other clasped his hand as if to console him. The following morning they joined their gang, which was felling trees on Mount Arthur, and the older man suddenly threw himself on the ground. His companion raised his axe to the heavens and brought it down with all his force on his friend's neck. The sharpened blade severed the head instantly; indeed, the violence of the blow threw it several feet from the rest of the body. Then the murderer hurled his axe into the undergrowth and wept.

'He must have been mad?' Dick asked one of the gang in the dormitory that evening.

'Oh, no,' said the man sadly. 'You could say they came to their senses. 'Tis known as a suicide-agreement and is not unknown here. Many a boy has jumped from Point Puer holding the hand of his friend.'

'But this isn't suicide,' Dick pointed out. 'The other man lives.'

'Aye, he won at cards, and has the sailing to Hobart Town to look forward to. At least he'll leave this cursed place. That's his prize.'

'God forgive them,' Dick murmured, and the man smiled.

''Tis us who should forgive Him.'

The winner of the card game retained his spirit unbroken to the end. Sympathisers who had heard of his action waited underneath the scaffold in Hobart Town to cheer him. As the convict climbed the ladder to the scaffold, a woman pressed forward with a Sydney orange sliced at the top, so he could suck the juice. Smiling, he said: 'Do not worry yourself over me; since Port Arthur this is the happiest day of my life.' There was a cheer as he waved the orange to the crowd. Then the chaplain pressed his other hand on the Bible before the calico hood was slipped swiftly over his head and the drum roll burst out. The convict dropped and so did the orange, rolling from the platform on to the ground below where boys scrambled to retrieve it.

To be able to break the spirit of a prisoner was the boast of O'Hara Booth. He relished the cruelty he inflicted, and could see no wrong in it. When a man had the courage to rebel, O'Hara Booth invented a new punishment to make him plead for mercy. One of his inventions was an instrument of torture: an iron collar attached to ankle fetters by a chain which was too short to allow the prisoner to stand upright. As spikes protruded from the collar it was also impossible for the victim to lie down and he was forced into a constant crouching position. When one convict died during this punishment, Dr Brownlow diagnosed heart failure and protested so bitterly that the collar was abandoned.

A man was hung by his hands from ring-bolts in the wall placed several feet apart for nine hours at a time, his feet dangling above the flags below, gagged to stop his screaming. When the doctor protested again, threatening an official complaint to Governor Franklin, O'Hara Booth indulged in his familiar brand of humour: 'I know people think this sort of punishment is bestial, but they forget I am dealing with beasts.'

The doctor regarded him coldly. 'No beast of the earth would treat another like this. It is *we* who are bestial.'

The commandant listened to the doctor with mixed feelings. He was a coward at heart and had no wish to provoke a scandal to cloud his retirement. So the two men lived in mutual disharmony, barely tolerating each other, and O'Hara Booth contented himself with more traditional means of breaking a man's spirit, such as having him chained to the floor and kicked at regular intervals to prevent his sleep, while cutting his rations to keep him hungry.

Stumpy Joe's privileges came to an abrupt end when no less a figure than O'Hara Booth himself was wheeled round the corner of the prisoners' block when Joe was resting on the ground after his return from Tongataboo, smoking a pipe. This in itself was forbidden, but the commandant found it even harder to forgive the man's insolence in failing to spring to his feet – a physical impossibility in Joe's case. Instead, Joe gave an amiable smile and lifted himself slowly off the ground. As his trousers concealed the stump, O'Hara Booth interpreted the movement as laziness and the smile as mockery, for the commandant was sensitive where his appearance was concerned. He gave orders that Joe should 'enjoy' the cure for incorrigibles.

That afternoon the convict boat rowed across the bay and dumped Joe on L'Isle des Morts with a piece of salt pork but no water, a calculated refinement at a time of year when rain was unlikely unless another freak electrical storm saved him. This was a long-accepted means of killing a man, but nine days later, thanks to the doctor's intervention, Joe was taken off. He was a changed man.

The days became weeks as Dick waited for his opportunity to escape, but he bore them with a lighter heart as he thought of liberty. It was liberty or death.

His chance came when he was assigned with five other convicts to a new gang fetching logs from Long Bay, three miles from the settlement. Joe was among them, the open smile replaced by a blank expression which irritated the new overseer, Cranky Jack Smith. One morning it was obvious to Dick that Joe's stump was hurting him acutely as he steadied himself for a moment over a log; unfortunately Cranky Jack Smith noticed this too and came over to strike Joe's chin with his fist. Losing his balance, Joe fell backwards. He seized his axe in an effort to rise, and Smith interpreted the action as a threatened assault. He ordered two of the guards to drag Joe back to the settlement. Returning to the chain-gang, Smith announced that Joe was receiving thirty-six lashes of the cat, and so would anyone else who dared step out of line.

Dick nodded obediently with the rest. That night a friend in the kitchen, already bribed with the promise of tobacco, brought him a piece of salt pork, and the moment of escape drew closer. It came the next morning, after Cranky Jack had ordered him into the water to shift some massive stones which were making it difficult for boats to moor alongside a jetty; arduous work which left him soaked. When he rejoined the gang on the slope above, he asked the overseer if he could remove his clothes and let them dry.

Cranky Jack Smith stared at Dick as if he had asked for hot buttered toast.

'You want *what*?' he cried, and went for Dick as he had for one-legged Joe. This time Dick struck first and it was Cranky Jack who was knocked to the ground. Before the others were fully aware of what was happening Dick had lifted the half-unconscious man, staggered to the edge, and hurled his body over the bank into the sea twenty feet below.

Cranky Jack Smith gave a cry of 'Help! I'm drowning', which brought the others scrambling to his rescue in the hope of ingratiating themselves with him – all except Joe, who caught Dick's hand as he bounded past, lifting his irons by the chain which stretched from the leather strap around his waist.

'Good on you!' Joe cried. It was the first time his eyes had brightened since his return from the Island of the Dead. Yet when the overseer and the prisoners returned, Joe pointed in the direction Dick had taken.

Instinctively, Cranky Jack Smith started to follow, but his cunning stopped him a few paces later.

'Ah!' he exclaimed. 'That's your game, is it? You don't catch Jack.'

Joe scowled, as if his ruse had been discovered, and Cranky Jack disappeared in the opposite direction with the guards. Joe smiled again.

With the semaphores in mind, Dick crossed Signal Hill keeping Norfolk Bay to his left, until he reached the range which ran parallel with the road leading to Eagle Hawk Neck. He forced himself through the scrub, determined to cover as great a distance as possible. Even so, having to hoist his fetters from the ground as he did, it was a shambling progress, and he had covered little more than a mile by the end of the day. He collapsed at the foot of a tree, and licked the blood from his bare feet. He woke before daylight, instantly aware of the great silence around him. After the clanking inferno of the settlement at dawn, the overwhelming absence of sound astonished him. 'I am free,' he murmured to himself. 'I am free.'

Ravenously hungry, he tore the salt pork apart and devoured more than he intended. He was left with a desperate thirst, and started to search for a landmark which would give him some idea of his bearings. After a short climb he came to a clearing and looked out at a hill rising steeply ahead, almost three miles away. Thirst made him long to descend, but he continued towards the summit, reaching it several hours later. As he hoped, the landscape stretched below him in a perfect panorama: the slender sand-bar of Eagle Hawk Neck stood out in sharp relief, with soldiers mounting guard, and a cluster of constables, doubtless assembled there for his benefit. Behind the guard house, on a slight incline, the semaphore was in a state of agitation, sending out a series of signals, presumably on his account as well. Dick crouched like a hunted animal – as indeed he was in the eyes of O'Hara Booth – and saw the commandant flanked by armed and mounted constables riding along the track below, apparently returning to the settlement after an inspection of Eagle Hawk Neck – the key to freedom.

Dick spotted three small huts on the other side of the road, a mile apart from each other along the coastline which skirted Norfolk Bay, ending with a stretch of water half a mile wide with the Forestier Peninsula on the opposite side. This water, resembling the estuary of a river, was the lair of the shark known as Government Billy. As Dick lay there motionless he chose the exact place where he would swim across as soon as it was dark.

Exhausted, Dick drifted into unwilling sleep, and it was dark when he woke. Judging by the moon, he guessed it was eleven o'clock, and he scrambled down as quickly as he could in order to catch the tide. Within a hundred yards of the second hut he approached the road quietly, recoiling when a convict constable walked past a few feet away as he crouched in the ditch. Hearing voices a minute later, he realised that a chain of patrols waited for him along the coast and blessed the cloud which suddenly obscured the moon.

Scurrying across the road, he reached the water. He tied his clothes in a bundle around his neck and struck out across the water to the opposite peninsula. The coolness enveloped him, soothing his scratched and bleeding body, so refreshing that he yielded to the ache and let it flow into his mouth as well. For a second he froze with fear as an object bumped into him, then gasped with relief as he felt the hardness of a log instead of the skin of Government Billy. The dogs howled mournfully on the distant Neck. Thankful for his strength as a swimmer and the cloud which stayed overhead, he moved steadily across the calm water until he felt a dense mass of seaweed and knew he had reached the other side. There had been no sign of the shark: evidently Government Billy was in pursuit of smaller fish elsewhere.

Dick dressed rapidly and headed for the cover of the undergrowth delirious with the knowledge that the most dangerous part of his escape had been successful. For two hours he forced his way through the prickly scrub on hands and knees until the exhilaration left him and he could bear the agony of his lacerated skin no longer. Then he flung himself on the gentler earth below a gum tree and waited for daylight to guide him in the direction of East Bay Neck. If he succeeded in crossing that as easily as he had Eagle Hawk Neck he would reach the safety of the mainland, though he had only the vaguest idea of what he would do then or where he would go. For the present, all that mattered was his liberty. 'I am free,' he murmured aloud, and fell asleep.

He walked, fell, and crawled throughout the next day through virgin bush until he collapsed on the ground, hungry and thirsty, but hopeful in spite of the raw flesh scraped so painfully by the irons and his bleeding feet. After a restless night he set out again, weaker now from lack of food and so uncertain of his direction that he started to retrace his steps in the afternoon in the hope of finding the road which led to East Bay Neck. He saw it several hours later, and concealed himself at a safe distance. He lay down to rest with a sharp pain in his chest, caused either by hunger or by the murky water he had drunk from a stagnant pool earlier.

On his fourth day he was weaker still, and blood was dripping constantly from his legs, but he consoled himself with the knowledge that the search for him would have been abandoned by now. Rashly he limped on to the road, and only a few minutes later found himself confronted by John Evenden, the chief convict constable, and five of his men. For a second, Dick looked around wildly; then he gave himself up.

'How far is East Bay Neck?' he could not help asking.

The chief constable looked at him with pity. 'Less than a mile away.'

'Oh, God,' sighed Dick. 'As close as that.'

They took him to the nearest hut. Dick was surprised when the chief constable offered him food and drink. 'Help yourself, but not too much too quickly or you'll make yourself ill.' Noticing Dick's surprise, he added: 'Most of you villains manage a few yards and put us to a lot of trouble for nothing. At least you made the hunt worthwhile.'

This was scant consolation for Dick. Success is nothing if you 'nearly make it'. Nevertheless he was grateful for the man's attitude and his order to remove the hateful irons. When he collapsed on the ground, Evenden sent a constable to the signal station on Forestier's Hill to semaphore the news of Dick's recapture, with the message that the prisoner would not be in a fit state to travel until the following day.

The next morning Dick was handcuffed and marched through Eagle Hawk Neck. Seen close to, in daylight, it was different from the imaginings of darkness. Eleven dogs were chained so that their muzzles nearly touched, but he was particularly interested in the two on either side tethered to large wooden stakes set in the water. They passed a gang of convicts on the road who surprised him with a cheer, for news of his escape attempt had spread throughout Port Arthur. Dick knew he would pay dearly for his reputation. Yet even in gaol he received an extra allowance of brown bread and a huge portion of skilley from the sub-overseer, who locked him in his cell with a cheerful grin. 'Well done, lad. You took the first key from Booth's pocket when you crossed the Neck. Few have managed that.' There was no answering smile from Dick, fearful of the punishment ahead.

The following day he was brought up for trial in front of O'Hara Booth.

'Richard Stanton 982!' The commandant was flanked by Lempriere, the officer in charge of the commissariat, and the muster master, who read the charge from a sheet of paper in front of him. As he did so, O'Hara Booth studied his prisoner with such intensity that Dick wondered if he recognised him as the convict who had laughed in his face. Then, as the pale eyes hardened, Dick knew that he had.

'I warned you,' the commandant whispered through the perfect teeth, 'yet you took no notice. Have you anything to say?'

'Nothing in my defence,' Dick replied with humility. 'It is the first and certainly the last time I shall be guilty of such foolishness . . .'

'Indeed it will be,' the commandant murmured. 'Is that all?'

Dick drew breath desperately. 'I shall tell my fellow prisoners that it's mad to attempt an escape which can only bring starvation and suffering, and the punishment I shall now receive. I give my word that I'm sorry for what I've done. I've learnt my lesson.'

O'Hara Booth stared at his prisoner, perplexed. The abject confession was unexpected, and he wondered whether the man was making fun of him for a second time. He was disappointed to be deprived of the chance to punish the convict for further insubordination. At the same time he was gratified to see such a strong young man grovel before him. His anger evaporated. Losing interest, he gave his verdict indifferently. 'A hundred lashes – six months' solitary – followed by eighteen months' hard labour in chains.' Raising a flabby hand, he had the convict removed.

Outside, Dick straightened with relief. At least he had been spared O'Hara Booth's latest instrument of torture, which his escort had described gloatingly as they waited beforehand. Now that Dr Brownlow had returned to Hobart Town and been replaced by Dr Furness, an inexperienced man who was feeling his way, the commandant was indulging his old pleasure in inventing punishments for the convicts. His latest was the 'Log': a vast block of wood secured to a man's irons by a three-foot chain so that the prisoner was obliged to carry the 'Log' with him wherever he went. Such a hindrance would make a second escape impossible.

Dick's irons had been left behind, so he was marched to the blacksmith for a new pair. The weight depended on the smith's tip, but as Dick had nothing to give him he was surprised and pleased when the satanic-looking man went to some trouble to provide him with the lightest irons possible. 'I've done them proper,' the man muttered as if to himself as he worked. 'That's for crossing the Neck. At least you got a taste of liberty.'

Dick nodded his head gratefully but made no reply, remembering Joe's advice: 'Trust no one.' The blacksmith finished his fitting and stood back admiringly. 'Fit for a bushman!' he grunted, and Dick realised this would be his label – Dick Stanton, bushranger.

Dick had hoped to see Joe again, and he did so that afternoon.

Cranky Jack Smith had been ordered to take charge of the flogging, a duty he accepted with glee. Here was Jack's revenge for the humiliation of being thrown into the sea, and all the subsequent fuss over the escape. Now, to make his vengeance doubly sweet, he appointed Stumpy Joe as flagellator.

When Dick entered the punishment yard, Joe stepped back in dismay. 'You expect me to flog him?'

Cranky Jack grinned. Joe shook his head, and Dick, sensing that he was going to refuse, muttered urgently: 'Go on, Joe. Better you than any other.'

For a moment Joe hesitated, deeply troubled, then he recognised the truth of Dick's words and took the cat held out by Cranky Joe.

The flogging triangle was seven feet high, consisting of three staves fastened together as if a gigantic cauldron was going to be boiled underneath. Instead, Dick was suspended in a manner which reminded the chaplain of the crucifixion, except that his feet were tied with thongs rather than hammered with nails, and his arms were stretched above his head.

Cranky Jack tore off Dick's shirt and his back gleamed in the sunlight that penetrated the yard, unblemished by previous weals. Christmas was only a short time away and the day was hot. The group sweltered as they waited for O'Hara Booth. When he was wheeled in on his barrow, his sluggish head shaded by a wide straw hat, Dick smiled so openly that young Dr Furness shook his head imperceptibly, warning him not to provoke the commandant further.

'Get on with it,' murmured Booth.

'One!' shouted Cranky Jack Smith.

As Joe hesitated, Dick urged him to start with a look of such desperation that Joe whirled the cat around his head and brought the knots down on Dick's back. It looked as if he used all his strength, but he had skilfully pulled back at the last second, lessening the impact.

After the twentieth stroke the pain was so fierce that it was numbing. The new doctor looked on in horror. After the thirtieth the pain returned with a new intensity, and Dick began to scream, mouthing obscenities as he struggled between the strokes, dreading the lacerating pain of the next. After the thirty-eighth stroke the doctor could endure it no longer, and turned away from the sight of Dick's back, which resembled raw meat.

'Thirty-nine . . .'

When Dick regained consciousness in his solitary cell he thought for a moment that he might be dead – the darkness and the silence were so infinite. Then the pain brought him back to a semblance of life, and he tried to fathom his new surroundings. The air was so damp that he could have been thrown to the bottom of a well, and for a moment he wondered if this was so. He touched the walls and *felt* the thickness of the stone. Then the peep-hole in the door slid noiselessly aside and he glimpsed the coldness of his gaoler's eye before it slid back again. Dick broke the tomb-like silence with a rage of invective, shouting the foulest abuse he could think of until his anger was replaced by despair. As he crouched in a corner, able to detect little in the dark, he realised the futility of rage, which would gain him nothing. From now on he would be devious, outwardly broken and contrite, winning trust as a prisoner who conformed, showing no insolence, no hint of courage, always respectful though careful not to say too much. He would learn the art of living deceitfully, accept the label of a 'no-hoper', be prepared to whine when necessary to prove his subjugation. He would do nothing remarkable which could mark him out as 'different'; he would become a forgotten man. And every minute of the day he would husband his strength and superiority, laughing at the others as he confided in himself alone, his only friend.

There was no hope of sleep that first agonising night, but his nerves began to settle and his mind grew calmer until at last a faint ray of sunshine penetrated some unseen crack and lighted on the wall beside him. Without having to move he could make out the scratchings etched on the granite in faint lettering by some unfortunate 'solitary' before him. *Words!* In such a place as this! When he had deciphered them Dick lay back with a sigh, marvelling at the resilience contained in the simple message – *Live in Hope*.

'I shall survive,' he told himself. 'I shall survive.' He repeated the phrase like a schoolboy kept in after school to do lines.

'I shall survive' – a hundredth and a thousandth time until there was no doubt left.

Faith in himself would provide the support he would need in the next six months – the 'python's tail' of his father's odd little sermon all those years ago.

'I shall survive' became 'Liberty or Death'. The in-between was a limbo not to be contemplated.

'Liberty or Death.' He vowed it to himself until the

fever passed and he came to terms not only with his dreadful new existence but with himself as well.

What an irony – what a glorious irony! – that Dick should not be afraid of death because he had realised the value of life.

PART 7

— 21 —
The power of The Times

The sickly youth who parodied the part of a page-boy in the Adelphi stopped Lionel Raxleigh as he left the hotel.

'You,' he declared. Lionel looked at the elegant envelope bearing the Governor's crest which had been delivered by hand.

'When did this arrive?' he asked, trying to suppress the irritation in his voice.

'Last night.'

'It should have been brought to me at once.' Lionel sighed, neither expecting nor receiving an answer. Retiring to the shabby smoking room he opened the envelope apprehensively, and then smiled with relief when he realised that Sir John Franklin was ready for a reconciliation.

My dear Raxleigh,
   Of course you may call at Government House. You are welcome both as a representative of the London *Times* and as a friend. It is too long since we last met. You must forgive Lady Franklin and myself if you find us in a state of some confusion, but as you may have heard I have been recalled to England and we are in the throes of packing up. However, I shall be happy to see you any morning this week at eleven a.m., if that should prove convenient to yourself.

                                        John Franklin

The letter was unmistakably cordial. Either Sir John had forgiven the Stowes for their behaviour at the Government House ball, or it had been forgotten in the bustle of departure. On reflection Lionel decided that the power of *The Times* was responsible. Sir John would be anxious to make a favourable impression on his premature return to England, the consequence of Sloley's indiscreet despatches. The irony was that Sir John detested the system almost as much as Sloley himself, yet was forced to defend it in his capacity as Governor. It was a bitter insult that Sir John had been informed of his recall only after his successor had been appointed. Sir Eardley Wilmot was due to arrive in the next few days, which was one reason why Lionel was anxious to make contact with Sir John as quickly as possible. Better the devil you knew . . .

Lionel hurried upstairs to his forlorn little bedroom to change into his best suit of clothes and make himself as presentable as he could. After his long spell of sobriety at Swansdowne, his return to the comparative civilisation of Hobart Town had felled him like an axe. Now, after several days of steady drinking, he had reached a no-man's-land where he was seldom hopelessly drunk but never entirely sober. He needed to conceal the cracks behind the veneer by plunging his face into a basin of cold water and sucking a fruit lozenge to disguise his breath. On the stroke of eleven he presented himself at Government House.

A new secretary led him to the Governor's study. Sir John rose from behind his desk and came round to greet him, shaking his hand so warmly that Lionel was disarmed, and wondered why he had ever doubted the man.

At first they spoke in pleasantries. 'You can imagine the commotion involved in our departure.' Sir John waved at the piles of papers round the room.

'Are you sorry to be leaving?' Lionel asked him directly.

Sir John frowned. He had never been consulted in the matter, but he was determined not to show his feelings. 'Of course we're thrilled at the thought of seeing England and all our friends again. And I've received word from

336

the Admiralty that they are prepared to supply me with a ship, the *Erebus*, for another expedition to the North-West Passage, so I'm delighted. At the same time, I trust that the seeds I have tried to sow in Van Diemen's Land will prove of some service in the future – but I must not say more on that painful subject. How is your brother-in-law?'

Lionel blinked, remembering Gussie's disastrous behaviour at Government House. 'He's settled down happily at Swansdowne,' he began, and then corrected himself. 'No, that's not quite true. I'm sorry to say that he's ill.'

'What's the matter with him?'

'If only we knew. The local doctor is unable to say, so you can imagine how worried my sister is. She thinks he's dying.'

'I'm sorry to hear that,' said the Governor sympathetically. 'If he comes to Hobart Town, I can recommend a good man. I'll give you his address. And do assure your sister that the incident involving Mr Stowe and that dreadful woman has long since been forgotten!'

'Dreadful woman?' For a moment Lionel was confused.

The Governor smiled. 'Surely you haven't forgotten Lynda Wynette? My wife's dearest friend at the time – much to her mortification now. She does tend to see no bad in people until she finds them out, and then she sees no good. Mind you, there was never much good in Miss Wynette that I could see.'

'What has she done?' Lionel asked, for the Governor was plainly in a mood to gossip.

'She was exposed. Not only did she run an establishment in Torquay, but she had every intention of doing so here in Hobart Town. What do you make of that?'

'An establishment?' Lionel asked vaguely. 'What sort of establishment?'

'Hardly a milliner's; a house of ill-repute, or whatever you choose to call it.'

'Good lord!' Lionel burst out laughing.

'You can imagine my wife's feelings! I know she wants

337

to extend an olive branch to your sister. May I tell her she might do so? Better still, have luncheon with us after our discussion and you can tell her yourself.'

'That will be most agreeable,' said Lionel gratefully.

'Now,' said the Governor, changing his tone, 'what can I do for you? I suppose it's the convict?'

With the candour that made him a foolish man, Lionel told the Governor the truth. He trusted Sir John and though he had an inkling that every confidence was relayed to Lady Franklin, the world's most accomplished gossip, he was reckless from anxiety. The Franklins were soon to leave Van Diemen's Land, so he rationalised that there was little to gain from discretion.

He leaned forward intently. 'First of all I should say that Dick Stanton has behaved impeccably. We regard him as one of the family . . .'

'Always unfortunate,' said Sir John in a tone of disapproval.

'I'm sorry,' said Lionel, surprising himself, 'but Dick . . .' (he added 'Stanton' hastily) '. . . *is* totally different from the usual convict.' The Governor smiled, as if to say he had heard this tune played before. 'His crime was negligible, and he was not to blame for leaving Swansdowne. I am sorry to say that my niece provoked him.'

'That's what comes of allowing a convict to become part of the family,' Sir John pointed out with a shake of the head.

'It was largely our fault. That's why I'm so concerned. I feel responsible for his welfare,' Lionel declared, 'and shan't rest until I know what's happened to him.'

'When I received your note I made enquiries. I believe he was captured after he absconded and was sent to Port Arthur.'

'Yes, I found that out. But what is he doing there?'

'I can tell you exactly,' said the Governor dryly. 'He's doing solitary after trying to escape.'

'Escape?' The news shocked Lionel. It was unlike Dick to act so rashly unless the conditions were worse than he suspected.

'Obviously he had to be punished. I cannot pretend that I share the commandant's zeal for punishment, but of course it's unavoidable when a convict misbehaves.'

'Oh, God,' said Lionel. 'May I see him?'

The Governor sighed unhappily, realising that such a visit was bound to cause trouble. Then it occurred to him that it could be profitable to himself if *The Times* published a despatch condemning the system, as Sloley had done, while absolving his own part in it, as Sloley had not. With a gesture he waved the new secretary out of the room.

'Very well, Mr Raxleigh,' he said. 'Let's talk man to man. You've spoken frankly, so let me respond in kind. You know the slanderous accusations spread by Sloley, who tars me with the same brush he uses to attack transportation. As Governor I have been powerless to defend myself or put my own point of view. He has the ear of the Colonial Office and deafens Lord Stanley with his complaints, while I am in the ludicrous position of having to defend the government without any thanks for doing so. Indeed, they blame me for their own mistakes. I shall be delighted to help you in every way I can. I'll authorise your visit to Port Arthur in your capacity as a writer for the London *Times*. Commandant Booth will block you all the way if he thinks you're nosing around, but he's as vain as the rest of us and he'll go out of his way to help you if he thinks it's in his best interest. In return I would ask you to make a point of quoting me to your readers as saying that the *abominable* – I use that word advisedly – the abominable system of transportation must be halted. Men should no longer be forced to suffer as they do today.'

'I shall welcome the opportunity of stating your views,' said Lionel. They spoke for a few minutes more, and then Sir John recalled his secretary and started to dictate the authorisation for Lionel's visit to Port Arthur.

'When do you wish to leave?' he asked.

'As soon as possible.'

'A boat sails in five days' time with provisions for the

settlement. You realise that means you'll be spending Christmas in Port Arthur? I can't imagine a more dreadful place to spend it.' '

'Perhaps I'll find a festive spirit,' Lionel suggested.

'I think that most unlikely,' said Sir John.

— 22 —

Christmas in hell

Lionel Raxleigh sailed into Port Arthur on Christmas Eve and found it beautiful. 'It's odd,' he told the captain of the *Tamar*, 'how one pictures a place beforehand, only to find the reality quite different. Because it's a penal settlement I thought it would be sombre. Yet that's a splendid church.'

'Yes,' the captain agreed. 'Tomorrow they'll have the Christmas service. You'll be surprised how big it is; holds more than a thousand. You know it's never been consecrated?'

'Why is that?'

'A prisoner escaped and ran inside for refuge, but they followed him in and shot him all the same.'

It should not be supposed that Christmas was just like any other time in the settlement. On the contrary, Lionel found the place in such a state of bustling anticipation that even the convicts looked cheerful as they shouldered the provisions to the shore.

There had not been time to alert the commandant to Lionel's visit, but the officer in charge was suitably impressed when he was presented with the envelope bearing the Governor's crest.

'I shall take this to the commandant at once, Mr Raxleigh. Would you like to accompany me?'

'I'm in no hurry. I can wait here and amuse myself quite happily.'

This gave him an opportunity to examine his surroundings, and he absorbed the scene until the officer returned with a note from O'Hara Booth welcoming him to Port Arthur and hoping that he would dine with him that evening after he had been settled in his quarters. Meanwhile, Lieutenant Cool would tend to his every need.

By now it was midday, and Lionel wiped his face with his handkerchief as he climbed the slope. He still found it difficult to reconcile Christmas with the heat of summer.

'Dashed hot, ain't it?' said the lieutenant.

'It certainly is.'

'Too hot for rum,' the officer said forlornly, 'but I'll see that a good French wine is sent to your cottage. I suggest I call for you at six. You might enjoy a stroll when the sun goes down. Then I can introduce you to the commandant.'

Lionel was left on his own in a room which bore itself with military severity and a minimum of furnishings: bed, table, chair and hideous wardrobe. No carpet, a cracked mirror, no pictures and certainly nothing so dangerous as a book. An ugly, utilitarian wash-stand contained a large china basin and jug, and Lionel dipped his towel in the water and wiped his face. At least the stone floor was cool, and he was grateful for the quiet and shade. The bottle of wine arrived with startling speed, or rather two bottles, brought by a servant – one of the 'educated convicts' – accompanied by Lieutenant Cool. The officer opened the second bottle for himself and drank with alacrity while he prattled on about nothing of importance, largely himself.

Lionel listened politely, blinking from time to time as he tried to look interested, but he found the lieutenant a superficial young man. He recognised the tell-tale signs of alcoholism in the listless eyes and insatiable conversation. He was unaware of Cool's disgrace after failing to report for duty when he lay in a stupor after consuming two bottles of black rum.

The officer lifted his glass with a hand which shook so violently that he had to steady it with the other. 'This place drives you to drink,' he confessed with a bitter laugh. Lionel responded nervously.

'I can well imagine.'

Regretting his indiscretion and finding the bottle empty Cool made his excuses and left stiffly, promising to return in time to escort the visitor to the commandant's Christmas Eve party. The moment of possible rapport between the expatriates was gone.

Lionel unpacked in a desultory fashion, opened the window as wide as possible, picked up the book he had brought with him, closed it again after struggling to concentrate on a single page, and lay down on the hard little bed. He seldom indulged in an afternoon siesta, usually waking exhausted rather than refreshed, and today was no exception. Having dozed for less than half an hour he was overcome with a feeling of nausea, and a terrible thirst which he tried to pacify with a copious draught from the jug of tepid water. He dressed slowly for dinner and waited outside the hut, relaxing in the slight evening breeze. By the time Lieutenant Cool returned, neither the better nor the worse for wine, Lionel had recovered and was ready for the confrontation ahead. As they strolled down the tree-lined avenue he wondered for the hundredth time about the man he was about to meet: Captain John O'Hara Booth of the 21st Fusiliers.

Everything about the man was to prove incongruous. Even his home was the opposite of the military establishment Lionel had been expecting: a small, almost dainty white-boarded cottage with black edgings overlooking the bay, surrounded by a low white fence and a jolly little garden with fuchsias dwarfing the roses, and lupins towering over the rows of pansies which lined the borders. A soldier posted outside the wide verandah with a loaded musket gave a shambling salute which Lieutenant Cool acknowledged with a languid wave, though he drew himself upright the moment he stepped inside.

Lionel would never forget his first sight of the commandant. Though there were several guests crowded into the room on this convivial evening, there was no mistaking

O'Hara Booth. Lionel paid his respects to Mrs John O'Hara Booth, a sharp-looking woman with suspiciously black hair and a very long nose. For this special occasion she wore an off-the-shoulder gown with puffed sleeves which fell like a cascade of large epaulettes as if to complement those on her husband's uniform. Three white rosebuds were skewered into the jet black hair and proceeded to wilt as the evening progressed. After the usual formalities Lionel turned to the commandant and blinked.

Ironically, O'Hara Booth was looking his best that night. The light from the oil-lamps was carefully controlled and far less brutal than the glare of daylight. Even so, Lionel found the hairless face so repellent that he had to blink to conceal his reaction. He managed to smile as he held out his hand in greeting.

'Please forgive me, Mr Raxleigh, if I remain seated,' said O'Hara Booth. 'I'm a martyr to gout.'

Lionel muttered something foolish, shaken by the glimpse of the shark-like teeth.

As the formal introductions were made Lionel tried to remember the names of the other guests who might prove useful to him in the future. They were a mixed bunch, as they usually are in a distant outpost, in awe of their host whose power was as inviolate as that of a captain in command of his ship at sea. O'Hara Booth did not have to play at God. He *was* God in Port Arthur. The new doctor, Andrew Furness, looked an agreeable man though curiously ill at ease, as if he had received bad news and wished he was elsewhere. Reddish hair fell over his forehead, and the lower half of his face was concealed by luxuriant moustaches and a beard.

In striking contrast, the chaplain was as bald as an egg. He smiled amiably, firmly on the side of authority, while his bird-like wife fluttered nervously when Lionel bowed to her courteously, sensing her loneliness.

The most impressive guest was the wife of Pierre Lempriere, in charge of the commissariat, a woman of striking beauty. Lionel had come across her like before: an exotic bloom in the wilderness of a military or naval settlement, though Françoise Lempriere was elegant rather than exotic.

'Lempriere?' he asked. 'It sounds French, yet you speak perfect English.'

'We're relics from the *ancien régime*,' she laughed. 'My husband's father and mine clung to the old traditions and gave us French pre-names. Captain Booth insists on calling my husband Peter, because he knows it makes him angry!' Everyone laughed, including the commandant, who plainly enjoyed the teasing.

'Now!' O'Hara Booth exclaimed, turning to the other guests. 'I have no doubt that Mr Raxleigh wants to see the worst of us – that's part of his profession – but I'm determined that he shall see the best of us as well. Happily he has arrived at the most convivial time of year. We must make him welcome.'

Lionel broke in quickly. 'As you'll appreciate, the convicts are my main reason for coming here.'

There was an imperceptible change in the atmosphere, overshadowed by the convicts – the be-all and end-all of Port Arthur. Lionel had prepared himself for this moment, realising how carefully he should feel his way instead of rushing in with his usual recklessness. He had decided it was vital to enlist the commandant's support and to this end he was prepared to be agreeable, even sycophantic. At the same time he wanted to ask about Dick.

'Obviously you have the place well guarded,' he went on casually. 'Do the convicts ever make a break for it?'

'Hardly ever. It gets them nowhere.'

'It got that man close to the mainland recently,' volunteered the doctor.

The commandant might have taken exception to this tactless reminder, but decided to turn it to his advantage instead. 'My semaphore system caught him, didn't it?' he pointed out triumphantly. 'That's something I must show you, Mr Raxleigh. Our private form of telegraph. If a man absconds we can signal the news to the guards

345

in minutes. Now, if you are agreeable, my dear,' he concluded, turning to his wife, 'let us go in to dinner.'

Lionel rose to his feet with mixed feelings. He wanted to learn more about the escaped convict, who he suspected was Dick Stanton, but he did not wish to admit that he knew the prisoner personally at this stage. As he followed O'Hara Booth's wheelchair into the dining-room, he knew he had to resist the questions which were uppermost in his mind.

It was inevitable, however, that questions were asked during the meal about his work for *The Times* – and about Swansdowne, which he tried to deflect in case they led inadvertently to Dick.

'What have you come here to write about?' the doctor asked at one point.

'That depends on what I find,' Lionel replied evasively. 'I'd like to know more about Point Puer: I understand why men are sent here, but surely the boys are simply those who have been unfortunate back home?'

'Not at all!' cried the commandant. 'People have no idea of the desperate element among the baby-faced villains sent out here from the dens of the East End of London. I assure you that even the most hardened criminal seems soft compared to some of those children.'

Lionel remembered the corruption among the younger passengers below decks on the *Countess of Bath*, and nodded his head. 'But once they're here, don't they reform?'

'They most certainly do not!' O'Hara Booth protested. 'You'd think they'd be grateful to be taken from the squalor of London and brought to a place like this – but not a bit of it.'

'You could hardly call them criminals,' said the doctor softly. 'One was convicted for the theft of a box of toys. I dare say he didn't know what a toy was. Hard to be taken from his family for something as slight as that.'

O'Hara Booth stared at the audacious doctor, genuinely baffled. 'I don't accept that at all. Most of them don't have families. They're the dregs of England, and they've grown up with none of the natural respect for the law that decent children possess. The first thing I have to teach them here is the concept of right and wrong. Do you realise, Dr Furness, that out of five hundred of those wretched boys I had to punish three hundred and sixty last year? That shows you what a bad lot they are!' Pleased at having made his point, he shoved a portion of lamb between those perfect teeth and proceeded to champ noisily.

'Punish them for what?' Lionel asked with apparent indifference.

'Insubordination. Attacks on the overseers. Things I can't mention here. Trying to abscond over the cliff. If you want me to encapsulate their offences in a single word, sir, I'd say "resisting". Resisting us, resisting the system.'

'Hear, hear,' said Lieutenant Cool.

'But what I fail to understand –' Lionel blinked to emphasise his naivety, 'is why they have to be sent to a settlement at all? Surely transportation is punishment enough?'

The commandant swallowed his chunk of meat in a single gulp and smiled at Lionel with tolerant good humour. 'You may be a clever man, sir, and no doubt you are as you write for the Thunderer, but you have an awful lot to learn about a place like this. What would you have us do? Cast them adrift? That would hardly be kind to them or healthy for us, letting them rob and murder as they please. But I see your point and agree with it wholeheartedly – I wish to God those wretched boys had never been sent here. I have enough to worry about as it is without their antics. If you can tell your readers that, Mr Raxleigh, I shall be indebted to you.' O'Hara Booth removed the napkin from his neck and leant across the table, tapping Lionel on the shoulder as if he had made a friend.

Lionel stopped himself from flinching. 'I'm beginning to realise that in many ways you're a prisoner yourself, trapped in impossible circumstances because of the whole policy of transportation.'

'Eh?' exclaimed O'Hara Booth, wiping his mouth suspiciously.

'I mean,' said Lionel, staring at him steadily, 'that you are a more merciful man than this place allows you to be.'

In the silence which followed, O'Hara Booth tried to work this out; Mrs Lempriere raised her fan to her mouth to conceal a smile, though her eyes betrayed it all the same; the doctor looked at Lionel with dismay bordering on contempt; and even the chaplain and his wife were genuinely surprised by this generous assessment of their commandant.

It was Mrs O'Hara Booth who broke the silence. 'You are most observant, Mr Raxleigh. My husband is much misunderstood.'

O'Hara Booth patted his wife's hand affectionately. 'I have to do my duty,' he declared. 'That's the price I pay for my privileged position as commandant of Port Arthur. The outside world has never understood – though thanks to the perception of our visitor it might do so in future.'

After saying good-night to their host on the verandah, Lionel and Dr Furness walked slowly back to their adjacent quarters, listening to the soft sound of the sea as it subsided on the shore.

'It looks like paradise,' said Lionel, 'and sounds like it, too.' The doctor sighed impatiently and turned to scrutinise the visitor in the faint light from the sky, wondering if he was really the fool he seemed.

'Mr Raxleigh, will you join me in my cottage for a night-cap? There are things I must tell you.'

The doctor filled their glasses with cognac and faced him earnestly. 'Mr Raxleigh, you have no idea what goes on here, have you?'

'I've heard rumours,' Lionel admitted guardedly.

'Whatever you may have heard, nothing can convey the horror of this place until you see it for yourself.'

'I hope I shall. That's why I'm here.'

'Don't you understand?' said the doctor impatiently. 'You won't be able to. They won't allow you to see the truth. If people back in England knew what happened in Port Arthur there would be such a stink that Parliament would *have* to call a halt to transportation.'

Lionel sighed with relief and shook the doctor's hand. 'Then you must help me.' In spite of the warm night air he shivered with excitement. 'With your help, I can tell the truth in *The Times*.'

'Booth is a monster, yet you called him merciful? You have no idea.'

Lionel smiled. 'He's everything I despise. That's why I flattered him. Booth must not become suspicious.'

'Of course.' The doctor suddenly understood. 'When my predecessor made an official complaint in Hobart Town it was hushed up. But you have *The Times*.' As the clock chimed, he raised his glass: 'To you, Mr Raxleigh! Tell me what I can do to help.'

'This man who escaped?'

'Stanton?'

'I know him. He was assigned to my family and I want to see him.'

The doctor's smile faded. 'Do you know what's happened to him?'

'No. Tell me everything.'

They talked long after the bottle was empty. Dawn was breaking by the time Lionel left.

One look at Lieutenant Cool's face two hours later told Lionel that the party in the officers' mess had lasted throughout the night, but at least he was a jollier man.

'Christmas service, don't you know?' Lionel recoiled from the fumes. 'One of the trials of the festive season. Usually I try to dodge the Sunday service, but not Christmas. Everyone goes today, as you'll find out. Quite an occasion. I brought this to help us on our way.'

The lieutenant produced a bottle of black rum from under his jacket with the proud flourish of a conjurer displaying a rabbit, but Lionel's head throbbed and the last thing he wanted was a swig of the evil-smelling spirit. Above all, he wanted to be alone while he washed and dressed.

He managed to muster a smile. 'That's kind of you. And a happy Christmas to you, lieutenant. What I'd really like is a pot of tea or coffee.'

The officer saluted. 'My pleasure, sir.' He went out, returning a few minutes later with a convict servant who carried a tea tray.

Lionel was refreshed but apprehensive as he approached the imposing church, said to have been designed by a convict. He drew a deep breath as he stepped inside, stared at by convicts and soldiers alike. Lieutenant Cool escorted him to the front pew, where the commandant was seated already in his mobile chair, surrounded by his family and senior staff. Lionel was relieved to find himself beside Dr Furness, next to the aisle. It was a conspicuous position, but it gave him the chance to look round and absorb the astonishing scene. The light which filtered through the fine stained-glass window at the northern end revealed a massive congregation; a thousand men at least, on this day of the year. Because the church had never been consecrated, they came from all faiths, Protestants and Catholics alike. Line upon line of convicted men, their characters signified by the colours of their uniforms.

Many were smiling, and Lionel realised that for them this was indeed a holiday, if not a holy one. Cool had told him how they had assembled at six in the prison yard, and each man had received an issue of tea, sugar, and – most welcome of all – tobacco, cut with a sharp blade in front of them so that they could see the fairness of their ration. For the next three days the convicts would be allowed to smoke, but if any tobacco was found on them after that they could be certain of a flogging. With the plug of tobacco in their pockets and the promise of extra food to come, their smiles were understandable yet disconcerting.

Lionel scanned the pews for a sign of Dick Stanton. Then sixty chained prisoners were led into separate stalls, divided from the body of the congregation. Lionel gasped with dismay.

'The "specials",' the doctor whispered. These were the 'incorrigibles', deprived of all contact with each other, sentenced to the model prison where even the gaolers wore felt slippers to make as little noise as possible and never spoke a word. Absolute silence and darkness. The doctor had described it as 'the cruellest torture of all – worse than the collar – because it unhinges the mind'. Each prisoner was isolated in one of the 'dumb cells' with double stone walls which excluded sound. Guards had to pass through four doors to bring the bread and water, so that no trace of the outside world – no ray of light, no distant sound of words or laughter – could enter with them. The model prison was a prison within the prison. There was a separate yard leading off each cell where the convict could walk for half an hour each day, but he did so alone and the yard was exactly that – one square yard. So the body survived. Encased in this tomb where time became meaningless, the mind could not survive so easily. 'I'm told that a man who does more than a few months in solitary becomes weak in the head,' said the doctor, 'and I'd be surprised if he didn't.'

From time to time the peep-hole in the door would slide back noiselessly and it might just be possible to meet the cold eye of the gaoler – the only contact.

Once a month the prisoners were placed in turn inside a large wooden box in a separate cell which served as a chapel. In this way the 'sinner' was excluded from the sight of the officiating clergyman, though able to hear the few words of admonition and the promise of torment for those who offended against Christ. Imagine, therefore, the excitement of these sixty unfortunate men on this day which celebrated Christ in a kinder light and allowed them to leave the model prison for one hour in the year.

But – and Lionel found this truly frightening as he

searched their faces in the hope of recognising Dick – *the men wore masks*.

'I know,' whispered the doctor at his side, realising the cause of his friend's distress. 'I didn't have the heart to tell you. They wear those things whenever they leave their cells. Even for their pitiful exercise they have to wear their masks.'

Lionel continued to search the faceless faces until one head turned towards him. He was certain it was Stanton's. The vast congregation rose and began to sing, but Lionel could not concentrate on the service. However, he joined in as best he could, sensing the eyes of the masked man upon his back. The masks were made of thick, dark-brown wool with narrow slits for the mouth and eyes. In the church they assumed an almost cowlish appearance, but this could not disguise their dehumanisation of man. Yet, when he turned again, Lionel could tell that the 'specials' were singing more lustily than anyone, in a positive orgy of noise after their 'silent treatment'.

All the time the image of Dick's face, his once broad and open smile, hidden behind that dreadful mask, tormented Lionel with guilt. What have we done to you? he thought. The hymn finished and he knelt down with the ranks of men, joining them in their fierce and angry prayers. 'O God, have mercy on my soul.'

After the service, Lionel requested an immediate interview with O'Hara Booth.

When he was shown inside the cottage he found the commandant on his own in the over-dressed parlour. 'Sit yourself down, Raxleigh,' Booth cried in his high voice. 'Now, wasn't that a truly excellent service! I hope you'll write about *that*. Did you see how the men enjoyed themselves?'

'I thought it was most impressive,' Lionel replied truthfully. 'I was deeply moved. In fact I've decided to base my despatch to *The Times* on Christmas Day in Port Arthur.'

'What a good idea. Capital. Is there anything I can do to help?'

'There is. I would like permission to visit the model prison.'

'When?'

'Today.'

'Why do you want to see the model prison?' Booth asked suspiciously.

'I've heard so much about it. Let me be frank,' Lionel continued, using the old preamble to a lie. 'If I use Christmas Day as my theme, I can show Port Arthur to its greatest advantage. I suppose it's inevitable that people have gained the wrong impression of the place and its commandant. To be blunt, your reputation is not of the highest in Hobart.'

Unwillingly, the commandant recognised a degree of truth in the statement. Dr Brownlow had done his best to stir up trouble even though his official complaint had been swept out of sight.

'People know nothing,' he exclaimed.

'That is my point,' said Lionel smoothly. 'They display the prejudice of ignorance. That is what I am anxious to correct.'

'Your consideration touches me,' said the commandant dryly. 'And how do you intend to do this?'

The moment of truth had arrived. 'There's a prisoner here who was previously assigned to my family. Sir John Franklin takes a personal interest in him, too, and has asked me to report back.'

'Has he?' said the commandant warily. The mention of the Governor had put him on his guard, as it was meant to.

'As you will know,' Lionel continued, 'Sir John is about to return to England. Indeed, he's taking my despatch with him to hand personally to the editor of *The Times*.' This was a blatant lie, but even as he said it Lionel decided that he would ask the Governor to do exactly that when he returned to Hobart Town.

The commandant made a sucking sound with his lips.

His eyes had gone dull. 'It sounds,' he said at last, 'as if you have a proposition . . .'

Lionel blinked. 'It occurred to me that I could present you in a sympathetic light by . . . by introducing a human touch because it's Christmas Day. Let us say a special leniency towards the convict I mentioned.'

'You take a particular interest in him? Why?'

'He worked for my family,' Lionel repeated. 'He's a good man, and we hoped he would be pardoned. That was John's intention.'

It was not lost on the commandant that Sir John Franklin had just been referred to by his Christian name; a shocking breach of manners unless he and Lionel were on terms of intimacy.

'What's the man's name?'

'Stanton.'

'Ah! The trouble-maker. What a *strange* coincidence!'

'He had a good record until he came here.'

'Why was he sent here?'

'He absconded.'

The commandant gave a long sigh. Lionel could not tell if he was relieved to see his opponent's cards laid out on the table, or annoyed at finding himself in a position he did not fully understand.

'Mr Raxleigh,' Booth said at last. 'You're a man after my own heart. You want me to make a deal?'

Lionel nodded, taken aback by such directness.

'Good. Now we know where we stand. You want me to bend the rules, and if I'm lenient to your man then you'll be lenient to me.' The smile was cut off abruptly. 'One thing worries me. How do I know I can trust you?'

Lionel smiled ingenuously. 'You don't. I can only give you my word as one gentleman to another.' As he looked steadily at O'Hara Booth he hoped the man could not read his thoughts.

The commandant gave a piercing giggle. 'So be it. After all, what's one prisoner among so many?'

'May I see him now? Dr Furness says he'll accompany me, so I need not upset your plans.'

'He does, does he? Yes, he would. Be very careful what you say to Dr Furness. He has an indiscreet tongue. But I thought the point of the game was to show *me* in a merciful light. No, sir, if you insist on your visit to the model prison I shall go with you.'

They were on their way in less than five minutes, the commandant's chair carried by four convicts. When they reached the prison, Booth said: 'Based on the one in England – Pentonville. The latest thing. Confinement replacing the lash for the good of the prisoner. That should please the readers of *The Times*, eh?'

The model prison was certainly pristine on the outside. The thick new walls, built of great slabs of granite, glistened in the sun. No speck of dust, no particle of dirt, would dare to linger here. They entered through the main gate and came to a halt under an arch which had been built in the classical style. Soldiers stood rigidly to attention in front of the steps which led to the duty-room. The solitary cells encircled the rest of the courtyard like a fan. The faceless steel doors had a few holes at the bottom so that a minimum of air could enter or escape. O'Hara Booth told one of the guards to fetch the prisoner Stanton. The man moved quickly in his felt slippers and Lionel waited apprehensively. The silence was broken by a hard, metallic screech as locks were opened. This was the moment he had been striving for yet feared, for he sensed that he had underestimated Captain John O'Hara Booth, and dreaded the possibility that he might reveal too great an emotion in front of him.

Lionel heard the clanking of leg-irons, by now horribly familiar, and Dick stood before him.

'Remove the man's mask,' the commandant ordered impatiently.

'Regulations,' muttered the gaoler apologetically as he hastened to unfasten the straps.

'I am the regulation here,' snapped Booth, though he knew that the man was obeying orders – all 'specials' had to wear the mask when they were led from their cells. When the mask was removed, the prisoner shielded his eyes automatically in the sudden brilliance.

'Stand to attention, arms by your side,' snapped the gaoler, determined to make a good impression on the commandant though going the wrong way about it.

'Don't bother about all that,' sighed O'Hara Booth. 'Stand easy. This is a courtesy visit.' He twisted his bulk to get a closer look at the prisoner, and then he turned to Lionel. 'Is this the man?'

Lionel nodded, too distressed to speak.

'A bad case. He's shown the wrong attitude ever since he got here.'

Lionel scarcely heard him, but spoke to the young convict. 'How are you keeping, Stanton?' In the circumstances a more fatuous greeting could hardly have been forthcoming, but what else could he say? He could not embrace the man as he wanted to.

For a moment, Dick said nothing, swaying slightly. The sickly pallor of his skin resembled the underside of a fungus.

'Answer him, man,' exclaimed O'Hara Booth impatiently. He was starting to sweat inside his tight-fitting uniform, wishing he was back in his cottage. He turned to Lionel with a sigh and a shake of the head as if to say, 'You see what I have to put up with?'

'Pleased to see you, Mr Raxleigh, sir.' The words were soft and slurred, out of pitch, like those of a deaf man who has lost the solace of hearing the human voice. Lionel was relieved to hear the note of respect which belied their former closeness.

'What brings you to Port Arthur, sir?'

'I'm here for *The Times*, Stanton. I'm writing a despatch on the penal settlement, and I wanted to see the conditions for myself. I heard you were here. The commandant has been gracious enough to give me permission to see you.'

'As it's Christmas Day,' O'Hara Booth added, in case anyone present should detect a sign of weakness.

'How is the family, sir? Mr and Mrs Stowe, and Master Roly?'

'Not good news, I fear. Mr Stowe's far from well, so you can imagine how distressed my sister is. To make it worse, Roly has disappeared. I believe he saw you in Hobart the night you were arrested; since then we've had no word from him. I suspect he took a boat to New South Wales.'

Dick absorbed the news and shook his head. 'And Miss Sally?' he asked softly.

Lionel answered him gravely. 'She's truly sorry for the harm she caused you. I know she would want me to tell you that. But she's gone too, to Sydney, so you can guess how lonely Swansdowne is without you all . . .' He turned round and saw that the commandant was involved in a heated argument with Lieutenant Cool. 'Have hope, Dick,' he said urgently. 'I'll do my utmost for you. We'll be together again before long. I pray to God you'll be able to return to us soon. Matilda is looking after Tim and being as cheerful as she can, but we need you.'

'Yes,' said Dick sadly, remembering. 'She has a good heart, that one. Please give her and Mrs Stowe my respects . . .'

A voice interrupted them. 'Mr Raxleigh, if your conversation is over, might I have your permission to return to my family and my Christmas luncheon?' He laughed to show that he was joking, but mirth was never convincing when it came from O'Hara Booth.

'Of course,' said Lionel. 'Would it be in order to give the convict a plug of tobacco?'

'I think that might be allowed,' said the commandant with a conspiratorial smile, 'seeing that it's Christmas Day. It will show your readers how merciful I am, won't it? And, to show how reckless I am in my spirit of goodwill, the prisoner may attend the entertainment tonight, unmasked. Right?' He turned to the officer in charge, who assured him that this would be taken care of.

Before the gaoler led Dick back through the locked doors, Lionel stepped forward and pressed a lump of tobacco into his hand. The rims of the two embedded sovereigns were barely visible but plain to the touch. For that brief moment they clasped each other's hand with an affection that did not escape the commandant, who found such familiarity odious. He clapped his hands and the servants lifted the mobile chair. The little procession started down the hill and the visit was over.

Lionel and the doctor were to lunch with the Lemprieres, and they arrived at the cottage in such a state of elation that at first Mrs Lempriere thought they were drunk. She did not mind if her guests became so during her parties, but she found it tiresome when they arrived either speechless or silly. However, she understood their excitement once she was told the cause.

'Those poor men.' She nodded gravely. 'I'm not allowed anywhere near them, except in church.'

Though Pierre Lempriere was too acquiescent for Lionel's liking, he understood that the man was content in his marriage and did not wish to jeopardise his position in Port Arthur. Unlike Dr Furness, his heart did not bleed for the convicts, probably because he would have found life unbearable if it had. Lempriere was an academic who had made a careful study of Van Diemen's Land and loved the place, as did his wife. They spoke of it possessively, critical of the worst, looking forward wistfully to a future when the island might be populated by free men. 'And this wretched place become a ruin,' added the doctor vehemently.

'Don't blame the place,' said Lempriere gently. 'The place is beautiful. It's we who have spoilt it.'

'I've always found it ironic that such a tranquil island should be so bloodthirsty,' said his wife sadly.

Lempriere told him of cruelties which Lionel could scarcely believe; how the early settlers, and the whalers in particular, had seized black girls from their families to satisfy their lust and clubbed any black man who dared

358

to protest, literally beating out his brains. 'We call them savages, but what about us? We threw their children into their fires and cut off their noses and ears as souvenirs and shot their dogs. The killing has continued ever since. I doubt if more than a dozen natives will survive the century.'

'Oh, God,' said the doctor, 'what a terrible place this is. By the time we're through, will anything be left?'

'You're dramatising,' said Lempriere. '*We* shall continue. I believe Van Diemen's Land will become a marvellous place. Let me explain . . .'

Lionel listened, moved by the zeal of the true colonist, which he had not comprehended before.

They talked and ate and drank throughout that Christmas afternoon. Lempriere asked Lionel if he was looking forward to the evening's entertainment.

'What entertainment?' Dimly he remembered O'Hara Booth's words. 'Entertainment – *here*?'

'Didn't anyone tell you?' asked Lempriere with surprise. 'Lieutenant Cool should have done. The Christmas entertainment is one of the traditions of Port Arthur, and we're invited.'

'Not the wives,' protested Mrs Lempriere.

'Some of the ballads wouldn't be fit for your ears, my dear. And your presence would be a distraction for the men. Even the commandant stays away, in case of violence.'

'Am I invited?' Lionel asked uncertainly.

'Any stranger who happens to be visiting the settlement on Christmas Day is expected.'

'What sort of entertainment can we look forward to?'

'Songs and ballads. For my sins, I have to perform the Ratcatcher's Daughter. I'm terrified.'

'Nonsense, he loves it,' smiled Mrs Lempriere. 'I've been rehearsing him for weeks.' She ran to the piano and started to play. Her husband clasped his hands in front of him and rendered the first verse in a surprisingly deep bass for such a slender man:

'Not long ago in Vestminster,
There lived a Ratcatcher's Daughter;
But she didn't live quite in Vestminster,
For she lived t'other side of the Vater.
Her father caught Rats, and she cried
    Sprats,
All about and over the quarter;
And the gentlefolks, they all bought their Sprats
Off the pretty little Ratcatcher's Daughter.'

Dr Furness and Lionel laughed and applauded while Mrs Lempriere looked up at them, beaming with pleasure as she refilled Lionel's glass once more.

Lionel would never forget the scene which greeted him that evening. Hundreds of prisoners stood four-square around a stage erected in the centre of the punishment yard and lit by oil-lamps. Surrounding them, like a frame for the picture, were lines of armed soldiers standing shoulder to shoulder to make escape impossible. They made way for Lempriere and his party, who were escorted through the prisoners to the benches below the stage reserved for administrative staff and senior officers. A few incapacitated convicts were allowed to sprawl on the ground nearby. Lionel looked for Dick but he was hidden in the multitude and the light was failing fast.

What astonished Lionel most was the overwhelming air of good humour, the open happiness on the faces of the men who applauded vigorously as their favourites climbed on to the stage. The Irish political rebel, Kavanagh, introduced himself proudly as 'Frank McNammara of Cashell County, Tipperary', and earned a deafening cheer as he swore 'to be a tyrant's foe, and while I've life I'll crow'. When he concluded with a sentimental ballad about a shepherd boy, there was a vast, attentive silence.

The Irish were the stars of the occasion, dancing hectic jigs to the violent scrape of fiddles, singing tearfully of beloved places they had left behind in Ireland, with gentle, lilting names. For this evening at least, performers and convicts were men again.

A Scouser elbowed his way on to the stage, threw his hat on the ground and started to sing his heart out:

> 'We had two Irish lads on board, Jimmy Murphy
> and Paddy Malone.'

He stabbed a finger at the convicts below, as if the two were there.

> 'And they were both the truest lads as any man
>   could own.
> The gamekeeper had caught them, and from
>   Liverpool's old Strand
> We three were then transported to plough Van
>   Diemen's Land.
>
> We had a lady fair on board, Lizzie Johnston
>   was her name,
> And she was shipped from Liverpool for
>   a'playin' of the game.
> She took the captain's fancy, he married her off
>   hand,
> But she gave us all good usage, going to Van
>   Diemen's Land.
>
> The minute that we landed upon this dreadful
>   shore,
> The planters they inspected us full twenty score
>   or more.
> They led us round like horses, they sold us out
>   of hand
> And yoked us to the plough me boys to plough
>   Van Diemen's Land.'

By now the crowd of men was joining in, shouting out the name of Van Diemen's Land with heartfelt detestation. Then they fell silent for the final, familiar verse:

'Last night as I lay in my bunk a'dreaming all
    alone
I dreamt I was back in Liverpool, way back in
    Marybone,
With my true love beside me and a jug of ale in
    hand –
But I woke up broken-hearted – in bleeding
    Diemen's Land.'

The tears were pouring down the man's cheeks as he
retrieved his hat and climbed down, to be greeted with
cheers and slaps on the back from his admirers.

Time passed quickly. Lionel was suddenly aware that
Lempriere was on the stage and had reached the last
verse of his song about the Ratcatcher's Daughter, accompanied by a fiddler who had been practising for the
past month. The laughter faded when she drowned in
the Thames, and Lempriere concluded the story quietly,
to great effect:

'Ven Lily-vite Sand he heard the news
His eyes ran down with water,
Said he, "In love I'll constant prove;
And bloody well blow me if I'll live long arter!"
So he cut his throat with a pane of glass,
And he stabbed his Jackass arter;
So here is an end of Lily-vite Sand, his
Jackass, and the Ratcatcher's Daughter!'

A moment's silence, then a great roar as the men
shouted out the chorus, 'Heu! tu diddle u!', repeating it
three times while Lempriere stood there bowing, flushed
with pleasure. Suddenly Lionel heard his own name
mentioned as Lempriere acknowledged the applause and
waved his hand in the direction of the 'man from the
London *Times*'. Lionel's fame had raced through the
settlement since the morning visit to the model prison.
Already the 'man from *The Times*' was welcomed as a
champion who could air their grievances in the greatest
newspaper in the world.

A chant began — 'The man from *The Times*', for they did not know his name — and hands stretched down and pulled him upwards while others forced him from behind. A silence fell, and Lionel stood on the stage alone. In desperation he remembered a song which had been all the rage when he left London.

It did not occur to him that it was a dangerous choice in such surroundings. Reaching down, he snatched a grimy cap from a convict pressed against the platform and stuck it on the back of his head. Then he faced the blurred lines of prisoners, and a challenging bravado possessed him. He staggered, and began his fearsome song:

> 'My name is Sam Hall, chimney sweep,
> My name it is Sam Hall.
> I robs both great and small,
> But they makes me pay for all.'

And then the last line of the verse, with unrepentant venom:

> *'Damn their eyes!*
>
> The parson he did come
> And he looked bleedin' glum
> He can kiss my tum-ti-tum
> *Damn his eyes!'*

As he continued the story of the murderer in his condemned cell, Lionel heard the prisoners join in with mounting enthusiasm until their final shout could be heard echoing around the hills above Port Arthur as every man cried out his bitterness — 'DAMN THEIR EYES!'

Lionel was woken by an angry knocking on his cottage door. Lieutenant Cool burst in, with a summons to see the commandant without delay. Cool's eyes were scarlet and his mood inflamed, having just been woken himself.

The commandant welcomed Lionel with a sly little smile which was quite devoid of humour. 'I hope you enjoyed yourself last night, Mr Raxleigh. I hear you provided an amusing divertissement. I had no idea you were an improvisitiore.'

Lionel said nothing.

'I think we'll give our sight-seeing expeditions a miss, eh, Mr Raxleigh? I believe we understand each other, so let's put an end to this charade. The *Tamar* sails for Hobart Town this afternoon, and I expect you'd like to be on board.'

Lionel would certainly be glad to leave the place, but he feared he might have done Dick Stanton more harm than good by his intervention.

With his disturbing gift for sensing the other man's thoughts, the commandant continued: 'As for the convict Stanton, let me be blunt. He stays here. There's no question of his release – plainly the point of your visit.'

'You have broken your word,' Lionel accused him, too hastily.

'Not at all.' The commandant smiled. 'I never gave it. We agreed that if you are fair by me in *The Times*, I will be lenient to your man. But until I see that story in print, he stays here. You must understand, Mr Raxleigh, I'm not the fool I seem.'

Lionel knew how crucial his reaction would be.

'On the contrary, Captain Booth,' he said carefully. 'Of course you are right in wanting to see my despatch. Meanwhile, however, I urge you to release Stanton from the model prison and send him back with the others.' He paused, and saw that Booth was about to object. Quickly but decisively, striking the surface of the table, he added: 'Otherwise the deal is off. And if that's the case, you'll suffer as much as Stanton.'

Captain O'Hara Booth raised the tips of his fingers slowly to his lips as he assessed the power of *The Times* and concluded that a damaging attack on himself could ruin his retirement. He yielded a carved grimace.

'We understand each other. Now it is up to you. Good

morning.' He rang a delicate bell on the table beside him and Lieutenant Cool opened the door of the parlour. 'Take Mr Raxleigh to the government brig as soon as she is ready to sail, and warn the captain of his passenger.' He closed his eyes and did not open them again until the door had shut behind his unwelcome guest.

In his cabin aboard the *Tamar*, Lionel laid some sheets of paper out on the swaying table beside his bunk and started to write:

Am I to tell the truth? If I do it must shock all of you who read this. The conditions I have witnessed here bear your name, for your courts of justice consigned the unfortunates to Van Diemen's Land as punishment for such heinous offences as the poaching of a rabbit. You bear your share of the guilt for the pitiless system of transportation by acquiescing in such an easy means of colonisation.

As you have no concept of the consequences once the prisoners are landed here, it is my duty to inform you. In years to come officialdom with its crew of parasites will attempt to deny the enormities committed in your name, but the grim truth of Van Diemen's Land will always remain. The stain is too deep. For the first half of this century your law has allowed convicts to be subjected to a lingering torment, to a monstrous system of punishment which is futile for good and horribly powerful for evil, and it is with profound passion that I urge you to demand of the government that this cursed system be abolished forthwith.

I write this on Boxing Day, on a government brig which has just left Port Arthur, the largest penal settlement in the island, where twelve hundred men are herded like beasts, and every kind of wickedness that imagination can invent is committed. Yet – a bitter irony – this dreadful prison is set in a landscape of rare beauty, which makes the suffering of the inmates all the more poignant.

What are the sins that have brought them here? Do they deserve such a dismal fate? Let me detail the case of one whose story I have followed with personal interest.

What was the nature of his crime? It took place on his seventeenth birthday, the day the young Queen went to Plymouth to inspect her Fleet. This young man accidentally stumbled against a midshipman on board the *Juniper* as the royal yacht was passing. For this 'insolence' he was sentenced to transportation to Van Diemen's Land, never to see his home or family again.

'Transportation' – it does not sound so dreadful a word, but this is what it means . . .

Lionel wrote throughout that lurching night, concluding with these words:

If man is treated without intermission like a brute, he becomes a brute. And if there exists one latent spark for good in his unhappy heart, then that faint chance of redemption will be extinguished. If all the decent citizens of England knew one hundredth of the outrage perpetrated in this colony, you would not, could not, feel indifference. I cannot impress on you strongly enough that the time has come to end the cursed system of transportation which is carried out in your name. Attention must be paid to the misery in Van Diemen's Land, before it erupts, and destroys all that is good in this otherwise peaceful island.

— 23 —

Rich dirt and good earth

It was a time of grief at Swansdowne. Gussie had grown increasingly incapable, scarcely able to tie up the laces of his boots, walking slowly with the support of a stick. His speech was slurred and his body twisted with pain. He knew the cause, but kept it secret. On his last visit to Hobart Town he had seen a doctor who was noted for his discretion. After a lengthy examination, the specialist had told Gussie the unwelcome truth – the unmentionable truth as far as friends and family were concerned.

Gussie was not surprised – he had guessed it for a long time. He blessed the fact that he had not inflicted the infection on Sarah, though if their physical relationship had been resumed after the birth of Sally he might never have caught such an infection in the first place. He assumed he had taken it from the woman in the London brothel shortly before he sailed from Gravesend, but the doctor assured him it went further back than that. It was on the way home to Swansdowne that he remembered, in a sudden flash of memory, the establishment in Torquay managed by no less than the monstrous Miss Wynette. Then he understood her coyness at the Government House ball, and cursed her for the connection.

With Lionel away, Christmas was a gloomy ritual at Swansdowne. No word had been received from Sally or Roly, and their names were seldom mentioned. The only distraction came from the antics of the happy baby boy. The tactile tenderness of touched fingers and tickled toes brought gurgles of delight. Timmy had a vile temper to balance his cherubic appearance, but when Matilda picked him up the howls of complaint turned to screams of pleasure on the instant. The child helped her to bear Roly's absence, and she made an effort to follow the usual Christmas traditions for his sake.

On Boxing Day Matilda played with Tim on the lawn outside the house. It seemed ironic that the building should have been extended to twice its original size, yet the new rooms were empty.

Partly to forget the haunting uncertainty over her son and daughter, Sarah rode off for the afternoon to supervise the convicts working on the land two miles away, and Gussie sat down and wrote a letter, steadying his right hand with his left.

My own darling Sarah . . . my dear, dear sweetheart. I wish I had words to let you know how much I love you and how very, very happy you have made me all these years. I wish too that I had brought you greater happiness in return and had not failed so often in my duty. Not a day passes without my feeling a bitter guilt over the loss of Raxleigh, our beloved home, which I mourn as much as you must, though you have never once reproached me. Loyal, stalwart woman, what a noble companion you have been to me in our journey through life! Now the time has come to end my part of that journey. Better than anyone, you know that I am not the man I used to be. My only regret is the fear that my departure may give you pain, but please, my dearest, do not grieve for me. It is for the best. I am finding life unbearable and seek peace at last. Remember the happier days; we did have them together, my dearest. I pray that our children return to you. My dear wife, be brave as I know only you can be. I bless and love you more than ever; let me always remain in your memory as

Your own, loving Gussie

He read the letter painstakingly with the aid of his magnifying glass, sealed it in an envelope, and left it on the table in the hall with his fine gold watch for Roly, should the boy return. Then he limped out of the house and down to the edge of the water.

When Lionel had said goodbye to the captain of the *Tamar* at Ferry Wharf, he walked up the hill to the Adelphi. Over the next two days he emerged from his room only for meals. On the third morning, as he lay on his bed reading his despatches for *The Times* yet again, the lugubrious porter knocked on his door and handed him a message which had just been delivered by hand. 'Come at once to Ma Sloper's. Most urgent. Flanagan.'

Though he doubted whether it was at all urgent as far as he was concerned, Lionel was sufficiently curious to go straight away. Roly's red-faced Irish friend was fetched the moment he reached Ma Sloper's, and shook his hand awkwardly.

'It's bad news, I'm afraid. Young Roland has been in a fight.'

'I thought he was in Sydney!' Lionel exclaimed.

'Melbourne. That's where it happened. He came off worst, poor soul. He's upstairs.'

In spite of the warning, Lionel was not prepared for Roly's injuries: the swollen eyes and mouth, hair thick and dark with congealed blood where his head had been kicked. Roly attempted a smile, and lifted his hand in greeting. Then, finding it painful to speak, he turned his head away towards the wall. The ever-faithful but now dishevelled Raxleigh lay beside him.

'I'll come back later, old boy,' Lionel whispered, shocked by his nephew's appearance, though thankful to see him again. 'We can have a pow-wow then.'

He left the room quietly and joined Flanagan who was waiting in the bar below, touchingly concerned about his young friend. 'Oh, it's a terrible thing,' he said. 'Indeed it is, though it was good news all the way before that.'

'What do you mean?'

'Shall I tell you from the beginning, as best I can?'

Flanagan described the sudden impulse which had prompted Roly to sail from Hobart Town across the Bass Strait to Melbourne. It was not distress over Dick's arrest, nor to join Sally as Lionel had assumed, but to look for gold with Flanagan, whose enthusiasm was so contagious that Roly had asked if he could join him. Flanagan had been brimming over with excitement, flourishing the news of the latest strike, reported in a Sydney paper, by a miner called Hargreaves who had also been lucky in the goldfields of California. The new strike was west of Ballarat.

'It's mug's luck, Roland,' Flanagan warned him, 'but we'll have a go.'

The strike was ninety miles from Melbourne and for two days they rode through the bush, a dull landscape of scrub and wattle known as 'mongrel mulga'. Raxleigh ran behind them until Roly took pity on the animal and lifted him on to the horse to ride with him. The pack-horses had been bought in Melbourne, and the rest of their funds went on supplies and equipment at the store in the village of Casterton Ararat, renamed Ophir – after the mines of King Solomon – by Jacob Solomon, who ran the Honey Pot Store and was growing rich on the fortunes of others.

Roly was disappointed to find that hundreds of other prospectors had poured into the area before them, and dismayed to realise that he was running out of money, but the fever gripped him when they started to choose their equipment. Most of the items were standard, though many of the miners made do with less. The most imposing was the 'cradle'. The clay was dropped into the 'hopper' tray at the higher end while someone else ladled water on to it. The cradleman then rocked the large wooden contraption to break up the earth and wash it away while the specks of yellow gold fell through the sieve on to a board below. These were washed in a pan and dried.

The cradles came in different sizes, and they chose one

the size of a tin bath which cost thirty shillings; picks and a crowbar to break up the rock; two shovels; and two zinc buckets to carry the earth to the cradle. In addition, they bought an elementary sieve and a pan for sifting the dust found in the river bed itself. An axe, nails, rope, and two tin milk-dishes came to seven pounds. Then there was the camping equipment: a strong tarpaulin tent and two opossum rugs, vital in the cold, wet weather; the all-important water bags; and an oven with basic cooking utensils. By the time they had bought their food, with extra roo-tails for Raxleigh, Roly's bill came to nineteen pounds and ninepence. 'For you,' said Mr Solomon with unctuous courtesy, 'I shall make it nineteen pounds exactly.'

'Bastard,' said Roly as they rode off, their horses sagging under the new weight, but he felt elated all the same although only a few pounds were left. All that remained for the partnership of Flanagan and Stowe was to strike some rich dirt.

They left Ophir behind them and rode on, reaching the goldfields of Ararat late in the afternoon of the third day. An encampment of tents stretched on either side of a rivulet, resembling two armies on the eve of battle, with many of the same sounds and a similar sense of anticipation. Flanagan and Stowe pitched their tent under the trees and began to make themselves known to their rival diggers.

Over the next few weeks, Roly relished the *camaraderie* as if this was the life he had been intended for. By day they crushed the stone and clay, panning for gold with Flanagan peering at the dirt through his magnifying glass. For thirty shillings they bought a stake of two acres four miles from the main goldfield. They had to pay the state of Victoria the same price for their licence; a cruel imposition on those who had not been lucky, for the licence was monthly.

At night they cooked their chops on an open fire and drank in the sly-grog shops hastily erected on the fringes of the field by owners eager to share in the boom.

Roly found himself an eccentric among eccentrics, popular in his own right for the first time in his life, thanks to his dark good looks, his elegant boots, and the comic-looking dog which rarely left his side. His laughter echoed across the camp fires in the evening and his gift for telling stories won him a ready audience. To know that he was liked for himself alone was an inestimable pleasure to Roly, who had had few friends up till then.

The diggers were a weird bunch, greedy for gold, certain they would strike lucky, always optimistic. These were men whose faces had fried in the sun, lining them deeply before their time; whose bodies were so ingrained with red clay that ounces of dirt came off them when they finally rode into Ophir for the luxury of a bath. Chance had brought them from all over the world. Sailors of numerous nationalities jumped ship the moment they docked in Melbourne, tempted by the great bonanza which was sweeping Australia. Afghans arrived on camels, and the Chinese sidled in softly, keeping scrupulously to themselves.

It was Raxleigh who found the gold. Wandering over to see what the dog was up to, Roly noticed a speck of yellow in a chunk of dirt and shouted to Flanagan to join him. Tense with excitement, they sifted the earth for a few minutes, and then the Irishman leapt in the air with a cry of 'Eureka!' and the team of Flanagan and Stowe danced a ridiculous polka around the river-bed, with Raxleigh jumping up beside them barking wildly.

They kept the secret to themselves. After a week of frantic digging they went to Jacob Solomon at Ophir and emptied their rich dirt on to his counter to be weighed. It came to twelve ounces, which they sold him on the spot. They did not tell anyone of the two massive nuggets which they received in exchange, keeping one each, but even so the news that Flanagan and Stowe had struck lucky raced through the camp. The next morning they found that miners were working the river-bed on either side of their claim. At the end of their second week they sold another fourteen ounces to Jacob Solomon at the

Honey Pot Store, but only eight ounces in the following fortnight, and four in the month after that. 'And that is that, my friend,' Flanagan announced. 'Not another grain of colour.'

Three months had passed. They were rich enough, and Christmas was near. They said goodbye to their friends, packed up their tent, and rode through Ophir, Bendigo and Ballarat to Melbourne. They arrived on 20 December, in time to enjoy the fun.

Melbourne that Christmas was in the grip of Yellow Fever. The atmosphere was one of promise, inflamed by a recent boast in the *Sydney Morning Herald* that the mountain ranges west of New South Wales, and the rolling hills stretching far into the interior, were one immense goldfield. Colonists thought nothing of spending a pound in a single night, when they thought a shilling was extravagant back home. Rumour claimed that one miner bathed with his mistress in champagne, and every clerk and grocer dreamed of leaving home armed with a blanket and a garden hoe and returning a week or two later with his pockets stuffed with gold. No one entertained the thought that bonanzas came to an end.

As Flanagan and Roly rode into Melbourne, they could almost see the boom town growing around them as new houses and shacks were thrown up on the outskirts. They booked into one of the best hotels, where the staff was used to dust-caked men who paid their bills in gold, and they re-emerged that evening relaxed and clean after scrubbing each other's backs in a long, luxurious bath.

Roly felt at ease in Melbourne, so much grander than Hobart Town. He was startled to discover how cosmopolitan the city had become. Entertainers from London sang in the new saloons, restaurants served continental food, and a splendid theatre promised the latest entertainment from Paris. The streets were crowded with smiling girls who stepped delicately over the sprawling bodies of drunken miners lying in the road.

News of their luck had preceded them, and partners

Flanagan and Stowe were welcome in a place where young men arrived with fortunes and lost them in a week. They enjoyed their wine, their women and their song, but Roly distrusted the gold-fever which tempted miners to spend so recklessly, and showed surprising caution.

As Christmas Day approached Roly began to wish he was spending it at Swansdowne. It would be pleasant to return as the rich, all-conquering hero, with his secret nugget of gold. And there was still New Year's Eve to celebrate.

'I'd like to take the next sailing for Hobart,' he told Flanagan on Christmas Eve. 'I ought to be at Swansdowne with my wife. I owe a lot to that girl. Now I can make it up to her.'

'That's fine by me. I'll travel with you, and we can say goodbye after a jar in Ma Sloper's. I'll book the places now, for I have a feeling there's a boat the day after tomorrow.'

Roly nodded contentedly. As Flanagan left the bar for the shipping office, with his unmistakable wide-apart gait as if his trousers were slightly wet, Roly smiled after him affectionately. They had become close friends, huddled together against the spring wind in their opossum rugs, lying side by side when it turned warm with the start of summer, talking freely under the stars. He knew that Flanagan would never betray his confidence. But for the moment he enjoyed his own company, planning for the future, thinking of the opportunities afforded by the secret nugget.

'Mind if I join you, mate?' He turned round, the mood broken, and recognised another miner from Ophir. He made room for him on the bench.

'Enjoying the view?'

The window of the saloon looked out on to the busy street. Across the road was the smartest hotel in Melbourne, a new building with an elegant façade and a delicate ironwork balustrade.

'God!' Roly exclaimed.

'What's that?'

'The girl getting out of that carriage. I know her.'

'Who doesn't?'

'What do you mean?' Roly asked tightly.

'Sally? Everyone knows Sally Smith. She came here from Sydney a month ago, only twenty-three but as eager as a filly. I wish to hell I knew her. I know what . . .'

Roly winced as the man described what he would like to do with his sister. 'Who's she with now?' He wanted to know the worst of it.

'Corbett. Not that he deserves her. A big bounce. Knew him in Bathurst. He's struck rich all right, as much with his fists as his fingers. There was trouble over his partner – he disappeared, and so did his gold. You know how crazy men get when they strike lucky? Well, I heard there was a cave-in at their mine, forty feet below, at the bottom of the shaft, and they say his partner's under the lot. No one's bothered to find out. He'd knock spots off them if they tried.'

'This Corbett, he's looking after her?'

'You could say that. He picks up the tabs. Hey! You haven't finished your drink . . .' With a shake of his head, the digger did so instead.

Roly raced out into the street and through the carriages to the hotel on the other side. He burst through the swing doors into the hall.

'Sally Smith,' he demanded, leaning over the reception desk.

'Suite five, sir,' said the Swiss clerk, obeying the voice of an English gentleman, 'but . . .' Roly was in no mood for buts and raced up the stairs. For a moment he wondered if he had made a mistake when he burst into the room and the woman turned towards him. He had never seen his sister dressed so elegantly. Her hair was curled up in the latest style, but he could see how heavily her face was powdered and smell the reek of sweet perfume. They stared at each other for a moment; then, as she whispered 'Roly?', the morality which lurked inside him broke out and he slapped her savagely on the cheek.

As she fought back he tore at her hair just as he had

when they were children, and stamped on the tortoiseshell comb which fell to the floor. It was a strange combat: screaming, hysterical, half hating, half loving; but it sounded real enough to Corbett who came running from the dressing-room. He was a large but nimble man with blazing eyes, luxuriant black moustaches and oiled-back hair. Presumably he had been changing, for he wore a scarlet waistcoat over a white silk shirt. Seeing the stranger as a half-crazed rival, he tore him off his woman, ignoring her cry that Roly was her brother, and punched him violently in the mouth with the other. He followed this up with a volley of blows that sent Roly reeling back against a glass-fronted cabinet, which splintered under the impact. Recovering, Roly rushed forward, charging at Corbett's stomach with his head, but another blow to his forehead hurled him back again. Sally, hysterical, ran downstairs for help, returning with the porter in time to see Corbett deliver a final, brutal kick to the unconscious body of her brother on the floor.

The whole incident had lasted for less than two minutes. Wiping his knuckles with a towel, Corbett pressed some coins into the hand of the porter and told him to 'clean up the mess'. Then he propelled Sally towards the door. When she managed to break free an hour later, she found the suite empty. The porter had recognised Roly as a guest from the hotel over the road, and with the help of two other men had carried him across the street and up to his bedroom. The horrified Flanagan, finding him there some hours later, was the only person to think of summoning a doctor. Then he sat by Roly's bed, holding his hand, and managed to piece together from his friend's disjointed utterances the story of what had happened since he left him in the bar.

The next morning, Flanagan had recognised Roly's sister as she crossed the hall of their hotel to leave a letter with the porter.

'Miss Sally?'

She swung round, eyeing him coldly: 'Yes?'

'My name's Flanagan. I travelled with your family in the *Countess of Bath* a few years ago. I thought you should know that your brother's upstairs.'

She shook her head as if to deny the reality. 'Let's go where we can talk.' He led her to a far corner where a waiter brought them coffee.

'Is he badly hurt?'

'Very badly. You can see for yourself.'

Again she shook her head. 'No, I can't do that. You must think ill of me, Mr Flanagan, but there would be no point in my trying to see him.' She looked around her as if for assistance. 'Roly has a stronger sense of right and wrong than anyone, in spite of all he says and does. He would not wish to see me.' Flanagan nodded, suspecting this was true.

'He hates the way I am,' she continued, 'hated it long before this . . .'

Flanagan studied the young woman in front of him. She had the forced intensity of someone who depended for her existence on her appearance, enhancing it with expensive clothes and perfume. But her mouth was petulant. He felt sorry for her, though sorrier for Roly.

'Is my father still alive?' He noticed that she made no mention of her child.

'I believe so.'

'Too late now,' she muttered, almost inaudibly. Then, turning to face him directly, she declared: 'I value my freedom, Mr Flanagan. I love the risk of it. I suffocated in Swansdowne, as if I was serving my own life-sentence for having associated with Tim Blake. Lord knows why I'm telling you all this, Mr Flanagan. I suppose it's easier with strangers. Don't tell Roly you've seen me. I'm dead as far as my family is concerned. Such damned bad luck that Roly tracked me down.' Flanagan winced at hearing her swear, but said nothing. She took his hand, caressingly. 'And in case you're wondering, I *am* happy, really!' She gave him a quick, bright, tiny smile as if she had reassured Flanagan rather than herself, and left the hotel.

*

'. . . So I helped Roland and the little dog to the ship on Boxing Day morning,' Flanagan concluded. 'He was awful sick, throwing up all over the place, but I thought it best to be off as soon as possible even though the doctor had said he shouldn't be moved. Anyways, Roland wanted to sail, and you know there's no stopping him. And if we had stayed I'd have thought it my duty to look for Corbett, and then I'd have been beat up as well.'

That evening Roly showed his uncle the letter Sally had left at his hotel when she learned where he was.

The message was simple, only two words: 'Forgive me.'

'Poor girl,' said Lionel instinctively.

'What?' murmured Roly, confused.

'The guilt she must feel over you. It must be terrible for her.'

'I hope so.' The old bitterness had returned, but withdrew as Roly spoke wistfully of Swansdowne. 'I want to go there, Uncle. Take me back tomorrow.'

'I'll do my best.' Lionel wondered about the best form of transport. He doubted if his nephew was fit enough to travel on horseback. Presumably they could put him on a mattress in a bullock-cart and stay somewhere overnight, but that was a lot to organise at such short notice. Also, he was anxious to visit Government House and see Sir John Franklin before he sailed.

'Please,' said Roly, sensing his uncle's hesitation. 'I ache to go home.'

Lionel was impressed by the longing in the young man's voice. He sighed. 'I can understand that. They'll be so pleased to see you.'

'There's a lot to make up for. I've given Tilly a wretched life, but I got rid of my demon in the goldfields. I found the python's tail that Dick was always on about. What about you, Uncle? Are you still trying to prove yourself?'

The old tinge of sarcasm made Lionel smile, and he told Roly about his Christmas in Port Arthur.

'Good old Dick,' said Roly softly. 'I hope they let him go.'

Lionel realised that Roly had little idea of the problems involved. 'I'm sure they will,' he said.

For a few moments they fell silent as they thought of Dick, then Roly asked quietly: 'Uncle?'

'Yes?'

'Will you give him this from me?' He produced an opossum bag from the side of the bed and brought out the gnarled, gleaming, golden nugget. Lionel gasped, never having seen such a thing before. It must have weighed five pounds or more. For a moment he felt a pang that he was not being given it himself, but Roly added: 'We owe a lot to Dick. Keep it safe for him. Will you make the plans for tomorrow? I feel dead tired.' He lifted his hand in a gesture of cheerful dismissal, and Lionel held it firmly for a moment before he left the room.

Raxleigh's dismal howls at four in the morning brought Flanagan and Ma Sloper to Roly's room. They found him sprawled across the bed, the pillow and blanket tacky with dark, red blood.

When the doctor came at daybreak he confirmed that Roly had died of a haemorrhage. Shaken and guilty, Lionel and Flanagan met in the bar downstairs.

'Who'd have thought it possible that someone so young should go like that?' said Flanagan. 'I can't believe it. I should never have moved him to the ship. I should have done as the doctor said . . . but I didn't think . . .'

'Don't blame yourself,' said Lionel, feeling equally guilty. 'If only I'd fetched the doctor yesterday. At least he was happy at the end, which is some comfort. You made a man of him in the goldfields. He said as much last night.'

'I'm glad of that,' said Flanagan, wiping his eyes with a large red handkerchief. 'I was fond of that boy. We were like brothers out there. He found his true self at last, among strangers.'

Flanagan offered to take charge of the transportation of Roly's body while Lionel called on Sir John Franklin. But when he arrived at Government House he was informed that the new Governor, Sir Eardley Wilmot, was already in residence, though tactfully absent on a visit to Launceston. To send out his successor before Sir John had even left the island was the ultimate gesture of contempt on the part of the colonial secretary, but Lionel found the Franklins in fine, rebellious spirit when he arrived at the hotel where they were staying.

'I'm frantically busy, Raxleigh,' Sir John warned him. 'Suddenly I'm popular. Did you see the *Chronicle*? No? They want me to stay for another twenty years. It's ripe, after all they've said before!'

Lady Franklin concealed her excitement under a pretence of irritation. 'They won't leave us alone. We've been pestered with addresses, from the bishop and the Royal Society and goodness knows who else. So flattering that they like us at last.'

They were genuinely shocked by the news of Roly's death. Lady Franklin left the room to write a letter of condolence to Sarah, and Lionel, left alone with Sir John, seized the moment to give him his despatches and ask if he would hand them personally to John Delane. 'You could find him a useful ally,' he added slyly.

'I shall be happy to meet him,' Sir John replied diplomatically. 'And I shall study your despatches with the greatest of interest during my leisure time in the *Rajah*.'

Lionel returned to Ma Sloper's, collected Raxleigh, who pressed himself against the coffin on the cart, and started his unhappy journey back to Swansdowne.

Sarah had searched the riverside for Gussie with the help of the servant convicts. They found his body not far from Swansdowne, snagged by a branch, floating under the water. The pockets of his favourite blue coat were weighted down with stones.

For the last two days Gussie's corpse had lain in his bedroom and, to Matilda's distress and private disapproval, Sarah had lain beside it, sometimes sleeping briefly in the knowledge that he would be there when she woke.

On New Year's Eve, hearing the horses and seeing the swinging lanterns approaching through the trees, Sarah hurried outside. She threw her arms around her brother, sobbing uncontrollably.

'Thank God you're back. Oh, Lionel, what is to become of me? I'm desolate. You got my letter, of course?'

'No,' said Lionel, confused. How could she have learnt of Roly's death so soon?

At that moment Raxleigh bounded into the house, barking with excitement as he recognised the old smells. Matilda ran outside. 'Roly,' she cried ecstatically.

Lionel slumped with fatigue, then shouted out in anguish. 'No! Come back, Matilda. Don't either of you understand? Roland's dead.'

When they entered the New Year a few hours later, there was no celebration. Too late Lionel felt a deep compassion for the formal man who had always kept his distance. He had suspected the cause of Gussie's decline, and knew how he must have suffered.

The funeral of father and son took place on 2 January, a day of bright sunshine which somehow emphasised the melancholy nature of the scene. There was no church service; the chaplain rode from Jericho to officiate at the simple ceremony held in the garden near the house. Lionel was touched that several farmers came to pay their respects to one of their kind.

The chaplain's address offered little comfort to Sarah, who was supported by Lionel and Matilda on either side. When the bodies of her husband and son were lowered into the massive grave dug by the convict servants, who stood respectfully at a distance, hats doffed and eyes lowered, Sarah gave a cry as if she had been wounded.

'I am the resurrection . . .'

Afterwards, she managed to thank the chaplain and the few neighbours for their presence, then retired to her room.

Her grief was terrible. Unable to accept her brother's

assurance that death had been a release for Gussie, the only consolation she could find lay in grief itself. She could not part with it. It festered inside her, consuming her strength. It became selfish.

Matilda confided in Lionel. 'She thinks she's alone in her feelings, but I loved the old man too. I really did. Oh, I know he didn't like me at first, but he grew so nice towards me. Always made me feel I was somebody, that I counted, you understand?'

'Of course,' he said gently, distressed by her self-deprecation when it was her strength that sustained them now.

'I've lost Gussie and Roly too. All I have is Timmy, and I suppose they'll take him away and send him to England to make him a *gentleman*. It's not fair. Nothing's ever fair.'

Lionel was depressed by this new note of bitterness, and blamed his sister. Her grief was starting to overwhelm him too. Restless with indecision, he began to hate Swansdowne, watching every post from Hobart Town for news from *The Times*. Before that came, however, he received a long letter from Lempriere in Port Arthur with the news that Dick had been released from the model prison and was back in the chain-gang.

The thought of Dick sustained him. If it were not for the prospect of seeing him again, he would have ridden into Hobart and sailed on the next vessel to England. Matilda had received a letter of credit from Flanagan for Roly's share of the profits, which she accepted with a wonder that was touching, but Lionel had not told anyone about the large nugget in the opossum bag which lurked richly among his shoes at the bottom of his wardrobe.

News from England reached Swansdowne at last. Everything arrived at once, but Delane's letter was the one that mattered.

My dear Raxleigh,

You will have no idea of the sensation your despatches have created in England. You are right to tell the truth about the transportation system and the vile inhumanities perpetrated in the model prison of Port Arthur. Liberty of thought is the very air which an Englishman breathes from birth, and it is the first duty of *The Times* to publish the truth of the events in Van Diemen's Land, thereby making them the property of the nation. Consequently, let me send you our congratulations. I believe that this may prove to be one of the rare occasions when we shall achieve some good. The enclosed transcript of the letter I have received from the Queen's Private Secretary reveals that Her Majesty has taken a personal interest in the matter, and I know that the contents will make your heart rejoice. In the case of one convict, good *has* been achieved already.

Lionel found himself shaking with nervousness as he turned to the enclosure, a brief but impressive communication addressed to John Thadeus Delane, Editor of the London *Times*:

Dear Delane,

I write to you in confidence to tell you that Her Majesty has expressed interest in the recent despatch from Mr Lionel Raxleigh published in your newspaper which described conditions in the penal settlements of Van Diemen's Land and raised the entire subject of transportation. I can tell you privately that Her Majesty was moved by the story of the young sailor who was transported following an alleged offence during Her Majesty's inspection of her Fleet at Plymouth, and she has asked the colonial secretary to investigate the possibility of an early release and pardon, unless there are circumstances unknown to us which make such a recommendation unwise. I shall keep you in touch with further developments in this matter. Meanwhile, may I add my personal congratulations on your treatment of this important and long-neglected issue.

Lionel gave a chuckle of delight as he turned back to the rest of Delane's letter.

Now that Earl Grey has left the Colonial Office, matters have moved in our favour. We have a new ministry, under Lord Derby, and Sir John Pakington, the Secretary of State, expresses genuine astonishment that so many shiploads of convicts are still being sent to Van Diemen's Land!

Trust me to pursue the matter, now that you have set the ball rolling. Given time and patience I believe there will be a successful outcome. However, before you pat yourself on the back with too hearty a blow, let me add that *if* the Colonial Office decides to abolish transportation it will not be for humanitarian reasons, as they will certainly claim. I hear on good authority that the feeling in the Colonial Office is that the system has run its course. The island is populated, the natives are subdued, and the French are no longer a threat. In other words, to keep on sending convicts is now an extravagance. I believe the experiment will die a natural death. Even so, you can be proud of the vital part you have played in consolidating this change of governmental heart.

Have you contemplated a return to England, I wonder? If so, I am sure that we can offer you a position on *The Times*.

Yours sincerely,

John Delane

Lionel opened the accompanying envelopes nervously, and read his published despatches with such intense interest that he could scarcely breathe. The thrill of seeing his words in print was indescribable. When he had finished, he read them through again – twice. Then he hurried into the garden to share his triumph with Sarah, and tell her the news of Dick's probable release.

Sarah spent most of her day in the garden, finding relief in the simple chore of weeding and planting, gaining solace from her contact with the earth. In addition to the long border near the house, formal with white viburnum and apricot foxgloves, she had created an English meadow which tumbled down to the water's edge near the place where Gussie had drowned; an echo of Devon in Van Diemen's Land, brimming with meadowsweet, scabious, and bright yellow splashes of cowslip and rattle, all sustained by a rainfall as heavy as it was back home.

She was so intent on her planting that she failed to hear Lionel until he stood beside her. Then she smiled up at him with the brave, martyred smile which made Lionel feel so guilty.

'Good news, Sarah. Dick is going to be released!'

'What?' She sounded confused.

'Dick Stanton. He's going to be free. The Queen herself has requested it after reading my despatch in *The Times*. It's caused a sensation! Read this letter from Delane.'

With a sigh, she read the letter carefully, holding the page some distance away from her face.

'I'm glad,' she said at last.

'Is that all you can say?' Lionel blinked, angered by her indifference. 'Good God, Sarah, it's time you stopped wallowing in self-pity and thought of someone else for a change. I don't matter, I'm your brother and it's my duty to stay in this damned place and look after you as I've done all along, but think of Matilda. She's lost a husband, remember, and she's doing her utmost with Sally's child. And now Dick's coming back, and a jolly home-coming it'll be if he finds you moping around all day like this. For God's sake, Sarah, this is a turning point for all of us, but unless you pull yourself together we're going to have a wretched time. Surely you have some regard for Dick? Aren't you pleased he's coming back?'

'Lionel . . .' For a moment she was on the point of revealing Dick's parentage.

'Yes?' he demanded impatiently.

'Nothing. Just that I care about Dick more than you realise. Leave me alone for a moment. I'll come to the house soon and read your despatches. I'm so glad . . .' She knelt down and resumed her planting.

Lionel hesitated, puzzled by her attitude, then walked back towards the house, tight-lipped with disappointment.

Sarah continued to plant for several minutes, then rose to her feet painfully, pressing her hand against the base of her spine. She looked around her, seeing the meadow as a whole, and drew a deep breath of satisfaction as she absorbed the scent of the wild flowers. Her brother's words had not been in vain: she realised how thoughtless she must have seemed to Matilda. Now Dick was returning to his rightful home, and as she thought of this her mourning came to an end at last.

A week later, Lionel received a curt but vital message from Captain O'Hara Booth. 'You failed to keep your promise, but I have received instructions from the Colonial Office which compel me to release the convict Stanton.'

Conditional Release: Ticket of Leave.

His Excellency, Sir Eardley Wilmot, Governor of Van Diemen's Land, has been pleased to authorise me to grant Reg. No. 982 *Richard Stanton*, convicted for *gross insubordination* at the *Plymouth Naval Court Martial* on the *2nd September 1845* and then and there sentenced to Penal Servitude for the term of *two years*, a Conditional Release from Prison during the remaining portion of his said term of Penal Servitude with the need to report his place of residence to the senior officer of Police in any district in which he may locate himself.

*

386

Their excitement at the thought of seeing Dick again faded when he returned. He had changed so much that he might have been another man. It was not simply his appearance, though he was dreadfully thin and his eyes looked out from sunken hollows. His hair was short, with no trace of the former lustrous curls, and the scar which had looked so conspicuous on the cheek of the boy was scarcely noticeable among the deep lines which ran down the face of the man. The change in his character was less easy to accept. All the hopes and plans which had sustained Lionel died when the two men came face to face. There was no trace of the open, outgoing youth; the man now standing before Lionel was silent, morose, drawn. And his role in the household had shifted. Sarah insisted that he should be treated as one of the family, and although Lionel had welcomed her decision at first he was shocked to discover that he was not as pleased as he should have been. He wondered uneasily whether he resented the fact that Dick no longer depended on him. Conversely, did Dick resent the knowledge that he was beholden to Lionel for his release? A man in debt to another finds it hard to forgive him. The very fact that Lionel entertained such ideas proved how far the two men had grown apart.

Sensing their estrangement, Sarah warned her brother: 'Give him time. After all he's been through – you should understand that better than anyone.' But Lionel had depended on Dick's release for too long, having idealised the moment of his return.

When Lionel showed him the copy of *The Times* containing the famous despatch, Dick read it laboriously and merely nodded his head gravely. He did not even say thank you.

Matilda understood Dick's reticence instinctively. She had not expected him to be the same person; she would have found it odd if he had been after his experience in the model prison. She was simply glad to have him back.

Sarah understood too, resisting the temptation to fuss

over him. She knew the truth in that trite old piece of wishful thinking – 'Time is the great healer.'

Raxleigh simply ignored Dick, behaving as if he had forgotten him. It was many months since the dog had seen him last, and he was pining for Roly. One day, however, as he dozed at Dick's feet in the garden, he gave a little jump and then leaped up, scrabbling wildly with his paws, yelping with excitement.

'Oh my!' called Matilda, who was playing with the boy. 'Isn't that nice! Raxleigh has remembered you.' And from that moment, switching allegiance in the instant, the dog accepted his new master and forgot the old, though sometimes puzzling memories returned.

Slowly, Dick came back to life. Preferring his own company, he rode off at dawn to explore the Swansdowne territory on the horse given him by Sarah. Gallant was dead, buried under the oak tree below a vast tombstone: *To the memory of a gallant horse. Bred in Bideford. And now lies here.* Gussie had chosen the words himself.

Raxleigh was Dick's sole companion on his explorations. When the dog grew tired, Dick would stop by a stream and they would share the food prepared for him by Matilda. Sometimes Dick rode to the Dromedary Range at the end of the valley, where others hunted for kangaroo and wallaby, returning with skins and hindquarters. When the range was covered with snow the hunt became a massacre, for the kangas lay close until the dogs drove them out and then floundered in the snow, unable to jump, easy prey for the men with the guns. Opossums were hunted at night. The dogs flushed them out of the bush and they scampered up trees to perch on branches while the dogs barked below, bringing the hunters running. They found the opossums outlined against the moon – a perfect target.

But Dick took his gun, given him by Lionel, to defend himself. He did not shoot for killing's sake. After Port Arthur he held all life in higher regard than that. Occasionally he shot for food, bringing home several bronze-winged pigeons which Matilda stewed in a rich brown sauce. Some days he fished the river Jordan for the small native blackfish, and eels by night. He found his own private places by the riverside, pools where he swam naked and afterwards dried in the sun.

In this way he rediscovered the grace of life. The secret of happiness is not simply to be happy but to know it while you are. One evening he returned with no game or fish but so radiant that Matilda and Sarah found themselves smiling.

'We had a fine day,' he exclaimed, slumping into a chair while Raxleigh fell exhausted at his feet. 'My word, this place is beautiful.'

'Don't you ever get bored?' Sarah asked.

'Bored? I wouldn't allow it. In a place like this, a man can achieve anything so long as he's a mind to.'

Matilda remembered Roly's surrender to boredom, and breathed a sigh of relief, tempered by regret.

As Dick began to heal, life improved at Swansdowne. Even the convict servants worked with more enthusiasm, respecting Dick as one of themselves who had licked the system instead of resenting his new authority as Lionel had feared.

By now Swansdowne was literally bearing fruit: the first warm peaches were taken from the north-facing espaliered wall, and fresh young vegetables were picked while they were small and cooked by Sarah in butter and scarcely any water, a luxury she had been denied since leaving Raxleigh House. In the late afternoons, Lionel played with Timmy. The family scene was peaceful. Yet they seemed to be living in a hiatus, as if they were waiting for some event to steer them in a positive direction. There had been a visit from Tony and Mabel Plunkett, but they were not the bright spirits they had been on board ship. Instead they seemed sedate and over-critical, expecting to be waited on hand and foot while they failed to lift a finger. They made it plain that Roly's caustic company was missed, and Dick remained a stranger. Even Lionel, who had enjoyed Tony Plunkett's conversation in the *Countess of Bath*, was glad to see them go. 'Guests are rather like fish,' he remarked. 'They go off after two days.' But when they departed they left a lingering sense of failure behind them.

Even Matilda became listless. Sarah looked for some sign that Dick felt affection for her, but it was not forthcoming. No longer Roly's 'Devon dumpling', she was now a mature woman, with a hint of wistfulness. But when the son of their new neighbour started to call, gazing at Matilda with obvious admiration, Sarah had mixed feelings. What would become of Timmy if Mr Rattle proposed and Matilda accepted? The child was the deciding factor in all of Sarah's plans for the future. He was five years old, a nice-looking boy with the smiling open features and curly hair of his father and the mischievous beauty of his mother. The combination was delightful in a child, but Sarah hoped it would not prove disastrous later. She was grateful to Matilda for bringing him up with such uncomplicated love, but it was time to take the boy back to England – his rightful home – where he could attend a proper school and learn to be a gentleman.

The sign they had been waiting for came in a letter from Delane, and provided the lifeline Lionel had longed for.

'Sarah!' he cried, running to tell his sister the good news. 'Delane wants me back in England. He thinks there may be a flare-up in Eastern Europe' – he referred to the letter in his hand – 'possible trouble between Russia and Turkey – he's preparing a team of ten "specials" to cover it if war should be declared. He's certain there's going to be one, and wants me to join them.' Lionel looked at her proudly. 'It's the chance of a lifetime.'

Sarah was shocked by her brother's reaction. Did he hate Swansdowne so much that he could leave it without a qualm? At the same time she felt guilty, for she had given Matilda and Dick no warning that she was contemplating her own return.

'I'm coming as well.'

'What?' The look of horror on her brother's face was so transparent that she laughed, but she was hurt and puzzled too. 'What do you mean? You can't leave Swansdowne.'

'Oh yes I can,' she replied coldly. 'But don't worry. I won't get in your way. I've been planning it for months.'

Lionel blinked in surprise. 'You never told me. What about Dick – and Matilda?'

'They can come with me.'

'And sell Swansdowne?'

'What of Sally?'

'She will have to follow, if she returns.'

'Good God!'

'I should get a good price.' With the naivety of someone who should have known better, it did not occur to Sarah that she was being cruel in selling Swansdowne.

'I can't believe it,' said Matilda, when she was told. She stood there flushed and miserable, feeling herself the outsider once again, inferior and unwanted. 'I really can't believe it. You're not serious?'

Sarah reproached herself instantly. How could she have been so stupid?

'But you'll come with us,' she explained, trying to make a joke of it. 'You didn't think we were leaving you behind?' She stopped as she saw the misery in Matilda's face.

'I don't know,' said Matilda grumpily. 'I don't know what to think. I'm not sure I want to leave.'

Sarah knew in her heart that she was failing the girl.

'You don't want to stay here without Timmy, do you?'

'No, of course I don't!' Matilda shouted angrily.

What am I doing to them all? Sarah wondered. Yearning for the Old Country as she did, it had not occurred to her that Matilda preferred the younger. Even Raxleigh's contentment made her feel guilty. He was stretched out on the floor, watching a bird which had flown through a window and was picking up crumbs just a foot away from his nose. The dog watched lazily, aware that he should attack but too relaxed to make the effort. Instead he closed his eyes, eliminating the need for decision.

The trouble lay, as it does so often, with the lack of

money. The return to England and Timothy's education could not be financed without the sale of Swansdowne, which Matilda now regarded as her home. The loyalties of the two women were torn by their sense of duty: Sarah had convinced herself that life for Timothy was too restricted in Van Diemen's Land; while the thought of leaving Swansdowne made Matilda wretched.

Dick's reaction surprised them all. His father had died in the meantime, and he felt no desire to return to England. As the holder of a conditional release it would be hard for him to do so in any case, but his opposition was stronger than that – emotional rather than practical.

'Go back to England?' he exclaimed vehemently. 'That's a ridiculous idea. Now father's dead no one will know me there – or care. The place will have changed, and so will my friends – not that I had many. I met a bloke once in Hobart who thought he'd make a pretty impression returning like the prodigal son, rich in money and experience, but he found he was more of a stranger back home than he ever was here. I'm staying. Sorry, but this is my country now and I wouldn't leave it for all the gold in Ballarat. I've worked on this land, I've ridden it, I've helped to build a home, and I want to see the reward in times to come. I want to see things *grow*! The trees and things I planted. I belong, I'm part of *here*. I won't go back to England, not now.'

It was the longest and most impassioned speech Dick had ever made.

'Hear, hear!' cried Matilda. 'That's how I feel. I love Timmy, but I love this land as well.' Her voice sounded shrill, and she knew why. Dick's outburst had been so uncharacteristic. She had accepted the change from easy-going boy into a man who was often distant, even dull, by comparison, but she had made no allowance for the layers of feeling just revealed. She had taken him for granted: someone who was always there. Now she suddenly realised how much they had in common.

Roly and her responsibility for Timmy had consumed her, but Roly had gone, and now she was threatened with the loss of the boy as well, unless she was willing to return to England.

No. She belonged *here* – as Dick did. Yet losing Timmy was such an unbearable thought that she raised her hands to her face in a vain attempt to stop the tears from pouring down her cheeks.

Dick came over to her at once with a look of awkward concern. 'Don't,' he whispered, vulnerable before her grief. 'It'll be all right.' And to comfort her he took off his kerchief and gave it to her to wipe off the tears. The simple gesture was so touching that she looked up and smiled. His answering smile unnerved her completely, for it suggested a warmth she had not contemplated. There was no passion between them, or so she told herself in sudden confusion, but she thought that passion was not what she wanted. She had known the pain of that emotion when she had needed so desperately to belong to Roly and all he stood for . . . But this was all absurd imagination! Dick was simply moved by her tears. Yet the incident forced her to realise how sorely she wanted to be the mistress of her own home, with a husband who was 'good' rather than 'mercurial'. Looking up at Dick she had no doubt of his goodness.

Watching them, Sarah was confused. She weighed again her responsibility to Matilda, to whom she owed so much, against her responsibility to Timothy. Was she in danger of ruining his life as well, by uprooting him? She knew what it was like to be *déraciné*.

Lionel had no hesitation whatsoever. Within days of receiving Delane's letter he had booked a passage on the next boat home and left for Hobart Town. Dick insisted on going with him to see him off, in spite of Lionel's protests. The longing that had once kept Lionel awake at night had given way to friendship, to the relief of both men.

As usual, the time before the boat sailed seemed interminable, and conversation between the two grew increasingly strained. They waited in Lionel's cabin, Dick sitting on the other berth. Lionel had the cabin to himself, as was usually the case on the return voyage.

Lionel prayed that the boat would leave as soon as possible. His innate weakness had forced him into shameful acts, but none more odious than his behaviour over the nugget of gold concealed in his duffle. He had tried to justify himself by rationalising the pros and cons, even persuading himself that Roly had meant to give the nugget to him. If the nugget belonged to anyone, it belonged in the family. Lionel had little enough to rely on apart from his salary from *The Times* and a share of the projected sale of Swansdowne.

'Better go now, Dick,' he said impulsively. 'This hanging around is wretched.'

To his dismay, he saw that Dick was crying. 'I'll be bereft without you.'

'Bereft?' Lionel was confused.

'I never could find the words, but if it wasn't for you I wouldn't be free ...' Suddenly Dick put his arms around him and kissed him gently on the cheek. 'I love you, Lionel.' Without looking back, the young man left the cabin.

Lionel stayed there motionless. He had despaired of hearing those words in his lifetime. Suddenly aware of cries on deck which warned him that the boat was sailing at last, he sorted feverishly through his duffle until he found the opossum bag, ran down the corridor to the deck, and pushed his way through the crowd of waving passengers to the rail. Looking around desperately, he saw Dick's back disappearing across the quay.

'*Dick!*' he bellowed.

Dick turned round to see Lionel waving frantically. He waved back, puzzled, and then retraced his steps.

'I forgot,' Lionel shouted when Dick fought his way through the crowd to stand below him. 'This is yours.' He held up the bag. 'Roly gave it to me the night he died. He wanted you to have it. *It's yours.*'

He threw the heavy bag carefully, and Dick caught it.

'Don't look now,' shouted Lionel. 'God bless you. Bless you, Dick.'

Again that heartbreaking moment as the vessel parted from the shore. But later, as the clipper sailed up river, he leant over the rail with a wry, contented smile.

'Goodness,' said the third officer, coming up beside him. 'You look pleased with yourself!'

He turned round and grinned. 'I am,' he said. 'For once, I like myself.'

The officer smiled. 'Mr Raxleigh, after what you've done for the people here, I can only say it's about time too.'

So Lionel left Van Diemen's Land unaware that the young man whom he loved was his own half-brother.

The unexpected weight of the bag made Dick curious, and he opened it. For a split second he was mystified; then, as he removed the large, twisted-looking stone, the sunlight struck the gold.

Dick did not call at Ma Sloper's that evening. When the transaction was completed and letters exchanged, he rode back to Swansdowne, only stopping to snatch a brief rest at the foot of a tree. A few years earlier he might have celebrated in the waterfront bars, but this was the sign he needed, just as Lionel had been waiting for Delane's letter.

Matilda sensed the difference the moment he galloped into Swansdowne. He took her arm forcibly to lead her, almost push her, into the garden where they could talk unnoticed, and blurted out his proposal. She tried to stop herself from laughing.

'Well?' he demanded angrily. 'Say something.'

'Do you love me?'

'Of course I do. What a question.'

'Not like you loved Sally?'

Dick seized her so violently that she knew it was time to end her mischief.

'Will you marry me?'

She kissed him so longingly that he knew the answer.

'But why have you asked me now?' She looked at him shyly as they walked back to the house, hand in swinging hand. 'Has anything happened?'

He smiled, looking down at her. 'You're marrying a man of means!'

That night they broke the news to Sarah, dreading her disapproval, some logical rejection of their plans. In the recent weeks of tension they had forgotten the intrinsic kindness of her nature.

'Oh, my two darlings!' she cried. 'Nothing could make me happier.'

Matilda ran to her, desperate for comfort. 'Oh, ma, but what are we going to do? We've talked it over and we want to stay here at Swansdowne and bring up Timmy as our own.' In the silence that fell then, the knowledge that Matilda had done just that hung between them.

'Yes,' Sarah replied at last. 'Yes, of course. You *must* do that. I understand.' And it was true. Suddenly it seemed so logical. After all, Dick had Raxleigh blood. She owed as much to him as to anyone, if not more. Again she was on the point of revealing his parentage, yet something held her back. It seemed too immense a revelation – almost an infliction. For all she knew it might be illegal to marry the widow of your nephew. It was kinder to keep the unnatural secret to herself.

'You see,' said Dick, 'I think we could buy Swansdowne, if you'd let us.'

'I don't understand.'

Dick told her about the nugget of gold, and produced a letter of credit for £1,700. 'With Matilda's money from Roly, and a loan . . .' His words died away as he saw her face.

'We could advertise in the *Courier* for a tutor for Timmy. We'd get him the best,' said Matilda imploringly.

'That's a good idea,' Sarah told them, considering her words carefully. 'I see you've made up your minds, so I'll let you have Swansdowne. But not like that. Not for the money which darling Roly left to you and Matilda. You'll need every penny of that. I'd like to give you Swansdowne. The land is making a profit, as you know, so you can send my share to England . . .'

'Oh, ma,' wailed Matilda, sitting at her feet. 'Don't you understand? We want you to stay.'

Sarah controlled herself. She had been longing to hear those words, though she had not dared to admit to herself that she was dreading her return to England. She had made her second garden and knew she would never make a third. Yet she felt it her duty to give the couple a chance to manage on their own. There was a time for sacrifice. 'No. Tim can stay with you, but I must go.'

She was startled to see Matilda burst into tears. Dick came and kissed Sarah on the forehead, something he would not have contemplated before. Bending over her, he whispered: 'Stay with us. We look on you as our mother.'

Sarah felt her resolve drain away.

'We couldn't be happy here without you,' said Matilda, who had no guile. 'This is where you belong, with us.'

Sarah looked at the child, asleep in the chair, and Raxleigh on the floor, thumping his tail contentedly as he heard them speak. 'All right,' she laughed. 'I suppose you are my family now.' And she picked up the stocking she had been darning before they interrupted her, in order to conceal her joy. As if he understood, Raxleigh subsided with his sigh as soft as the surf on a sandy shore, and closed his eyes.

The embossed invitation to Mr and Mrs Richard Stanton arrived at Swansdowne a week after their third wedding anniversary.

On the occasion of the Jubilee to celebrate the foundation of the colony, and the cessation of transportation, The Mayor and Members of the Launceston Legislative Council request the pleasure of the company of

Mr and Mrs Richard Stanton

at a Luncheon on the 10th day of August 1853

Dick was reluctant to accept, but Matilda persuaded him. 'The whole island's going to celebrate. Let's go – it will be such fun!'

'But why have they invited *us*?'

'Because you're famous' – the circumstances of Dick's release had made him something of a celebrity – 'and anyhow, I expect they've invited *everyone*.'

Matilda had never been to Launceston, the second largest town in Van Diemen's Land, though she had been to its namesake in Cornwall. She looked forward to the expedition with an excitement that finally affected Dick as well, though he grew exasperated by the constant argument over what she should wear. Sarah had received an invitation too but refused to go. 'I'm happier here,' she told them. 'I don't suit the town, nor the town me.' She knew they would prefer the adventure on their own. 'I can look after Tim and Raxleigh, and the swans.'

'You and your swans.' Matilda smiled with relief. 'You speak as if they're human.'

Sarah did not attempt to explain that the swans who nested nearby had a special significance. To go down to the river where Gussie drowned and see the cygnets, almost as large as their parents, gave her a satisfaction which soothed the frown-lines from her face.

They stayed the first night at an inn in Jericho, and the second in the pleasant cedar-lined rooms of the Half-Way House at Antill Ponds, having been wise enough to make their bookings in advance. Every inn was crowded with families converging for the Jubilee celebrations in Launceston.

On the cold Tuesday night, Dick and Matilda left their hotel in Launceston and promenaded through the park, newly planted with English oaks and elms, and marvelled at the firework display which burst into the sky above them.

'Oh, my! What it must have cost!' Matilda exclaimed. She looked at her husband proudly. She would always miss Roly, but loved Dick for his greater simplicity. He looked so handsome. The curls ran down his face and around his chin once again, though he kept his upper and lower lips bare. The small pig-tail knotted at the back was not for vanity's sake but a symbol of his pride at having served in the Queen's Navy.

Yet it would be misleading to say that the riding, rustling years at Swansdowne had restored him to his former self, for there was no vestige left of that. Forged by his experience, he was a new man, suddenly jaunty in the contagious atmosphere of celebration which brightened the streets. In spite of the crowds they were on their own for the first time in their lives, and felt a childish glee in the unexpected liberty.

'I'm glad we're together,' he whispered, abashed by such emotion. 'I'm glad I have you.' With a rare show of affection, he tightened his arm around her. 'But as the old Duke might have said, it was "a close-run thing".' News of the soldier's death had just reached them, and the passing of 'the hero of his time' seemed to mark the passing of an age as well.

They made a striking couple: Dick with his kangaroo-skin cap and waistcoat; she with her radiant complexion wearing a brand-new dress bought in the town that morning; and their obvious happiness was reflected in the faces of the passers-by who smiled and sometimes touched their caps in recognition.

Never had Van Diemen's Land known such exuberance: all the excitement of *Le roi est mort, vive le roi!* – off with the old, and on with the new! Fifty years had passed since the colony was founded and every man in Launceston was determined to honour the coming of age of his country.

Matilda was woken early by the peals of the church bells and looked with infinite tenderness at Dick sleeping in the unfamiliar bed beside her. She nuzzled her nose next to his shoulder. Later, they attended the thanksgiving service at ten o'clock, after which they made their way to the impressive town hall for the luncheon, suddenly awkward as they stood in line, Dick waiting to present their card. By now they knew that Dick was a local hero, but Matilda was dismayed when they were led to the top table and several men rose to make way for her, bowing respectfully as if she was someone of importance too.

Oh my, she thought, they must have made some mistake. I shouldn't be up here like this. She looked appealingly at Dick two places away, wishing they had not been separated, but he shook his head slightly with a helpless smile. She could tell he was nervous too. Then the meal began, and she decided to forget her fears and enjoy it.

The luncheon was marred for Dick because he was seated next to Mr Sloley. He revived painful memories by asking after Sally, a subject which Dick avoided so brusquely that Sloley realised he was trespassing on dangerous ground and turned instead to his new appointment as commandant of Port Arthur; for Captain O'Hara Booth had retired at last. Sloley mistook Dick's look of dismay.

'Yes, I know it seems a strange appointment to most people. The Minister has an inflated idea of my capabilities; at the same time it marks his new policy towards the punishment of prisoners. He knows I am a moderate in that respect.'

'No, sir, it's not that,' said Dick, embarrassed. 'I thought Port Arthur was going to be abolished.'

'Because transportation has come to an end? Oh, no, the settlement will still be used as a place of correction, though I hope that a new system of trust will now prevail.' Sloley insisted on asking Dick's advice, which he gave reluctantly, looking enviously at Matilda, who was starting to enjoy the company of the men on either side of her.

The toastmaster's shout subdued the din of conversation, and Matilda rose with the others to drink the toast – 'Her Majesty, The Queen' – which she did with all her heart. There was a thunderous clatter as everyone sat down again. Only the Honourable Richard Dry, member for Launceston and Speaker of the Legislative Council, remained standing, looking down at the gathering and smiling benevolently.

'What a proud and happy occasion this is! We are fifty years old and today we enter a new era. The hostile aboriginal tribes have long ceased to inflict terror, while the bloodthirsty depredations of the bushrangers are now tales of the past. The colonists of New South Wales may be intoxicated by their surfeit of gold, but we are the recipients of an even greater blessing – great because it affects the intellectual, social, and moral well-being of the colony – the decision that has come from Downing Street that transportation should cease at once and for ever!'

He was stopped, as he intended, by loud and long applause. As it faded away, he continued:

'At such an auspicious moment in our brief history, may I abandon the name given to us by the old Dutch navigator – so evocative today of crime and wretchedness – and adopt the more euphonious one of *Tasmania* . . .'

The following words were drowned by a roar of cheering as men rose to their feet, waving wildly, calling out, 'Tasmania! God bless Tasmania!'

At last the Honourable Richard Dry was allowed to continue, paying tribute to those leaders of the anti-transportation cause present, with Sloley receiving a special mention.

'But now,' Richard Dry concluded, 'we take this opportunity to pay a special tribute of a different kind, to honour two men in particular who have helped to bring the pernicious system of transportation to an end. This address is signed by the magistrates of the city and members of the council to express the high esteem in which they hold Mr Lionel Raxleigh, whose despatches to the London *Times* first shocked the conscience of

England and have *shamed* the Colonial Office into taking action at last.'

More respectful applause.

'We are arranging for the London Agency Association to present this address to Mr Raxleigh in the offices of the London *Times*, to assure him that we are not unmindful of his continuing exertions in our cause since his much-regretted departure from our colony.

'Meanwhile, however, we have with us today a young man well known to Mr Raxleigh, whose case won the hearts of the English public, including Her Majesty the Queen, who requested his rightful pardon.

'We are proud to have Richard Stanton as our special guest of honour.'

Richard Dry stood aside, applauding Dick as he did so. The entire company started applauding too, then scraped back their chairs and rose to their feet while Dick sat down again, overwhelmed, unable to respond. Richard Dry saved the moment by continuing, as soon as the uproar died down, as if no answering speech was called for.

'Richard Stanton, we tender you our best thanks and request your acceptance of this casket, which encloses a purse of two hundred and fifty sovereigns – not as any degree of compensation for the ordeal you have endured, but as a small token of the admiration in which you are held by your fellow Tasmanians.

'I call on your wife to accept this casket with our blessing. Mrs Matilda Stanton.'

The assembly rose again, shouting, clapping, smiling sympathetically at Matilda's confusion, cheering loudly as the Honourable Richard Dry gave her the casket and kissed her impulsively on her bright red cheeks. She looked at Dick who was on his feet as well, nodding to her proudly.

'Oh my,' she exclaimed, when the applause died down and everyone looked up at her expectantly as she clasped ᵗʰᵉ casket.

ᵧ!'